PRAISE FOR
JOANNE KENNEDY

"A delightful read full of heart and passion."
—Jodi Thomas, *New York Times* and *USA Today*
bestselling author, for *Cowboy Fever*

"HOT, HOT, HOT…with more twists and turns than a buckin'
bull at a world-class rodeo, lots of sizzlin' sex, and characters so
real, you'll swear they live down the road!"
—Carolyn Brown, *New York Times*
bestselling author, for *Cowboy Fever*

"Wit and charm suffuse this well-plotted story about remembering what's most important in life."
—*Publishers Weekly* for *Cowboy Summer*

"Joanne Kennedy creates the kind of cowboys we wish existed. Her
heroes are strong, honest, down-to-earth and sexy as all get-out."
—*New York Journal of Books* for *Cowboy Crazy*

"A witty, sizzling contemporary western romance that will have
you eagerly turning the pages."
—*Romance Junkies* for *Cowboy Crazy*

"A light and wonderfully enjoyable read."
—*The Romance Reviews* for *Cowboy Crazy*

"An emotional, tender romance with just the right touch of intensity, intrigue, and humor."
—*Fresh Fiction* for *Cowboy Crazy*

"A sassy and sexy wild ride that is more fun than a wild hootenanny! Don't miss it!"

Also by Joanne Kennedy

Cowboy Crazy

JOANNE KENNEDY

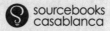

sourcebooks
casablanca

Published by Sourcebooks Casablanca, an imprint of Sourcebooks
P.O. Box 4410, Naperville, Illinois 60567-4410
(630) 961-3900
sourcebooks.com

Originally published in 2012 in the United States of America by
Sourcebooks Casablanca, an imprint of Sourcebooks.

Printed and bound in Canada.
MBP 10 9 8 7 6 5 4 3 2 1

*To my hometown, the city of Cheyenne, and especially
to the volunteers whose dedication and community
spirit have made Cheyenne Frontier Days the ultimate
outdoor rodeo for over 115 years. Cowboy up!*

CHAPTER 1

Win or lose, a bull rider always ends up in the dirt. Sometimes he jumps off and sometimes he's tossed, but either way he winds up scrambling around on all fours trying to save his own life.

For some reason, Lane Carrigan never got tired of it, despite the fact that the pay was mostly cuts, bruises, and broken bones. On this hot July night, he'd scored a paycheck along with a shot of adrenaline that hummed through his veins like a shot of strong whiskey.

After shoving his riding glove in his gear bag, he hoisted it to his shoulder and strode out from under the stands. A faint feeling of unease pricked the hairs at the back of his neck when he spotted a woman lounging against one of the makeshift pens that held the roping steers. She was dark-haired and shapely, dolled up like a barstool cowgirl in clean pressed jeans and a sparkly shirt. Her pretty, practiced smile was fixed on his face, and she held her hands behind her back like she was hiding a surprise.

He hoped she wasn't going to jump out with a bunch of flowers or something. He was more in the mood for beer than buckle bunnies tonight, and something about her expression made him feel more like a lamb being led to slaughter than a man who'd just bested a bull. His thigh ached from an old injury and he just wanted to hang out with the guys and maybe hit the hay early.

Besides, he was embarrassed by the way girls fawned over him. It would have been all right if he'd earned their adoration with his riding skills, but he knew his fame stemmed from two accidents of birth: the Carrigan name, and the square-jawed, laser-eyed Carrigan face. The Carrigan money didn't hurt either, but the recent deal he'd struck with his brother left him land-rich and cash-poor, which wasn't exactly bunny bait.

That was fine with him. His brother was the one who cared about money, riding an executive office chair and mahogany desk at Carrigan Oil with as much confidence as Lane brought to bull riding. Eric was carrying the company into the twenty-first century with grace and style, decked out in high-fashion suits and driving high-priced cars. Lane was only graceful when he was on the back of a bull. The rest of the time he was just another cowboy, a little beat up from hard landings, with a slight limp from a long-ago wreck that had broken his right leg and set short.

The mystery woman stepped forward, her hands still behind her back. When she flicked out her tongue to lick her glossy lips, Lane felt a tightening down below, but it was more reflex than anything. She wasn't his type. Not many of them were these days.

"Lane Carrigan?" she asked.

"That's me."

She whipped out what she was hiding and shoved it in his face. *Microphone.*

When a man emerged from under the stands balancing a television camera on his shoulder, Lane almost groaned aloud—but he smiled instead, flashing the famous Carrigan grin he'd inherited from his dad. He hadn't done anything newsworthy today, not with that mediocre ride, but this babe was probably a rookie reporter with no rodeo knowledge looking for a story and figuring the rich guy would fill some airtime.

"Congratulations."

He cast her a sheepish sideways grin. "Wasn't my best, but I made the buzzer."

He spoke with the slow, easy drawl expected of a rodeo cowboy, though he'd spent most of his childhood in swanky boarding schools. He'd had just two weeks every summer at his grandfather's ranch near Two Shot, but he'd been determined to memorize the way the hired help walked and talked so he could be a cowboy himself someday. He'd worked as hard at the lingo as he had at his roping and riding skills, developing his aw-shucks charm with the same care most people put into learning a foreign language.

The woman dimpled. "I was talking about your new endeavor."

He searched his mind for any kind of endeavor at all. He felt like an idiot when somebody asked him about real life while he was in rodeo mode. For him, riding *was* real life—more real than any business deal or snooty high-class party. His father had believed the Old West of cowboys and cattle needed to step aside for the new world of oil rigs and energy booms, but Lane knew the old ways were worth saving. His rodeo career had been the first step in freeing himself from what he considered his family's money-grubbing, oil-soaked legacy, and trading his company shares for control of the family ranch was the next. He'd sworn to himself that the former Carrigan Ranch—now the LT Ranch—would be the one stretch of Wyoming untouched by the oil industry. No bobbing oil rigs, no transmission lines scarring the hillsides.

"I'm wondering how you reconcile raising organic, grass-fed beef with the upcoming energy development on the ranch," she said.

"I don't. There is no energy development on the ranch." He slid his thumbs into his belt loops and grinned. "Though I suppose you could call raising Grade A beef developing energy."

Nudging her stylish half-glasses down to the end of her nose, the reporter whipped out a sheaf of notes. "It says here the production plan for the Carrigan ranch calls for fourteen wells. Estimated output will be ten to fifty barrels per day."

"On the ranch?" He swallowed a whole lot of cuss words they probably didn't allow on TV. His mind was going a million miles an hour, trying to figure out what was going on and screaming *shit, shit, shit. He wouldn't. He couldn't*, over and over.

He and Eric competed for everything. That's why they'd split things up—so they wouldn't be stepping on each other all the time. But though Lane was in charge of the ranch, the company still owned the mineral rights. If Eric was planning to exercise those rights, he wasn't just stepping on Lane's toes. He was stomping all over them.

The reporter was still smiling expectantly. Lane edged toward the exit but she followed, trotting alongside him, holding the microphone like she was trying to get him to eat the damn thing.

When in doubt, a Carrigan always had one line to fall back on, and this seemed like the perfect time to use it. "No comment, ma'am."

She narrowed her eyes, sensing his confusion and homing in on it like a coyote sniffing out a weakened calf. "Were you unaware of your brother's plans?"

She cocked her head to one side, her smile fading into an expression of concern that would have made his leg ache a little less if there'd been a shred of sincerity in it. He turned away, but the woman dodged around him like a square dancer executing a slick do-si-do.

"You're the face of Carrigan Oil, yet you're left out of the loop." She was on a roll now, unearthing a real story, and the hand holding the microphone shook just the slightest bit as she suppressed her excitement. "Does this make you realize how other landowners feel when they fear Carrigan will exercise their mineral rights without regard to family ranching legacies? Does it make you sympathize with the little guys?"

"I've always sympathized with them," Lane said.

What was she going to do next—get out a stick and poke him in the side? He knew she was manipulating him, but the anger roiling in his gut was rising, spilling into his brain. The implication that his wealth made him different from his fellow ranchers always annoyed him.

Besides, he'd expected his brother to keep his money-grubbing hands to himself. It had been an unspoken agreement, a point of honor—the kind of thing their father would have respected. But while he'd been off riding bulls, Eric had apparently been making plans.

He dredged up the Carrigan grin again. If his brother's betrayal hurt, he sure as hell wasn't going to let it show. Lane Carrigan didn't get hurt. Not by bulls, not by women, not even by family. He was the definition of cowboy tough.

And he always fought back.

In this case, the weapon he needed was right in front of him. The public viewed oil company CEOs as cartoon villains to rival Lex Luthor. If there was one thing Eric couldn't deal with, it was bad publicity.

The reporter edged closer, again sensing the tension in the air. Maybe she wasn't a rookie after all. She had the slick, self-conscious presence of Katie Couric or Ann Curry. He glanced down at the microphone. CBS.

He smiled. This was national media. Anything he said was liable to hit the ten o'clock news in a matter of hours.

He probably should think about what he was going to say. He should go back to his trailer and come up with a formal, carefully constructed statement.

But that wouldn't be any fun.

"You know, I'm used to those bulls being out to get me," he said. "I guess my brother's not much different."

The reporter nodded eagerly.

"He'll tell you they've found a safe way to get the oil out, but the truth is, that's basically a big pile of—excrement." He brushed off the seat of his Wranglers with an exaggerated motion. "The truth is, any drilling process is hazardous—to the land and the people who live there. Carrigan might think they have the science down, but nobody knows what the long-term effects are going to be. And these projects just kill small-town communities. You seen Midwest? Or Pinedale? I'm not letting that happen to Two Shot."

"How do you plan to prevent it?"

"Whatever it takes, I guess." He looked straight at the camera. "Whatever it takes. Those rigs are not going on my land."

CHAPTER 2

SARAH LANDON STEPPED INTO THE CARRIGAN TOWER AND flashed a smile at the receptionist that felt about as deep as her silk camisole and as steady as her high-heeled pumps. When she was a little girl, she'd dressed up as Wonder Woman for Halloween. Now she dressed up in a costume every day, smoothing her flyaway red hair, basting foundation over her freckles, and pasting on that confident, take-charge smile. While she might not leap tall buildings in a single bound, she managed to scale the tallest one in Wyoming every morning en route to her boss's tenth-floor office.

But that wasn't her greatest feat of strength. She'd climbed the hallowed towers of two Ivy League colleges too, earning a master's degree in political science with a focus on energy policy and leaving her small-town roots behind forever.

Or so she hoped. Her hometown of Two Shot was only an hour's drive from Casper, but it held so many memories she did her best to stay away. Even when she visited her sister Kelsey she avoided the place, keeping herself cloistered in the tidy single-wide at the edge of town.

Of course, Kelsey was always urging her to eat at Suze's Diner, shop at the candy store on the corner, do all the things they'd done as kids. But Sarah knew better. When she left Two Shot, she'd left behind a lot of disapproving glances, gossip, and snide whispers about who she'd been and who she planned to be. She wasn't about to let all that into her life again. The past was gone, and she was keeping it that way.

She pressed a button and stepped into the steel-sided elevator. The construction of the sleek, modern tower that housed Carrigan Corporation had been trumpeted as the start of a new age of prosperity for Casper, but most of the dollars drilled out of the ground bypassed the city, winging their way to various executives and speculators back East. Casper's only skyscraper still stood alone, looming over crumbling brick storefronts and proving what everyone already knew: the Carrigans owned this town.

The building was cutting-edge architecture, spacious and contemporary, but entering Eric Carrigan's office was like stepping into the past. The room was carpeted in plush hunter green and decorated with dark wood, leather, and brass in the style of a Victorian gentleman's club. It was jarring to look through the window behind his hulking mahogany desk and see cars and trucks passing on the street below. It would have been more fitting to view a host of hackney cabs dodging Dickensian urchins.

A copy of the *Casper Star* flew through the air as she entered. It would have hit her if she hadn't caught it. She bobbled it in the air a couple of times before clutching it to her chest.

"I saw the story," she said.

She wasn't the only one. Everybody in town had seen it. OIL HEIRS BATTLE OVER RIGHTS TO RANCH, bellowed the oversized headline. It topped an account of Lane's interview with the reporter from Channel 10 and a detailed history of the brothers' lifelong rivalry.

"Looks like a job for the public affairs manager," Eric said.

It looked to Sarah as if Eric needed a private affairs manager to deal with his brother, but she waved one hand with a suave confidence she didn't feel and stepped up to the task. "I wouldn't worry. A fight with your brother gives you a public forum to explain the process."

Eric shot his cuffs and adjusted his tie. In some men the gesture would have looked vain and silly, but Eric moved with such assurance that it only emphasized the square strength of his hands and the chiseled masculinity of his jaw. With his dark good looks and designer duds, he looked like the boardroom hero of a romance novel. Female interns and administrative assistants fluttered around him like moths to a lightbulb, but Sarah wasn't interested. For one thing, he was her boss. For another thing, she'd sworn off men, and Eric didn't make her heart flutter anyway.

"The way I see it, your brother's handed you publicity on a silver platter," she said.

"Lane would never touch a silver platter. If he gave us anything, he shoved it at us with a manure fork." Eric tapped a remote and his brother's image appeared on a big-screen television mounted in a discreet wooden frame above a carved credenza.

"I'm not letting that happen to Two Shot," the image said.

Sarah shifted uneasily. The reference to her old hometown had kept her awake half the night. Why was Lane Carrigan talking about a Podunk little town twenty miles from the ranch? What did he care about Two Shot?

"Really, your brother's doing my job for me." Sarah felt like she had a manure fork herself, only she was using it to shovel actual bullshit. "You wanted publicity, and there it is."

The two of them watched the screen in silence as the camera shifted to follow Lane and his cowboy cohorts across the packed-dirt parking lot in back of the arena. The lens zeroed in on the fringe framing the West's best-known Wrangler butt and she shifted in her chair. "Proving the process doesn't affect Lane's cattle operation will be a major public relations victory. They can't complain when we're willing to risk your family ranch, right? And everyone will be talking about it now. It's just what we wanted."

Actually, she suspected everyone was talking about the way Lane Carrigan's butt looked in those chaps. Everyone female, anyway.

She slapped the thought away and turned back to her boss, who was tapping a pencil on the desk top and scowling.

"We'll make it work," she said, shoveling on more fake confidence. "We'll talk to him."

"How? I left message after message. No response." Eric lurched out of his chair and started to pace, raking his fingers through his dark hair. "Now that he's been attacked by that reporter, he'll probably claim we sandbagged him. He's impossible, Sarah. It's going to be a tough fight."

His shoulders slumped, and for a moment Sarah saw past the professional facade. Eric was only human, and being vilified as a land-raping oil executive while your brother reaped glory as a rodeo star couldn't be easy—especially when that brother slammed you on national TV.

No such thing as bad publicity, she told herself. *No such thing.* Somehow, she'd turn it their way. She had to. This job was a perfect match for her skills. It would carry her far beyond her past and into a world where she could finally stop worrying—about herself, about her family, and about her place in the world. In the business world, hard work paid solid dividends nobody could ever take away.

Nobody. Not Lane Carrigan, or anybody else.

Late afternoon sun slanted over Sarah's desk, casting the long shadow of her mile-high in-box over the paperwork she was trying to finish. Eric appeared at her door just as she was about to dot an i and cross a final t.

"He's coming in."

The drama in his tone made it sound like he was talking about a fugitive from justice.

"Lane," he clarified. "He'll be here in ten minutes. I'd like you to be there."

She started to protest, but he held a hand up to stop her. "He's turned this into a public relations issue, and that means you're going to be involved."

She followed him to his office and perched on the chair in front of his desk, back straight, legs crossed. Her pose radiated poise and self-control, but she caught herself covertly biting her cheek the way she always did when she was tense. Sometimes she worried she'd chew her way right through it, but until then nobody would know how uptight she was. The nervous habit kept her hands steady and her gaze level.

"It's good he's willing to talk," she said.

"Not really. He says he's not going to allow the drilling."

"He doesn't really have a choice." Sarah felt a stab of remorse. Sometimes she felt like she was on the wrong side of these arguments. She'd driven past the Carrigan Ranch a hundred times, maybe a thousand, admiring the smooth, concentric curves of plowed land that traced the contours of the earth. Now those graceful lines would be replaced by long, random scars and right-angled roads that cut through the land with no regard for dips or valleys, rocks or trees.

But she couldn't think about that now. She needed to keep her mind on her job. "The company owns the mineral rights. What's he going to do—chain himself to a tree?"

"He says that reporter wants to talk to him again."

"I'll bet she does." Sarah blushed, hoping her boss hadn't caught the sex-starved subtext in her words.

"Well, look out." Eric patted his hair into place and crossed his legs. "He tends to bowl people over. Especially women."

"I know the type," Sarah said. She'd met enough professional cowboys to understand that the macho, rough-and-tumble rodeo life had probably puffed up Lane's ego to the size of a mushroom cloud from an atomic bomb. And no doubt he'd try to blast her to kingdom come along with his brother.

Eric grimaced and adjusted his tie again, then shifted a trio of pens around his blotter. He lined them up parallel to each other, then shifted them to an angled arrangement. Picking up a stack of papers, he riffled through them and placed them to the left side of his blotter. After a second or two, he picked them up, tapped them on the desk to square the edges, and moved them to the right side. She'd never seen him like this. One of the reasons she liked working for Eric was his self-assured, take-charge confidence. The only time it seemed to waver was when the subject of his brother came up.

The door swung open and his helmet-haired assistant Dot tipped her head in.

Eric straightened. "Yes, Dorothy?"

"Mr. Carrigan, your brother…"

Lane Carrigan filled the doorway, standing with his legs slightly apart and his arms folded over his chest. He was taller than Eric by a couple of inches, but what made her jaw drop were the muscles straining his worn denim shirt and the uncanny vibrancy of his blue eyes. Eric had those same eyes, but in his aristocratic face they were merely interesting. Contrasted with Lane's deep tan, they were striking. Eric was handsome, lean, graceful. Lane was a force of nature.

She wondered how old he was. Eric was the little brother, so that made Lane what? Twenty-nine? But he looked older. While Eric's face was unlined, Lane had faint crow's-feet when he smiled and long furrows that bracketed his mouth when he didn't. Eric's face was genteel and perfectly proportioned; Lane's was craggier, with a nose that was just a little too big and brows that jutted over his eyes, making the blue of them seem all the more piercing. It was like you'd taken the same man and let one live a refined, easy life while you put the other one through the wringer. She wondered if it was just outdoor life that made Lane look so much older, or if the lines on his face had been written there by some kind of stress or even sadness.

She folded her hands in her lap, doing her best to look prim and professional and praying she'd managed to wipe the lust from her face. Her tummy wasn't just doing a happy dance; it was cutting a rug in an all-out, hell-for-leather tango.

Lane nodded politely at the secretary. "Thanks, Dot."

The assistant made a high-pitched giggling sound that was totally at odds with her usual stolid personality and fluttered away. Lane headed for a chair, his stride a little uneven. Somehow the slight limp only made him seem more masculine—maybe because Sarah knew it was the result of an encounter with an angry bull.

But he was clearly at ease in the corporate surroundings, maybe because he overwhelmed them. His presence dominated the room in spite of Eric's imposing desk, and his animal intensity made the fluorescent light seem suddenly pale and artificial. He glanced at Sarah and her belly twisted again, hard this time, with an urgency that was almost painful. The man's eyes seemed to see right through her skin and into her soul—or maybe just into her underwear. Certainly the spasm of heat that bolted through her made her feel naked.

But she didn't like rodeo cowboys, she reminded herself. Not anymore. They'd been her heroes once upon a time, but since then she'd seen firsthand what their devil-may-care attitude and risqué charm could do to a woman's life. She'd sworn off men in general and cowboys in particular—at least until she got her career rolling.

Lane lowered himself into the chair beside her, shoving it backward so he could stretch out his legs. Now she couldn't see his face, and she felt immediately uneasy, as if he'd somehow earned an advantage.

"Lane." Eric reached for the pens and aligned them in a new, precise arrangement on the left side of the blotter. "This is Sarah Landon, our new public relations consultant. We're glad you could make it."

"Are you?"

Lane stared at Sarah with an unwavering and decidedly hostile gaze. She wished she had some pens to fool with, but all she could do was tighten her interlaced fingers in her lap and hope the heat in her face didn't show. The man was so loaded with pheromones that his gaze burned like a branding iron. She told herself the tugging low in her belly was just a reaction to the famous Carrigan charm, but her inner hussy was sashaying around her innards like the boogie-woogie love child of Richard Simmons and a TikTok dance star.

It took all her self-control to give Lane a cold, formal nod. Normally she would have offered her hand, but his gaze made it clear they were already in a fight of wills and she wasn't about to give him the chance to snub her and score a point.

"Nice to meet you." He pushed his chair further back and crossed his scuffed cowboy boots at the ankles. They weren't the tooled, polished fashion statements the wannabes wore to happy hour. They were plain brown leather, rough, scuffed, and unadorned. Working man's boots.

But he didn't work, she reminded herself. He played, riding real-life rocking horses like a three-year-old on steroids.

She worked her way up the faded denim of his jeans, flicking her attention to his face when she found herself eying his belt buckle. His answering gaze slid down the lapels of her jacket and dove into the modest neckline of her camisole. From there, it drifted from side to side, making her renegade nipples perk up and stand at painful attention.

He probably expected her to flutter girlishly like Dot and fall apart, but instead she looked away, pretending something outside the window was holding her attention. There was a cloud shaped like a duck drifting in the wide blue sky.

Think about the duck. Think about the duck.

"So." Eric shifted uneasily. "I understand you have a problem with the drilling on the Carrigan Ranch."

Lane hacked out a sound that might have been a laugh but sounded more like the bark of an angry dog. "I sure do. But it's not the Carrigan Ranch anymore. It's the LT."

"It'll always be the Carrigan Ranch."

"That's not your decision," Lane said. "It might be family land, but the ranch operation's a partnership now."

Sarah quickly turned her attention to Eric. He was a master of the poker face, but it was obvious the news surprised him. He'd told her the ranch was everything to Lane. So why would he sell out to someone else?

Maybe he needed money. Maybe he had some kind of gambling addiction, or a drug problem. Her eyes lingered on the bulge of his biceps. Were steroids addictive? Were they expensive? Because he was way more muscular than your normal rodeo cowboy. Riding and roping gave a man long, lean muscles. He was built like a weight lifter, solid and powerful.

His eyes fixed on the hem of her trim tapered skirt. The fabric ended just an inch above her knee, so she didn't know what he was staring at, or why it made her so uneasy. Checking out an associate's clothing was a valid means of judging their professionalism, but his gaze followed the line of her calves as if he was assessing her for some other purpose, and she doubted he was judging her chances in the Boston Marathon.

She clenched her knees together reflexively, regretting the reaction when faint crow's-feet gathered at the corners of his eyes. He'd goaded her into reacting—again.

By her count, the score was Lane three, Sarah zero.

CHAPTER 3

"SO WHY IS SHE HERE?" LANE SPOKE TO HIS BROTHER, DELIBER-ately turning away from the woman in the chair beside him. He didn't see why the company needed a public relations consultant. Did Eric want a witness to this conversation for some reason? Or did she have something going on with Eric? He normally went through women like Kleenex and seemed to have about as much respect for them. But maybe this one was better at gold digging than the past dozen or so. She certainly looked a lot smarter than any of them, so maybe she'd conned her way into the boardroom.

Well, she wasn't staying. He'd see to that.

"I'm a public relations consultant." The woman shifted in her chair, facing him and demanding his attention. "I develop strat-egies for dealing with legislators and community leaders to safe-guard and enhance corporate images."

She was obviously an expert at the kind of business-speak Eric used at every meeting. This might be a woman to be reckoned with—but he'd handle her. He doubted she was any tougher than a rodeo bull.

"That's a mouthful," he said.

"It's really fairly simple." She leaned toward him, speaking slowly as if he was some kind of idiot. "I find ways to help people understand what we do."

"What *Carrigan* does."

"That's what I said."

"No, you said *we*. And you're not a Carrigan. You're a publicity flack."

Eric stirred. "She's part of the team. And she's worked miracles for other companies. New West Corporation. Holt Communications."

"Isn't New West the company that developed a hundred thousand acres of Texas hill country into an industrial park?" Lane asked. "Shame about all the green grass and bluebonnets. And didn't Holt Communications string transmission lines over half of Colorado?"

The woman straightened her shoulders and gave Lane a tight smile. He could tell her nervous tension threatened to pull it out of shape. "Green grass and bluebonnets don't provide jobs for people," she said. "And those transmission lines helped bring high-speed Internet to the reservation, among other things."

"Oh, I get it. You're one of those people that sees the bright side." He gave her a teasing smile and knew he'd scored himself a point when she looked away, frowning. "I should have known. You seem like a real Little Miss Sunshine type."

He could see why Eric was attracted to her. She was pretty in a buttoned-up, businesslike way, but there was a lot of energy crackling behind those cool, expressionless eyes. Her tightly controlled demeanor was a challenge, and he wondered what it would take to get her out of that square-shouldered, double-breasted suit.

"I'm not Little Miss anything, Mr. Carrigan. And I'm definitely not sunny." She seemed to realize how silly the statement sounded and shifted uneasily. Another point for him.

"You're not, are you?" Lane settled back in his chair. "Well, sunny or not, digging up the LT Ranch isn't going to help anybody but Carrigan and its shareholders."

"We're hardly digging anything up," she said. "The process can move forward with minimal environmental impact."

"Really. Who told you that?"

"The company engineers."

"Wow. I wonder who paid them to say that."

Eric bristled. "The methodology of our scientists is unassailable."

"You always did go for the ten-dollar words," Lane said to his brother. "Environmental impact. Methodology. Unassailable. You sound like you're reading from a report by one of those engineers you're so proud of."

"Where do you want us to get our information?" The woman tilted her pretty nose in the air. "*Pro Rodeo News*?"

He narrowed his eyes and shot her a glare. So she thought he was just a stupid cowboy? He'd show her different.

He'd show her a lot of things.

"Mr. Carrigan, it really won't be a problem." She seemed to realize she'd stepped over the line and sounded a little less patronizing. "You'll be able to graze cattle even as they set things up, and you'll barely notice the difference once drilling is under way. There will be some extra traffic on the ranch roads initially, and we'll have to dig a shallow pipeline trench, but the land will be restored to its original condition almost immediately."

Lane set his elbows on his knees and looked her in the eye. "You really believe that, don't you?"

"I do."

"Well, I don't."

She lifted her chin. "What part of it is a problem for you?"

His eyes met hers with a discomfiting intensity that shot straight to her core. She squeezed her legs together and saw a faint smile tweak his lips.

"The problem is the part where you invade my land, construct a series of eyesore oil rigs, dig trenches across my pastures 'til the place looks like France in World War I, and scare my cattle into miscarrying with your construction racket," he said. "And then you overrun my hometown with transient workers who degrade the community and bleed law enforcement dollars without paying a dime toward local taxes."

"Your hometown?"

"Two Shot," he said. "It's a little place on…"

"I'm familiar with Two Shot," she said. "Do you really think it's worth saving?"

———✦———

Sarah cursed herself inwardly for rising to the bait. Her intimate knowledge of Two Shot was the last thing she wanted to talk about.

But how could Lane Carrigan call it his hometown? It was *her* hometown, and she'd never seen him there. Not once. The Carrigans had lived miles away, isolated on the elegant, state-of-the-art Carrigan ranch, and from what she'd heard the boys had only visited occasionally.

It surprised her how proprietary she felt about a town she'd been so anxious to leave behind. "I'd say the town would benefit from some new development," she said.

He was obviously one of those rich people who thought everyday life in a small town was an episode of *The Andy Griffith Show*. It had probably never occurred to him how tough it was to make a living in Mayberry. She could rock his reality if she told him what it was really like growing up in a place like Two Shot, but Eric's image of her—and his respect for her—would be in tatters if he knew she'd grown up in a trailer.

Dot poked her head into the room. "Mr. Carrigan," she whispered.

Lane and Eric both started to rise, and Dot gave Lane an apologetic smile. "I meant *Mr.* Carrigan. He has a meeting. But it's good to see you, Lane."

He grinned, seeming totally unaware that Dot had just defined the difference between the two brothers. Eric was Mr. Carrigan, taking charge and giving orders. Lane was just Lane. Dorothy's tone was warmer when she talked to Lane, but Sarah knew the oil business was a cold, hard world where warmth didn't hold much sway. Eric was the one who commanded respect.

Eric cocked his wrist and winced at the time on his watch. "I've got to go, Lane. If you'd give me a little advance warning, we can have a longer talk. Maybe lunch?"

Lane made a noncommittal grunt.

"Meanwhile, Sarah can answer your questions."

As he left the room, Sarah tried not to look as panicked as she felt. Lane might not command the respect of the Carrigan workforce, but his physical presence was intimidating and she didn't want to be alone with him.

Besides, the whole Two Shot situation was complicated. Normally companies like Carrigan just threw money at small towns, and folks were so grateful to get funding for schools and street repairs that they didn't question the project itself or who was involved with it.

But Lane was going to make it an issue, and that could be a serious problem for her. She'd led Eric to believe she'd leapt fully formed from the ivied bastions of Vassar and Harvard, but if he talked to anyone in Two Shot he'd get a very different picture of her past. Hiding her history had been an innocent lie of omission at first, but since then he'd made so many references to her inborn style and high-class roots she'd ended up with an origin myth worthy of Wolverine.

As her boss left the room, she squared her shoulders and faced Lane. She felt like a tiny bird fluffing up its feathers to intimidate a cat.

"So you're familiar with Two Shot?" Lane's voice rumbled deep in his chest, and his slow drawl made even the most innocuous phrases sound sexy.

"I've—been there. And I do feel the town would benefit from the prosperity this kind of project would bring."

He pushed back his chair and stood. Sarah immediately shot to her feet so she wouldn't have to look up at him, but even standing toe-to-toe her eyes were about level with his shirt pocket. She took a step back so she could look him in the eye.

"Yeah, well, I disagree," he said. "And anyway, I'm not discussing family issues with a stranger."

She thought of her hometown, with its pitted streets and crumbling buildings. "I'm sorry, but this is about much more than family."

"How would you know? Trust me, it *is* about family. And you're not a part of that."

His dismissive tone jabbed a man-sized hole in her self-control. She felt the real Sarah coming out to kick butt and was powerless to stop her.

"There are real people in Two Shot, Mr. Carrigan. People who need jobs."

"Money isn't everything."

"It is when you're hungry. When you're losing your home. When things go wrong and..."

She stopped herself. This was getting way too personal. He'd tilted his head to one side and was looking at her intently, and this time he seemed to be probing her mind instead of her clothes. She needed to get the conversation back on track before she gave something away.

"Extracting oil from the land isn't always pretty, but the company does its best to keep it clean, and if we do it on Carrigan land people will trust us to do it right." She cleared her throat nervously. He was still staring at her as if he was trying to figure her out.

She didn't like being figured out.

"I'm sure your brother will see to it that the ranch's historic heritage is preserved."

His eyes slid away and he pretended to be absorbed in brushing imaginary dirt off the thighs of his jeans. He was playing casual, but she could tell by the short, vicious strokes that the mention of his brother made him tense. Unfortunately, she was tensing too. The gesture emphasized the muscles bulging beneath the denim and made her conscious, again, of a testosterone aura that glowed with the steady intensity of a neon sign.

"Dad doesn't like my view of what it means to be a Carrigan. I always thought the name had as much to do with cattle as it did with oil. But what would I know? I'm just a dumb cowboy." He tugged at the collar of his blue chambray shirt. "My father hated the color of my collar, and I guess my brother does too."

"This has nothing to do with that," she said. "We're just saying—"

"What's this *we* shit?" Lane was more than angry now. "You're not part of *we*. Unless—are you something more than an employee?"

"I beg your pardon?"

"Are you having some kind of relationship with my brother?"

She felt like she'd been punched in the stomach. "Of course not," she said, struggling to keep her composure.

"No, you're right. He's not your type, is he?" He gave her that look again, the one that seemed to laser its way right into her mind. "You keep saying *we*, but you're not one of *them*. Where are you from?"

"That's none of your business."

"Well, it's the company's business," he said. "If you're going to go to bat for Two Shot, you ought to have some idea what makes a small town tick. But you don't, do you?" He nodded toward the window. "You try to act like you care, but you're ten stories above the street while I'm down there in the dirt with the rest of them. I can tell you real people don't want you and your minions coming in and ruining their land and their towns."

She should have defended her position, said Carrigan wasn't ruining anything, but she was overwhelmed with a rush of relief. He wasn't even close to figuring out she'd spent her childhood and adolescence rolling around in the dirt he thought was so all-fired picturesque. Even a no-kidding cowboy couldn't tell who she really was. And that meant she'd succeeded in leaving her past behind.

"Ever been to Midwest?" he asked.

Of course she had. Midwest was just north of Two Shot, an isolated outpost in the middle of nowhere that had struck it rich in the last oil boom. She hadn't been there lately, but she'd heard the boom had subsided. "They had a boom, didn't they?"

"And a bust. Now it's the world capital of substandard housing." He scowled and folded his arms across his chest. "All those cheap rentals they put up are falling apart, half of 'em boarded up. Guys came in and worked Monday to Friday, then went home to their families like they'd had their nose to the grindstone all week, when really they spent half their time with a snootful of beer. God only knows where their other body parts ended up. They're hell on local women." He shook his head. "Two Shot doesn't need your kind of prosperity."

"Why don't you let the people make that decision?" she asked. "Ask them if they want to keep trying to raise cattle on yucca plants and cactus, or if they'd rather sit back and enjoy life while Carrigan pumps out black gold, day after day, whatever the weather."

"And I suppose you care about what they want."

"Yes, I do." Those were the truest words she'd said since the conversation started. She didn't have many fond memories of Two Shot, and the few she had were clouded by failure and shame and a lot of uncomfortable truths. But deep down, she still cared about the people there.

"Well, I'm not letting the company ruin my land. I'll put up razor wire and go all Ruby Ridge if I have to, but I think there's probably an easier way." As he headed for the door, he tipped his hat in a snide mockery of cowboy etiquette. "See you on the nightly news."

She took a step toward him, then realized how close he was and stepped back. Unfortunately, she backed right into the door and slammed it shut. Next thing she knew, she was plastered against it like the heroine in a melodrama vying to keep her hero at home. He was standing so close she caught the clean laundry scent of his shirt and something else, something masculine—pine, wood smoke, leather. Maybe horses. Wind. She could feel him—not just physically, but deep down inside, the way you felt danger or heartache.

"I'm not here to play games," he said.

"Me neither." She grabbed the doorknob to steady herself. This was no time to go all girlie.

"So you weren't keeping score?"

How did he know about that? Her body language must have given her away somehow. What had she been doing—counting on her fingers?

He seemed to enjoy watching her flinch as he gently pried her hand from the doorknob and held it in his.

"I've got better games to play." His voice rumbled so deep in his chest she could feel it in her own.

"On the nightly news?" She slipped her hand out of his grip and wiped first her palm, then the back of her hand on her skirt with elaborate care, as if she'd accidentally touched something slimy. "I'm sure your brother would appreciate it if you kept your family business to yourself."

"Okay. Good advice. I'll start right now." His eyes met hers. "Stay out of my family business."

"Sorry." She snatched at the last shred of her self-control, but he'd gotten her riled up and she couldn't seem to stop herself from fighting back. "I'm paid to be in your family business. If you got along better with your brother, maybe you could talk him into firing people who annoy you. As it stands, you're going to have to deal with me."

"Okay." He shoved his hands in his pockets and relaxed his stance. "Good."

"Good?" She felt as if the plush carpet was suddenly moving under her feet like a grocery store conveyor belt. Surely he hadn't felt the same instant attraction that had struck her the moment he'd walked into the room.

Had he?

The answer came a little too quickly and shattered that notion like a bullet hitting a beer bottle.

"Yeah, good." His brows lowered and he looked like one of the bulls he rode, glowering at the world through the rails of the chute gate, ready to bust loose and raise hell with anyone who crossed him. "I like to know who my enemies are."

CHAPTER 4

LANE LOOKED DOWN AT THE WOMAN BARRING THE DOOR AND struggled to keep his composure. He wasn't sure what would happen if he let loose. Maybe he'd shove her aside and walk away, maybe he'd laugh, or maybe, just maybe, he'd push her up against the door frame and work his way past all that uptight professionalism to the real woman underneath. He'd work his way past that stick-in-the-mud suit, too.

She wasn't at all what he'd expected. Eric's previous public affairs manager had been a bitchy blonde who was all bones and teeth and blind ambition. This one was a very intriguing redhead, and there was nothing brittle about her. In fact, there was something almost admirable in the way she fought for the company. She seemed to honestly believe the project would be good for Two Shot, too. Her passion might be misguided, but it was sincere.

He stepped back from the door. How could he get to her? He didn't want to win the argument so much as he wanted to knock away that stiffly held shield of self-control. Or maybe kiss her.

Yeah, he wanted to kiss her.

He assessed her like a horse or a bull, trying to see past the hard shine in her eyes to find a weakness. She was on the defensive here, protecting her turf. He needed to get her out of this office and into his world, where he felt comfortable and in charge and she wouldn't be so damn sure of herself.

"What you need," he said, "is an education."

She tossed her head, as if she was used to wearing her hair long. Her tight French braid had loosened during their debate, and all the head toss accomplished was to loosen a random strand that dangled over one eye so she looked like an angry little terrier with one floppy ear.

"I don't think so," she said, her brows arrowing down. "I'm highly educated and highly qualified."

"And that makes you right." He leaned toward her and rested one forearm on the door frame. He knew he was big enough to be intimidating, but there wasn't a hint of fear in her eyes as she nodded her head sharply. Yup, she was right. All the time—or so she thought.

This woman would be incredible in bed.

He wiped that thought away and got back to the game. Winning required focus, and thinking about sex with his opponent was a sure way to derail his concentration.

Of course, he'd never had that problem with a rodeo bull.

"I'm not talking about book learning, here," he said.

The words came out "book larnin.'" Dang it, he sounded like an ignorant redneck. He'd spent his whole life shifting from one world to another, from the rich world of his family to the rodeo ring, and he'd become adept at taking on the qualities of the people he was with. But lately he'd spent so much time in the chutes that it was hard to shed the careless grammar and casual syntax of the rodeo. That could be a good thing. Sarah obviously set great store by schooling. If she thought he was stupid, she was liable to underestimate him.

But for some reason, he wanted her respect even more than he wanted to win.

"What I'm talking about is experience." He straightened and lowered his arm, concentrating on enunciating his *ings*. "Eric says you're an expert on small-town sensibilities, but your schools were back East, right? I'm not sure you understand what people are like in the West."

He scanned her eyes, noticing a smile behind her skepticism— almost as if she thought she'd already won. She was wrong, but he realized he'd take a smile from her wherever he could get it.

"Ranch life is different," he continued. "It depends on the land and the seasons, so it moves a little slower. And the things that matter are lasting things. Some folks might be willing to go for the quick buck, but cowboys think about the future. About their legacies, the land. Future generations."

She looked up at him and he saw sympathy in her eyes, as if she knew what it was like to worry about those things.

"I know." She looked away quickly, as if she'd given something away.

"You do?"

Her gaze flicked around the room, lighting on the desk, the bookcase, the carpet—everywhere but his face. "Not really. I mean, I know lots of people think about that, but, um, I don't know anything about cowboys. Not—not personally, I mean."

"See? You need an education." He shoved his hands in his pockets and rocked back on his heels, pretending a casualness he didn't feel. "Why don't you come to the rodeo with me tonight? I'll introduce you to some of the guys, and you can mingle with the crowd, get a sense of what people are like here. I can give you a real inside look at the West."

She shook her head so hard that another section of her hair escaped the braid. "No, I don't think so. Thank you, but no."

"We could talk about the ranch too. You could tell me more about how the drilling would help Two Shot."

Now he had her attention.

"I'd be interested to hear what you have to say," he continued. "My decision isn't cast in stone, you know."

Her brows slanted down again, making a little crease appear between her eyebrows as she scanned his eyes. He did his best to look guileless and a little stupid.

"Really?"

"Really. You just might be able to change my mind."

Sarah stared into her tiny closet and swore under her breath. Ever since Lane's visit, she'd felt as if her old life in Two Shot was bearing down at her like a speeding semi on a two-lane road, swinging wide on a turn and threatening a head-on collision. She could practically hear the air horn blaring.

The Humboldt Rodeo was the last place in the world she wanted to go tonight. Well, second-last. Two Shot, which was only a few miles farther on, was the last.

But it wasn't like she had a choice. She'd tried to turn down Lane's invitation as politely as she could, but he'd evidently appealed to Eric. Her boss had called her in and told her she had to go, his eyes shifting around the room, looking everywhere but her face. He probably would have bartered her as a bride if he'd thought it would help his cause.

Shoot, at least then she'd know what to wear. Choosing a wedding dress would be easy compared to finding an outfit that fit this occasion. She needed something professional yet casual. Chic, but with a touch of country. So far, she'd gotten as far as a white lace bra and panties.

Skidding wire hangers from one side of her closet to the other, she considered pencil skirts, blazers, little black dresses, and trousers. Everything she wore was aggressively proper because she didn't dress for success, or to express her fashion sense. She dressed to convince herself that she really had changed from a rough-and-ready country girl to a perfectly poised professional.

As she scanned the closet's contents and dealt with the sinking feeling in her stomach, her roommate Gloria flounced into the room and pitched herself onto the bed. Blond curls bounced on impact, along with a bunch of other body parts. Gloria was a bouncy kind of girl, all roundness and curves, with eyes as blue and innocent as a newborn's. But for once, she wasn't smiling. She eyed the trousers Sarah was holding as if she'd just pulled a dead animal from the closet.

"I thought you were going to a rodeo."

"I am."

"Well, you can't wear those. You need jeans. Where are your weekend clothes?"

Sarah sighed and hauled an ancient Samsonite hard-shell suitcase from under the bed. When she flipped open the latches, she felt like she was releasing her old self. She'd almost thrown out her ranch duds when she'd left for college, but her sister had pressed and folded everything, convinced Sarah would come to her country-girl senses and ditch her dressy ways once she graduated.

Sarah had sworn never to go back to her old life, but she'd broken that vow when Kelsey needed her. Then she'd been glad the clothes were there. Her sister would have had a fit if she'd worn her stuck-up city clothes on the weekend visits to help with her niece.

Stuck-up city clothes. Like the other 244 residents of Two Shot, Kelsey seemed to feel betrayed by her sister's determination to move beyond the town's barbed wire borders. Even though Kelsey herself was struggling to survive as a single mom in a single-wide trailer, she expected Sarah to share her knee-jerk loyalty to the town where they'd been born.

Sarah sorted through the suitcase. "I only wear this stuff on weekends," she told Gloria.

Gloria spread her hands in a don't-you-get-it gesture. "It's Friday night."

"I know, but I'm kind of working."

"Working?" Sarah could practically hear the grind of meshing gears as her roommate made the connection. Gloria widened her eyes. "You're going to see Lane Carrigan."

"Sort of," Sarah muttered. She didn't normally tell Gloria much about her job. The two of them had met through a Craigslist ad and agreed to share a loft-style apartment in one of the old brick buildings not far from the Carrigan tower. They were different as cats and dogs, but something in Gloria's carefree ways meshed well with Sarah's straitlaced personality. Gloria acted like a teenager set loose on the staid world of grown-ups, and Sarah ran her life like a geriatric business executive. Between the two of them, they made one pretty good twenty-five-year-old.

But as a Starbucks barista, Gloria was gunning for a golden future as a trophy wife. She envied Sarah her career, but only because it gave her such a great platform for husband hunting. Letting Gloria anywhere near the Carrigan brothers was a recipe for trouble.

She was sitting up now, wide-eyed and flushed. "Oh my God, Lane Carrigan would be perfect for you."

"No, he wouldn't."

"Yes, he would." Gloria nodded toward the worn Wranglers Sarah had just pulled out of the suitcase. "You're a cowgirl at heart."

"Am not."

"Yeah, you are. Me—I'd go for the other brother." Gloria's blue eyes took on a faraway focus, as if she was seeing the future. "He's so tall and dark and *rich*." She ran the tip of her tongue over her upper lip like a cat licking cream. "Like a venti French roast. Bet he goes down *smooooth*."

"Gloria, that's my boss you're talking about."

"Yours, not mine." Gloria tossed her curls and gave Sarah a mischievous smile. "But he could boss me if he wanted." She shimmied her shoulders in a move straight out of the stripper handbook. "I'd do whatever he said."

She watched Sarah struggle into the jeans. It took a few hard tugs to get them up and over her hips.

"Those are getting tight," Gloria observed.

"It's your fault. You and your Very Berry Coffeecake." Gloria had a habit of bringing home the excess treats from the coffee shop. It was probably a conspiracy to make Sarah as round and bubblicious as Gloria was.

"We should go shopping," Gloria said. "At that Western place. We could get you one of those sparkly shirts to draw attention to your boobs."

"Are you kidding? I've got enough Western duds to stock a Boot Barn tent sale." Sarah slipped into a silky peach-colored tee. "As soon as my sister gets back on her feet, I'm taking all this stuff to Goodwill."

"How come Kelsey's hubby left her, anyway?" Gloria settled back on the pillows heaped against the headboard, folding her hands behind her head. "She seems so nice."

"She is. He's just a jerk." Sarah couldn't even think about her former brother-in-law without a hot tide of anger sweeping over her. "That's how rodeo cowboys are. And he's not even a good rodeo cowboy. He doesn't make any money at it. Kelsey's raising my niece all on her own."

A pang pierced her heart when she thought of Katie. She'd heard how love overwhelmed you when you looked at your own baby for the first time, but she couldn't imagine a love stronger than she felt for her niece. It was a miracle to see her troubled family living on, surviving into another generation—but now that Mike had left, she was worried that old patterns were repeating themselves.

"She ought to take the guy to court," Gloria said. "Make him pay child support."

"Yeah, if she could find him. Mike's been MIA for months."

Gloria's wide eyes widened even more. "Wow. And she was a stay-at-home mom, right?"

"Was. Now she works at Katie's school."

"Well, it's good for a girl to have a career, right?"

Sarah wanted to agree. She'd been trying to nudge some

ambition into Gloria that reached beyond finding a rich husband to support her. But for Kelsey, being a mom *was* a career. She cooked like Rachael Ray, organized like Martha Stewart, and sewed all her own clothes and Katie's too. She'd decorated the trailer with all sorts of crafts, including a hand-embroidered set of sofa pillows that said *Home is Where the Heart Is, Love is Family, Family is Love*, and *Home Sweet Home*. Sarah had always envied her sister for having a philosophy of life so simple it fit on a throw pillow.

But Mike had torn that philosophy to pieces. If Kelsey made a pillow for him, it would say *I Just Want to Have a Good Time. Beer and Buddies Matter Most.* Or maybe something more direct, like *Who Cares About the Kid?*

She kicked around the footwear heaped on the floor of her closet, passing over sandals and pumps until she found her old boots. They were worn and scuffed and even a little dirty, but nobody would be looking at her feet. Not with Lane Carrigan beside her.

She toed into them and tugged at the backs to sink her heel.

"Boy, you really are a cowgirl, aren't you?" Gloria said, grimacing at the boots. "You can take the girl out of the country..."

"And you can take the country out of the girl," Sarah said, adjusting her jeans so they stacked over the boots just so. "They're just boots. And I'm only wearing them one night."

She stuck her wallet in one back pocket, shoved her cell phone in the other, and turned to check herself head-to-toe one more time.

"Wow," Gloria said. "You look like a completely different person."

Sarah had to agree. The woman in the mirror wasn't Sarah Landon, public affairs manager. She was Sarah the rancher's daughter, all dolled up and ready for the rodeo. Her hands were on her hips, her shoulders back, and her chin tilted up like she was ready to hold her own against the world.

She hated to admit it, but she kind of liked the real Sarah.

"Have fun," Gloria said. There was a hint of envy in her tone, and Sarah realized with a start that she could have fun tonight. She was going to a rodeo with Lane Carrigan. How many cowgirls would kill for a chance to do that?

Sure, she'd left her inner cowgirl behind when she'd left Two Shot, because you couldn't be a country bumpkin and gain the kind of respect she was shooting for. But maybe she should let a little of her real self out for just one night.

A horn blared outside and she glanced out the window to see a beat-up Dodge dually parked at the curb. It was definitely a cowboy truck, battered and bent, pieced together from so many parts it was hard to tell what its original color had been. The hood was red, the quarter panel blue, and hints of yellow paint showed through the rust on the tailgate.

Sheesh. Eric drove a Lincoln; his brother drove a disaster. Gloria was right—Sarah was hanging out with the wrong brother.

CHAPTER 5

LANE STOOD BESIDE THE TRUCK, LEANING AGAINST THE CAB with his arms folded over his chest and his ankles crossed. He should really pick Sarah up at her door, but there was a camera perched over the entrance to the apartment building and a bell on the door frame. It irked him to stand on the doorstep with his hat in his hand like a supplicant, waiting for Sarah to buzz him in. That would put way too much control in her hands. And while he'd started to like her and even respect her, he wasn't about to hand over the reins.

He shouldn't have even invited her to the rodeo. While it would give him the advantage of pulling her out of her world and into his, he wasn't sure he could endure the ribbing he'd get from the other competitors when he turned up with Miss Priss. She'd stand out like a long-haired cat at an all-dog poker game, and he'd never hear the end of it.

But it would almost be worth it to watch her climb into the truck in that sleek little skirt of hers. He was thinking so hard of the view that would offer that he almost didn't recognize the woman who whirled out the door and down the steps. Either she'd stopped at the Boot Barn on the way home or she had a hidden cache of cowgirl clothes.

He should have known she'd dress right. She was obviously the kind of woman who had to be the master of any situation, so she'd hardly dress inappropriately for any occasion. That realization made him want to take her to a pool party, or maybe one of those skeezy bars where the girls dressed like hookers. See if she was up for a challenge.

He opened the truck door and held out a hand for her but she

ignored him and hauled herself up into the passenger seat on her
own. He couldn't help noticing the way the jeans stretched over
her curves as she climbed in. They were lightweight denim, faded
to a summer shade of pale blue and worn in all the right places. She
caught him staring at the big Wrangler *W* on the back pocket like
he was trying to relearn the alphabet. She scowled, and he shot
back a know-it-all grin just to annoy her.

"You look nice. Thanks for dressing down."

"I like to fit in," she said.

"You do, don't you, princess? Not me. I like to stand out."

She'd practically handed him that point. He was starting to
enjoy this game.

"Do me a favor," she said. "Don't call me princess."

"Sorry." He gave her a full-bore Carrigan grin, the one that had
charmed rodeo queens and barrel racers from Tennessee to Texas.
"Just trying to be nice, that's all. I said I'd show you the good side
of the West, and that's what I aim to do."

"All right." Her girlish brand of spunk made him want to tease
her, in a big-brother, kid-sister kind of way. He half expected her to
stick out her tongue or punch him on the arm.

"Maybe in exchange you could show me the good side of Sarah
Landon," he said. "Assuming there is one."

"I don't know." She folded her arms over her chest and
skootched down in her seat, frowning at the city as it petered out
on either side of them and gave way to open fields. "If there is one,
you're sure not going to find it at a rodeo."

———

Settling back in her seat, Sarah tried to ignore the flutter of appre-
hension as she and Lane headed toward her hometown and the
past she'd worked so hard to leave behind. *There's nothing to worry
about*, she told herself. *Concentrate on Lane.*

It was just for one night, after all. She'd listen and fake interest in what the man had to say, and then she'd go back to work and find ways to get Two Shot to roll out the welcome mat for the Carrigan Corporation. She had to get that done no matter what Lane Carrigan wanted.

And being with him wasn't that much of a hardship. He might be arrogant and obnoxious, but he seemed to have a sense of humor. And he was, without a doubt, the sexiest cowboy ever to strap on a prize buckle. She ought to just relax and enjoy herself. But it was hard to relax when the air in the truck cab shimmered with vitality, and it was even harder to ignore the squirmy sort of warmth that was coiling deep in her belly. She turned her head, pretending to stare out the window, and hoped he couldn't see her reflection. Because she was pretty sure her tongue was hanging out.

It always surprised her how quickly you could get out of Casper. After a quick trip on the freeway, they cruised through an almost featureless landscape where broad plains stretched out from the road, bordered on both sides by a motley assortment of fence posts that proved ranchers were willing to staple barbed wire to anything that would stand still. She counted the posts as they flashed past. *One. Two. Three, four, five.* The truck picked up speed as the traffic thinned.

Unclenching her hands, she tried to relax. She leaned against the door. She propped one foot on the seat with her knee bent under her. That was uncomfortable, so she shifted and crossed her legs. Finally, she found herself back in her customary position, legs parallel at a graceful diagonal, ankles primly crossed, hands folded.

Shoot, she was such a tight-ass these days.

She hadn't always been that way. Riding across the plains in a pickup reminded her of riding to town with her stepdad in the days before child safety seats and seat belt laws. She and Kelsey had ridden in the truck bed with their backs to the cab and feet stretched out, letting the wind whip their hair around while they whooped and made faces at the cars behind them. Sometimes they'd stand up, resting their elbows on the top of the cab and bracing their feet, leaning into the wind like figureheads at the prow of a rusty, rattletrap ship.

"I'm the king of the world!" Kelsey would shout, spreading her arms.

Sarah wondered what had happened to Roy's old pickup. Sold, probably, along with everything else. Her mother had driven a series of nondescript sedans that had degenerated from simply used to derelict, reflecting the declining path her life had taken after Roy had died and she'd started finding comfort in the bottle again. She'd passed on two years later, and everyone at the funeral had called it "a blessing." Sarah thought the blessing came a little late. Her mother could have used God's grace a little sooner.

The crunch of gravel under the tires brought her thoughts back to the present. As they turned into a wide, flat parking lot, the rodeo grounds loomed before her like a slice of her past plopped down in the middle of the open plains. There was no good reason for the arena to be where it was except that some enterprising rancher had decided to use some extra lumber to build a set of bleachers. From that small beginning the place had grown into pretty respectable rodeo grounds, with fenced corrals for livestock, a high booth set on stilts for the announcer, and a playground for the kids—though why ranch kids would want to ride plastic ponies on springs was anybody's guess. As Lane and Sarah passed the chain-link fence that kept the kids corralled, Sarah saw a little boy throw out a loop and snag one of the play ponies like a pro, dallying his rope on the handle of the teeter-totter.

It was summer, so a carnival had sprung up around the grounds. Trailers advertising hot dogs and turkey legs were parked in ragged rows, and a few rickety rides competed with the playground. There was a beer tent on the far side of the arena, and a few enterprising women from the Wind River Reservation had set up tables in the parking lot to sell jewelry.

Lane checked his watch and cussed under his breath. "We're running late," he said. "I'll meet you after the bucking. You want to watch the barrel racing then, or hit the beer tent?"

"Beer tent," she said quickly. It was an easy decision. Watching the girls urge their horses through the cloverleaf would bring back memories, while tossing back a beer would help stave them off.

She headed for the stands, enjoying the way her old boots crunched on the gravel walkway. A bunch of girls dressed in sparkly rodeo queen attire were loping their horses up and down behind the concession trailers, showing off for the cowboys who lounged carelessly on their truck tailgates and pretended not to notice.

She took her time strolling to the entrance gate, dawdling over the jewelry tables. A young girl dressed in a tourist-pleasing buckskin dress smiled at her over a display of fetish necklaces and squash-blossom pendants. Sarah fingered a cheap silver necklace that was obviously made for the tourist trade. A tiny running horse dangled from the chain, frozen in motion, its silver mane streaming from its neck.

The child behind the table dimpled, smiling so hard her eyes almost disappeared behind her plump cheeks. "Only five dollars." She gave Sarah a sly sideways look, her eyes gleaming mischief.

"Three," Sarah said, catching on to the game.

"Okay."

Dang. The kid was sharp. Sarah hadn't really intended to buy anything, but she handed over a few crumpled dollars from her wallet and strung the necklace around her neck. *Silly, cheap thing. And a horse, too.* She shoved the charm inside her shirt and hurried over to the ticket line.

The voice of the rodeo clown crackled from a tinny speaker mounted high on a light pole, bantering with the announcer about goats and what great girlfriends they made. She could picture him in his baggy pants and wide suspenders, boogying on a barrel in the middle of the arena while he kept up a constant patter between rides. Shifting from one foot to the other, she breathed in the familiar odor of popcorn, beer, and nachos and flashed her companion pass at the sleepy cowboy slouching against the gate.

"Got yourself a cowboy? Better get in there," he said. "Buckin's 'bout to start."

She nodded her thanks and walked inside, pausing at the rail that edged the grandstand as rock music blared. The clown jumped off the barrel and crawled inside, his painted face scrunched up in exaggerated terror as a gate across the arena swung open. A bull stormed out, leaping like a cat on a hotplate, hitting the ground so hard with his front hooves that the cowboy on his back almost fell onto his neck. Sarah clutched the top rail with both hands, her lips moving in a silent prayer. Rodeo always stirred her emotions. Much as she wanted to be the bored city girl, she could feel the excitement as the rider struggled for balance with the bull's every buck.

Tilting sideways as the bull humped up his forequarters and leapt into a clockwise spin, the rider righted himself with a mighty heave of his muscled arm. He seemed totally in control now, his free hand held high, his outside leg spurring while the bull whirled in a frenzied blur. His hat shaded his face, but the size of him made her pretty sure it was Lane.

The announcer yammered with excitement and the crowd cheered as the bull stopped dead, snorted once, and spun the other way. The cowboy slid down into the spin, his arm muscles bulging as he strained to haul himself back up on the bull's back, but it was no use. Centrifugal force pulled him into the well like a leaf sucked into a whirlpool, and he hit the dirt shoulder first.

His hat flew off as he struck the ground and Sarah saw that it was Lane, scrambling to get his feet under him and run for the fence. Two bullfighters in baggy plaid shorts and red T-shirts rushed the bull, waving their arms in a frantic dance of distraction, but the animal dipped one blunt horn under Lane's ribs and tossed him into the air with a quick twitch of his head.

Sarah clapped her hand over her mouth to stifle a scream as his body rose into the air. There was a flurry of activity and when the dust cleared, Lane lay motionless on the ground. His hat lay in the dirt just inches from his outstretched hand, a massive hoof print crushing the crown.

Sarah stared down at the hat. The image of it lying there in the dust echoed an image from her past and opened her mind like a key sliding into a matching lock. Memories flooded into her mind. Another accident. Another man.

Another hat lying in the dust.

That day, Sarah had been a typical high schooler leading a typical high school life. As usual, she'd rushed through the hallways at school and daydreamed through her classes, anxious to get home.

Being eager to get home was a new thing for her. Before her mother met and married Roy Price, it had just been her mother, her sister, and herself, three women struggling to survive on the next-to-nothing wages her mother made as a waitress at Suze's. Actually, it had been three girls, not women. Kelsey was only twelve, and their mother had never acted much like a grown-up. Sarah had played the part of the adult in the family up until Roy swept all three of them out of their trailer-park life and moved them to his small ranch at the edge of town. To some people, it might not have looked like much, but to Sarah it was heaven. Not only did she have a dad now, she had a horse.

And it was one heck of a horse. Roy had been a horse trader all his life, but Chromium Flash was his biggest, best buy ever, a quarter horse stallion from champion performance stock with explosive speed and gorgeous conformation. Roy wanted to stand him at stud for a steady income, but first he needed to prove the animal could perform. He thought the horse would be good at barrel racing, and he wanted Sarah to ride him.

Sarah loved the speed of the race, the excitement of taking the tight turns at top speed, the shotgun run for the finish. She practiced every day in the small corral beside the barn, but Roy said she needed to work out in a regulation-sized arena. So that afternoon, they were taking Flash to the Humboldt outfit outside of town.

She'd practically leapt off the bus and flown to the house that day, tossing her backpack on the floor in the entryway and rocketing up the steps to her bedroom. She was excited to train in a regulation arena, but the best part would be spending time at Humboldt's.

"Hurry up," Roy hollered. "We've got to get Flash over there before four so you can practice. You want any time to talk to that Humboldt boy you're so sweet on, you'd better run."

"I'm not sweet on him," she hollered. But she could feel a blush warming her face. She'd always been shy with boys, but talking horses with Brian Humboldt was like talking to a friend. Maybe even a boyfriend. "I have to change."

"Well, change fast."

Though Roy had way more bark than bite, she changed as fast as she could. It wasn't like she had to decide what to wear. She'd thought through half a dozen outfits during algebra class, settling on a sparkly T-shirt that would glitter in the sun as she let Flash out of the trailer. Maybe Flash would rear and prance a little. She'd told Brian how hard he was to handle, and she'd seen a spark of admiration in his eyes.

But when she scanned herself in the mirror, turning right and left, she looked disappointingly childish. Brian was a senior. He'd never ask an unsophisticated freshman tomboy out on a date.

Makeup. That's what she needed. Opening her underwear drawer, she rummaged around and found a bag that held her meager supply of beauty aids: a sample of foundation from the Clinique counter at the Casper mall, an almost-empty tube of mascara she'd nabbed off her mother's vanity, and a compact of brush-on blush. Leaning into the mirror, she dabbed foundation in her T-zone, just like it said in *Seventeen* magazine, and brushed a little blush onto the apples of her cheeks.

She was just about to open the mascara when Roy pounded on her bedroom door. "You ready yet? We need to get that horse in the trailer."

"Just a minute."

For once, she was glad Roy was just her stepfather. A real dad would have charged right into her room and seen what she was doing, probably yelled at her for wearing makeup. But Roy always respected her privacy.

"I'll load him," he grumbled.

She heard him thump down the stairs and turned back to the mirror, opening her eyes wide to stroke on a coat of mascara as she thought about how Brian would fall in love with her new longer, blacker lashes.

She was on the second coat when a high-pitched shriek pierced the quiet afternoon. It was followed by a clanging, pounding racket and then another scream, lower this time. A man's scream. *Flash. Roy.*

She dropped the mascara brush and ran down the stairs. Flash was high-strung and nervous, and he hated the trailer. She'd always coaxed him in with treats, letting him take his time. He'd do anything for her, and secretly, she enjoyed the fact that he wouldn't behave for anyone else. Roy told her she was spoiling him, but he could never get the horse to load.

He must have tried, though. When Sarah ran out the door he was curled in the dirt at the foot of the ramp, blood pooling around his head. One hand was extended toward the trailer, where Flash stood trembling, glossy with sweat. As Sarah watched, he tried to rear and hit his poll on the top of the compartment, then flung up his back hooves in protest.

Somehow, Roy must have gotten in the way of those hooves. His gray felt hat lay in the dust beside him, its crown crushed by a perfectly shaped hoofprint.

Sarah ran to him, but one look at his ashen face told her he needed more help than a teenaged girl could offer. Slamming the trailer door shut on the trembling horse, she ran to the house to call 911, the newly applied mascara turning her tears black as they streamed down her face.

CHAPTER 6

SARAH DIDN'T KNOW WHERE BRIAN HUMBOLDT WAS NOW. FOR all she knew, he was in charge of the arena, but this was the first time she'd been to the rodeo grounds since the accident. With Roy gone, she'd focused on a new future—one where fortune didn't turn on the whims of a nervous horse. Once she'd loved rodeo and ridden horses every day. Now even the smell of saddle leather made her shudder.

She stared at Lane's hat lying in the arena and mouthed a quick prayer as a couple of cowboys ran over and knelt beside the unconscious cowboy. Lane's hand twitched, then waved away his would-be rescuers.

Thank God, she thought. *I couldn't take it if it happened again.*

The minute the thought crossed her mind, she wanted to smack herself. How could she think of her own feelings at a time like this? She forced herself to focus on Lane's body, lying in the dust. She thought about his eyes, his smile, his face. His butt in those jeans.

No, wait. That was almost worse. Self-preservation and sex— were those the only things she ever thought about?

Yes.

Lane rose to his hands and knees, his head hanging low, his back arched in pain. Silhouetted against the sunbaked arena, the man who'd been the picture of confidence that afternoon looked as utterly beaten as any man Sarah had ever seen. She felt tears prick the backs of her eyes.

That was more like it.

She swatted at her eyes with the back of one hand and sniffled. *One extreme to the other.* What was she crying about? She didn't know Lane, not really, and what little she knew about him she didn't like. But he seemed so strong that seeing him hurt was almost physically painful.

His first try at standing failed and he fell to his knees. His chest heaved as he braced himself and tried again, slowly rising to his feet. He lifted one hand over his head and waved to acknowledge the cheers of the crowd, then stumbled a few steps in the wrong direction. Sarah clasped her hands to her chest and watched him fall again just a few yards away from her spot at the fence.

She was jolted back to reality by the pounding of hooves. A pickup man on a sturdy gray gelding loped up and skidded to a halt right in front of her. Sliding down from the saddle, he scanned the crowd and finally nodded to Sarah.

"You," he said. "Come on through and hold my horse."

His tone was so authoritative she obeyed without thinking, ducking between the metal poles to stand at the horse's head. A medical team surged into the arena and the pickup man helped them lift Lane onto a backboard. He seemed to regain consciousness and tried to sit up. *Too ornery to die*, Sarah thought. But then he collapsed again.

It was hard to watch. Sarah stroked the neck of the horse who stood motionless beside her, regarding her stoically through a pale blue eye set in his white face. She was surprised by the softness of his sun-warmed pelt and how comforting the horsey scent of him felt.

The medics lifted the backboard and she realized with a start that Lane's eyes were open and fixed on her. God, she was probably the last person he wanted to see. He probably thought he'd died and gone to the Carrigan Corporation version of hell.

Tears threatened again, but she blinked them back and gave him a tentative smile. The medics whisked him away before she could tell if he'd been looking at her or simply staring at the sky.

"Let's have a round of applause for our boy Lane Carrigan," the announcer said in his down-home twang. "That's what we call the cowboy spirit here in Wyoming, the real cowboy spirit."

Sarah braced herself for some mention of the corporation or a comment on his interview the day before, but the announcer was apparently done with Lane. The pickup man came back for his horse, and the crowd's attention returned to the clown, who had brought out a goat on a leash and was kneeling in front of it as if proposing marriage. He presented a bouquet to the animal, who stretched his neck out and took a big bite of the flowers. The crowd laughed and Lane's wreck was forgotten as if it had never happened.

Sarah ducked back under the fence and edged through the crowd, following the signs that pointed toward the Justin Sports Medicine Clinic under the grandstand. The venue had turned a concession stand into a makeshift hospital, with a few folding cots laid out for the inevitable cowboy casualties. The scent of anti-septic burned in her nostrils, making her stomach tighten and twist. The scent of blood and sweat overlaid the smell of horses and cheap concession food, and she wished she'd taken one more breath of fresh air before she'd stepped into this space.

Maybe she should just go back to the truck and wait. Lane was sitting on the edge of a cot with his back to her, so he hadn't seen her yet. He'd doffed his shirt and his bare shoulders were hunched slightly, as if protecting his ribs.

A short, bandy-legged doctor in a cowboy hat glanced up from the bulb of a blood pressure cuff and Sarah realized with a start it was a woman, dressed in the cowboy uniform of chambray shirt and jeans. Only her white coat and the stethoscope draped around her neck separated her from the rest of the crowd.

The world of rodeo was still overwhelmingly male, and Sarah felt a stab of something like sisterhood as the woman grinned, bright eyes dancing, and set one hand on Lane's bare shoulder. "Well, this'll make you feel better. You got a visitor. And it's a girl!" She widened her eyes in mock wonder. "There's a surprise for you."

Lane turned and Sarah was stunned by the way the harsh fluorescent lights emphasized the prominence of his cheekbones and the deep set of his eyes.

"You okay?" she asked.

Dumb question. The man had just been gored. Of course he wasn't okay.

"I'm fine." Lane tried not to wince as he said the words. His shoulder was killing him, and his ribs hurt every time he tried to breathe. But he was fine, he really was. Pain was a part of rodeo, going hand in hand with the adrenaline and the cheers of the crowd.

Sarah looked appalled and he wondered just how bad he looked. "You got some dirt on your pants," he told her. "Makes you look almost human."

He gestured toward a row of plastic chairs set against the cinder-block wall, using the arm opposite the bruise. He kept the other one cradled in his lap, holding it motionless until he could figure out just how badly he'd been hurt.

"You might as well sit down," he said. "Doc Myrna's probably going to torture me for a while."

The doctor swatted his good arm. She was a fixture at rodeos and could set a broken bone faster than most doctors could take your temperature. But she wasn't much for sympathy.

"Sit still," she ordered.

He stared straight ahead while she shined a little light in his eyes. "Didn't anybody ever tell you to first do no harm?" he asked.

"Didn't anybody ever tell you not to insult the lady with the white coat?" She poked him in the ribs with her index finger. "That hurt?"

"You bet it does. Sadist."

"Whiner." The doctor turned to Sarah. "You the girlfriend?"

Sarah straightened, ready to issue a denial, but Lane beat her to it. "No, she works for my brother. I think she's supposed to make sure I behave like a good little Carrigan."

The doctor slapped her leg and hooted. "You need a keeper all right."

To his surprise, Sarah grinned. "I'm not keeping him. I'm throwing him back."

Maybe she wasn't such a priss after all. He'd sensed a sharp intelligence under her tightly wound demeanor, but he hadn't expected her to tease him with the kind of good-natured joshing the other cowboys dished out.

"She's giving up," he told the doctor. "Can't handle me."

"She's gonna have to learn," the doctor said. "You're gonna need a ride home."

"I'm driving." Lane grunted.

"Not after I get done with you, you're not," the doctor said. "This is gonna hurt." She looked up at Sarah. "Pulled a tendon in his arm, maybe tore it. Bruised those ribs real good too, but I don't think they're broke."

She busied herself fashioning a sling with competent but not terribly gentle hands while Lane tried to figure out which hurt worse—the wreck itself, or the doctoring afterwards.

"Take two of these." The doc handed him a small white envelope. "And let your lady friend take that beat-up carcass of yours back home."

"Keep your pills. I'm not taking that stuff." He slid off the table, which jarred his injured arm and sent a bolt of pain rocketing through his ribs. Sarah grabbed his good arm, but he shook himself loose.

"Yeah, you are." The doctor snatched the envelope from him and shook two into her palm. "It's an anti-inflammatory. You want to ride tomorrow, you'll take it."

He grumbled but obeyed when she handed him a Dixie cup of water.

"Tomorrow?" Sarah turned to the doctor.

"You can try and stop him, but I doubt you'll have any luck."

Sarah's eyes widened. "How can he be that...that..."

Lane tried not to look smug as she fished for the right word and resisted the impulse to help her out. *Brave*, maybe. *Courageous. Indomitable.*

"That *stupid*," she blurted out.

"It's a cowboy thing." Doc Myrna walked Sarah to the doorway, both women ignoring Lane as he trailed behind them. "You can't do a damn thing about it. They got to learn on their own." She shrugged. "Just get him home and take good care of him. That's about all you can do."

"I'm right here," Lane protested. "And I can take care of myself."

"Right. That's why you're thinking of getting back on a bull tomorrow," Sarah said. "But Doc, I'm not taking care of him. I told you, I'm not his girlfriend."

The doctor gave her a saucy wink. "Give him a couple of these and he'll think you are." She handed Sarah another pill envelope. "They're for pain."

Sarah glanced back at Lane. He'd hunched his shoulders, probably to protect his injured ribs, but he straightened up and did his best to look unconcerned when he caught her gaze.

"I'm fine," he said again.

The two women eyed him, then looked at each other and executed simultaneous eye-rolls.

"Anything wrong with leaving him alone for the night?" Sarah asked.

"Not for his sake, but maybe for yours." The doc winked again. "I saw you looking, girl. That's some prime, Grade A cowboy you got there." The smile faded along with the good-natured gleam in her eyes, and she patted Lane's good shoulder with a surprisingly gentle hand. "Take care of him, okay?"

CHAPTER 7

"How bad is it?" Sarah asked as soon as she and Lane were out of the doctor's earshot.

Lane scuffed his feet and shrugged, wincing as he lifted his shoulder. "I'm okay, but I could use some help getting my gear. Somebody probably grabbed it for me, but by morning they won't remember they have it." He tugged at the sling. "And carrying it's going to be a problem."

Great. She was with the most powerful, muscular man she'd ever met and she was going to have to carry his bags.

He strode confidently toward the area past the stands where the cowboys parked their trucks and horse trailers, forcing her to trot to keep up. Vehicles were scattered haphazardly around the wide, dusty lot, some lit only from within, some running with lights beaming out into the night. The sharp, acrid scent of exhaust overlaid the earthier scents of cows and horses as a big diesel pickup rumbled past.

"Hey." A cowboy seated on the tailgate of a parked truck gave Sarah a friendly smile. He was rolling a cigarette, something he'd evidently done many times before, since he didn't watch his hands as they pinched and twisted. He watched her instead, his eyes flicking up, then down, scanning her from head to foot. "Who's your friend, Carrigan?"

Lane ignored the question. "You seen my stuff? Those EMTs hustled me out of there without my gear bag."

"I got it." The cowboy reached back into the bed of the pickup with one hand and tossed a green canvas duffel at Lane. Instinctively, Sarah stepped in front of him and caught it. It was surprisingly heavy and she stepped back so fast she almost fell. Lane caught her, holding her tight against his chest.

"Who's this?" the cowboy asked. "New girlfriend?"

Lane didn't seem to be in any hurry to answer—or to let her go. She could feel his breath stirring the hair on the back of her neck, tickling her ear. She jerked away and slung the bag's frayed canvas strap over her shoulder. "Nope."

"Good." The cowboy thrust the finished cigarette between his lips. It bobbed as he spoke. "You want to go get a beer, hon?"

"She's with me," Lane growled.

"Thought you said—"

"I said she's with me." Lane grabbed Sarah's arm just above the elbow and half pushed, half pulled her away from the cowboy. She shrugged him off, but it was too late to stop heat from rocketing through her body, beginning at the place where he'd touched her and bouncing around to various body parts like a pinball racking up a high score.

What was *that* all about? Sure, he was sexy, but he was everything she didn't want. A cowboy. Worse yet, a rodeo cowboy. They were adrenaline addicts, risk takers. The last kind of person she wanted to let into her life.

It was just chemicals that made him seem so—so tempting. Testosterone and estrogen, scientific and inevitable. The setting, the scent of leather and horses—it was all so dang masculine. And the touch of his hand was a turn-on for the same reason it annoyed her: he was domineering, overpowering.

It made her want to prove him wrong. Do a little domineering of her own.

Where the hell had that thought come from? She didn't go for domination on either side of a relationship, did she? She liked men like Eric—polished and civilized.

"You cowboys have a little problem with testosterone, don't you?"

"Some of us do. I don't."

"Oh, really."

"Really." He looked down at her, then back at the cowboy who was craning his neck to ogle her. "You want me to go back there and knock him out?"

She rolled her eyes. "Oh, right. No testosterone problem here."

"What's that supposed to mean?"

"It means you're being irrational."

"What do you mean? He was rude to you."

"Why would that bother you? You've been nothing but rude to me since we met."

"Not that kind of rude." He looked almost contrite, staring down at the gravel-strewn dirt lot as they walked. "Well, not really. Besides, I have reason to be rude to you."

"Really?"

"Yeah. You came in here from God-knows-where, cozied up to my brother, and messed up my family. Messed up my life."

"I'm not cozying up to anybody. And I'm not the one messing up your life. You're the one who trashed your own company on TV." She slipped her hands in her pockets. "And don't try to tell me your family is your life."

"Isn't yours?"

She winced. *Only my sister. She's all I have left.*

"Family's always part of your life, whether you want them to be or not." She shoved her hands deeper in her pockets. "But if a messed up family means your life is messed up, I'm a train wreck like you've never seen."

"What's wrong with your family?" He actually looked concerned, and she had to squelch an impulse to tell him—about her sister, about herself, about all the ways she'd failed her own family after her stepfather died.

"Never mind." She tossed her hair and hoped she looked casual and at ease, not nervous and flighty like she felt. "We're not talking about my family. We're talking about yours."

"Right. Because your family's probably not exactly fascinating.

Where you from? New York or something? Your family's probably got the permanent pinkie cock."

"The *what*?" So far as she could see, it was the cowboys who had the permanent—whatever.

"The pinkie cock." Lane lifted his hand and mimed sipping from a cup, his little finger thrust out in an exaggerated imitation of an aristocrat drinking tea.

She smacked him on the arm, then remembered she was hitting an injured man and laid her hand over the spot she'd struck. "Sorry. Forgot."

"Didn't hurt." He sounded unconcerned, but he was speaking through clenched teeth. "But for a pinkie-cocking girl, you pack a wallop."

"I'm tougher than I look."

"You're different than you look." He gave her one of those appraising stares, but this one felt even more intimate than before. It was like he was seeking out who she was deep down, not just what she'd be like in bed. She fumbled with the gear bag so she didn't have to look back.

"If this business with your brother ruined your life, you're not tough at all," she said. "He figured you didn't care about it. You never returned his calls."

"I didn't know what he wanted. Figured it was just more Carrigan bullshit."

"Oh, yeah," she said. "I can tell your family's everything to you."

"Well, it seems to be everything to *you*. And I still don't understand that."

His fifth wheel was parked on the edge of the lot, the gaudy gold Carrigan logo glinting in the fading light of the sunset. She remembered how he'd asked if she was "something more than an employee" and stopped feeling bad about hitting his hurt arm.

"I'm not taking anything from your family, Lane. An honest paycheck, that's all. I'm just doing my job."

"And that makes everything okay, right?"

"It's what I have to do, so yes, it does." She tightened her lips. "If you've been shut out, it's not my fault."

"I wasn't shut out. I was never in. My father just trotted me out like a prize pony every once in a while."

"Like Whiplash." She couldn't help smiling.

"What?"

"Whiplash the Cowboy Monkey. He rides a dog around the arena, does some rope tricks. They trot him out—I don't know, what you said just made me think of him."

He lowered his brows. "How do you know about that? You a rodeo fan?"

She flushed. "Of course not."

"Hardly seems like your kind of thing. And anyway, I'm not a monkey."

He reached for the gear bag, lifting it as effortlessly as if he'd never been hurt.

"Where's the sling?" she asked.

"Took it off." He flung it on the bed along with the gear bag.

"Doesn't your arm hurt?"

"Nope. You want to come in? I need to check on my dog."

"No, I'll wait." What did he think she was, stupid?

Lane stepped inside and whistled. "Willie? Come on, Willie."

Sarah laughed. "Does this work very often?"

"What?"

"Getting girls to come to your trailer to see your Willie."

He didn't answer, just called again, sounding slightly muffled from the back of the trailer. "I can't find him."

"And I suppose you want me to help you look."

He reappeared at the door. "He's probably out visiting the barrel racers."

"Yeah, right. I bet he does that a lot."

"He does, actually. Sociable little dude."

Sarah snickered, but he didn't seem to notice as he jumped the steps and relocked the door.

"So," he said. "Beer tent?"

"I don't know," she said. "You were going to show me something good about your world tonight. You had all that talk about community, but the only cowboy I've met tried to steal your girl." She grimaced. "Worse yet, he assumed I *am* your girl."

He grinned. "Well, you are a woman, princess. And you are walking beside me."

"Behind you, actually."

He paused and waited for her to catch up. "Sorry."

He sounded like he meant it, but she couldn't tell if he was going to fling another zinger her way because his eyes were hidden in the dark shadow cast by the brim of his hat. "You know, you're right. This hasn't exactly been the best of the West."

He set off again, but this time he eased his pace so she could keep up. They passed the grandstand, heading toward the pens where competitors kept their horses. "Want to take a look at the horses?"

She shook her head so fast she almost gave herself a case of whiplash. "No. I'm…" *Dang. What could she tell him?*

Maybe it would be good to tell somebody the truth for a change. "I'm afraid of them."

"Really? I didn't think you were afraid of anything."

She shrugged, suppressing a faint glow inside at the compliment. *Fearless.* That's what she wanted to be. What she'd been, once. But fear ruled her life these days. Fear of poverty. Fear of losing control. Fear of failure.

Because she'd failed her family back when Roy died. All the way home from the hospital after his death, she'd listened to her mother rant about Flash, about how dangerous he was. He should be put down, she'd said. Sarah had convinced her to call the sale barn instead of euthanizing the horse, but her mother had still insisted that Flash would stay in the trailer until they came to take him away.

It was the one time in Sarah's life she was glad her mother reacted to stress by drinking herself into a stupor. With her little sister asleep and her mom passed out, there had been no one to stop her from sneaking out to save Flash.

—⁓—

The stallion's coat had been hot and damp, lathered with sweat from the stress of staying so long in the trailer. She'd whispered soothing words to him until he calmed, nudging her pockets for treats like his old self. Then she'd walked him to the barn and groomed him slowly and carefully in a slip of moonlight that slanted through the door. At first he'd spooked and sidestepped, but she'd stroked him until he stood quietly. Nothing but the tension rippling under his skin told her how the day's tragedy had affected him.

"I'm scared too," she'd told him. "But it's going to be okay."

She'd saddled him slowly, methodically, taking comfort in the familiar motions and hoping the horse did too. It seemed like it, because she could feel the knotted tension in his mind giving way as she slipped on a bridle with a sweet iron snaffle bit and led him outside. Then she'd slipped her foot in the stirrup and grabbed the saddle horn, just like she had a hundred, maybe a thousand, times before.

She'd visualized this ride all the way home from the hospital. She'd ride him up to the house, spin him right and left in the front yard, then holler to her mother to watch so she could prove he was safe as a child's pony. Or maybe she'd ride him into the sunset like a movie cowboy, leaving her old life behind and taking him with her into some unknown future.

Somehow, some way, she'd save him from going to the sale barn.

But as she shifted her weight to the foot in the stirrup, Flash rolled his eyes back and whinnied, a hoarse scream tearing through the night. She'd clung to the reins, knowing that if she let him go he'd bolt off and run until a semi on the highway stopped him or a barbed wire fence cut his legs and tangled him to a stop.

He spun to face her and reared, and in that instant she could only think of Roy, broken in the dirt at the foot of the trailer ramp.

She'd been afraid of a horse for the first time in her life. She'd barely been able to hold him, but he'd finally bucked out and stood trembling, docile as a kitten. With shaking hands, she unsaddled him and led him back to the trailer.

He'd loaded without a fuss, just like he'd always done for her, and she'd thought again of how different things would be if she hadn't been so selfish, if she hadn't thought it was so important to primp and preen for some boy she barely knew. Roy was dead. It was her fault. And the next day somebody from the sale barn hitched the trailer to a growling diesel pickup and took Flash away for the last time.

Flash had sold for two thousand dollars—a tenth of his value. And no wonder: the last thing he'd done was kill a man. It didn't help that the various stories Sarah had told Brian Humboldt about how hard he was to handle had made their way around the small world of horse traders.

Everything Roy had brought into their life was gone, swept away by his death and her foolishness. Everything he'd worked for was gone.

All because Sarah couldn't work up the courage to ride a horse.

CHAPTER 8

SCANNING THE SCATTERED LIGHTS FROM HORSE TRAILERS AND RVs decorating the rodeo grounds, Sarah let the hum of engines and the buzz of generators chase the memories out of her mind. Somehow, she needed to change the subject and get Lane talking about something other than horses.

"You know what would be good right now? A turkey leg. And maybe some ribs." She wasn't the least bit hungry, but it would provide a distraction.

"A woman who eats real food. I like that." He stopped and touched her shoulder, and she felt the mood between them shift. She should have kept walking, pretended she didn't notice, but something in his tone made her stop and turn toward him. He wrapped his hands around her biceps and ran them down to her arms, leaving a shimmering trail of sensation in his wake.

"I like *you*," he murmured, taking her hands.

She stiffened, trying not to react to the scent of him, the warm awareness of his body inches from hers. "Come on, Lane, stop. You're not my type and I'm not yours."

He scanned her face, his eyes probing hers. "I'm not so sure of that. You're pretty spunky once you get out of that straitlaced suit."

She pulled her hands away, wondering just what he'd meant by that comment, and was surprised to see he was flushing a little. The double entendre must have been unintentional.

"Sorry," he said. "But you were right—testosterone runs high around here. Girl dressed like you might as well be running a gauntlet."

"Dressed like me?" She was suddenly conscious of the way her old jeans clung to her flesh. Maybe it wasn't that the cowboys were overloaded with testosterone. Maybe she just looked like a woman who was willing to help them work some off.

He glanced down at the jeans, then caught himself and returned his gaze to her face.

"Didn't mean it that way. You just—you look good, that's all. Really good."

―――

Lane could have kicked himself for being so clumsy. Sarah looked great in her jeans and T-shirt. There were plenty of buckle bunnies prancing around like prize ponies for sale, dressed in slutty midriff-baring tops and jeans so low you could see butt cleavage. Compared to them, Sarah was a thoroughbred.

But she wasn't the tight-assed professional type his brother usually hired. She was funny, smart, and sassy. She'd joined in on the banter with Doc Myrna like she'd known her all her life.

He was attracted to her—and not just to her body, though that was damn near enough. Unlike most women, she could carry on a conversation and he actually enjoyed being with her.

Too bad it was all about Carrigan. She wouldn't even be here if it wasn't for business.

They'd strolled into the shadow of a shuttered concession stand, and the faint light glinted on her cheekbones and the delicate curve of her shoulders.

Damn, that filmy, silky shirt was pretty. He didn't usually notice a woman's clothes, but the pastel peachy color brought out the delicacy of her complexion, and the fabric skimmed over her skin so smoothly he could make out the lacy borders of her bra. He wondered what it would feel like if he took a slip of the cloth between his fingers. It was so finely woven it would probably catch on his rough hands, maybe even tear. He wasn't the kind of man who could handle delicate things. Fine china broke in his hands, and delicate women didn't last long either.

And for all her spunk, he sensed a fragility behind Sarah's professional facade, a hidden store of secrets and insecurities. Not that she'd ever admit it. He could tell she was a regular warrior princess when it came to shielding her feelings.

"Princess." He realized too late he'd said the word out loud. Worse yet, his hand had followed his thoughts, reaching out to touch the silky surface of her shirt.

"Don't call me that."

She might be objecting to the name, but she wasn't pushing him away. He ran a cautious, gentle fingertip down the faint outline of her bra strap, tracing the delicate line of lace down to the place where her breast swelled in a sweet, sensuous curve.

"Sorry." He toyed with the necklace that dangled between her breasts. At the office she'd been wearing a dignified diamond chip in an abstract setting. Now she was wearing a little silver horse charm on a chain. It looked like a kid's necklace.

He lifted his finger to touch the point of her china doll chin. "Can't help it. Can't help—any of this."

He tipped her face up to his. With her pale skin and wide eyes, she made him think of a fawn, sleek and soft and Bambi-eyed. Was this the same Sarah he'd met in the office? She seemed so hesitant now. So—womanly. A tangle of conflicting feelings welled up in his chest, a need to protect her combined with an urge to dominate her now that she'd showed a hint of submission.

He smoothed a lock of hair behind her ears. He hadn't intended it to be a sexual touch, just a comforting one, like you'd use to calm a skittish horse. She tilted her head and for a moment he held her cheek in his palm. She closed her eyes and drew in a soft breath, her lips parting, and there was nothing he could do but kiss her.

Her lips were so delicate, so perfectly shaped. He'd just meant to touch them with his own, but he couldn't resist flicking out his tongue to trace the smooth curves of her upper lip and that sweet little dip in the middle. When he felt its pillowy, velvet texture give way, an arrow of desire hit his heart as surely as if she'd aimed it. But she hadn't aimed it. She wasn't half-trying. She was giving in to him, surrendering.

So why did he feel so damned helpless?

He buried his fingers in her hair and deepened the kiss, wrapping his other arm around her shoulders and pulling her to him. Sure enough, the silk shirt snagged on his rough skin, but when he slid his grip down to her waist the cloth wafted weightlessly over his hand and he was touching her skin, smoother than any silk and warm, so warm under his fingertips.

She shifted in his arms and he started to pull back, but she was moving toward him, not away. He realized with a start that her lips were seeking his as desperately as he'd sought hers. His palms cupped her waist and her body bent backward, arching not to escape but to press herself against him. He moved one hand up her side, savoring the way she shivered as his fingertips ran along the edge of her bra. The other drifted low, stroking the perfect curve of her ass, and she let out a sound that was feminine and wild and totally uncivilized.

Her little tongue touched his and slicked along the side, then dipped teasingly past his lips and flicked out again. That might have been an accident, but then she did it again and they were past kissing. This was something far more, him thrusting, her parrying, and he felt desire spiral up in his loins and make him so hard so fast he thought he'd die if he didn't reach down and release the pressure. But his hand got sidetracked on the way, sliding over her breast, feeling the soft flesh yield while the lace teased his fingers.

Smoothing his thumb over the curve, he felt her nipple hardening to his touch and had a flash of what she'd look like naked, all that smooth perfect skin and hard, pink nipples begging to be kissed and licked and more. He wanted to take her back to his trailer, pull that slippery little shirt off over her head, and shimmy her out of those tight jeans. He wanted her legs around his waist and her breasts in his hands. He wanted to keep on kissing her, but he wanted more than that—a lot more.

A car door opened in the alley behind them and a slash of yellow light sliced into the shadows. It slanted across her body, traveling from her white throat up to the soft curve of her jaw, rising to light her flushed cheeks. With her swollen pink lips and wide eyes she looked like a sexy Madonna, Venus in blue jeans, tempting and sultry and sexy as hell.

A little wild, too. Her hands raked his chest and he took them in his own so he could kiss her better, but now she really was pushing him away.

"Lane, no," she hissed. "Wait!" She snatched her hands away and skittered backward, smoothing her shirt, tucking her necklace beneath it. She was buckling her belt too. When had her belt come undone?

"Sorry." His head was spinning. "What…"

"It's okay. I—I—it's okay. I mean, it's not, but it is." She was twirling her hair in a frantic effort to redo the ponytail at the back of her neck. He bent down and plucked her barrette out of the dirt.

"Oh. Thanks." She clipped up her hair with a practiced twist and straightened, smoothing her shirt and squaring her shoulders. "Do I look okay?"

He grinned. "Do you mean like normal-okay, or sexy-okay? Because I'm not sure I'm qualified to judge the kind of okay you want to be."

He felt suddenly energized. The kiss had made him forget his aches and pains. He'd been hoping this jaunt was something more than a job for her. He'd caught a distinct hum in the air at their meeting this morning, a sexual tension between them that ran both ways.

If only she wasn't scared of horses.

But wait. That had to be a lie. He'd woken from his bull-riding wreck to see her standing over him, her eyes glowing with an other-worldly light as she held a white horse like some equestrian angel who'd come to carry him to heaven. Maybe he'd imagined it. Maybe it was wishful thinking. But if he was going to indulge in wishful thinking about Sarah Landon, wouldn't she have been naked?

And there was that necklace. A horse. She was lying when she said she didn't like horses. He was sure of it.

She frowned and that little crease appeared between her eyebrows. "Button your shirt."

He looked down to see his chest exposed nearly down to the waist, bandages and all. "Hey, I didn't unbutton it."

She let out an exasperated breath and leaned toward him, her fingers brushing his sore ribs as she struggled to fasten the buttons she'd clawed loose. He took pity on her and helped, which probably slowed things down as their fingers tangled together. Her gaze flashed up to meet his and skittered away again. She bit her lip and concentrated on the buttons.

When she finished the last one and started to pull away, he took her hands in his own, holding them against his chest.

"Does this mean we're not having sex?"

"Lane, shh." She nodded toward a group of men emerging from the nearby car. "Tuck in your shirt and let's go." She was all business now, except for the flush that reddened her neck and cheeks. He wondered if it was embarrassment or passion or if she was just pissed off. Probably all three.

He shoved his shirttail into the waistband of his jeans, wincing as his hand hit his still-eager buddy down below. She turned to him, her eyes stern, and he had to resist the urge to kiss her into submission again.

She smoothed her shirt and he almost groaned as the fabric tightened over her breasts.

"Is there any sign of…anything?" she asked. "Can you tell what happened?"

"Not by looking at you. Maybe by looking at me, though."

Her eyes flicked downward and away, her cheeks flushing.

"Want to go for that beer?"

She swallowed. "Sure."

She gave him a stiff little nod and he wondered what had happened to the woman who'd kissed him a moment ago. She was all tense now, and he couldn't think of a thing to say to her as they headed past the bright lights of the midway and made their way through the dimly lit parking lot. He usually found it easy to talk to women. He talked, they giggled. Then they went to bed, and he didn't have to talk anymore. But that obviously wasn't the way it was going to go tonight.

Most of the concession stands were closed for the night, but a string of plastic chili pepper lights glowed red against the buff canvas of the beer tent. The catcalls and whoops of celebrating cowboys drifted through the canvas and swirled on the night air, mixing with the sharp scents of spices and barbecued meat. Sarah kicked a stone with the toe of her boot and sent it skittering across the walkway. Lane looked down and froze.

"What's with the boots?"

She pulled her wallet out of her pocket and took out a five for the cover charge, ignoring Lane's efforts to pay. "Nothing."

She edged through the crowd and plopped down in a folding chair, swinging her feet under a long table that looked like it had been borrowed from a school cafeteria. A couple of guys waved at Lane, but he nodded and sat down beside Sarah, bending down to tug at the hem of her jeans. "Let me see those."

They were brown leather cowboy boots, square-toed and unadorned. They weren't girlie fashion footwear with fancy tooling; they were working boots. Judging from the worn, scuffed leather, they'd been used and used hard.

She pulled her foot away. "They're cowboy boots. Is that a problem?"

"Real cowboy boots."

She tucked her feet under her chair and he knew he'd scored a point. He just didn't know how.

"No city girl has boots like that."

"This city girl does." She shrugged and looked away. "They come that way these days."

This was getting interesting. He'd seen the so-called "distressed leather" boots they sold in stores. Sarah's were the real thing, broken in, broken down, and used damn near to death.

He was sure now that she was lying about the horse thing. And he definitely wanted to go on with the game.

———

Sarah glanced around the crowded interior of the tent, searching for familiar faces. Humboldt was far enough from Two Shot that she might go unnoticed—but there was a chance somebody would turn up who knew her *when*.

When she'd been dirt-poor trailer trash. When she'd been the daughter of a drunk, the only defender of a family that fed the gossip vine like Miracle-Gro fed potted plants.

"Shit," she muttered, then winced. She wasn't thinking. She hadn't been thinking when she let him kiss her, and she hadn't been thinking when she swore like some spunky heroine in a Reba McEntire song, either. He was scoring points right and left, and she was losing the game big-time.

"Sorry," he said, surprising her. "It's not exactly the Ritz. I just thought this would give you a sense of the kind of people you need to deal with, the kind of minds you're looking to change."

She nodded, realizing she'd almost forgotten the whole purpose of the evening. It was hard to squelch her old self—the self that would have given her right arm to go to the rodeo with a guy like Lane, share a kiss in the shadows, go for a beer and maybe a dance. It was a redneck girl's definition of fun.

But Sarah knew now that there was a price to pay for fun. Her sister had paid that price and Sarah had been careful ever since—the responsible sister. She tipped out one foot, frowning down at her worn-out boot. When things went wrong, you had to have a plan. That's where Roy had gone wrong. He hadn't planned on the accident. He hadn't planned on Flash selling for next to nothing. He'd bet everything and lost, so they'd had nothing to fall back on.

That was never going to happen to her again. She'd worked hard to become a new person. A successful person, a *rich* person who could take care of herself and have enough left over to help her family.

She needed to get back to work, where she only had the younger brother to contend with. The safe one.

Because being with Lane was not safe. She could feel her old self clawing at the cage she'd created, trying to break through the layers of sophistication she'd built up over the years. And if her old self got loose, she was liable to do a lot more than kiss Lane Carrigan the next time they ended up in a dark alley.

CHAPTER 9

LANE WATCHED SARAH SIT PRIMLY IN A FOLDING CHAIR AS THE band cranked out country's greatest hits on the platform at the front of the tent. Her lips were pressed tightly together, her hands knotted in her lap. She was probably afraid the locals would eat her alive.

He smiled at the thought. As far as he was concerned, her world—the business world—was full of piranhas and barracudas. Worse yet, the predators there dressed like regular folks. In his world, people might look a little rough but at least you knew what to expect. Bikers wore leather, and cowboys wore hats. Easy girls wore low-cut tops, and good girls—good girls dressed like Sarah.

The top of the tent was a tangle of electrical wires, each one leading to a paper lantern. The individual circles of light made each table a mini-stage, highlighting the various dramas taking place. At one, a woman sat slouched over a beer, watching with wounded eyes as the cowboy beside her chatted up a woman at the next table. At another, three women watched the band, their eyes fixed in identical predatory squints on the lead singer. At the one closest to the door, a man and woman conversed in furious whispers. Lane couldn't hear what they were saying, only the faint hiss of anger in their tone.

He let his eyes roam down the bar, where cowboys and cowgirls perched on tall stools, boy-girl, boy-girl. Some of the women leaned close to the men beside them; others seemed determined to shrink into the smallest space possible as eager cowboys waved imaginary lassos in the air, recounting their glory days.

Everyone was trying a little too hard, including the band up on the makeshift stage. A singer with serious dental issues was rasping out the lyrics to "Sweet Home Alabama" with his stance spread wide and his skinny hips thrust forward. Behind him, a fiddler sawed determinedly at a battered violin. Everything was a little too loud, a little too desperate.

Sarah's eyes flicked from one face to another, then slid back to a thirty-something cowboy who was standing a few feet from the bar, talking with a bunch of other guys. Lane had seen the guy ride a few times, and his mental tape loop pictured him getting bucked off a lot. He remembered a fatal tendency to misread the horse's cues, a habit of letting his shoulders tilt into the spin and pull him off center.

The guy sure wasn't making much of an impression on Sarah. Lane hoped she never looked at him like that, with her brows lowered and her lips tightened in disapproval. He scanned the luckless cowboy from head to foot, wondering what annoyed her so much. He wasn't bad looking—reasonably fit, dressed in the typical cowboy uniform of striped shirt, Wranglers, and boots. The shirt was faded as if it had been washed about a hundred times, but Lane didn't think Sarah cared about the condition of a man's clothes. If she did, his own would never pass muster. And however cold she was now, she'd kissed him like she wanted him. He brushed a finger over his lips and she flashed him a glare almost as cold as she'd given the other guy.

Maybe coming to the beer tent was a mistake. He should have kept her in the shadow of the potato skins stand.

As Sarah swung her gaze back to the cowboy, the guy turned like he could feel the chill. When his eyes lit on her face he froze as if he'd been turned to a pillar of ice.

"Sarah Landon," he said. "Shit."

So he knew her? That was odd. Though she'd seemed remarkably comfortable at the rodeo, she sure didn't seem like the type to spend time in the kinds of places where this guy probably hung out. Unless he was from Texas or Colorado, where she'd stomped out a couple of small towns at the bidding of the corporations she'd worked for. Maybe that's what this was about.

"Mike Sullivan." Sarah spat out the name like it was a cuss word. She turned to Lane. "Could you get me a beer, please?" She said it curtly, still staring down the mystery cowboy. Suddenly, she seemed less like a delicate flower and more like a cactus blossom, beautiful but ringed by thorns. He felt like saying no, but maybe it was better to get away before she started scratching the other guy's eyes out.

Starting toward the bar, he wove his way through the crowd of cowboy-hatted men and tight-jeaned women. Halfway there, he turned and saw the guy striding over to her, fists clenched at his sides and a pugnacious scowl on his face. Lane paused midstride to listen in.

"What are you doing here?" the guy asked Sarah.

"Working," she said. "And I suppose you're having a *good time*."

She said it like it was the worst thing a guy could do. Lane definitely needed to rethink hanging out with this woman. She was even more straitlaced than he'd thought.

"I suppose I am."

The guy's chin jutted in defiance, his hands still clenched into fists. Something was wrong with this picture. Maybe it was the familiar way the guy spoke to Sarah. Maybe it was the way he stood, stiff and hostile. He looked like a man about to start a fistfight. Surely he wouldn't hit a woman. Lane walked back to Sarah and stood just behind her. The guy's eyes flicked toward him and he did a quick double take.

"Hey, you're Lane Carrigan."

Sarah turned and scowled at Lane. "I thought you were getting a beer."

"Thought you might need me."

"I don't." Her tone was frosty as a chilled mug.

"You sure?"

"Hey, run while you can, buddy." The guy barked out a bitter laugh. "Sarah's liable to spit in your eye before she even knows your name."

"Spit?" Sarah snorted. "That would be too mild."

"Yeah, well," the guy said. "Having second thoughts isn't a capital offense, you know."

"No?" Sarah lifted her chin imperiously. "Well, it should be." She waved the guy away. "Have a *good time*, Mike."

What the hell was she so upset about? And how did she know this guy? The mystery was intriguing, but if she had a problem with a guy having a good time Lane was done with her. Sarah might have softened when he'd kissed her, but now she was all sharp edges.

He'd get her the beer she'd asked for, but then he needed to get her home and get away from her. No matter how much he'd enjoyed that kiss.

"Who was that?" Lane had returned from the bar with two beers, making his way through the crowd in record time despite the shout-outs of half a dozen cowboys and an equal number of eager buckle bunnies.

"He's nobody." Sarah downed half the beer in one gulp, determined to finish it and go. She'd thought she could get away with coming here. Because of the lack of jobs, there was hardly anyone under the age of sixty left in the Two Shot area.

But Mike didn't care about jobs. The guy had all the ambition of a cat in the sun. He'd seemed smitten with her sister, and he'd done the right thing for a while, sticking around after the baby was born. He'd found a steady job at the feed store and come home to Kelsey's cooking every day. He didn't spend much time with Katie, but Kelsey thought parenting was the woman's job.

Then the feed store had shut down and instead of finding another job, Mike had left his family for the rodeo road. Said family life was too "confining." He'd married too young, he said. He needed to "have a good time."

Sarah wanted to kill him. He'd left Kelsey with a two-year-old daughter and Kelsey started the single mom struggle for yet another generation of the Landon family.

She threw back another slug of beer as Lane hailed a waitress who was edging through the crowd with a tray full of oversized shot glasses. Grabbing one, he shoved it at Sarah.

"Drink up," he said. "I'm driving."

She sniffed the amber liquid and the scent of tequila almost knocked her head back. A shot was the last thing she needed. She'd already loosened up way too much, kissing Lane in the alley, letting Mike get her steamed. Or was she already drunk—on Lane, on all the testosterone he put out? Could pheromones make you dizzy?

Maybe. He gave her a smile and a wink that made the rage ebb a little, raising his beer in a toast.

"Come on, it'll do you good," he said. "You're a little tense. I'm afraid to get back in the truck with you."

She didn't blame him, but there was nothing to worry about. She'd spent all her anger and adrenaline on Mike, and now she felt like she was made of glass and might shatter any second.

Bringing the glass to her lips, she tilted her head back and drank. The liquor traced a fiery path down her throat and coiled in her belly, spiraling up to warm her from the inside out. She set it on the table and wiped her mouth with the back of her hand. Dang. What a redneck move that was. But Mike had already blown her cover, and Lane didn't seem to care. He grinned and draped an arm over the back of her chair.

"See? Having a good time isn't such a bad thing."

He had a point. She let herself lean into him a little. It felt good to have a big, muscular man beside her. And Lane really was trying to show her a good time.

That kiss. Now *that* was a good time.

She turned and scanned his face, wishing she could just give in to the urge to nestle into the crook of his arm, tuck her head under his chin, and enjoy the music. But what must he think of her? He didn't know Mike had walked out on her sister. He probably thought the guy was an old boyfriend. He must think she was a total bitch.

As a matter-of-fact, a lot of people thought that. And maybe they were right. When had she changed so much? She just wanted security, financial and otherwise, for herself and for Kelsey, but most of all for Katie. She didn't want her niece growing up with the same doubts and uncertainties she'd had.

But sometimes it seemed like her ambition had taken on a life of its own. It was eating up her life and her personality until she'd become a woman she barely recognized—and one she didn't like very much.

She wouldn't blame Lane if he let her go, but he pulled her a little closer and she went limp, tucking her head under his chin and resting her cheek on his chest. She felt safe for the first time in years.

"That guy," she said. "It's not what you think."

He shrugged. "Whatever. You don't have to tell me anything."

"No, I do," she said. "*I'm* not what you think." She hailed the waitress. "Bring us another shot."

CHAPTER 10

LANE SAT BACK AS THE WAITRESS IN THE TIGHT CUERVO T-shirt and denim short-shorts slid two more shots across the table. "On the house," she said with a flirty little curtsy. "Just let me know if you need anything, Mr. Carrigan." She winked and walked away, twitching her tight little behind.

The glasses skidded on the moisture glossing the table. One almost landed in Sarah's lap, but she caught it deftly and downed it in one easy motion.

"So," she said. "Let me tell you everything."

"Everything?" He grinned. "You're giving me whiplash."

She arched an eyebrow. "The kiss was good, buddy, but I'm not buying you a monkey."

He laughed. "Not that Whiplash. Emotional whiplash."

"You're right." She sighed, staring down into the empty shot glass. "I'm running hot and cold tonight. Part of it's Mike."

"Bad memories?"

"Like I said, it's not what you think," she said. "He's my sister's ex. Knocked her up, made a big deal out of 'doing the right thing' and marrying her, and then last year he walked out. Said he'd married too young and needed to have a good time."

"Oh." Maybe he'd misjudged her. She had every reason to hate that guy. But what was her sister's ex-husband doing here in Wyoming?

"How…"

He didn't even have to finish the question. It was like she couldn't wait to tell him. "I'm from here. Well, near here." The words tangled on her tongue. The tequila was talking, but she didn't seem to care. Stiff, stuck-up Sarah was gone. He could almost believe she was from Humboldt.

"I thought you were from New York or something."

"That's what you're supposed to think." She sighed. "For God's sake, don't tell Eric. He thinks I'm just like him. Like you. From a wealthy family. But I'm—I'm actually from Two Shot."

She said it like she was admitting to mass murder. Now it was his turn to look away as he tried to figure out how to respond. He kind of wanted to laugh, but that would obviously hurt her. She was confiding in him, letting him into her life as surely as she had when she'd kissed him. And it was becoming more and more obvious that letting people in wasn't easy for her.

She was watching his face, her eyes flicking up to his to gauge his expression.

"You sure don't seem like a small-town girl," he finally said.

"Thank you."

"That's not necessarily a compliment."

"I know."

The waitress set down a pitcher of beer and two plastic cups, shooting Lane a sexy little smile. Sarah grabbed the pitcher and started pouring. She'd filled the cup halfway with foam before Lane took the pitcher from her and finished the job, holding the cup at an angle so the beer poured smooth and clear.

"I hated it, Lane." Sarah took the cup from him and sipped. "You think Two Shot's so great, but I couldn't have spent my whole life there."

"I wish I had."

"I know. You call it your hometown. But you never—I mean, I'm from there, and I never saw you there. We would have known each other."

She stopped short of accusing him of lying, but he could see the doubt in her eyes.

"I wasn't there much," he explained. "It was as close to being home as anything I had, but I spent most of my time in boarding schools back East."

"Boarding schools?"

"Exeter."

She drew back and scanned his face like she was looking for the stuck-up preppie hidden under his cowboy facade. "You're kidding."

Apparently she couldn't even imagine him at a swanky school. He should probably be insulted, but as far as he was concerned that was a good thing.

"I hated it," he said. "I might not have spent much time at the ranch, but it was home. My real home. The two weeks a year we spent on the ranch were the best times of my life." He took her hand and laced her fingers in his own. "The prep schools were my dad's idea. He wanted nothing more than to leave the ranch behind." He flashed her a questioning look. "Kind of like you."

"What I'm leaving behind isn't twenty thousand acres and a family empire. We didn't even have a home—just a series of trailers and apartments. We had a ranch for a while, but…"

He could almost see the shield going up. The light in her eyes dimmed and she swallowed, turning her attention to their interlaced fingers, staring at them as if they were so absorbing she couldn't possibly continue the conversation.

"The ranch?" he prodded gently.

"We lost it. So there's nothing in Two Shot for me but a bunch of bad memories."

She dropped his hand and straightened in her chair. Obviously, talking about Two Shot was not the way to win her over.

"I suppose I shouldn't claim it as my hometown," he said. "I didn't actually grow up there."

"That's okay." She sipped her beer and rolled her eyes. "You can have it. I don't mind. And I'm sure they'd be happy to put up a sign for you at the city limits. You know, *Home of Rodeo Champion Lane Carrigan.* Something like that."

"That's not what I want," he said. "I just want to belong there."

The minute the words were out, he wanted to take them back.

How pathetic was that? He'd just given away far more than he'd intended. She was probably picturing him as a kid, slouching around the campus at his prep school, friendless and homesick for a place he'd never really lived.

"I guess boarding schools wouldn't be a great place to grow up," she said.

"Not really. But I could see where a small town might be tough too."

She sighed. "There's nothing there. No jobs. No money." She sipped at her beer, then licked the foam mustache off her upper lip. "And poverty sucks."

"I wouldn't know."

"No, you wouldn't." There was no bitterness in her voice; they were both just stating facts. "When you don't have money, you don't have options. You get trapped."

"So how'd you get out?"

"Scholarschlip. I mean scholarship." She slumped back in her chair and traced her finger down the side of her cup, revealing the golden liquid through the condensation. "I went to Vassar."

"Well, they sure put a sheen on you."

"Yeah, they did."

"*That* was a compliment."

She smiled, which was definitely an improvement over scowling into her beer.

"Thanks. But I'm still the same person underneath, you know? And places like this remind me of that."

"Sorry."

"Don't be," she said. "Telling Mike what I think of him felt really good."

"You miss cutting loose."

"I miss my old self. I watch every move these days. I have to test every word before I say it, make sure I'm still in character. I miss saying what I think, being myself. I miss being *fun*."

—⁓—

Sarah felt like her thoughts were a runaway horse, breaking through fences and running for freedom. She'd never told anybody these things before, but somehow telling them to Lane felt right.

"It must have been hard—getting out," he said.

"It was."

"Bet you broke a lot of hearts."

"No. I didn't get attached to anyone. No boyfriends or anything. I didn't want anybody to tempt me to stay." She didn't know why it suddenly felt so important to explain things to this man. Maybe it was because he straddled both worlds: her old world of cowboys and country and her new world, which consisted mostly of Carrigan Corp. these days. "I didn't want to hurt anybody."

"But you did." His voice was surprisingly gentle. "You hurt yourself, hon. The person you used to be."

"It's no big deal. People change every day. It's how you survive. I built a new image for myself, just like I'm building a new image for Carrigan."

"So your life is like a publicity campaign. Everything planned out and calculated."

She'd never thought of it that way before. He was right. She controlled every aspect of her life like she was producing a movie, and that meant she was faking it 24/7. There was a tension inside her that simmered just below the surface, a panicked, desperate feeling that needed an outlet. She'd been able to tamp it down until tonight, but somehow he'd opened a door to her true self. Maybe it was being here in the beer tent. Dressed like everyone else, she felt like one of the crowd, anonymous and strangely free.

Or maybe it was that kiss. Lane was watching her with those ice-blue Carrigan eyes, focusing on her face as if reading the thoughts behind her expression.

"Do you watch the bulls like that before you ride them?" she asked.

"Like what?"

"You look like you're trying to figure out how hard I'll buck. I'll save you the trouble. I buck hard. So you can stop watching me like you're going to break me or something."

"I don't want to break you." He put his hand on hers. "I was trying to figure out how I could gentle you a little bit."

She felt the hard shell around her heart crack like the candy coating on an M&M. Lane moved his thumb over the soft spot on her wrist and she felt suddenly vulnerable. *Melts in his hand, not in his mouth*, she thought. *No, melts in his mouth, too. His mouth…*

"What are you thinking, Sarah?"

She tossed her hair and looked away. "Thoughts."

"What kind of thoughts?"

Crazy thoughts. Sexy thoughts. Leaning into him, she caught that masculine scent cologne companies could never quite manage to cram into a bottle. The light bounced off the sun-bleached streaks in his hair and sculpted his face, highlighting a scar that ran from his temple to the top of his right cheekbone. Without thinking, she reached up and traced a finger down the length of it. The band stopped playing just then and everything in the room seemed to freeze, as if time had been temporarily suspended. Lane's gaze was expectant, his breathing slow. The moment was hushed, like something that mattered was about to happen.

"Let's dance," he said.

"Okay." She flashed him a smile. "Let's."

~~~

The woman saying yes to a dance seemed like a completely different being from the woman Lane had been talking to a moment ago. He'd watched a riot of emotions play across her face as she went through some complicated process that evidently ended with a decision to trust him. Now she was smiling and bright-eyed as she cocked a hip and held out her hand.

"Can't think of anything I'd rather do," he said. Actually, he could think of a lot of things he'd rather do with Sarah, but he couldn't do any of them in public. Dancing would have to do—for now. It was an excuse to touch her, and touching would help him figure her out. Sometimes before a ride, he'd lay a hand on a bull, feel the tension in its muscles and the blood pulsing through its veins. A skipping heart and twitching muscles told him the bull was nervous, maybe even scared. A steady heart told him it was ready for the ride. A scared animal bucked to shake you off, while a relaxed animal bucked for the joy of winning—and joy bucked better than fear.

He needed to get Sarah to trust him. Then they could get back to their game, and maybe there'd even be some…bucking.

The fiddler stepped down to cheers and backslaps, and the band swung into their next song, a limping but serviceable rendition of a George Strait ballad. Lane led Sarah to a dim corner of the dance floor and took her hand, pulling her toward him while he wrapped his good arm around her waist. He'd expected her to tense, but she melted into him like a stick of sweet butter, her curves conforming to his muscles, her head resting on his chest. He could feel her tension ebbing away as he held her and swayed, and when he looked down her eyes were closed.

A wave of tenderness swamped him and he wondered what was happening. He was an old-fashioned guy, and it was a natural impulse to want to protect women. But this was more than your standard manly protective urge. There was no threat here, no ex-boyfriend, no predatory Lothario or evil ex-husband. There was just this woman, this soft tender woman, who thought she had to be tough to survive. Who thought she had to cover up her true, generous, sweet nature in order to succeed.

He wanted to protect her from herself.

And the only way to do that was to make her feel safe. What was it she'd said about poverty? *When you don't have money, you don't have options.* He wondered when she'd learned that lesson and held her a little closer, lowering his head so his lips rested gently on her glossy hair. She smelled like peaches and flowers. He rested his cheek against her head and swayed with the music, closing his eyes as she relaxed into him.

When you trained horses, there was a point where the horse stopped fearing you and started to trust you. He'd learned to feel the subtle shift in energy as the change took place and the animal opened up its heart.

He felt that now.

When the music stopped, they stood still in the moment. Somehow, in the course of one song, everything had changed.

Sarah let Lane lead her through the crowd on the dance floor. They followed a serpentine path through the scattered chairs and tables, most of which were empty since the band had struck up a Chris LeDoux song that flooded the dance floor with swirling girls and stomping cowboys. When they stepped out of the bar, the lights of the rides and concession stands were out, leaving the rodeo grounds in shadow. The reflection of the moon floating in a silvery pillow of cloud was duplicated over and over in the empty windshields of parked cars.

Sarah jumped as a ghostly white blob shot out from the shadows.

"Willie." Lane bent and picked up a dog, white and woolly. Someone had tied the hair up over its eyes with a pink bow.

"That's your dog?" She stifled a laugh.

"Yeah." He looked as sheepish as a too-tall cowboy with a sissy dog could possibly look. "One of the wives must've got hold of him. I don't do bows."

"No, I didn't think you did."

"Mind if we take him back to the trailer?"

The music from the beer tent, the muffled voices rising from the flap, the hum and thump of various engines and compressors around the rodeo grounds—all the sounds of the night seemed to pound in a steady rhythm that matched the beat of her heart. *Lub-dub, lub-dub.* It sounded faintly ominous, like the music from *Jaws.* She could take it as a warning, or she could see it as a challenge.

She'd always loved a challenge.

"Sure," she said. "Why not?"

He hoisted Willie under his good arm and they strolled in silence back to the trailer. Unlocking the door, he set the dog inside and held out a hand to Sarah. She glanced up at the moon and felt suddenly adventurous, like her old self. Taking his hand, she climbed in after him.

She scanned the snug, shipshape interior. There was a tiny breakfast nook with leather-padded benches on each side, but Lane had set his gear bag on one and Willie claimed the other, turning in tight circles before lying down.

"He parties all night with the ladies, then comes back here to sleep," Lane said.

"Wonder where he learned that routine." Sarah sat down on a foldout bed that doubled as a sofa. She felt surprisingly comfortable, considering she was in a very small space with a very large man. Maybe it was the dog. "He doesn't seem like a cowboy kind of dog."

"He's not." Lane shot the dog a scowl. "He turned up in the back lot at Fort Worth. I figured I'd pawn him off on some buckle bunny or something. Named him Willie as a joke. But nobody ever wanted him and now he won't answer to anything else. Guess I'm paying for my sins."

Lane lowered himself onto the bed beside her, which was understandable since he couldn't stand fully upright in the small space. The moon cast a cool, soft light through a skylight, silvering his face to the tones of an old tintype and accentuating the timeless masculinity of his features. He looked like he'd just come in from playing cards with Wild Bill or chasing after Butch Cassidy. His eyes met hers and she realized she'd been staring.

"What?" he asked.

"I was wondering…"

"Wondering what?"

"Would you kiss me again?"

He reached for her and pulled her close—but not close enough. Leaning backward, she pulled him down on top of her and slid her lips over his jaw to whisper in his ear.

"When you kiss me, I remember who I really am."

CHAPTER 11

SARAH FLEXED HER HIPS, PUSHING HER PELVIS AGAINST LANE'S. That was probably his belt buckle she was feeling.

Or maybe it was him. She sure as hell hoped so.

Because cutting loose from her uptight city-girl persona had loosened something else, too. Some people might say it was her morals, but she felt relaxed and a little euphoric, and it wasn't just the tequila. Maybe it was her inner hussy, or maybe it was her true self.

It felt good to tell her secrets. Of course, there was nothing to stop Lane from telling Eric she wasn't what she seemed, and while Eric might not fire her, he wouldn't trust her anymore. How many times had he mentioned how lucky he was to find a girl with so much inborn class and culture? How many times had she led him to believe she was the real thing?

She felt a stab of panic, then shrugged it off. There was no point in worrying. What was done was done. She didn't know if it was the heat of Lane's body or the warmth of the tequila running through her veins, but something was torching all her inhibitions and igniting all kinds of delicious new possibilities. She'd resolved never to mix business with pleasure, but Lane didn't want any part of the business, right?

Besides, the rodeo arena, standing isolated on the highway to nowhere, seemed somehow separate from the rest of the world. Cars and trucks whipped by on their unknown business, oblivious to the lights and noise, the little dramas playing out behind the rough wood ranch-style entrance. Once the dramas were played out, people drove out of the lot and back into everyday life. It was like stepping out of time and into a fantasy world.

Suspended in a ray of moonlight, she felt the world outside the trailer slow, then stop.

Maybe, just for one night, she could step out of the life she'd constructed so carefully and be herself. She took Lane's face in her hands, nesting her fingers in his hair as she bent down and ran her tongue over the curve of his lips. As her breasts flattened against his chest and his hips flexed to meet hers, she spilled everything she felt out into a hot, fiery kiss that burned through the last of her scruples.

Sarah Landon, Two Shot cowgirl, had returned. And surprisingly, Sarah Landon, prissy professional, was really glad to see her.

Talk about shifting gears. Lane had never seen a girl change from prim and proper to sweet and sexy so fast in his life. He drew back, partly to appreciate the sight of Sarah sprawled beneath him and partly to make sure it was really happening.

Her eyes were half closed, her hair a tangled mass framing her pale face. Her T-shirt had ridden partway up and somehow the top button of her jeans had come undone. She was an open invitation any man would accept.

He stroked a finger across the waistline of her jeans. His finger dipped down into the V created by the undone button and her skin rippled in response.

Bending down, he kissed her again, his hand skimming up her body. Her abs didn't feel like a city girl's; they were taut and strong but not hard like a gym six-pack. He kissed the spot at the juncture of her ribs, then lifted the shirt higher. She sighed and arched her back, her breasts straining at the confines of her bra, and he deftly undid the front clasp and peeled away the thin fabric.

The sight of her lying half naked on his bed in the moonlight was something he never wanted to forget, and for a minute he just drank her in. She twisted her body, closing her eyes and parting her lips as if not having his hands on her was torture. He cupped both hands around her breasts, squeezing them gently, and licked a slow circle around each nipple. She gasped and made a pleading sound, a little cry that flooded him with feeling. He'd been hard since they danced, but now he was balanced on the thin line between pain and pleasure, his skin stretching over muscles so taut and tense that the slightest touch would send him over the edge.

He made a conscious effort to slow down, flicking his tongue over the rising peaks of her breasts, giving each one his full attention. She squirmed her approval and her jeans edged lower, the zipper parting to reveal a hint of lace and a few reddish curls. His hand drifted down and touched her there and he felt that ripple run through her body again as she threw her head back and bit her lip.

He wanted to have her, take her, now. He wanted to claw off her jeans, rip away the lace, spread her open, and bury himself inside her. The urge was so strong it shocked him.

She reached up and pulled his face to hers, kissing him with a wildness that echoed his own, and suddenly they were writhing like animals, clawing at each other's clothes.

Slow down, he told himself. *Slow down*. But she buried her fingers in his hair and slid her tongue into his mouth, gliding it out and in again in an unmistakable demand. Slowing down was out of the question.

He reached down to unfasten his belt and her fingers tangled in his, clawing and tugging until she managed to release him, and then her hand skimmed up the underside of him and her thumb swept over the top. He was afraid he'd be finished before they even started, so he sat back, resolving to savor the way the moonlight polished her body and shaded her curves.

But when he stopped, the world rushed in and reality hit. He stopped with his shirt half off, and when she reached up to finish the job he trapped her hand in his.

"Sarah, you—I think you might have had too much to drink." He breathed out a long, shuddering breath. "I'm sorry. I lost control."

She sat up and yanked at the shirt, hauling it away from his bruised shoulder.

"I am not drunk," she said. "I can hold my liquor. I'm from a town called Two Shot, for heaven's sake."

"Honey, you're no bigger than a minute," he said. "There's no way…"

"Do you want me to walk a straight line down the middle of the trailer? Look." She closed her eyes and spread her arms, then touched the tip of her nose with each index finger.

It was silly, but somehow ridiculously erotic. At that point, she probably could have stood on her head and it would have turned him on.

He closed his eyes, then realized that if he left things up to his imagination they'd only get worse. But when she threw off her shirt in a gesture straight out of a strip show, he had to close them again.

Sarah didn't know if she wanted to screw Lane or strangle him. For the first time in her life she had a man she really wanted, right where she wanted him. He was so aroused he was shaking. She'd been about to have the best sex of her life.

And he'd decided to go all conscientious about her level of inebriation.

"I'm fine," she said. "And if you don't touch me again I'm going to go over there and find a kitchen knife."

"Yikes," he said. "How do I know you're not just a mean drunk?"

"You don't. But how pathetic is it that I have to threaten you before you'll have sex with me?"

"I don't want to take advantage."

"Take advantage, all right?" She realized she was screeching and took a deep breath. "Stop making me beg. Let's just pretend we can't help ourselves, okay?"

He smiled. "Okay. If we can't help ourselves, that would mean we have to help each other."

"Right. You rip off my clothes and I'll rip off yours."

"Yours are already gone."

"Then catch up, cowboy."

She heard a distinct tearing sound as she tugged at the sleeve of his shirt. Well, maybe she should rip off the other sleeve too. That was kind of a cowboy thing, wasn't it—wearing a shirt with the sleeves ripped off? It should be, anyway, if the cowboy had muscles like Lane's. The preppie types she'd dated the past few years hadn't even come close to this.

She pulled him down on top of her and then they were both naked and he was kissing her and she was sinking her fingertips into the hard muscles of his haunches and steering him right where she wanted him.

"There," she said. "Go. Please. Go."

The muscles flexed and she felt him there, right there.

Still there. No further.

She opened her eyes to find his face inches away. His gaze was so intense she closed her eyes again.

"Open your eyes," he whispered. "Look at me."

She didn't want to do it. If she looked into his eyes there'd be more than a meeting of bodies going on; there'd be a meeting of minds, and that was the last thing she wanted.

"Just go," she whispered.

He started to pull away and her eyes flipped open like a doll's. "I'm here," she said.

"Good." He moved into her, then out, watching her face. His gaze was tender and hot all at once, and she felt her shield slipping. She could almost believe this meant something to him, but that wasn't possible. They barely knew each other. This was a one-night stand, a brief, hot interlude of mindless sex, a slaking of both their appetites and nothing more.

Besides, he was Lane Carrigan. He could have damn near any woman he wanted. A small-town girl turned spinster business-woman was hardly what he'd choose.

"Nobody ever felt this good," he whispered. "Nobody."

She tried to say something witty, but what came out was a pleading animal noise as she pulled him into her again. After that she stopped thinking and simply moved. It was like music, the way they dipped and soared, asked and answered, over and over, until she cried out again with a scream that released all the darkness inside her and let his light flood in to take its place.

When she opened her eyes again, the moon had slid into the small skylight and was looking down at her with its blank, serene face. It felt like a blessing. Lane lay beside her, sleeping. She hadn't noticed what long lashes he had. They softened the masculine planes of his face, making him look less like a mythical outlaw and more like a man.

A man who made love to her like there was actually love involved. But then, Lane did everything all-out. When he rode, he rode wild animals; when he made love, he chose a woman determined to resist him. Even when he slept, he slept hard. She shimmied out from under the arm he'd tossed over her waist and slipped off the bed, gathering her clothes. When she'd finished dressing, she tapped him on the shoulder.

"Lane, I need to go home."

He rose and dressed without a word, as if he was still asleep—or maybe he knew talking would break the spell. As he dressed, his shadow shifting in the moonlight, Sarah sat on the edge of the bed and slowly came to her senses.

What the hell was she thinking? Real life didn't end at the entrance to the rodeo grounds. You couldn't step outside your life. You couldn't stop time and do what you wanted and expect no repercussions.

What was done was done, and there was no point in regretting it. But she needed to figure out how she was going to move on. For instance, what she was going to tell Eric in the morning. She was supposed to be changing his brother's mind about the drilling, not seducing him.

Hopefully Lane would agree to keep their liaison under wraps. Maybe he'd understand that this had been a one-time thing, that she wasn't that kind of girl. That she'd slipped, and she simply needed to right herself and move on.

Lane pretended to be absorbed in finding his scattered clothes, but he watched Sarah's face surreptitiously. She looked confused, impatient, and regretful—and none of those expressions boded well for the future.

Didn't she know what they'd just shared? It didn't matter that she worked for his brother. It didn't matter that they were different kinds of people, with different goals. She was driving on a fast road to prosperity, and he was fleeing just as fast in the opposite direction. Maybe the fact that they'd collided head-on was a sign that both of them needed to stop and think about where they were going and why.

Talking about Two Shot with her made him realize he might have idealized the notion of small-town life. But she was being just as unrealistic about wealth and prosperity. Being well-off might mean you'd never starve, but it didn't guarantee happiness.

"Okay." She pasted on the same smile she'd worn at the office, before she'd let down her guard. It was about as bright and meaningless as the painted smile on a Barbie doll. "I'd better get going then."

"Sarah." She'd let her hair fall over the side of her face and he swept it back with one finger. "Don't shut down on me."

"I'm sorry, Lane. I have to go back to work tomorrow. With your brother." She reached up and pushed his hand away. "It was—fun, you know? But it's time to get back to reality."

"That *was* reality."

"It's not the reality I had planned."

She draped her purse strap over her shoulder and opened the door, slipping down the steps and into the dark night without looking back. He followed, his boot heels crunching on the gravel walk. They'd passed the beer tent, the potato skins stand, and the shuttered booth where she'd bought the running horse necklace before he spoke again.

"You know, it's funny. I've been trying for years to shed that veneer you've been working so hard to build up. Trying to get real."

She kept walking.

"It's an advantage, you know—coming from Two Shot. The whole reason you understand rich people so well is because you can see them from the outside. And you know all about small towns."

"Way more than I want to know."

They reached the truck and he opened the door for her. He put out a hand to help her inside, but she pretended she didn't see it and climbed in on her own.

He slid behind the wheel and turned to face her, propping one leg up on the seat. "Two Shot made you who you are. If you'd been born rich, you wouldn't be you. You wouldn't have all this ambition and drive."

"So you're saying it's good to have something to run away from?"

"I doubt you ever ran away from anything." He leaned over and took her chin between his thumb and forefinger, forcing her to face him. "Except me."

He could tell she wanted to swipe his hand away, but he held her with his eyes as well as the touch of his hand. The only way she could get loose was to shake him off, and she was too dignified to do that.

"Look, Lane, you can't possibly understand. When you wake up Monday morning, you'll still be a Carrigan. You'll always be a Carrigan."

"And you'll always be you."

"I can't afford to be me." She blinked, avoiding his eyes, and the connection fizzled and shorted out. "And please don't talk to Eric about me—about the things I told you." Suddenly she seemed a whole lot less sure of herself. "I kind of misled him about where I come from."

"You lied on your resume?"

"No." She shifted uncomfortably. "I didn't have to put down where I was from. But he's always assumed I was born to—you know."

"Privilege?"

She nodded. "I never lied to him, but he made assumptions and, well—it's gone way too far. If he found out I'm from Two Shot now, he'd feel like I lied."

Lane shook his head. "I don't understand why you try to hide it."

She sighed. "I don't either, sometimes. It just happened. One thing led to another, and now it's like his whole concept of me is that I'm this high-class society girl."

"You know, he might be impressed by how far you've come."

"I doubt it." She pulled the seat belt across her body and fastened it, letting the sharp click punctuate her answer. "Please don't tell him, okay?"

He pressed the clutch and started up the truck, driving out of the gravel lot and swinging onto the dark empty highway without a word.

CHAPTER 12

THE NEXT MORNING, SARAH STARED INTO THE BAKERY CASE AT Casper's only Starbucks as if the fate of the universe depended on the choice between Very Berry Coffee Cake and a banana nut muffin. But she wasn't thinking about breakfast; she was thinking about Lane. The evening at the rodeo had stirred up memories and misgivings and way more hormones than she could handle. She'd slept uneasily, waking to realize she'd dreamed of him.

He'd gotten bucked off again in her dream, and she'd crawled under the fence and run to him while the noise of the crowd roared in her ears and the clowns lured the bull away. Bloody white bones stuck out of his chest, and she'd knelt in the arena, hurrying to force the broken ends together while the bull pawed the dirt. The bones kept snapping apart in her hands and she woke with her mouth dry as dust, her arms aching as if she'd worked out all night.

The dream and the night that inspired it proved she'd made a mistake by getting personal with a cowboy. With Lane, there was too much risk. Too much feeling. Too much everything. She was her normal, rational self until he touched her, or looked at her in that intense way that made her feel like their souls had met and mated in some previous life.

She couldn't erase what had happened, but she needed to forget it. She'd avoid Lane and make a solemn vow to keep herself on track. From now on, she would keep friendships and business relationships separate.

"Never again," she muttered to herself, making a quick and very vague sign of the cross.

"Warding off temptation?" She turned to see Eric standing behind her, holding a steaming venti cup that gave off the sweet, milky scent of a latte. Damn. It was like seeing the Devil's brother beside you when you'd just sworn off sin.

But Eric didn't have the effect on her that Lane did. She wondered why. He was just her type—classy and sophisticated. Why did her heart beat so fast for the yahoo brother? If she was going to screw up her life, why couldn't she choose a guy who fit into the future she had planned?

"How did it go with my brother last night?"

She moved up a spot in line as a guy in a denim jacket finished giving his order and moved to the pickup counter. "Well, let's see. He got bucked off his bull and we spent most of the night in the medical unit." She caught a flash of concern in Eric's eyes and hurried to say, "But he's okay."

"Did you change his mind?" His posture stiffened slightly. "Or did he change yours? Please don't tell me he made you long for the romance of cowboy life?"

It wasn't the cowboy life Lane had made her long for; it was the cowboy himself. But that was the last thing she wanted Eric to discover. The rivalry between the two brothers was probably a holdover from adolescence, but it was obviously still strong. Shifting her loyalties to Lane wouldn't just make her less effective on the job; her boss would see it as a betrayal.

All the more reason to step away from the cowboy.

She shrugged one shoulder in what she hoped was a casual gesture. "As far as I can tell, there is no romance in the cowboy life." She faked absorption in the menu, as if she hadn't already memorized the coffee shop's offerings. "Basically, the whole thing just proved what I already knew. That cowboy culture he's so set on is a dying concept, and the people clinging to it aren't exactly enriching the community. Bringing in oil workers would probably improve things. But I doubt anything can convince Lane of that."

Eric took another sip of his latte and pulled his wallet out of his back pocket. Flipping it open, he fished out a gold Starbucks card and turned it in his long, slender fingers like a street-corner magician. The metallic surface of the card caught the sunlight streaming in the window behind them and arced glints of light off the wall behind the bake case. Everything about the man was accomplished and graceful. The fact that she was attracted to the cowboy brother and not the executive just proved she hadn't left her old self behind as effectively as she'd thought.

"So let me buy you a coffee. And maybe a doughnut?"

"No, thanks."

"Oh, that's right, you just swore off those." He shot her a sharp glance. "Or were you swearing off something else?"

The card in his fingers caught the light and flashed in her eyes. She felt like she was under interrogation, but Eric was just making conversation.

Wasn't he?

"No, I was just warding off the coffee cake."

"Good. I was afraid Lane had inspired you to swear off the Carrigan brothers, and I want you to go to the Petroleum Club with me tonight."

"The Petroleum Club?" Sarah could feel another unkept vow winging away to join the ones that had fluttered off the night before. The club was a massive cedar-sided building on the edge of town, a complicated structure with elaborate gables jutting from the roof and subtle lighting fanning over the walls. Membership fees were astronomical, and nonmembers rarely passed through its intricately carved doors. The food was rumored to be incredible, the atmosphere posh beyond belief. Sarah was dying to go there.

And maybe spending time with Eric would help exorcise whatever evil impulse was urging her toward Lane.

"You know you want to go," Eric said. "And I need a date. It's a benefit dinner." He flashed her a knowing smile. "The chef there is incredible, and their wine list is a mile long. I know you appreciate good wine."

Sarah did like good wine. Unfortunately, she usually liked bad wine too—especially the super-sweet pink stuff. Learning to tell the difference was part of her scheme to infiltrate the upper classes.

"It might look bad," she said reluctantly. "Other employees might get the wrong idea."

"It won't be just you and me," he said. "I bought a whole table, so I actually have three seats to fill."

She turned to see Gloria standing behind the pastry case, staring expectantly at her, then flicking her gaze to Eric. Her roommate scanned Eric's expensive haircut, then licked her lips at the cut of his Armani suit.

"Well, hello," she said in a Mae West purr.

"Hi, Gloria. Eric, this is my—friend Gloria. Gloria, this is Eric Carrigan. He's…"

"Oh, I know who he is." Gloria's dimples deepened as she gave her blond locks a peppy Meg Ryan toss. "It's just *wonderful* to meet you. I *so* appreciate all you do for this town. I mean, half our customers are Carrigan employees. If it wasn't for you, we'd all be drinking our coffee at home." She giggled and Sarah winced at her slightly maniacal pitch. Gloria had a tendency to try too hard with men. "I mean, I like the finer things in life. Don't you?" She cocked her head and pressed her arms to her sides, turning slightly from side to side in a gesture that appeared little-girl bashful but actually emphasized her own "finer things." Both of them.

"Maybe you'd like to go with us tonight too," Eric said, obviously charmed by Gloria's puppylike friendliness.

Sarah could feel her two lives colliding again, but she was helpless to stop it. Gloria never saw a party she couldn't liven up with a little table-dancing, and she'd never met a man she wouldn't try to seduce—especially if he happened to have a tight butt and a loose wallet.

"A bunch of my golf buddies are going to be there." Eric named a couple of higher-ups from other energy companies. "All men, though. We could use some female company."

Gloria was practically drooling on the counter at the prospect of man hunting at the Petro Club. "I'd be happy to come," she said primly. "Thank you *so* very much!" She tilted her chin down, angling it toward the swell of her breasts, and fluttered her lashes up at Eric.

"Great." Eric grinned. "My friends are going to love you."

"I sure hope so." Gloria tapped Sarah's regular order into the register and beamed. "I'll do my very best to make that happen."

CHAPTER 13

LANE IGNORED THE STARE OF THE RECEPTIONIST IN THE lobby of the Carrigan building and hit the "up" button on the elevator. He'd woken exhausted by dreams of Sarah and had resolved that if she was going to wear him out, he'd rather she did it in person. Hopefully he could talk her into lunch, because five o'clock would be way too long to wait. He'd play on her conscience, point out that they'd never gotten around to talking about the drilling.

Stepping into the elevator, he tipped his hat to two giggling young women as they exited. City girls in Casper were mostly country girls trying out town life. Eventually, they'd finish with the outside world and return to the small-town cycle of relationships, work, marriage, and children—who would repeat the cycle all over again. They all giggled when they saw a cowboy—except for Sarah. She wasn't a giggler, which was part of the reason he'd been compelled to come back.

Compelled. How long had it been since a woman compelled him to do anything? He hit the button for the tenth floor and eyed his reflection. The wavy stainless steel walls of the elevator gave his image an amorphous fun-house twist, stretching his legs and widening his shoulders and hat so he looked like a cartoon cowboy. Ducking down to check his reflection in the smoother panel that housed the controls, he realized he hadn't shaved that morning, and maybe not the day before, either. Stubble shaded his chin and his hat was bent where the bull had stepped on it. He looked like a refugee from Wyoming's outlaw past, not an heir to one of its most successful companies.

At least, it used to be successful. Eric had been grumbling about the dwindling supply of oil in the West for years, and now he claimed that if they couldn't access deeper reserves under the rocky Wyoming plains, they were going to run out of product. Their methods had to change.

Well, they could change without Lane's help. He wasn't coming along for that ride.

But he'd been thinking about his family, and a few things were bothering him. Sure, he hadn't asked for a life of ease, but he'd lived one. He'd ridden the Carrigan gravy train straight to stardom, and yet he'd gone on the nightly news to bite the hand that had fed him all his life.

The elevator beeped and the doors slid open, revealing a gleaming modern hallway. Lane took a deep breath and a right-hand turn toward his brother's office. Rapping on the door, he opened it without waiting for an answer. "Hey, bro."

Eric leaned back in his padded leather office chair and smiled. For half a second Lane felt like he was looking in another fun-house mirror—one that made him look nattily dressed, slimmer, and altogether tidier than usual.

And a little on the smug side.

"Well," Eric said. "I thought you'd be back."

Lane eased into the chair in front of the desk, suddenly conscious of the ache in his ribs.

"I realized the other day that I hadn't been much of a brother lately. Thought I ought to stop by more often."

Eric's grin widened. "What you realized the other day is that I have a gorgeous woman working for me. Who's way out of your league, but that never stopped you before." Lane started to protest and Eric held up one hand like he was stopping traffic. "I saw you looking."

"Who wouldn't?" Lane shrugged one shoulder and winced. "But she's not going to change my mind about the drilling."

"So she told me."

"She tell you anything else?" Lane suddenly felt like he was back in middle school, asking if a girl liked him.

"Nope. But I can give you some hints and tips. First one is to shut that door so she doesn't know you're here. She's got a thing about not fraternizing with the boss, and seeing you's liable to remind her of that. You'll lose me my date to the benefit dinner tonight."

"Your date?"

"I talked her into coming to the Petro Club tonight. And that's your next tip. You show up there and make an effort to fit in, she might see you a little differently. It's her kind of place," Eric said.

Lane was tempted to laugh. With its smoked windows and brass accents, the Petro Club was all glitz and somber glamour, a symbol of smug wealth and exclusivity. Eric didn't have a clue that Sarah didn't entirely belong in that world. He only knew the straitlaced, stylishly suited corporate creature she played by day, but Lane had caught a glimpse of a rodeo natural who dressed, walked, and talked back like a no-nonsense cowgirl.

He liked the cowgirl best, but that buttoned-up suit was a challenge as tempting as a bull that had never been ridden. Maybe if he dressed up and stopped by the Petro Club, she'd see he was more than a cowboy.

"All right," he said. "I'll come."

"Good." Eric's sharp, fox-like grin set off a warning bell in Lane's head, telling him he was being manipulated.

"You think she's going to change my mind about the drilling."

"I think she gets whatever she goes after," Eric said.

"Yeah, but so do I." Lane gave his brother a wolfish grin of his own.

"Well, I guess that's one strategy for getting a high-class woman to date you. Although deep down, I think she's really your kind of girl."

"Oh." Maybe Eric wasn't as clueless as he seemed. "So you know where she's from, then?"

"No." Eric looked past him. "Hey, Sarah, where are you from?"

Lane spun to see Sarah, decked out in a prim navy suit and heels, standing in the doorway. She was looking at Lane with murder in her eyes. She probably thought he was telling Eric all her secrets.

"I went to Vassar." She turned and walked out, leaving the door wide open.

Eric shrugged and looked back at the computer screen. "That's all she'll ever tell me. Sometimes I think that girl's got secrets."

"Would that matter?"

"No." Eric clicked the mouse a few times and leaned sideways, his eyes on the doorway. "Sarah, come here," he said loudly. "This spreadsheet's acting weird."

She reappeared and walked over to the desk, edging around the side to join Eric without so much as looking at Lane.

"Here." She clicked the mouse a few times, biting her lower lip. She'd done that the other night and Lane had bitten it back, nipped her, and she'd kissed him, and then...

"Hit this, and then this. See?" Sarah bent over the desk to demonstrate, revealing a scrap of lace in the V of her lapels. He shifted forward for a better look and she straightened and shot him a look that reminded him of a bucking bull's killer glare.

—∾∾—

Sarah struggled to keep the mouse from shaking in her hand. It was obvious she'd interrupted Lane in the midst of spilling her secrets to his brother. Why else would Eric suddenly be asking about her past?

The whispers had been all over the office five minutes after Lane had arrived. *The cowboy brother's back. That's twice in two days.* She'd taken yoga breaths to hold back the blush heating her face and still she'd had to turn away from the whispering interns as they speculated on his reason for being there. She wondered if he'd come to see her, and dread of what he might say or do warred with vivid memories of the night before.

Seeing Lane again could only lead to trouble. What was done was done. She was moving on.

She'd resolved to stay holed up in her office until he left, but she needed to make a copy and the machine was down the hall, past Eric's office. She'd zipped past the open door as fast as she could, but she'd stopped short when she heard Lane talking to Eric.

You know where she's from?

The air had whooshed from her lungs as fast as the pleasant short-term memories fled her thoughts. It was really her own fault. What kind of a professional slept with her boss's brother?

Then again, what kind of a man kissed and told without even waiting a day?

She'd asked him to keep her secrets, and he hadn't answered—but he was answering now. Worse yet, he was doing his best to peek down her cleavage. And while any reasonable woman would be contemplating a sexual harassment suit, she could feel her skin heating and her nipples tightening. She had to concentrate so hard on suppressing her body's instinctive response that she didn't hear what he said next—something about rodeo and her bust.

"What?"

Eric cast her a curious look and she realized she'd dropped her mask and was getting red in the face.

"He said your rodeo expedition was a bust."

"Oh." She let out the breath she'd been holding and her heartbeat slowed a little. "Yes, it was."

"I think he wants another chance."

She felt like a trapped animal with Eric watching her expectantly while Lane worked the Carrigan charm for all it was worth. Obviously his ego had swelled to the point where it put pressure on his brain. How could he think she'd get anywhere near him now that she'd caught him about to betray her confidence?

She remembered the vow at the Starbucks and repeated it to herself. *Never again.* No more following her impulses. No more letting down her guard. No more sex with cowboys in moonlit trailers at the rodeo grounds.

That last thought brought another flood of heat to her face and she turned away so Lane couldn't see it as she edged out from behind the desk. The space between it and Eric's neatly organized bookcase was narrow, and knowing Lane was watching her backside didn't make her face cool down any. The room felt close and hot and she just wanted out of there, but her heel caught on the leg of the desk and she tipped off balance, grabbing at the chair for support.

But the chair wasn't there; Lane was. He stood quickly and caught her hand in his, putting the other hand on her waist to steady her. In an instant Eric was gone, the office, the tower, even the humiliation and dread that had filled her moments before. Suddenly she was back on the dance floor at the beer tent and she had a crazy impulse to melt into him the way she had the night before.

She glanced up, praying he hadn't caught her reaction, but his eyes were inches from hers, fixed on her face. He wasn't smiling like she expected; he looked intensely serious, as if he was forcing her to take notice of this moment.

She jerked away from him and hooked her shoe with her toe, sliding her foot back inside and righting herself. Backing up a step, she smoothed her skirt and then her lapels, wishing she could smooth down her feelings as easily as she straightened her clothes. She was being a fool. He was a rodeo cowboy—a player. All those tender words, those sensitive responses—they were simply designed to get her naked.

And she wasn't going to fall for them again.

CHAPTER 14

LANE LOOKED DOWN AT HIS HANDS AS SARAH stalked out of the office. He could swear his fingers were tingling from where he'd touched her. For half a second, the two of them had replayed their brief dance at the bar, his hands steadying and supporting her, her flesh yielding under his palm.

He looked up to see Eric watching him, eyes narrowed. "Did something happen between you two?"

"No." Lane's voice came out thick and hoarse. "Nothing. I just—I need to talk to her."

He almost overturned the chair in his hurry to follow Sarah, but she was already halfway down the hall. He called her name and she hastened her steps, turning into an office and swinging the door shut behind her.

Lane caught it just before the latch clicked.

"Hey." He edged through and let the door close behind him. "We need to talk."

"There's nothing to talk about." She stood with her back against a desk, her hands gripping the edge on either side of her hips. He had no doubt she was trying to look tough, but the pose was more alluring than fierce.

"There's a lot to talk about," he said.

"I noticed you had a lot to talk about with Eric."

"Not really."

"You were talking about where I was from." She tossed her head in a move worthy of a soap opera star, but he saw more fear than anger in her eyes.

"I wasn't going to tell Eric a damned thing. I was trying to help." He took a step toward her, but her knuckles whitened on the edge of the desk and he took the step back and spoke in the soothing cadences he used on frightened horses. "Eric's a detail guy. I was trying to see if he'd checked you out. If he had, I could have saved you from worrying about keeping secrets. As a matter-of-fact, he knows you're keeping something from him, and he says it doesn't matter."

She scanned his face and he stared back, willing her to believe him. Her jaw was tense, but he sensed that sudden shift of energy he'd felt the night before, and he thought he saw that straitlaced professional mask slip for a moment.

She wanted to believe him. He just needed to keep pushing. Like he did with the horses—if he asked for a little more each time, eventually they'd form a true partnership.

"We can keep what happened this weekend a secret," he said. "For a while."

"Forever," she said. "I've worked in places where…" She swallowed hard. "Where women had sex with the boss. I'd lose everyone's respect."

"I'm not your boss. And that wasn't just having sex," he said. "It was a whole lot more than that."

That wasn't what he'd intended to say, but it was true. Because—what was it? Why was he so smitten with her? Why was he even here?

"Because I've been running away from who I am all my life, just like you." He was sensing the truth as he formed it into words. "You're a class act, Sarah. No one would ever know you weren't born to wine and fine china. But underneath all that, you and I are a whole lot alike—it's just that we're moving in different directions." He smiled. "Maybe we could meet in the middle."

His words surprised him as much as they'd surprised her. He hadn't realized his feelings until he put them into words, but what else could have made him come to the office on a Friday morning, like a regular nine-to-five wage slave?

He peeled one of her hands off the desk, then the other. She didn't help him any, but she let him. As he looked down at her, the office seemed to fade away. He could smell flowers. Hear music. What the hell?

He looked her straight in the eye. "Look, if you want to keep this a secret, we can do that. Whatever you want—for a while. But eventually, your coworkers are going to have to get over the idea of us being together."

The scent of flowers hit him again, along with the hum of voices. *You may kiss the bride.* He heard the words as clearly as if they'd been spoken and stepped back, dropping Sarah's hands.

A wedding? What was he, a woman?

Now he knew how a horse felt the first time it saw the halter. He'd never had thoughts like that before. Maybe he had one of those biological clocks or something. Next he'd be picturing kids. A little boy, maybe, or a girl like Sarah. He could see the little tomboy she used to be in her face right now, as she looked up at him and struggled for composure.

Aw, hell. He ought to stay away from this woman. He'd always figured on finding some starry-eyed buckle bunny to marry someday, one of those girls who looked at him like he was some sort of hero. He wanted a passel of kids, a little home on the range. Sarah was hardly what he had in mind.

But taking the easy road with women had never gotten him anywhere. Maybe it was time for something different. More of a challenge.

Bending his head, he cupped the back of her head in one hand and kissed her, gently at first, then harder. She stiffened against him but he persisted and finally she relented, letting him wrap his arms around her and pour his soul into figuring out just what it was about her that had him so damn confused.

—∿—

Sarah held onto her anger as long as she could, stiffening in Lane's arms and resisting his kiss. This man was going to ruin her life, she was sure of it. He was a cowboy, after all. His life was one long road trip, and he liked it that way. He'd never settle down with one woman. If she was stupid enough to risk her job for him he'd be gone in a month, off to the next town and the next woman, leaving her life in ruins with that sexy sideways grin and a wave of his hand.

And her job—how could she trust him? She'd caught him asking Eric if he knew where she was from. He'd proven he couldn't be trusted.

She told herself all these things, blocking her emotions with logic like a fighter pilot throwing out chaff, but the kiss shot right through her defenses and made a direct hit on her heart.

Yes, he was a rodeo cowboy and a ladies' man. But he was a study in contradictions: a gentle, kind man who rode wild animals to a standstill, a rich man who loved the grit and grime of the rodeo, a cowboy with class. And job or no job, this kiss was sincere.

As the kiss deepened, she struggled to remember why she cared so much about her career. She didn't need to be rich. She didn't care about wearing fancy clothes or living in splendor. She wanted safety and security, but what was safer or more secure than the arms of this man? She gave half her money to her sister anyway.

She froze and stiffened in his arms. *Her sister.* How could she forget the one thing that mattered most? She could take risks with her own life, but she couldn't take risks with Kelsey's—or Katie's.

"Lane, stop." She pulled away, but his arms were like iron, holding her like he'd never let her go. She looked up into his face and saw tenderness in his eyes, but there was determination there too—the kind of determination that could glue him to the back of a bucking bull for eight seconds.

She put her hands on his chest and shoved—hard. He let her

go, but he didn't step back. He still stood close, looking down at her with equal parts tenderness and amusement.

"Sorry," he said. "I guess this isn't appropriate office behavior." He gave her a charming, hangdog look from under his brows, then swabbed at her smudged lipstick with the pad of his thumb. "I'll try to be good."

She closed her eyes for a second, marshaling her defenses against the feel of his rough fingertip against her lips. She leaned back against the desk again, but there was no gripping the edge this time. She'd studied the body language of successful women and how to radiate authority, and clinging to the furniture was not the way to do it.

Folding her arms over her chest, she crossed her feet at the ankles and tilted her head, arrowing her brows down over her eyes in an expression she hoped was confident and commanding. Her heart was hammering double-time in her chest, but he didn't have to know that.

"Lane." She put a frigid bite into her tone. "I'm sorry, but I think you misinterpreted what happened between us."

He stilled. "Really? What part of 'You rip off my clothes and I'll rip off yours' did I get wrong?"

"I did not rip your clothes off."

"You came damn close."

He was right. Lane one, Sarah zero for this conversation. But she continued as if he hadn't spoken.

"I know you're used to getting what you want, but I think the other girls have spoiled you." She tossed her hair and shifted slightly, propping one hip up on the desk and allowing herself a small, sardonic smile. "I think you overestimated my…"

"Enthusiasm?"

She cleared her throat. "I was going to say you overestimated my feelings."

"Which are what?"

She lifted one shoulder in what she hoped was an eloquent shrug that precluded the need for words.

"Sarah, don't bullshit me. You felt it too."

"If you're trying to woo me with your eloquence, you should leave out the references to animal excrement."

"Like you never heard the word bullshit before. Like you never dished it out. Hell, you're shoveling it on now, and you know it."

He was right. She hated this side of herself, prim and proper and phony as hell. But it was her best defense.

She couldn't look at him, so she pretended to study her nails— but her hand was shaking. She quickly folded her arms again. "It was fun, but it's done. Come on. People don't fall in love in one night."

"Yeah, they do. I've seen it happen. A guy meets the right woman, and *boom*. It's over."

"Well, it's not over for me." She walked to the door, shoulders back, and held it open.

He stayed right where he was.

"Lane, please. My career is important to me, and I'm not going to ditch it for a man."

"I'm not asking you to ditch it."

She clenched her jaw to keep her chin from trembling. What was wrong with her? It had just been a fling. If she hadn't deprived herself for so long, it wouldn't have felt like such a cataclysmic event. She was being such a *girl*.

"How could I stay on here and date the boss's brother?"

"Grit and determination. Seems to me you've got plenty of both."

"Yes, I do, and I'm using it now. A relationship with you is out of the question."

The tenderness had completely faded from his face. The power that had seemed strong and comforting the night before now seemed almost threatening.

"The question is when you'll let yourself relax and have a life."

"That's my decision," she said. "The only question I have is whether you'll break my confidence."

Everything rested on that question. She'd just about finished the initial three-month tryout Eric had asked for, and though she felt like she hadn't accomplished much, she was pretty sure the company would renew her contract—unless he found out she wasn't the woman she seemed to be.

If this job didn't work out, her next one might be in San Francisco, or Boston, or New York. That would mean leaving Kelsey and Katie, and she couldn't do that. Kelsey was doing a great job raising Katie without Mike, but lately the stress was getting to her and she was having migraines. She needed Sarah close.

"I won't tell your secrets," he said. "But you need to stop lying to yourself." He reached up as if to tip the brim of his hat, but the hat wasn't there; he'd left it in Eric's office.

He made the tipping gesture anyway, gave her a wry smile, and walked out of the room.

Lane scooped his hat off his brother's desk.

"You coming tonight?" Eric asked.

"Don't think so. I ride this afternoon."

"So you're giving up on her?"

Lane gritted his teeth. He didn't believe in giving up, and Eric knew it.

"Dinner's at seven if you change your mind. I'm having a limo pick up the girls."

"Girls? Plural?"

"Sarah and her friend Gloria. She's a barista at Starbucks. Peppy little thing. Think I might get lucky." Eric ran a hand through his dark hair. "But hey, let's pretend I didn't tell you Sarah'd be at the

club though, okay? She'll be furious if she finds out I set her up."
He laughed. "Never thought I'd have to get a woman for you, that's
for sure."

Lane had a sudden urge to lunge over the desk and sucker
punch his brother—not to hurt him, just to take him by surprise
and remind him who was the stronger brother. They'd tussled
all the time as kids—Eric with his brains, Lane with his brawn.
Which brother won didn't mean anything; it was the sparring that
mattered. It was a tradition, a ritual that defined all their differ-
ences and confirmed their strengths.

"So did you get what you came for?"

Lane scowled. Sarah had him spinning in circles, but nobody
else needed to know that.

"I came to talk to you."

"Right. Why? Did Sarah change your mind about the drilling?"

Lane looked down at the toes of his boots. She hadn't changed
his mind, but she'd hijacked it. He'd practically forgotten how this
whole thing started. It was about the ranch, the landscape, the tra-
ditions of the West. It was about Two Shot, even though Sarah
didn't want it to be.

In fact, she'd only increased his determination to save the town
from the curse of an oil boom. Sarah might be ashamed of her
hometown, but it had made her the woman she was—resourceful,
hardworking, and ready for anything. The world needed more
people like her, and more places like Two Shot.

"Don't you care about Two Shot?" he asked his brother.

He knew the answer to the question. Lane had always longed
for a hometown, a place to belong, but the small town near their
grandfather's ranch had barely been a blip on Eric's radar.

"Not really," Eric said. "I know you don't want it to change, but
it's inevitable. It'll either die and be absorbed back into the prairie,
or it'll grow and thrive. Which would you prefer?"

"I'd like it to thrive, but not the way you mean. The guys that work the platforms don't care about the towns or the people. They're there for what, six months, maybe a year? They move into trailers and cheap rentals, work all day, and screw around on weekends. Then they leave."

"They leave a lot of money there."

"They do more harm than good, and you know it." Lane set his fists on the edge of the desk and leaned forward, looming over his brother. For the second time in under an hour, he wanted to punch his little brother.

But dominating Eric physically wouldn't change anything. It didn't matter that he was the bigger brother anymore. They were grown-ups now, and for once, he was going to have to act like one.

He was going to have to learn a whole new way to fight.

CHAPTER 15

SARAH SPENT THE DAY IMMERSED IN WORK, FIGHTING thoughts of Lane with facts and figures. It was well past five when she glanced at her watch and realized she was going to be late. She barely had time to rush home, shower, and slip into a little black dress before the company's long black Town Car rolled to a halt outside the apartment building.

The stolid, expressionless driver didn't even blink when Gloria tumbled into the back seat, giggling and kicking up her heels to offer a paparazzi-worthy panty-flash.

"Gloria," Sarah hissed. "Don't forget this is a work thing for me."

"What?" Gloria giggled and fluttered her lashes at the rearview mirror. "I just want to see if I can get a rise out of him." She giggled again. "You know, a *rise*?"

Sarah had a sudden vision of herself standing in a line at the unemployment office. "Did you have a drink while you were getting ready or something?"

"Two." Gloria stuck out her tongue. "Stop being an old schti… schti…" She giggled. "Schtick-in-the-mud."

Sarah slumped in the seat. She hated being a stick-in-the-mud. She really did. But Gloria was like a peppy little puppy, bright-eyed and stumbling into trouble at every turn. Bringing her to a work function was a disaster in the making.

But it wasn't like Sarah could snap a leash on her. She'd just have to do damage control as the occasion arose. And she had a feeling there were going to be a lot of occasions arising.

The driver evidently wasn't one of them, though. His expression was unchanging as he pulled up outside the club, came around to the passenger side, and opened the door. He stayed stoic even when Gloria stumbled into him accidentally-on-purpose.

Was there any way to rescue this situation? Short of shanking Gloria with her nail file and shoving her body into the shrubbery, Sarah couldn't think of a solution. And the place was so neatly landscaped, there really wasn't anywhere to hide a body.

"Okay, Gloria, I just have one rule for tonight," she said as the Town Car drove away.

Gloria smiled at her, swaying on her feet. "Jus' one?"

"Well, there were two, but the first one was 'no drinking before dinner.'"

"Too late!" Gloria did a little soft-shoe in the loose gravel of the parking lot, ending with a jazz-hands flourish.

"Yeah, I know," Sarah said. "So there's just one rule left, and you'd better follow it or I won't let you go to dinner with my friends anymore."

"Okay." Gloria seemed to sober instantly and stood at attention.

Sarah stifled a smile and pointed a stern finger at her roommate, whose curls were still bouncing from her impromptu tap performance.

"Eric is off-limits, okay? He is my boss, and my paycheck depends on him. You mess around with him, I'm liable to lose my job and then you'll lose the rent money." She quirked a little smile to soften the negativity. "*Capiche?*"

Gloria made a cross over her heart. "*Capiche.*"

Stepping inside the club, they paused to absorb the softly lit, walnut-paneled splendor of the Petroleum Club. Even Gloria was hushed by the dignified brass sconces, the elaborate paneled woodwork, and the elegantly carved doorway. Sarah breathed in the scent of the world she'd worked so hard to earn, a sweet-smelling combination of candlelight, furniture polish, and money.

Eric was seated at a long table near the back of the restaurant along with a half-dozen other men, enveloped in the faint musical

sounds of clinking china, clanking silverware, and low conversation. Levering himself out of the chair, he pulled out the one
beside him while two of his friends stumbled over themselves to
help Gloria.

"You look terrific," he said as he pushed Sarah's chair in. He
leaned over to whisper in her ear. "I'm so glad we found a Vassar
girl like you to tell us how to class things up."

She smiled, remembering all the hot summer afternoons she'd
spent on the back step of her mother's trailer, daydreaming while
she watched her little sister frolic in her plastic Walmart wading
pool. She remembered feeling her polyester T-shirt sticking to her
back and wishing it was silk, wishing she were rich, wishing she
was anywhere but in Two Shot.

That was the one thing she'd succeeded at in Two Shot: leaving. She'd failed miserably at everything else—holding her family
together, holding onto Roy's legacy, making his life count for
something. All her success was on the surface.

But she couldn't think about that now. She needed to concentrate on making sure Gloria behaved herself.

"And *you*." Eric turned to Gloria. "You look amazing."

Gloria giggled and shook her shoulders, making her breasts
bobble. She was always bobbling and bubbling, putting on a show.
It seemed to be an instinctive response. Apparently, she believed
in the survival of the sexiest.

She'd seated herself between two of Eric's golf buddies.
One, a youngish guy who almost rivaled Eric for good looks,
was being politely attentive while she told a story with a lot of
bouncing around in her seat to punctuate the good parts. The
silver-haired but fit-looking guy in a plaid sport jacket on her
right wasn't even trying to hide the fact that he was trying to peer
down her dress.

Sarah tried to remain poised, but she was still prepared to
pounce if Gloria started in on any cringe-worthy anecdotes. Eric,

oblivious to her nerves, poured her and Gloria each a generous glass of Burgundy, then topped off his own and lifted it in a toast.

"To the West and all its riches," he said. "Including my two lovely dates."

The other men lifted their glasses. The plaid-jacketed man managed to get through the entire toasting and drinking process without raising his gaze from Gloria's breasts. Evidently he wanted two dates too. Sarah really couldn't blame him. Gloria's rather generous endowment was enhanced, shaped, and lifted by her dress to the point where she might as well have presented it on a platter. Sarah frowned and took another sip of wine, then another. Then another.

"Rough day, Sarah?" Gloria cast a lash-fluttering look toward Eric, who raised his glass in flirtatious appreciation.

"No, it was fine," Sarah said. "Just the usual meetings and stuff. Fun, actually. Why? Do I look tired?"

"No, you look terrific. But you just drank an entire glass of wine in three sips, and you didn't even read the label first. That's not like you."

Sarah pushed her wine glass away. Gloria was right—she was going too fast. She'd never learn about wine if she chugged it like soda.

"So how did your date go last night?" Gloria turned to the plaid-jacketed man. "Sarah had a date with Lane Carrigan."

The man jerked upright as if he'd been caught ogling her breasts, which, in fact, he had.

"Urp?"

Sarah figured he hadn't heard Gloria's announcement, but the other men at the table turned her way, obviously curious.

"It wasn't a date," she said.

Gloria slapped Plaid Jacket Man playfully, apparently as a stand-in for Sarah. "Shut up. It was so." She leaned across the table to address Eric and the silver-haired man lapsed back into his breast-induced reverie. "It's, like, impossible to fix her up, you know?" She turned to Eric. "I mean, what more could you do? Your brother is hot, hot, hot." Fanning herself theatrically, Gloria simpered as he topped off her glass. "So are you, but she said I shouldn't say so." She shrugged, which made Mr. Plaid Jacket nearly fall out of his chair. "So what's Lane like, Sarah?"

"He was—fine."

"*Mighty* fine," Gloria said with a Groucho-style waggle of her eyebrows.

"It really wasn't a date, though." Sarah wasn't about to trash her boss's brother in front of this crowd, but thinking about the night before made her want to down the glass in one gulp, like a cowboy downing a shot of whiskey in a Wild West movie. "And he got bucked off his bull, so we spent most of the night at the medical tent."

Gloria simpered and flung a sultry glance across the table at a middle-aged guy wearing a bolo tie. "I'd like to spend a night in a tent with a cowboy, I can tell you that. I bet they're really good at—you know." To Sarah's horror, she raised one arm and pulsed her hips like a bronc rider. "Yee-ha!"

A faint "yee-ha, baby!" echoed from the corner. Sarah was pretty sure it came from a young guy in a pin-striped suit who looked like he was probably scared of horses. He'd probably be scared of Gloria, too, if he knew her. He certainly should be.

But Eric wasn't. The Carrigan eyes were fixed on Gloria like rifle sights.

"Well, you ought to know about all that stuff," Gloria said to Sarah. "You rode in the rodeo yourself, didn't you?"

Sarah clamped her lips tight and gave Gloria a quick head shake, but the girl was on a roll.

"You'd never guess it, but Sarah grew up dirt poor!" She announced it as if it was something to be proud of. "And now here she is, a corporate big shot, getting me invitations to the Petronia—Petrolia—*Petrolinum* Club." She giggled.

"Really? You grew up poor?" Eric turned to Sarah, his eyebrows lifted in surprise.

She waved a hand carelessly, hoping he couldn't see it was shaking. "That's kind of an exaggeration."

"Did you two grow up together?" he asked.

"Oh, no way. Sarah lived in a *trailer*," Gloria crowed. "My mom didn't have squat, but it was never *that* bad."

"Really," Eric said.

"Really." Gloria was off and running on her own childhood now, and Sarah started to relax as she began talking about the trials of single motherhood and how they'd made her mom's eyes bag and caused her breasts to sag before she turned fifty.

"But Sarah knows all about that single mom stuff," she said. She was referring to Kelsey, but judging from how startled Eric looked, he probably thought Sarah herself had a child named Cosette hidden in some back alley with a cruel hotelier.

"My sister," she said quickly. "She separated from her husband, and she has a little girl."

The good-looking man to Gloria's left seemed to sense her discomfort. Leaning across the table, he shot her a sympathetic smile. "So Lane got bucked off? Was he hurt much?"

"Not too bad." Sarah flashed him a grateful smile. "He's fine."

"How fine?" Gloria made the question as suggestive as possible, lowering her voice into a sultry purr and fluttering her lashes.

"Fine enough to be his typical cowboy self," Sarah said, trying for a light tone.

"Oh, you would know about cowboys," Gloria said. "Being a cow*girl* and all."

Sarah narrowed her eyes and gave Gloria a hard stare, but her roommate chattered on, oblivious.

"But he's probably not into art and wine and all that crap." Gloria waved at the elegant tabletop dismissively. "I guess that's why you came home alone." She simpered and flashed Eric a cute little kitten smile. "*I* think you chose the wrong brother." She set her glass down on the table with an audible *thunk*. Evidently the tabletop was higher than she'd thought. Eric flagged down a waiter and ordered another bottle while Sarah sipped ice water and stared into space, hoping no one would notice she was struggling to figure out damage control strategies to counter Gloria's revelations.

She idly fingered the running-horse necklace, which she'd slipped inside the modest neckline of her dress. She was wondering how things could possibly get any worse when a ruckus near the door upped the club's noise level. The men at the table swiveled their heads to stare at the doorway, which framed the impressive figure of none other than Lane Carrigan.

He looked like a bull in a china shop—a rodeo bull, far too big and brutal for his delicate surroundings. Dressed in full formal cowboy regalia, he was holding his hat to his chest. As he strode toward them, his boots thudding on the hardwood floors, he reminded her of the hero of an old-time Western. Shane, striding in to clean up the town. The Outlaw Josey Wales, stopping trouble with his trademark glare.

Sarah took another quick sip of her water, glancing over at Eric. Her heart sank at the self-satisfied smirk on his face. He'd set her up, dammit. She'd told him his brother was hopeless, but apparently he wasn't giving up on the idea she could change the man's firmly made-up mind about drilling on the ranch.

She ducked her head, but melting into the shadows was not an option. Gloria was practically jumping out of her seat, leaning across the table and waving frantically at Lane, and her big eyes and bigger smile drew every eye in the room that wasn't already fixed on the cowboy.

"Lane!" She leaned farther forward, offering the entire room a generous glimpse of cleavage and almost knocking over the bottle.

Lane gave her a cool stare, then smiled as he recognized Sarah.

"There you are, babe," he said.

Gloria arched her eyebrows and slid her gaze toward Sarah. "*Babe?*" She rolled her gaze to the ceiling and made a dramatic swooning gesture, her arm flailing overhead. The plaid jacketed man made full use of the opportunity.

Lane strode toward them, his eyes fixed on Sarah, and the room went quiet as a Hollywood main street at high noon.

Sarah tensed and reminded herself that she'd gone too far with him once. Twice, really, if you counted that kiss in the office—and how could you not count that kiss?

But it was starting to feel like dating the boss's brother was a job requirement. Eric was sitting with one arm flung carelessly over the back of his chair, watching her with an annoying, smug expression. She was starting to understand why Lane didn't get along with him. Eric was a schemer and a plotter. She had to admit that whatever his other flaws, Lane was honest and direct. It made her wonder why he was making such an effort to pursue her. He knew she was riding high on a pack of lies, fooling everyone into believing she was something she wasn't.

She felt everyone's eyes on her face as Lane stopped at their table, shoved his thumbs in his belt loops, and grinned. He'd been just one more cowboy at the rodeo—maybe the biggest and best, but still in his element. Here he stood out like a wolf in a dog kennel, filling up the room not just with his height and bulk, but with his masculine confidence and the intensity of his stare.

"Sorry," he said. "Didn't have time to change. Made the short round today." He grinned. "The better you ride, the harder you work."

He assessed the room with narrowed eyes like he was thinking about buying the place—or like he already owned it. Pulling out the empty chair beside Sarah, he lowered himself into it and turned toward her, his arm resting on the table. She felt like she was already in his embrace.

Not that she was going to end up there again. Nope, never again. She was the responsible sister. The responsible roommate.

He leaned toward her and she caught the scent of aftershave, a hint of cinnamon blended with leather and wood smoke. He hadn't been wearing that last night. All this "I didn't have time to change" stuff was a load of bull. He'd wanted to make an entrance—and it was working. Every eye in the place was on him—the women covetous, the men envious.

"How are you, princess?"

Sarah bristled. "Don't call me that."

She reminded herself that she didn't like rodeo cowboys. Didn't like them at all.

You liked the way he kissed you, though. You liked the way he—

She shut down that line of thinking as he gave her a lopsided grin that made him look surprisingly boyish despite the breadth of his shoulders.

"I thought maybe you'd give me a second chance."

"That's assuming you ever had a first chance," she quipped.

The men at the table guffawed, but Lane seemed unaffected by what she'd thought was a killer zinger. He scanned the room and its business-suited clientele with obvious scorn, looking rough, battered, and one hundred percent cowboy.

Being responsible sucked.

She was grateful when the waiter interrupted, bringing course after course of beautifully presented, perfectly cooked food. The conversation started up again around them, and Lane's white teeth flashed as he good-naturedly answered question after question about rodeo from Eric's friends. Sarah did her best to shrink into the shadows, concentrating on her food so she wouldn't have to look at him.

Gradually, the questions slowed and finally ceased as one man after another got up to leave. Lane scooted his chair back a bit, clearly looking to engage Sarah in conversation. They listened to each other breathing for a while. Obviously Eric had invited her here to persuade Lane to do the drilling. And he wanted her to use every possible means to do the persuading.

She had a job to do, and that job didn't just matter to her. It mattered to Kelsey and Katie, too. She took a deep breath. "We need to talk."

"You're right," he said. "We do."

CHAPTER 16

"Why won't you let them drill on the ranch?" she asked.

"That's what you want to talk about?"

"Of course." She leveled what she hoped was a dispassionate stare. "What else would we talk about?"

"Us."

"There is no us. There can't be. It's not just my job, either. You're a cowboy, and I'm—not. You like Two Shot, and I don't."

"How can you not like your own hometown?"

"Easy. If you'd really grown up there, you'd understand. Trust me, you'd be all for making some changes. I know it looks all quaint on the outside, but people there really struggle to keep going."

"Is that such a bad thing?"

"It is when you're the one struggling."

He sighed. "Do you really want to pave over your past like that?"

She thought of the town as she'd left it. The abandoned school building, with its broken windows and chipped facade. The town library, filled with out-of-date fiction by Frank Yerby and Anya Seton. The streets, pockmarked with potholes.

Then there was the gossip. The meanness. Her mother hadn't been very well equipped for life, but instead of helping her, folks in Two Shot had whispered and lied. Even the smallest mistake got blown up into a drama worthy of Shakespeare in that town. And Sarah's mother had made a lot of mistakes, mostly under the influence of alcohol.

"Yes," she said. "I do want to pave it over."

"Why?"

She glanced around the table, almost hoping Gloria would say something embarrassing so she wouldn't have to answer the question. But at some point, probably while Sarah was listening to Lane talk about rodeo, Gloria had left. So had Eric.

As a matter-of-fact, only the middle-aged cowboy with the bolo tie remained.

"Excuse me." Shoving back her chair, Sarah set her napkin on the table and headed for the front lobby. Maybe Gloria had just felt the call of nature. She glanced right, then left as she exited the restaurant. No Eric, no Gloria.

"Where's the ladies' room?" she asked a uniformed waitress.

"Down the hall."

She headed down the hallway and ducked into the door marked "Ladies," but it was empty, the stall doors standing open. Any other time she'd admire the plush carpet, elegant settees, and posh potpourri bowl, but she had to find Gloria. She went back to the lobby, where a black-jacketed server was manning the maître d' stand.

"Is there another ladies' room?" she asked.

"No, ma'am."

"Have you seen a blonde? Petite, big—hair?" She fluttered her fingers around her face to illustrate Gloria's poof of curls.

"She left with the gentleman," he said.

"What gentleman?"

"I'm sorry, ma'am. I believe they—never mind." He skittered off to the kitchen as if he'd just revealed the hidden life of Brad Pitt to a paparazzo.

Sarah hovered in the hallway, unsure how to proceed. Should she run outside, try to catch Eric and Gloria? For all she knew Gloria was puking in the bushes.

Then again, she might be in Eric's Porsche, making out. Or worse.

She stepped outside, holding the door open behind her with

one foot while she scanned the parking lot. The highway hummed just over the hill, the steady sound broken by the occasional rumble of a big rig and the rush of wind in the grass.

Eric's Porsche was gone, and so was Gloria. He'd probably have to help her up the stairs, and then he'd discover Sarah lived there too.

Not that she was going to live there for long. She'd given Gloria one rule, and the girl had broken it as quickly as she could. Heck, Sarah never should have moved to Casper anyway. It would be easier—and cheaper—to live with Kelsey and commute.

She'd tell Gloria in the morning. Or maybe she'd just pack her stuff and go. All her belongings would fit in the Malibu's backseat and capacious trunk. How pathetic was that? She was living a mid-size life.

Something needed to change.

Reluctantly, she returned to the dining room. As she emerged from the hallway, she slammed into a familiar figure, bumping her nose into the unyielding plane of Lane's chest. He steadied her with one hand, but she quickly skittered backward.

"You want dessert?" he asked.

"No," she said. "No, I want to go home." She scanned the empty dining room. There were only a few diners scattered around the room, and Eric's table was occupied only by a busboy who was clearing dirty dishes.

"Let's go, then," Lane said. "I'll take you home."

The two of them strolled in silence through the parking lot, a lone cricket announcing their arrival. Lane was all cowboy confidence and swagger, and that testosterone aura Sarah had sensed the night before surrounded him like smoke from a campfire.

He unlocked the passenger side door of his beat-up pickup.

"I thought you were doing well with rodeo," she said. "This looks like the Clampetts' truck."

"It gets me places and carries my stuff," he said. "Is there something else trucks are supposed to do?" He opened the door to reveal a bronc-riding saddle set fork-down on the passenger's side. The stirrups were looped over the seat, and a coil of rope was tossed haphazardly on top. His gear bag was on the floor.

"Oops, no room," Sarah said. "Better call a cab."

"There's room." He hoisted the saddle against his chest, then set it in the truck bed. There was no sign of the previous night's injury, and she wondered if he'd really needed help with his bag even then.

He brushed off some of the dust with the flat of his hand. "Come on, princess."

She climbed into the truck cab, feeling awkward in her short dress and heels. The scent of the saddle lingered in the interior— leather and metal and horse. There was dried mud on the floor mats and a stack of papers shoved between the window and the dashboard.

Considering the amount of space Lane seemed to take up in the restaurant, Sarah had expected to feel cramped in the confines of the truck cab. But with one hand on the wheel and one on the shift lever, he fit far better than he'd fit into the cavernous walnut-paneled dining room at the club.

"Stick shift," she said, thinking aloud.

"You're not the only one who likes to control things, princess."

"Don't call me that. And anyway, I'm just doing my job." Suddenly conscious of her posh dress and demure pose, she looked down at her hands, which she'd folded in her lap like a good little girl on a trip to the fair. "I don't like to control things. Not really."

"Well, you're controlling me."

She let out a quick, short laugh. "I can't control you."

Not only couldn't she control him, she couldn't control herself. Ever since he'd turned up at the club, she'd felt like everything was spinning out of kilter. The idea of spending time alone with him made her want to screech to a halt like the Road Runner coming to the edge of a cliff, but she couldn't seem to stop herself—maybe because she was hanging out with Wile E. Coyote. Lane might not have the cartoon critter's knack for disaster—in fact, he seemed to live a uniquely charmed life—but he had the same scrappy optimism as a coyote, the same trickster mentality, the same devil-may-care determination to get what he wanted.

She'd been like that once—a girl who ran horses hell-for-leather, who cussed and kicked and spoke her mind. Sometimes she wondered if all the phoniness she'd let into her life was really worth the paycheck. The new Sarah might be successful and secure, but she wasn't really very likable.

———

Lane rested one hand on the steering wheel and stared straight ahead. Sarah was gazing out the windshield too, as if they were already on the highway. As if the two of them were actually headed somewhere together.

Actually, they were. He just wasn't sure where they were going to end up.

"So tell me again why you want to destroy Two Shot. What did that town ever do to you?"

She heaved a heavy, weight-of-the-world sigh. "It didn't really do anything to me. I didn't let it. But my mom, my sister—things didn't work out there for them."

"Would they have worked out differently anywhere else?"

"*Yes.*" Her vehemence surprised him. "You probably think everybody in a small town pulls together, right? That everyone knows everybody else's business, and they just can't wait to help their neighbors?"

He shrugged. She was right—he did think that. If you all lived in the same place, you'd care about the same things. Surely that would bring people together.

"Well, you're right on the first count, wrong on the second. Everybody's got their nose in your business, but when things go wrong, they just crinkle it up like you smell bad and pull away."

He couldn't help chuckling at the metaphor and she scowled, making a little crease appear between her eyebrows. He figured she was probably trying to look mean, but mostly she looked hurt.

"And that's the good part," she said. "After they pull away, they all go whisper about you together and point fingers and judge you. Remember in high school how there were cool kids and outcasts? Well, in small towns that never ends. Cliques and power plays, winners and losers—it's all there. If you make a mistake, just one mistake, you're done. Done."

"Surely not everyone's like that."

She turned away as if something fascinating was going on outside the passenger side window. "No. Some people pretend they feel sorry for you so you'll let them help you. That way they'll have more to whisper about." The hand resting in her lap curled into a fist. "You bet I want to pave it over."

She turned quickly to face him and he was surprised to see a teardrop hovering on her lower lashes. He brought his hand up to brush it away and remembered how he'd cupped her cheek the night before, just before he'd kissed her.

She must have remembered that too, because she reached up and grabbed his wrist to pull it away. But when their eyes met, she stopped, the two of them barely breathing. Her eyes were wide, and her lower lip trembled a little until she nipped it in her teeth and looked away.

"You *are* a winner, Sarah," he said in a low voice. "You made it out in spite of it all." He kissed her, just brushing her lips. "Forget Two Shot. Just be who you are."

CHAPTER 17

SARAH WHIMPERED—ACTUALLY WHIMPERED, DAMMIT—AS Lane's eyes flickered over hers like he was seeking permission to touch her again.

Why couldn't he just take what he wanted? Why did she have to decide everything? Her whole life was a series of vows and decisions, all designed to minimize the risk of failure, and where had that gotten her? She'd been working her butt off all her life, but had it made her happy?

Nope.

Lane's words rang in her head. *Be who you are.* She'd done that last night, and she'd been happy—truly happy—for the first time in a year. And despite the second thoughts and regrets that had plagued her all day, she wanted to feel that way again.

Yes, she thought. *Yes.*

She kissed him back, tentatively at first, but then pleasure set her heart thrumming like a plucked string. Next thing she knew she'd climbed over the gearshift and was straddling his lap, kissing him with every ounce of her real, true self. It felt so good to let go.

He gripped her hips in his hands. God, his hands were huge. His thumbs rested on the soft spot just below her hipbones, and his fingers spanned the curves of her bottom. When she bent down and gave his upper lip a tentative, teasing lick with the tip of her tongue, his fingers dug into her flesh, pulling her against something she was pretty sure wasn't a belt buckle.

"Sarah," he murmured against her lips. "Do you know what you're starting?"

She licked him again, teasing him with her tongue, coaxing him to let her in. It felt good to be the aggressor, demanding what she wanted, and it felt even better when he kissed her back.

She could feel tension building in his muscles, need spiraling up on need as the kiss deepened and his hands moved up to clutch at her hair. He was pushing against her now, nipping at her tongue, trying to take over the lead in the spicy back-and-forth tango she'd started. She pushed her pelvis forward and rubbed against him like a cat, feeling the outline of his arousal through the thin fabric of her dress.

He pushed back, writhing underneath her, and she knew he was losing control. A man who could ride a bucking, twisting, two-thousand-pound animal was losing control to her, Sarah Landon.

He groaned against her lips, and she felt a surge of excitement deep in her belly. Moving her lips up to his cheekbone, then flicking her tongue in his ear, she reached down to the side of the seat and hit a small lever near the back. The seat whirred and tilted backward, taking her and Lane with it. She pulled open the top snaps of his shirt and felt his skin warm under her hands. She'd never done this before. She'd let men touch her, allowed them to make love to her, but she'd never taken what she really wanted.

In fact, none of them had been anything close to what she'd wanted. They'd been appropriate men, men who fit into her future. Lane was anything but appropriate. He was an accident, a glorious, serendipitous accident that was going to free her from all her self-imposed restraints tonight.

Just tonight, she told herself. Tomorrow she'd get back on track.

She had a vague memory of making that choice once before. A foggy recollection that maybe it hadn't worked out so well. But she was in charge now. How could that be a bad thing?

She tightened her thigh muscles, pressing her hands to his shoulders to hold him down. She might have lost control over her life lately, but she was definitely the boss in this situation. This was what she wanted, to have her way with this man, to have...

Blaaaaaaat.

She shrieked as the harsh blare of a horn cut through the night air. Falling against Lane's chest took her butt off the truck's horn, but as she thrashed to rise, her legs tangled with his and her foot hit the stick shift, shoving it out of gear. The truck rolled backward, slowly at first, then faster. Grabbing her around the waist, Lane pushed himself off the seat with one hell of an ab crunch and cranked the wheel to the right. Hauling himself upright, he reached for the knob and floundered for the brake. The crunch of gravel under the tires gave way to rougher ground and the truck bounced over rocks and stones. Tree branches slapped at the windows. Finally there was a faint crunch and their backward motion stopped abruptly.

"Oh, God." Sarah struggled to extricate her arms and legs from his, twisting herself out of his arms and into her seat. She looked over her shoulder. "What did we hit?"

"Tree," he said. "Good thing, too. We were headed for the ditch."

"Oh, no. Your truck. I'm so sorry." She pawed at the door, but the handle flexed uselessly under her hand. She was locked in. She tugged at the handle in a panic. She couldn't get out. She couldn't...

"Wait." He grabbed her hands and held them both in her lap. She stiffened, her back tight against the back of her seat, her spine rigid. They'd ended up under a tree that shut out the moonlight so she couldn't see his face, but she had no doubt he was frowning. Of course he was. She'd wrecked his truck. Ruined the evening, and probably his bumper, too. She wondered if the taillight was smashed. Taillights were expensive.

He shifted her two hands into one of his and pulled her toward him so she could see his face again in the faint glow of the parking lot lights, which seemed oddly distant and far away.

He was, incredibly, laughing.

Lane looked over at the terrified woman on his lap and tried to stifle his laughter. She seemed to think denting the truck bumper was some kind of disaster, which only made it funnier. He was anything but angry. In fact, he was right where he wanted to be.

When the truck had flipped out of gear, it had drifted backward across the sloping parking lot, rolling across a small patch of grass and into a grove of trees. They'd almost hit somebody's SUV, but he'd cranked the wheel in time and the truck had come to rest against the trunk of an enormous pine. The tree's branches draped around them, drooping almost to the ground. He could barely see the club with its tasteful landscape lights glowing in the distance more than fifty yards away.

Nobody was likely to notice him here. Or Sarah. Or the truck, hidden under the boughs of the tree. He'd yanked the headlights on as he'd floundered for the steering wheel and now he shut them off. It felt like they were deep in a forest, sheltered by the ancient tree, safe in a cave of branches.

"Don't you want to check the bumper?" Sarah asked.

"No," he said. "But if I don't repair this night right away, it's a goner."

"This—what?"

"This—I don't know what to call it. Whatever's happening between us."

He kissed her, kneading the back of her neck with his fingers as he slid his lips over hers. She was tense as a jackrabbit caught in the open, frozen but ready to bolt. Teasing her lips with his tongue, he felt her nervousness drain away. Then a new kind of tension took over and it wasn't nerves but need that made her tremble as she kissed him back.

He moved his lips down her neck, pausing to nuzzle the curve where her shoulder met her neck. She was running her hands over his back, over his shoulder blades, tracing his muscles. When she cupped his hips in both hands he felt a stab of urgency that almost hurt. He pulled at the straps of her dress, tugging them down to admire the simple black lace of her bra. It was plain, but not prim—just practical. What it held, though, was heaven. A few faint freckles spattered her skin as if they'd been poured down her cleavage. They faded where her breasts swelled over the lace and her skin turned to smooth white perfection. He kissed her again and slipped one hand past the lace. Her breast fit his hand perfectly, the nipple hard against the center of his palm.

She gasped and he pulled away to make sure it was a gasp of pleasure. It was. Her head was tilted back, and the dim light from the moon spilled over her shoulder and made her skin glow magically silver, just as it had the night before. He reached up and tugged the straps from her shoulders, moving them slowly down her arms and enjoying the slow revelation of her breasts while he expertly flipped open the clasp at the back.

He bent his head to lick a slow circle around each of her nipples, pink as her lips and perfectly round. His hand moved down to fumble with the hem of that sleek little dress—so professional, so prim. He wanted it gone. He wanted her naked, and he wanted her *now.*

And she wanted him too. She was pulling at his shirt, tearing the snaps open, but when she hit the last button the console got in the way. She hit it with the heel of her hand and made a little mewl of frustration.

"Does this thing come out?"

"No." He opened the door. "But we do."

Before Sarah had time to think, Lane was out of the truck and around it, opening her door. She tumbled into his arms and clung to his neck, her dress hanging off her shoulders, her bare breasts brushing his chest. He lifted her like she weighed nothing and strode around to the back of the truck.

The bumper was dented, all right. The tree had caved in the tailgate and he had to set her down to jerk it open. It fell with a clang that resounded through the night and made the crickets hush their chirping.

She shivered.

"You cold? Hold on."

Lane set her on the tailgate and ducked into the cab. A second later he tossed her the silky tasseled wrap she'd carried along with her purse. She pulled it around her breasts and held it at her throat, dangling her legs over the tailgate and looking up at the tree branches that ascended like a spiraling ladder up the rough trunk. A few stars peeped through the filigree of needles, and the moon perched high above as if impaled on the topmost spike.

"Merry Christmas," she whispered to herself. It might be July, but she was giving herself one heck of a present. She pushed back all the cautions poking at the back of her mind—*someone might catch you, he's your boss's brother, you shouldn't do this, it's not professional*—and she laughed, because all those things mattered so little compared to the way Lane was looking at her.

"Something funny?" He climbed up beside her.

She smiled. "You."

"That's just what a man wants to hear."

He scrambled up to his hands and knees. He'd brought a blanket from the truck cab and he draped it carefully over a couple bales of hay at the front of the pickup bed. One bale had broken open and spilled straw in a smooth cascade, and the blanket turned it into a sloping chaise lounge. Lane sat back against the intact bale, and propped one arm behind his head. His shirt was open to the last button and the flat plane of his chest glowed in the moonlight. Sarah thought he looked like a shot from a cowboy calendar. Mr. July.

She scurried up beside him and he crooked the other arm around her, lazily stroking the wrap she'd pulled over her breasts. She wasn't sure where her bra had gone, but the feel of his hand sliding over her taut nipples with nothing but the thin fabric between them raised goose bumps on her chest and arms. He pinched a bit of fabric between his fingertips and she let out a shuddering breath and arched her back.

"You like that?"

"I'd like it better without the shawl," she whispered.

"You sure?" His hand paused. "We don't have to do this. It's kind of in the open. We could…"

"Don't." She pulled his hand back to her breast. "Please don't. I want this. I want the moonlight. I want *you*, Lane. Just one more time."

He pulled the fabric gently away from her body, first one side, then the other. "One more time? Are you thinking this is a two-night stand, Sarah Landon?"

She sat up and shrugged off the shawl. "Yes."

Then, to his surprise, she shimmied out of her dress so fast he barely had time to enjoy the show before she was lying beside him again, clad in nothing but a pair of black bikini panties.

She splayed her hand over his chest. "I work for your brother. I work for your *father*, Lane. In a way I work for you, except we're not on the same side. Remember?"

"No," he said. "I don't take sides. And I don't want to talk about work right now. Besides, you know I don't care about the company."

"I think you do," she said. "You told me last night I messed up your life."

He knelt beside her and ran a gentle finger across the top edge of her panties, stroking her belly from one hip to the other, then skimming back again. Her skin quivered under his touch. He reached the side and slipped his finger under the waistband and tugged it down, then stroked from one side to the other until he'd uncovered her and she kicked the panties away.

"I have a feeling you're going to make up for messing up my life," he said. "But it might take more than once."

CHAPTER 18

SARAH WATCHED LANE'S FINGER TRACE THE CURVES OF HER body, moving up over her belly, between her breasts, and over her throat. When it lit on her lips she opened them and sucked it inside, gazing brazenly into his eyes while she swirled her tongue up and down and around.

God, she was naked in the back of his truck, giving him a pretty obvious prelude to a skill she'd actually never performed. She'd had an old boyfriend who always wanted her to use her mouth, but it seemed dirty somehow with him and she'd never done it, distracting him by offering the rest of her body. He'd been perfectly happy to settle for straight sex, and she'd been perfectly happy to endure it.

But the thought of doing something different with Lane made her salivate. *Salivate*, for God's sake. She'd never drooled over a man before.

He pulled his finger from her mouth and moved it down to her breasts, tracing a wet trail around each nipple. A faint night breeze and the thought of what might happen later had raised them both into aching, pleading pebbles. His lips followed his finger and he licked, sucked, and swirled, squeezing her breasts together to make the tips even more full and sensitive.

She tugged at his shirt and he pulled it off, his lips never leaving her breast. Tugging at his belt, she struggled with the zipper to his jeans and finally slipped two fingers into the waistband, gasping when she felt the bead of liquid swelling at the tip of him.

"Sarah." He'd been on his hands and knees, bending over her, but now he reared up and fumbled at his jeans with shaking hands, finally managing to pull down the zipper and strip them off.

He was wearing briefs. Brief briefs, the briefest imaginable. Most guys looked ridiculous in tight underwear, but Lane looked like a pinup, especially since he was so ready for her that the tip of his cock had slipped past the waistband. He stood to shed the jeans and she rose to her knees, tugging the fabric down to set him free and running her palm up the length of him before she closed her hand around him and stroked. Once, twice, and then he pulled her hand away and grabbed for his jeans, fishing in the pocket and finally pulling out a condom.

Tearing the packet open, he slipped it on quickly, then fell to his hands and knees and pushed her down with him, straddling her and looking into her eyes. His eyes were intense, focusing on her with the rapacity of a predator, and his biceps bulged as he bent to kiss her.

It was a kiss that changed everything. She wasn't Sarah Landon anymore; she was barely human. She was a tight bundle of nerves and sensation that had no thoughts beyond giving herself to this man so she could take what she needed. Stripping off the Speedo or whatever the hell it was, she slid down the hay bale until she was sprawled beneath him and he was poised at her entrance, a breath away from sliding inside her.

His face was inches away from hers, their noses and lips almost touching. He closed his eyes.

"I can wait," he said. "I can wait and make it last."

"Don't," she said. "I don't want to wait." She reached down and put her hands on his hips, pulling him into her, and he slid inside and she confirmed what she'd discovered the night before: He fit her. He was made for her. He filled her like a missing piece.

Lane closed his eyes and gave himself up to the sensation. Sarah was rippling beneath him like water, moving with an unexpected grace. She wasn't the stiff little professional anymore, that was for sure. She'd pulled down all her barriers and let him in.

And tonight she looked him in the eyes without being asked. He felt that joining of minds again, a union that went way beyond the physical act. Tenderness swept over him in a wave, and gratitude for the generosity of her trust.

He moved slowly, holding his breath, watching her face to gauge her reaction. He was watching and waiting and testing and *thinking*, but she had completely given herself up to feeling. Her brows tensed for a moment, dipping downward. That little crease between them appeared and he thought he'd hurt her, but she grabbed his hips and pulled him into her.

"More," she said. "*More*. Let go."

He wanted to—God, he wanted to—but he couldn't help remembering what she'd said: *just one more time*. He wanted more than one time. He wanted all time. Forever—so he needed to make this as good for her as he could.

The crease between her brows deepened and she reached up, pulling his head down to hers and pressing her lips to his, flicking her tongue out to tease him, advancing and retreating until he forgot all his resolutions and let loose, plunging into her. He'd reached a crossroads between tenderness and animal instinct he'd never experienced before. Every nerve ending in his body crackled to life and demanded more, more sliding, more friction, harder, faster, *deeper*. He wanted to be inside her, surrounded by her warmth, the slick sweetness at her core.

This was more than sex. Sex was detached, controlled. You took pleasure and gave it, thinking about what your partner wanted, but not who she was, or who she would be tomorrow.

But he had to think about who Sarah would be tomorrow. Because somehow, some way, she needed to still be his.

—⁓—

Sarah woke to see the moon through a lacy network of pine boughs. It took her a minute to remember where she was, what had happened.

Oh, yeah. She'd slept with her boss's brother. Again.

Lane lay beside her, the moonlight casting deep blue shadows that defined his muscles. His eyes were closed, his expression serious—more serious than she'd ever seen him. When he opened his eyes, the playful gleam she'd come to expect had given way to something deeper.

Uh-oh.

He took her hand and held it in his, then spread his fingers and set them palm to palm so his brown, rugged hand contrasted with her small, white one.

"You're so tiny," he said, a note of tenderness in his voice.

For a moment, she felt like leaning into that tenderness. It would be so nice to have someone to depend on.

But Lane Carrigan didn't seem like a likely candidate. He cared about her now, in the aftermath of their lovemaking. But tomorrow or the next day, he'd hit the road again. He'd be gone, and she'd be here dealing with the fallout from her dumb decisions.

"I might be little, but I'm tough," she said. "Tougher than I look."

"I know." He brushed her hair back from her face and she almost looked away. She wasn't sure she wanted to know what was behind the intimacy of his gaze. "I know you're not looking for somebody to take care of you."

"No, I'm not." She laid back on the blanket, staring up at the sky. "I take care of myself. Counting on other people doesn't work."

"You sound like you know that from experience."

She nodded as he crooked one arm behind his head.

"Who left you, Sarah?"

She surprised herself by answering. "My dad. My stepdad, actually, but he was the best father. Really the best. My mom—she wasn't a bad person, but she wasn't very well equipped for life. He saved us. And then he died."

Because of me. The image of her stepfather's face flashed across her mind, pale and drawn on the gurney as they slid him into Two Shot's one and only ambulance, a battered old thing that should have been a collector's item, not a working emergency vehicle. He hadn't survived the long trip to the hospital.

"I don't want to talk about it."

"Okay." He threw his other arm over her waist, pulling her close. "We don't have to talk." He nuzzled the curve of her neck, and she brushed her lips over his hair. "We have other ways to communicate."

"I need to get home. I have a lot to do."

Like getting a good night's sleep. And going to work in the morning, pretending she hadn't spent most of the night naked with the boss's brother.

She sat up and scanned the truck bed for her clothes. Her panties were draped over the tailgate, her dress hooked on a branch above her head. She reached up and pulled it down, tugging it over her head, shoving her arms through the straps. Lane watched like she was putting on a show.

"Okay," he said. "Let's go."

She tossed the wrap over her shoulders and clutched it at her throat, a look of horror crossing her face. "You're not thinking of staying, are you?"

"Not at your place." He slid off the tailgate and put his jeans back on. "I was thinking you could come home with me."

He held out a hand to help her down, but she ignored it, resting one hand on the side of the pickup while she jumped lightly from the tailgate. She hurried around the side of the truck and climbed into the passenger's seat, trying to pretend she hadn't heard his answer.

Staring out the window, she avoided his eyes as he slid behind the wheel and shoved the key in the ignition.

"Lane, I told you. We can't do this. It was good, it was really good, but you're leaving, and I'm not one of those clingy types."

"It was beyond good. And it'll be even better next time." He reached over and flipped her hair back over her shoulder, forcing her to look at him. "I'm sorry I didn't take as much time as I should have."

She gave him a wry smile. "Trust me, it's not a matter of the performance. It's just—we need to get back to reality now."

"That was real. That was as real as anything could be."

"My job is real. I work for your brother."

He stared through the windshield, his jaw working as if he was trying to keep from getting angry. He cranked the key in the ignition and the truck started up, the engine throbbing like an angry animal that couldn't wait to get moving. "I can't believe this."

"What?"

"I can't believe I'm competing against my brother for a woman and losing. You care more about what he thinks than you do about me. And I don't have much left in my arsenal of charms. I kind of shot off every weapon I had."

"It's not just that. It's—I don't want a relationship right now." She gave him a rueful smile, the closest she could come to throwing him a bone. "Not even with you."

"So you've made your choice."

"I have to choose my job. Eric can help me survive."

"Yeah, but I can help you *live*."

"I'll take survival," she said. "Please, Lane. Take me home."

—◦◦◦—

Lane kept his eyes on the road and his hands on the steering wheel, but his mind was on the woman who sat stiff and silent beside him. Was this the real Sarah—the woman in the little black dress? He didn't think so. He'd seen the real Sarah in the back of the truck.

It was like the moonlight was magic, releasing a luminous secret goddess from the buttoned-up businesswoman.

Or maybe the magic worked the other way. It was obvious something had happened in Sarah's life that imprisoned her in a hard, brittle shell. Tonight, something had broken through it and set her free, but now she was closed up tight again like a princess in a tower.

Well, he was going to storm the ramparts. Somehow, he was going to figure out how to open the castle door.

No. Scratch that. He wasn't just going to open the door; he was going to tear down the damn castle.

"What is it you're so afraid of?"

She shot him a hard glare. He wasn't sure if he'd struck a nerve or simply struck out.

"I'm not afraid of anything."

"Then come home with me."

"I'm not saying no because I'm afraid. I'm going home because I don't want a relationship with you."

"Look, I have no idea what flipped your switch, and I'm not going to chase after you. But it's a hell of a way to treat a guy. If a man treated a woman this way, you and your girlfriends would tear him to pieces."

She brought a hand to her forehead and for a moment he thought she was going to cry, but she sucked in a deep breath and steeled herself. He had a feeling she did that a lot.

"You're right. Lane, I'm sorry. I let my—my needs get away from me. I shouldn't have let that happen." She breathed in a shuddering breath and let it out. "You can let me out here."

"I'm not leaving you on the street."

"That's my apartment." She pointed to a three-story brick building that looked like it had once housed a bank or maybe a law office. It was one of those buildings someone had bought and renovated back when the oil boom hit, filling it with high-class loft apartments that were ugly, overpriced, and mostly empty.

He pulled to the curb and parked under a streetlight that cast deep shadows on her face, making her look drawn and haunted.

"I'll walk you up," he said, shoving the gearshift into park.

"No need."

He looked past her at the darkened building. The place looked practically abandoned. "Don't you have a doorman or anything?"

"Of course not. This is Casper." She floundered for the door handle, her hand shaking. "And I'll be fine. I'm used to being on my own, Lane, and I'm staying that way. I can't continue to be in any kind of relationship with you, and I hope you'll be a gentleman and let it go."

He leaned over and opened the door for her, but his arm blocked her exit.

"You of all people know I'm not a gentleman. 'Gentlemen' are those shysters in suits that sat across the table at dinner. And I don't know what makes you think any kind of man would let this go." He eased back, letting her slide out of the car, but the hem of her dress caught on the door handle and she tugged at it, frowning.

"Don't worry, princess. Your secrets are safe with me." He reached over and pulled her dress free, brushing her thigh in the process. "I just wonder what they're doing to you."

CHAPTER 19

SARAH CLUTCHED HER PURSE CLOSE TO HER BODY AS SHE headed for the front door of the condo building. Fishing for her keys, she glanced back at the curb where Lane's big diesel idled, growling like a monster in a kid's nightmare. He'd parked at a slant to light her way. It was a nice thing to do, but in her agitated mental state, its lights seemed mercilessly bright, blinding her view of the man in the driver's seat.

Which was just as well. She'd be better off if she never saw Lane Carrigan again. Somehow, he'd turned her from a dutiful, rational publicity executive into a wild woman with all the poise and judgment of a rabid squirrel.

She found her key ring and fumbled to find the front door key. Somehow they slipped from her fingers, and she bobbled them frantically before dropping them on the doorstep. She bent to pick them up, angling her body and stooping so she wouldn't flash her panties at Lane. As she shoved the key in the lock, she turned and gave him a dismissive wave.

The truck stared back, its lights bright, its broad grill grim and threatening. Turning, she jerked the door open, eager to escape into the sanctuary of her apartment.

Whap.

She'd jerked the door right into her forehead. The impact knocked her backward and her heel hit the edge of the step. Flailing for balance and cursing her own clumsiness, she grabbed the door and dodged inside, hastily turning the dead bolt.

As she climbed the steps, harsh white light from Lane's headlamps still lit the hallway. She couldn't believe he'd asked if she had a doorman. How much did he think the company was paying her?

Of course, he couldn't know she gave half her money to her sister, which was why she'd had to give up her paid parking space in the well-lit lot next door. Lane would really freak out if he saw her usual nighttime arrival, dodging in the back door from the dark alley, hoping no late-night drunks or homeless vagrants happened by.

Wearily, she crossed the second floor landing and traipsed up the final flight to her apartment. She should have been home hours ago. She had to work tomorrow, then make the two-hour drive to Two Shot in time to get there before Katie's bedtime. Kelsey managed to play happy housewife without a husband from Monday to Friday, but working in Katie's preschool, shuttling her to half-a-dozen after-school activities, and then chairing PTO meetings in the evenings took everything she had. By Saturday, she was a basket case. When Sarah found out Katie was spending entire weekends in front of the TV while her mom lay half comatose on the sofa with a migraine, she started going home to help out every Friday night. She played with Katie on Saturdays, giving Kelsey a break, and drove home Sunday morning. Two Shot wasn't exactly her dream destination for weekend vacations, but so far she'd been able to hide out in Kelsey's battered single-wide.

Flicking the light switch on the third floor landing, she peeked out the window to see Lane's truck pulling away from the curb. She sorted through her keys, then tripped on the top step and dropped them again. Was she drunk or just tired?

A little bit of both, maybe, plus weak in the knees over Lane. She yawned as she found the apartment key and swung the door open. Dim light spilled into the hallway. Gloria must have left a light on for her. That was thoughtful. A light and…

Music?

Something soft and new-agey filled the air. That was odd. Gloria usually listened to bouncier stuff—Lady Gaga and Duffy. Stuff like that. Unless she was with somebody. Sometimes she played soft music when she had a boyfriend over and they were…

Oh God. What was that on the sofa?

Gloria.

Gloria naked.

Oh, shit. Sarah's roommate was lying on the sofa in a tangle of naked limbs—too many limbs for one woman to have. She was using her body to shield the rightful owner of the extra arms and legs.

"I thought you'd be late," Gloria babbled. "What are you doing home? I left you there with that holy-shit-mother-of-God stud, and I figured you'd have more sense than to come back here." She stood, totally unembarrassed by her nakedness as a pale figure darted off the sofa and scampered down the hall, dodging into a doorway. Sarah had done her best not to watch, but she was pretty sure Gloria's man-toy had just run into the closet. A thump and the sound of hangers clanging confirmed her theory.

She looked back at Gloria, who was trying to cover herself with her guest's jacket, which was a dark, distinguished charcoal gray. Perfectly cut. Armani.

Eric's.

Holy crap, she'd just seen her boss's naked backside. Suddenly, she wished she was back in the truck with Lane, speeding to his place for another round of holy-shit-mother-of-God sex. Because sleeping with her boss's brother suddenly seemed like the least of her worries.

She strode down the hallway without a word, passing the closet and turning into her own room. Grabbing her overnight case, she shoved bras, panty hose, and underwear inside. She flung open her closet and grabbed an armful of hanging suits and skirts, and then ran across the hall to the bathroom. It didn't take long to toss her makeup and toiletries into the case. Hefting the overnight case on one arm and the hanging clothes on the other, she stomped down the hallway and out the door.

"Sarah, wait!"

"No." Sarah spun to face Gloria, so mad she could hardly see. "I told you there was one rule, Gloria. Just one. And you went ahead and did it anyway."

She clutched at a pair of panties that was slipping out of the bundle of clothes in her arms and slammed out of the apartment, almost running down the steps.

Opening the building's back door, she looked both ways. No drunks. No vagrants. She hit the beeper on her keys and started across the alley as the light inside the Malibu glowed to life. Just as she started to cross the alley, a deafening rumble filled the air.

A truck sped directly toward her, lights blazing, dust billowing from its tires. Skittering backward, she dropped the clothes in the dirt and flattened herself against the brick wall by the door. She let out a squeak of alarm as the vehicle skidded to a stop right in front of her, but then she realized who it was.

"Lane," she said. "Lane?" The night's event whirled in her brain, and before she had time to think she stepped up to the pickup and smacked the hood. "What the hell are you doing here?"

Lane winced as Sarah punched the pickup. Most women screamed when they were scared, or fainted. Sarah stepped up and smacked something.

He hadn't meant to scare her. He'd watched her unlock the dark apartment building and his protective instinct had gone into overdrive, making him wonder what she did when he wasn't there. He'd been just about to go around to the back and see if that was where she parked when he spotted Eric's car parked out front.

Shit. What the hell was his brother doing there? Waiting for Sarah?

Maybe there really was something going on between them. He'd thought that at the start, but had he listened to his gut? No.

He'd wanted to believe Sarah was his, only his. That she couldn't resist him.

When really, she was playing him for a fool.

"What the hell am *I* doing? Maybe I should ask *you* that." He leaned across the seat and swung the door open. "What's my brother doing here?"

"What do you think he's doing here?" She backed away from the truck. "You think…oh my God. What do you think I am?"

"No, I…" He opened the truck door and slid down from the seat, but she was already scooping up the clothes she'd dropped and crossing the alley, her keys clenched in her fist.

Her hands were shaking as she tossed the clothes in the car and slammed the door shut. Sliding into the driver's seat, she shoved the key in the ignition and revved the engine.

She shouldn't be driving. She was way too upset—and no wonder. He'd practically accused her of sleeping with his brother.

He didn't know why Eric was here, but he knew that wasn't the reason. Sarah would never do that. He was a jerk to even consider it.

Running to the car, he rapped on her window, but she looked over her shoulder and backed away at top speed, running over a few scraps of clothing she'd missed. She tore out of the alley, back tires spitting gravel, and he watched her taillights disappear.

CHAPTER 20

SARAH STEPPED OUT OF HER CAR AND TRUDGED TOWARD Kelsey's dark house. After a half hour of listening to the highway hum beneath her wheels, the quiet country night was a little unnerving. A cricket scraped out three hesitant notes as she approached the house, then fell silent.

In a way, the silence was welcome. At Kelsey's she could be herself, nothing more or less. She was needed and loved, and she didn't have to worry about impressing anyone. Just walking up the driveway made her feel like a princess changing back into the carefree goose girl in a fairy tale.

Lately, she could feel her past barreling up behind her like a racehorse pounding into the homestretch. Her professional poise sometimes felt like a heavy crown that weighed her down, and one that kept slipping to one side when she accidentally dropped a G or sat down at the conference table with her legs astraddle like the cowgirl she used to be. One of these days she was bound to blurt out a cuss word at a meeting or bring up Whiplash the Cowboy Monkey again.

Not that it mattered anymore. Gloria had spilled most of her secrets last night at the dinner table, and no doubt she'd leaked more during the pillow talk portion of the night.

She eased Kelsey's front door open, slipped inside the darkened house, and closed it carefully behind her so the latch wouldn't click. She was sure she'd carried off her stealth mission until Katie's little black terrier mix rocketed down the hallway and skidded to a stop at her feet. The dog whined and wriggled, all bright eyes and pink panting tongue.

"Shhhh, Corky. Shhhh." She picked up the puppy and carried

him over to the sofa. Cradling him in one arm, she settled into Kelsey's needlepoint throw pillows.

A shadowy form appeared in the dark hallway. "Sarah?"

"Fortunately, yes. But I could be Ted Bundy. You really ought to lock your door."

"We're in Two Shot."

"We're in the twenty-first century."

"Good point, I guess." Kelsey sat down on the edge of a rocking recliner that used to be Mike's TV chair. Actually, it had been more like his throne. He'd held court there every night, king of the remote, flicking from football to fights and back to football while Kelsey waited on him.

At least now that he was gone she wore comfortable pajamas. After their marriage, Kelsey's entire nighttime wardrobe had consisted of sexy sheer nighties with scratchy lace inserts. Sarah had wondered how she ever managed to sleep in them.

Kelsey had always been the pretty sister, while Sarah was the smart one. Kelsey was taller and curvier, with a generous figure that inspired envy in their girl classmates and lust in the boys. She'd had her pick of dates, and Mike had been her choice. At the time, Sarah thought it was a good one. The handsome, easygoing football player seemed like a good match for bright, bubbly Kelsey.

Except that he couldn't seem to hold a real job and was a self-centered bastard. But they didn't know all that until six months ago, when he'd walked out and left her on her own with two-year-old Katie.

"So how's it going?" Sarah asked, keeping her voice low so she wouldn't wake Katie. "You feeling okay?"

"So far. But I've got the flickering." Kelsey fluttered her fingers on either side of her face. "I'll have a migraine tomorrow."

"Can't you take something for it? I think there's something you can take when you get the warning signs. You need to go to a doctor, Kelse. It's not fair to Katie."

"What wouldn't be fair to Katie is getting hooked on some drug." Kelsey's pretty face creased into a frown. "You know what it's like to deal with a mother who's impaired half the time. I won't let that happen."

"It's not booze, it's migraine medication. There's no danger of addiction, and…"

"Sarah, I'm working on it, okay? You think I don't care about Katie? You think I want to spend all day Saturday on the sofa nursing a headache while my kid spends the whole day having fun with you? You think I like taking my sister's money so I can keep a roof over our heads?" She swiped at her eyes. "I'm trying. I'm doing deep breathing, and I'm rewiring my brain."

"Rewiring your brain?"

"Thinking positive thoughts. It creates new neural pathways and actually makes you intrinsically happier."

"New neural pathways, huh?"

Maybe that was why Sarah couldn't stop thinking about Lane. He'd made her intrinsically hornier. It was a good thing she had Kelsey and Katie to distract her, or she'd become a sex maniac by Monday.

She pulled her legs up onto the sofa and sat with her legs crossed facing her sister. "So what did you do this week?"

"Worked."

"No, I mean what were your days like? We talked about trying to simplify things, remember?"

"My life is simple. I take care of Katie. I work. It's not rocket science."

"It is when you try to do it perfectly."

"I know." Kelsey kicked idly, hitting the front of the recliner with her heel as she furrowed her brow in thought. "I gave Katie cold cereal on Tuesday and Wednesday. But I could tell she didn't like it, and when I made pancakes Thursday morning she was so happy."

"What time did you have to get up to do that?"

"Five." Kelsey sighed. "And the night before was the PTO meeting. I had to go, because they were working on the fund-raiser for new safety equipment for the playground. There's this new surfacing material made from recycled Styrofoam..."

"Can't other people take care of that? Just until things get easier for you?"

"They need my support. And besides, things aren't going to get easier."

"But you'll learn how to balance things. And Katie's growing up."

"Too fast." Kelsey rose from the sofa and began picking up the plastic Weebles scattered around the floor. The little round toys were a hazard, but Sarah couldn't help feeling that Kelsey was only picking them up so she wouldn't have to look Sarah in the eye. "I do all right." She tossed the Weebles into a basket that was already brimming with stuffed toys, board books, and plastic cars. "In fact, I can pay you some of your money back."

"You don't have to do that. It wasn't a loan."

One of the Weebles rolled off the heap of toys and fell to the floor. Kelsey scrambled after it on her hands and knees as it rolled under the sofa. "Well, I can't just take it."

"You need it to pay bills."

"I did. But I'm doing better now." She held up the Weeble as if capturing the renegade toy was evidence of her newfound success.

"How? Did you get a raise?"

"No. I just—I have some extra, okay?"

"Well, spend it on Katie, then."

"Yeah, 'cause she needs more toys." Kelsey lurched to her feet and sighed. "I'm all right, Sarah. I appreciate your help, but I'll be okay."

"Well, I don't mind helping." Sarah scratched the dog under the chin and the puppy grinned and panted. "I just don't think you should have to work so hard. You don't have to be perfect, you know."

"You're telling me this? Picture-perfect professional Sarah?"

"Oh, I'm definitely not perfect." Sarah shifted the dog in her lap and gave his collar a totally unnecessary adjustment.

Kelsey cocked her head and studied her. "You're not, are you? What happened? Why are you here in the middle of the night?"

"Nothing. I just—roommate problems."

"That Gloria girl? I wondered about that. She sounded like a wild child."

"You have no idea." Sarah shuddered, remembering the tangle of naked arms and legs on her sofa. "Kelsey, I don't think I can room with her anymore."

"I don't think you should have to." Kelsey started kicking the recliner again. "I can make it, Sarah. And Mike will start paying his share soon."

"What makes you think that?" Sarah asked.

Kelsey shrugged and looked away. "I just—I just think he will."

"Listen, what if I stayed with you? Just for a while. That way I could get away from Gloria and still help out."

Sarah had thought Kelsey would be thrilled to have help every day, but she just shifted in her chair and looked uncomfortable. "Isn't that an awfully long drive?"

"Kind of, but I'd see more of Katie."

"Yeah."

Sarah wondered if Kelsey was already getting a headache. She was frowning as she shoved the basket of toys under the coffee table with one foot.

"What else is wrong?"

"Nothing," Sarah said.

Kelsey used two fingers to point from her eyes to Sarah's and back again. "Big sister radar, remember? It's a man, isn't it?" She closed her eyes in mock concentration. "I see a tall, dark asshole in your future…"

"He's got brown hair." Sarah wanted to kick herself the moment she said it. She and her sister had always competed in the Golden Girl Sweepstakes to see which of them could live the most perfect, enviable life. Kelsey had dropped out of the race when Mike left, but Sarah was still competing, almost subconsciously. Admitting to a relationship—no, not a relationship, a *fling*—with the kind of cowboy she'd always scorned would be like throwing the game.

"So who is he? What happened?"

"Nobody." Sarah put her hands up, palms out, to stop the onslaught of questions. "Nothing."

Kelsey gave her a suspicious look, then slumped. "Well, it's about time you had some fun. I just wish you'd tell me about it so I could live vicariously, that's all."

"Nothing to tell." Sarah set the puppy on the floor and stood up, brushing imaginary crumbs from her dress. As she bent forward, her necklace swung forward and almost hit her in the face.

"What's that?" Kelsey reached over and took the charm between her fingers. "Oh, Sarah, a little horse. Are you going to start riding again?"

"No." The vehemence of her denial surprised her, and it made Kelsey take a step back.

"Sorry, I just—it was your thing, you know? You loved it so. And just because things didn't work out back then doesn't mean you can't ride anymore."

"I can't," Sarah said. "Trust me, it's not going to happen."

"Okay." Kelsey winced and raised a hand to her forehead. "Oh, shit."

"It's starting?"

Kelsey closed her eyes tight and clutched her stomach. "Yeah."

"Go lie down, hon. Try to get some sleep. I'm here."

"Okay." Kelsey gave her a weak smile. "What time do you have to leave in the morning?"

"Early. Like seven. But if Katie's up, I'll give her breakfast."

"Okay." Kelsey stood, her shoulders hunched against the pain. "So, on Saturday…"

Sarah knew what was coming, and she could feel a headache of her own coming on. They'd had this conversation before.

"What about it?"

"Maybe you could take Katie to town. Some of the other moms in the PTO go to the playground in the afternoon."

"Like who?"

Kelsey listed a couple of girls they'd gone to school with who were grown now with kids of their own.

"I don't think so," Sarah said. "We can play here."

"Sarah, you have to go to town sometime. You can't just hide out here. Especially if you're moving back."

"Why? They won't have anything to say to me. I couldn't get out of this town fast enough, and people here couldn't wait to kick me in the butt on my way out."

"That's not true, Sarah."

"Then why didn't anybody talk to me after Roy died? Why did every room go quiet when I walked in? Why didn't one single person offer to help us?"

Kelsey stomped her foot. "Because you scared them all away!"

"I was a fifteen-year-old kid. How scary is that?"

"Pretty damn scary when it's you, Sarah. It was like you had your own personal thundercloud you carried around with you. Nobody knew what to say to you. You never reached out. Never gave anybody a chance."

"A chance to what? To come watch our mother drink herself to death? To see how our lives were falling apart? Why? So they could gossip about us again, the way they did before Roy came along and made us respectable?"

"So they could help."

"I didn't need their kind of help."

Kelsey stood in the door to the hallway looking defeated.

"You're just making it worse, you know. Everybody sees your car here. They're all wondering why you don't come say hello."

"Well, they can keep on wondering." Sarah sighed. "I'll be late tomorrow, okay? I have a lot to wrap up."

"You work too hard," Kelsey said.

"Look who's talking. Taking care of a three-year-old and working full-time is a lot harder." Sarah smiled, trying to break the tension. "Besides, I love my job."

As she said it, a bolt of dread shot through her and she thought she might get a migraine herself. She used to love her job. But with all that had happened that night, she was hardly looking forward to her next day at the Carrigan Corporation.

CHAPTER 21

"I FIGURED IT OUT," ERIC SAID.

Sarah perched in the chair in front of his desk in her usual posture, straight up, knees slanted to one side, hands clasped in her lap. She was doing her best to look poised, but deep down her stomach clenched with dread. Eric hadn't mentioned Gloria yet. He hadn't mentioned the revelation that Sarah, his "Vassar girl," had grown up "dirt poor." He hadn't asked her how things had gone with Lane, or mentioned the fact that she'd seen him naked scampering down the hall in her seedy, poorly furnished apartment.

She'd been hoping he was embarrassed. Maybe the two of them could just silently agree to pretend the night had never happened. Maybe if she kept her polished, professional mask on, he'd follow suit.

But judging from the got-it-going-on grin on his face and the theatrical pause she was suffering through, things were about to change.

They were certainly changing for Sarah. She'd packed the rest of her belongings into the Malibu on her lunch hour, while Gloria was working. Gloria was fun, Gloria was sweet, but Gloria was a lousy roommate. Sarah had overlooked the late hours, the loud music, and the frequent male visitors—but she couldn't overlook the business with Eric. She simply couldn't trust Gloria, and there was no room in her life for people she couldn't trust.

Eric broke into her thoughts, leaning back in his chair. "We need to talk about Two Shot." He paused, his gaze intensifying. "I think it's the key to everything."

Oh, shit. He was so right. Two Shot *was* the key to everything. Her evasions. Her many, many sins of omission. Her lies.

Well, not exactly *lies*. She'd never told Eric where she was from. She'd just let him believe her life had begun at Vassar. It was as if she'd been born into the world at the age of twenty-five with a master's degree instead of an umbilical cord.

She'd started hiding her roots soon after she'd started college. She'd listened to her new classmates describing their summers in the Hamptons and winters in Gstaad, and she'd launched into a narrative about tipping cows and John Deere joyrides that earned her raised eyebrows rather than laughter. When the girls edged away almost imperceptibly, she'd realized fitting in would be a challenge. So she'd studied the rich girls harder than she'd studied Econ 101, memorizing the effortless way they walked, copying the subtle simplicity of their clothes, imitating the faint note of ennui in their voices. By her second semester, she'd changed from a wide-eyed country girl into an upper-crust sophisticate.

But now she'd been busted.

"Yes, it's all about Two Shot." Eric picked up a gold-plated Mont Blanc pen and tapped it on the desk, first one end, then the other. "Lane really cares about that town, and he's afraid the drilling operation will change it." He set the pen on the desk and rolled it right, then left. "I don't know why—it's not much of a town. Just a crossroads, really."

She nodded.

"Your friend said you'd lived in a trailer."

Here it came. She was going to get fired. "Yes, I did. For a while."

"Was it in a small town?"

She nodded, unable to speak past the lump forming in her throat. He was toying with her, sure as he was toying with the pen. Or did he really not know about her connection with Two Shot?

"I think you'll be just the right person to solve the problem."

She lifted her head, blinking. "Really?"

"Sure." He set down the pen. "Lane seems to think our workers will come into town and shoot up the place like outlaws in a Sergio

Leone movie." He leaned toward her, steepling his fingers. "You and I both know that's not true. We're going to bring money into that town. Money, jobs—prosperity. And I suspect the people of Two Shot will welcome that kind of change."

His intent expression darkened and his heavy brows arrowed down. She could almost hear distant thunder. "Besides, it's not up to Lane to decide what should happen. It's up to the people. And that's where you come in."

"Really?" she said again.

She needed to shut up and listen. She sounded like an idiot.

Eric didn't seem to notice. "Lane can't turn up on TV talking trash about the drilling if the whole town wants it to happen, right? So you'll go to Two Shot and talk to everybody who counts—the mayor, the police chief. But in addition, you'll talk to the regular folks. Ranchers, waitresses, hairdressers—everybody."

Could the world come up with a worse nightmare to impose on her? Talking to everyone in town would definitely lead to some one-way conversations, because she doubted anyone in town was speaking to her.

"No. I—I can't."

"It's okay. You won't be missing all that much at the office. This is so much more important."

He'd completely misinterpreted her refusal. Eric thought he knew her, she realized. He thought she was simply a dedicated worker who didn't want to take a business trip because she was worried about falling behind on other projects. He had no clue she was a liar and a fake.

"There's a little diner there. Suze's." He settled back in his chair. "Lane reminded me of it, said it's still there. It might be a good place to start spreading the word about what Carrigan can do for the town. Get people talking about how many jobs it'll create, how much money it'll bring in. See if there's a pet project—a library, a meeting hall, something like that—and show how we can make it happen. Maybe a shooting range, or a motocross track. That's what those people like, right?"

He looked at her expectantly. Much as she wanted to call him out on his stereotyping of small-town people, she felt like she had no room to take risks, no room to run. She'd been a little worried about the project's proximity to Two Shot, but she'd expected to work behind the scenes, lobbying the legislature, attending meetings. She hadn't expected to have to go right into town and talk to the people she'd left behind all those years ago.

"I don't know..."

"It'll work," Eric insisted. "All you have to do is your job." He fished a set of keys out of his pocket and slid them across the desk. "I even arranged a place for you to stay so you won't have to make that drive. Go on home and pack your bags."

She felt panic rising in her chest. "Where do you want me to stay?"

"There's an old cabin at the ranch. I think you'll find it quite comfortable."

Her eyes widened. "Doesn't it belong to Lane?"

"It's on a separate plot of land, across the creek. You won't be sharing a room with him or anything."

No, but she might end up sharing a bed with Lane again if she got within a stone's throw of him. His energy, his charisma—hell, maybe it was just his muscles. Or his kindness. Whatever it was, she was helpless to fight it.

"Don't worry," Eric said. "It's fully renovated into a top-notch guest house. You'll have your own kitchen, and there's a sitting room and a loft bedroom. It hasn't been used much since we were in high school, so I called Lane's foreman and asked him to send somebody over to clean."

"You used it in high school?"

He smiled nostalgically. "Lane and I used to call it the Love Nest."

Lane hunched over his laptop at the tiny desk wedged below the microwave in his trailer, reading the latest PRCA statistics. He was near the top of the pack in bull riding, but there were a couple of young guys pretty close on his heels.

He sighed. Both guys were talented riders, but neither was a true cowboy. One was from New York City, of all places. The kid didn't know a damn thing about ranching and probably couldn't ride a horse. He'd trained on machines in schools designed just for bull riders.

Now the kid was a star on the Professional Bull Riders tour, taking home purses that made the National Finals prizes look like chump change. Lane didn't begrudge him the money, but the PBR pulled the good bulls away from the small-town rodeos Lane loved.

And no real rancher ever needed to ride a bull. Lane had started rodeoing because he loved the way it preserved traditional ranch skills, so maybe he should go back to bronc riding. He'd quit the bareback event because it was too hard on his body; even the roughest bull ride didn't dish out as bad a beating as the crack-the-whip action a good bronc dealt out.

But saddle bronc was a possibility. The purses weren't as big as bull riding prizes, but it was the event that required the most artistry on the part of the cowboy. Riding a bull was about flair, skill, and confidence. Riding a saddle bronc was about balance, spurring, and finesse. Cowboys still had to make the buzzer, but they had to do it with grace. A great bronc ride was beautiful, pure poetry.

Beautiful. Pure poetry. His mind's eye flashed to Sarah lying in the bed of his truck, dressed only in shadows and moonlight. Now *that* was poetry. He allowed himself a moment to sit back, close his eyes, remember. Dangerous stuff—more dangerous than any rodeo bull.

Usually, women weren't a problem for him. Their expectations of a rodeo cowboy were low on the romance side, and though a few women had tried to snag a piece of the Carrigan fortune, not one had succeeded. He loved 'em and left 'em, and nobody was surprised—least of all the women.

But Sarah was turning things around. She'd left him standing in the alley with his hat in his hand—and he couldn't blame her. After all his talk about understanding her real self, he'd practically accused her of sleeping with his brother. Deep down, he knew that was something she would never, ever do.

But why had Eric been there? The question was driving him crazy.

He turned back to the screen, telling himself it didn't matter. By this time tomorrow, he'd be on the back of a bull in Amarillo. He wouldn't be thinking about Sarah and how he'd blown the one relationship he'd ever hoped would last. He'd be thinking about hanging on. Surviving.

Maybe he and Sarah had more in common than he'd thought.

"She said she'd take survival," he told Willie, who was curled up at his feet. "Guess that's about all we've got too."

He tapped the mouse pad, bringing the screen to life. He had mail—including a reminder that draws for Amarillo were up on the Professional Rodeo Cowboy's Association website. Clicking into the list, he grinned. Rusty Nail. The big brindled animal could spin like a tornado and jump like a jackrabbit—all at the same time. He was a high-score bull, the kind a cowboy wanted to draw. Lane had ridden him to a buckle in Cheyenne last year, and he was willing to bet he could do it again.

His cell phone jumped to life, jitterbugging across the table and falling to the floor. He stared down at the screen. *Eric*. He clicked the green "go" button and grunted a hello.

"Hey, Lane."

"Hey."

"Thought I'd give you a warning. There's a hurricane headed your way."

"What?"

Eric chuckled. He sounded smug, like he'd won an argument or proved what a yahoo Lane was somehow. Too many of their verbal battles had ended with that chuckle.

"Hurricane Sarah's coming to Two Shot. I thought I'd better let you know, since she'll be staying at the Love Nest."

The light seemed to fuzz and blur in Lane's head, and his skin prickled despite the heat. Eric had Sarah at the Love Nest? The cabin had a nest, all right, though the "love" part wasn't quite accurate. He and his brother had played host to a number of girls there during their adolescent Two Shot vacations. They should have called it the Lust Nest.

"Tell me she's on company business."

Eric snorted. "Sarah's always on business. She's probably on business when she's—well, never mind." The smile came back into his tone. "You probably know all about that."

Lane wanted to make a smart remark, some kind of rude comment, but he couldn't speak. Eric must have caught the tension, because his voice sounded wary when he asked, "What's the matter?"

"I saw your car."

"Yeah, good." Eric sounded positively smug. "And you were struck with envy, right? Don't blame you, driving around in the rattletrap Dodge. You ought to get yourself something better."

"No, I mean I saw it at Sarah's."

"What, last night? Shit, you weren't with her when she got home, were you?" He laughed uneasily. "Now that was embarrassing. I know Gloria's hardly the kind of girl I ought to go for, but I couldn't help myself. Well, actually, I could *help myself*. And I did."

"Gloria?"

"Yeah. You know, the blonde. Sarah's roommate."

"Sarah's *roommate*." Suddenly, everything was sharp and clear in Lane's mind. "It's her apartment too."

"Yeah, and let me tell you, there's not a surface in there we didn't—never mind. I should be ashamed of myself, right?"

Lane felt suddenly giddy with relief. "Why? Gloria's nothing to be ashamed of."

"Well, she's hardly my type. I don't know why I always end up with the wrong kind of woman."

"Maybe because they *are* your type," Lane said. He remembered the blonde doing her rodeo rider imitation and smiled. "I think she's just what you need. Step outside your comfort zone and live a little, why don't you?"

"I suspect that with Gloria I'd be living a lot."

"And it would be about time."

Eric paused. "Oh. I get it."

"What?"

"You thought I was with Sarah." Eric sounded more appalled than amused.

"No, I…"

"You did. And then I tell you she's at the Love Nest." He chortled. "Had you going, bro."

"So she's there because…"

"She's working on something."

Lane slapped the desktop and Willie jumped up, giving him an irate look before curling up again a few feet away.

"So you're not only planning to drill on the ranch, you're putting up employees there without even asking. I thought we had a deal, Eric. The ranch is mine. The company's yours. Maybe I ought to come over there and take over your office. See how you like it."

"The Love Nest isn't yours. It's not on the ranch."

"It figures you'd find a technicality. What's she doing—taking measurements? Plotting out a trailer park for the yahoos you're going to bring in to work the wells?"

"I hate to tell you this, Lane, but I suspect our workers will raise the level of class and culture in Two Shot."

"How would you know? You barely talked to anybody there." Lane slid his rolling desk chair over to the trailer's mini-fridge and pulled out a Bud Light. Popping the top, he swallowed a good slug, but it didn't cool the heat of his anger one bit.

"That's why I'm sending Sarah to get to know the area," Eric said. "Meet some of the people, get acquainted with the town."

Lane set his beer can down hard on the desktop. "Hell, Eric, she doesn't need to get acquainted with Two Shot. She grew up there."

He closed his eyes and smacked his forehead with the heel of his hand. Shit. He needed to erase those words somehow. In the irrational heat of his petty anger, he'd just betrayed Sarah's secrets.

There was a long silence, which gave Lane plenty of time to curse himself.

"What are you talking about? She's not from there," Eric finally said. "She's from—well, I don't know where she's from." There was another long silence. "If she's from Two Shot, that puts us way ahead of the game. She'd already know everybody. Wonder why she didn't mention that when we talked?"

Lane didn't respond. He'd said more than enough already.

"There's something strange going on with that girl," Eric said thoughtfully. Lane could picture him tilting back in his chair, staring up at the plaster medallions on his office ceiling, clicking the pieces of the puzzle together. "If she grew up there, she's not being honest with me. She let me think…"

"Grew up?" Lane barked out a laugh he hoped sounded halfway convincing. "I said she *threw up*. I shouldn't have let that slip, though. I'm sure she'd be embarrassed."

"She threw up? What did you do the other night—ply her with alcohol and take her home? I can't believe she'd be that careless about drinking. She…"

"I think it was stomach flu," Lane said. "She didn't drink that much."

There. Now he'd saved her secrets *and* her reputation.

"Well, whatever. I just thought I'd let you know she's there. I saw a spark between you two, but maybe you'd better just leave her alone if things ended that way."

Lane hung up after a few minutes of awkward small talk. His brother was right—he should leave Sarah alone.

But he'd planted a seed with Eric and he needed to warn her. It shouldn't matter to anybody where Sarah was from—what mattered was who she was now. But Eric was big on class and status. He looked down his nose at Two Shot and the kind of people who lived there. People like Sarah.

He clicked back into the rodeo site and stared at the message again. Rusty Nail would put him on the road to the finals. He was sure of it. But going on with his own life seemed selfish when he might be leaving the wreckage of Sarah's behind.

A cowboy could "turn out" for a rodeo—opt not to attend—without losing any points or even respect. Some did it when they had a bad draw, leaving the dud bulls for the neophytes who would ride anything anywhere. But you'd have to be crazy to turn out when you drew a bull like Rusty Nail. Crazy, or in love.

Love?

No. He just felt duty-bound to find Sarah and warn her there was a good chance he'd screwed up her life.

He sent a quick message to the rodeo committee bailing on his ride and shrugged into a Carhartt jacket. Grabbing his hat from the table, he tipped it onto his head with a practiced flip and strode from the trailer.

Maybe he could find Sarah before she left town. Otherwise, he'd have to catch her at the Love Nest.

CHAPTER 22

SARAH ROLLED INTO TWO SHOT WITH WHITE KNUCKLES ON the steering wheel. She wasn't looking forward to this assignment, and worse yet, she couldn't get hold of Kelsey. She'd tried to call her sister at work and they said she'd taken the day off.

Kelsey never missed work, any more than she missed any of Katie's activities or play dates. Maybe she had one of her headaches. Up until now, she'd somehow held them off until the weekend.

Pulling up to the curb outside the trailer, Sarah threw the Malibu into park. Sure enough, Kelsey's car was parked in the driveway. There was another vehicle there too—one Sarah had never seen before. It was a pickup, an old Chevy from the '80s with a two-color paint job and chipped fenders. It was the kind of truck a cowboy drove when he wasn't winning at the rodeos. Sarah stared at it a moment, foreboding roiling in her stomach.

No. It couldn't be. Tossing her purse over her shoulder, she practically ran up the walk to the front door. Giving it three quick raps with her knuckles, she barged in.

Kelsey sat at the kitchen table, a cup of tea halfway to her lips. Kitty-corner from her, at the head of the table, sat Mike. He paused midmotion too, a forkful of Kelsey's famous made-from-scratch coconut cake raised halfway to his lips.

Sarah hung onto the door frame, barely able to absorb what she was seeing. Mike hadn't sent a support check in six months. Why the hell would Kelsey be feeding the bastard?

"Sarah!" Kelsey clanged the teacup down on its saucer and jumped to her feet, almost knocking her chair over backwards. "What's wrong?" Her eyes widened. "You should be at work."

Sarah ignored her and turned to Mike. "What the hell are you doing here?"

"Eating." He hoisted his fork in the air as if she might not have noticed the massive sugary slab in front of him, white cake with white frosting coated in snowy white coconut curls. "How 'bout you? You didn't get fired, did you?"

"Of course not. I can't *afford* to get fired." She was ready to fling some real zingers at Mike, but Kelsey hooked the leg of a chair with one foot and jerked it out from under the table, almost tipping it over.

"Sit, Sarah. We need to talk."

Sarah sat, a little stunned. Kelsey normally didn't order her around.

"He's been working," Kelsey said. "All this time."

"Working? Let me guess. At the rodeo?" Sarah rolled her eyes. "Eight seconds at a time? Or—wait a minute. You didn't make the eight seconds most of the time, did you? It's probably a challenge for you to ride that kitchen chair."

He took the insults in stride. "No rodeo," he said. "I'm working for the Carrigan Corp. Got a job on the oil rigs. We've been up north of Bismarck, building roads and digging trenches."

Sarah glanced down at his hands. He'd always had the typical cowboy calluses on his riding hand, but now he had them on every finger. Grime was etched deeply into the whorls of his fingertips and the lines in his palms. They were the hands of a working man.

"I didn't want to go," he continued, setting down his fork. "I mean, I wanted to go. I felt like the marriage wasn't working, and—well, that's personal. I know she's your sister, but what happens between Kelsey and me is none of your business."

"I..."

"No." He held up a hand with such an authoritative gesture she swallowed her retort. "We were married, me and Kelsey. You weren't in that marriage, and you don't know how things were between us. I left because it wasn't working, but I always meant to take care of Katie. I just didn't have any luck."

"Or skill," Sarah muttered. "You couldn't stick the coin-operated pony at Walmart."

"You think I don't know that?" The anger in Mike's tone surprised her. He was usually such a mild-mannered guy. "But there are no jobs here, Sarah. I couldn't find a ranch job after the feed store closed, and rodeo was the only thing left. Kelsey didn't want me to leave. She thought I ought to be in Katie's life, and I think she was right, but that didn't leave me a whole lot of choices."

Sarah shifted in her chair, starting to feel uneasy. Maybe she'd made too many assumptions about Mike.

"I could only deal with losing for so long, even for Katie. Carrigan had a couple guys quit on 'em and they wanted workers right away."

Sarah reached for her only remaining shred of righteous anger like a drowning woman reaching for a scrap of flotsam. "You could have told us."

"I don't have to tell *you* anything. But I tried to tell Kelsey. I had to leave right away, but I called." He flashed her a furious glare. "Thanks to you, she erased the message without listening."

Kelsey nodded, looking down at her folded hands. "You kept telling me I shouldn't listen to him, shouldn't let him sweet-talk me. So I didn't play the message. I just erased it."

"Oh, shit," Sarah said softly.

"Yeah, exactly," Mike said. "I figured she didn't want to talk to me, and the oil fields up there are out of cell range anyway. So I just kept working. And I saved almost all of it." He cast Sarah a hard look. "That night you saw me was the first time I'd been to a bar in three months."

"He thought he had to earn his way back to us," Kelsey said. "So he came home and slapped—how much was it?" She looked at Mike and the two of them laughed.

"Five thousand dollars," he said. "Slapped it right down on the table in cash. Her eyes sure got big when she saw it, and there's more where that came from."

"And then I cried."

"I can't believe you thought I'd never come back." Mike stroked Kelsey's arm and cast her a lovelorn look that reminded Sarah of a cow. Not a steer or a bull, but a dairy cow, all soft brown eyes and foolishness.

"Why wouldn't she think that?" Sarah asked. "How many nights did you go to the bar while Kelsey stayed home with Katie?"

"A lot. I was a lousy husband, okay?" Mike straightened in his chair and lost the lovelorn look as he turned to Sarah. "I married too young, and I was a jerk. I thought I wanted to hang out with my buddies more than I wanted to be with my wife and kid." He reached over and placed his hand over Kelsey's, and Sarah felt her stomach flutter with unease. She'd seen Mike as the villain so long that her protective instincts were still running full strength. She wanted to smack him away from her sister, drive him from the house, but now she had no reason to hate him. She felt limp as a hot-air balloon with the air let out.

"But let me tell you, you spend three months with nobody but a bunch of oil workers and you get pretty damn sick of hanging with the guys." He interlaced his fingers with Kelsey's and they sat there like a couple of newlyweds, beaming at each other. "I missed you and Katie so much, honey. So damn much. I never knew how much I loved you 'til I couldn't get to you."

Sarah blinked, surprised to find tears in her eyes.

"I know I was a jerk, Sarah, but I've learned my lesson and I'm back to stay."

"To stay?"

Kelsey melted into Mike's arm, still clinging to his hand. "We're going to try again," she said, flashing Sarah a heartbreakingly hopeful smile. "Be happy for me, Sis."

Sarah looked from one to the other. She hadn't seen Kelsey look so happy in months—not since Mike left.

"Isn't this kind of sudden?" she asked.

"We had a long talk."

"Just now? How can you forgive him so fast?"

Kelsey blushed. "And—and last night. And a few nights before that."

"Oh, no. Has Katie seen him?"

The sound of a rumbling engine filled the room as air brakes gasped on the street. Sarah glanced out to see her niece hurtling down the steps of the school bus and tearing up the front walk, an oversized sheet of construction paper flapping in her hand.

"Daddy," she shouted as she charged in the door. "I made you a picture!"

Without even glancing at Sarah, she threw herself into her father's lap and held up the paper as proudly as Christopher Wren revealing the plans for a new cathedral. "Look, it's a tree! And this is a cat, and a dog, and a woodchuck."

"A woodchuck," Mike said. "Nice."

Katie went somber. "He's going to eat the tree, though."

"No, that's beavers," Mike said. "Woodchucks eat beetles and stuff."

"Oh! Okay." She slid off his lap and ran to her room, as if all the world's problems had been solved by animal identification.

She still hadn't noticed Sarah, who hiked her purse up on her shoulder and turned to go.

"Wait, Sarah," Kelsey said. "You haven't told me why you stopped by."

"It doesn't matter," Sarah said. "It doesn't matter a bit. I just thought—I thought you needed me."

—m—

Sarah swung open the door to Lane's cabin and ran her hand up and down the wall to the right of the door until she found the light switch. She hadn't wanted to stay here. She hadn't wanted to come to Two Shot either, but seeing more of Katie and Kelsey had made the concept of melding her two lives a little more bearable. She'd been looking forward to being there all week, really being a part of their day-to-day lives.

Now that her sister didn't need her, she realized there wasn't much point to all her panic about her job. Without Kelsey and Katie to take care of, her work seemed kind of pointless. She'd thought it was about money and security for herself, but here she was, homeless and on the verge of being unemployed, and she didn't really care.

But Eric was counting on her. She'd been hired to do a job, and she was going to get it done.

She flicked on the light switch and her jaw dropped. The cabin really *was* a love nest. A huge stone fireplace dominated the far wall, surrounded by a cozy grouping of two chairs and a love seat upholstered in a warm-toned Native American pattern. The bright fabric contrasted with subdued throw rugs in red and ochre, and while the light she'd turned on was a slightly tasteless antler chandelier, it hung over a golden oak dining table that was polished to a high shine. Soft woven blankets that complemented the upholstery were draped over the back of the love seat and one of the chairs.

But what made it a love nest was the candles. They were everywhere, their wicks and wax in various stages that proved they'd been used frequently. She pictured the golden log walls lit by flickering golden light and thanked God and good luck Lane wasn't there.

She'd seen him in the cool silver light of the moon. What would he look like in candlelight? She pictured a warm glow glossing his muscled shoulders, shadows defining the ridges of his torso, and then she was in the danger zone.

Get out of there, she told herself. *Think about his face.*

Obediently, her mind's eye focused on the way his deep-set blue eyes would dance in the flicker of candle flames. Something much hotter than a candle flame shimmied around inside her when she thought of the jut of his cheekbones, the hard set of his jaw, and the sensitive lips that were such a subtle contradiction to the harsh masculinity of the rest of his face. Then she remembered what he'd done to her with those lips and decided she ought to stick with the torso.

The truth was, she shouldn't be thinking about Lane at all. The man accused her of sleeping with his brother, for God's sake. She'd thought he had feelings for her. She'd even thought he understood her. But clearly he'd just seen her as another floozy.

And Eric had said his brother was headed to another rodeo, all the way down in Texas—so he'd probably move on to a new floozy by tomorrow.

At least she could be sure he wouldn't show up at the ranch—not for two weeks. She had fourteen days to win hearts and minds in Two Shot. Fourteen days with no interference from the other side of the argument.

So why was her heart fluttering like a bird in a cage as she looked around the comfy cabin? Lane wasn't going to show up here. Sure, his mark was all over the place: in the rodeo posters on the wall, in the prize saddle mounted on a carved sawhorse in the corner, in the framed photos of him with various rodeo royals like Ty Murray and Trevor Brazile—but he was on the road and she was on her own.

And if he did turn up, he'd be angry, not amorous. He already thought she was having an affair with his brother, and he'd be even madder when he discovered she was working behind his back to get the townspeople on her side. By the time he got home he'd have lost the battle without getting a chance to fight. And Lane didn't like to lose.

Judging from the intensity of all his other emotions, his anger would not be pretty. The notion should make her cringe, but it actually kind of turned her on. What the hell was wrong with her? She was picturing a six-four cowboy coming to the door of this tiny, isolated cabin, walking in and finding her there. He'd push her down on that sofa, and he'd…

Stop it.

She sucked in a deep breath to clear her mind. Then she took another one. It took six or eight breaths to banish Lane to the back of her brain.

Resting one hand on the door frame, she kicked off her heels and tossed her messenger bag on a chair, heading for the kitchen. She'd make sure there was a microwave, and then she'd head into town to buy supplies—some frozen entrees, crackers and cheese, maybe some fruit. Definitely coffee.

A harsh series of knocks struck the door and she froze.

He *was* here. She wasn't nervous; she was psychic. What was she going to do? They'd be alone. Alone with that sofa, that fireplace. In the Love Nest.

He'd push her down on that sofa, and then he'd…

No. He wouldn't do anything. She'd simply tell him, brusquely and without emotion, that he needed to leave her alone. She'd cut him out of her life as quickly and efficiently as a bruise on an apple. She was here working for Carrigan, and besides, she could never forgive him for what he'd implied about her and Eric.

Quickly, she slid her feet back into her high heels. She'd have a better chance of standing up to him if she didn't have to hike herself up on tiptoe to meet his eyes.

CHAPTER 23

SARAH FELT LIKE A BIRD WAS FLUTTERING AROUND IN HER chest, banging off her heart and lungs and thrashing her breath away. She put her hand to her chest and swallowed, struggling to compose herself, then opened the door.

She'd expected to confront Lane's shirtfront despite the high heels. Instead, she stared at the crown of a man's hat. Beneath the black Stetson was a handsome, dark-haired cowboy in a wheelchair. He wore a Western shirt right out of a George Strait video, along with black jeans and boots that made him look like a Nashville refugee. All he needed was a guitar and a mass of squealing fans.

"Hello," she said, taking a step back. She felt a faint stir of unease. This cowboy looked familiar, but she didn't know why.

"Howdy." He moved the chair back a bit, as if sensing her nerves, and negotiated the uneven ground with the skill of a cowboy on a cutting horse. "I'm the foreman for the LT Ranch. Can I come in?"

"Sure." She stepped back to let him in, a little nervous about being alone with a stranger out here in the back of beyond. But the guy apparently worked for Lane, and he seemed friendly enough. And that face—it was so familiar. She had to know him somehow.

"I'm Sarah Landon." She put out a hand and got a firm grip in return.

"Trevor Ross. Eric let me know you were coming. I just came to check if the cleaning got done."

"It did, I think. I just got here, but the place looks great."

Actually, it looked beyond great. The slightest fleck of dust would have shown in the warm sun spilling in the windows, but every surface gleamed and the log walls glowed like burnished gold. A stack of logs sat in the fireplace, waiting for the touch of a match.

"I'll just check it out if you don't mind," Trevor said. "I have a girl from town that does it and I want to make sure she's doing her job. You know how teenagers are." Trevor motored into the galley kitchen, surveying the gleaming countertops and opening the refrigerator, which she saw was fully stocked with milk, eggs, and butter. She wouldn't have to run to town after all.

Backing out of the kitchen at top speed, Trevor took off for the living room, spinning to face her in front of the fireplace. "You don't remember me, do you?"

She considered him a moment. He was a handsome man, but thin, and his face seemed prematurely etched with lines that spoke of suffering. That probably had something to do with the wheelchair, but his smile was self-assured, as if he'd made it through a long struggle and come out victorious.

"You look familiar, but I can't quite…"

"'Fraid I gave you a lot of shit in high school."

The memory of a tall, muscular cowboy flashed through her memory. In her mind, he was leaning up against the brick wall of Two Shot High and giving her an insolent once-over that had made her hunch her shoulders, clutch her books to her chest, and scurry past like a fleeing mouse.

"I do remember." She frowned, wishing she hadn't let him in. She remembered Trevor Ross now. In fact, she was surprised she'd forgotten him. His teasing back then had cut deep, taking a chunk out of her self-esteem. If she'd recognized him she probably never would have opened the door.

"Guess I owe you an apology." He spread his hands, indicating the chair. "Obviously, I'm not the guy I used to be."

"I guess so. I mean, sorry. That's not…that's not right." She flushed. Whatever had happened to Trevor, nobody deserved to be hurt. And she had no doubt the change was especially hard on this man, who'd been a sports star back in the day—basketball and football as well as rodeo.

"You're thinking I got what I deserved." His tone was flat, as if stating a fact.

"No. Seriously, not at all." She flushed again, wishing she'd never had those thoughts.

"It's okay if you did. I was so damn arrogant I thought I could do anything—ride like Ty Murray, drink like Johnny Cash, and drive like Dale Earnhardt. It was the last two that got me in trouble." He looked down at his legs. "I was pinned in my truck for three hours before they found me. Gave me a lot of time to think."

She nodded, lost for words.

"At least I hit a tree and didn't kill anybody."

She stared down at the floor, still at a loss for a response. What was wrong with her? She could make cocktail party chitchat with millionaires, stand up in front of a roomful of congressmen, and hold her own with businessmen twice her age. But the past felt like a brick wall between her and this man. He'd been a boy back then, so why should it matter?

Maybe it didn't. Maybe she'd just distanced herself so thoroughly from her old life that she couldn't talk to regular people anymore. That didn't bode well for her success in Two Shot.

"Anyway, your boyfriend took a chance on me and gave me a job here. We're raising quarter horses—good ones. You still ride?"

"No. And he's not my boyfriend."

"Too bad. I heard you were pretty damn good."

She froze. Had Lane given this guy a play-by-play or what?

"You rode Chromium Flash, right?"

Oh. He was talking about riding. And he evidently had a memory like a steel trap, because she'd ridden Flash twelve years ago and only at a couple of rodeos.

Oblivious to her confusion, Trevor chattered on. "How come you quit?"

"My dad—Roy Price—he got killed."

"That's right. But you were good. I saw you ride that horse

at Humboldt. You must've been what, fourteen maybe? Fifteen? Everybody said that horse was crazy." He flashed a quick grin. "I thought you both were."

Her mouth was dry and she could feel that bird thrashing in her rib cage again. Couldn't he tell she didn't want to talk about Flash? She wished she still had some good memories of that time. She vaguely remembered the triumph she'd felt when Flash did her bidding and the glow she'd felt when Roy talked to her about barn management with all the respect he'd give to a grown-up. But ever since that day, any mention of horses took her back to the day Roy died and the sad aftermath of the accident.

"I remembered hearing you were going to ride that horse at Humboldt just a couple days after the accident. Couldn't believe how brave you were riding a killer horse like that."

"He wasn't a killer," she said. "It was an accident. He saw something that spooked him and—it just happened in a bad spot, that's all."

Trevor shrugged. "That's not what people were saying."

"Anyway, I wasn't so brave. I didn't ride him that day, or ever. I don't ride anymore."

"Why not? It's not like you can't." He scanned her head to foot and she felt a blush rising. It wasn't a sexual look, it was one that took in the fact that she had all the working parts she needed and wasn't using them, and it made her ashamed. "It's just your mind that's holding you back."

He had a point, but her mind wasn't holding her back from success. It was just holding her back from riding horses. And what did that matter? She'd moved on. Millions of people never rode a horse in their life.

Trevor's gaze lost focus and seemed to turn inward. There was a long silence before he shook his head sharply, as if to clear out old cobwebs.

"Well, I'm sorry for how I was back then." He wheeled toward the door. "I had a crush on you the size of Texas. I just didn't have a clue how to treat women, or I would've been nicer. And I guess Lane beat me to it anyway." He gave her an exaggerated version of a lovesick grin and backed the chair up so he could wheel straight for the door. "So you're happy with the cabin?"

She was relieved that she wouldn't have to talk about Lane. "It's great."

She was tempted to ask why it had enough candles around to supply three Italian restaurants and a bordello, but she wasn't sure she wanted the answer to that question.

"Well, enjoy your stay. Feel free to use the fireplace. Gets cool at night." He spun the chair and eased down the ramp, bouncing over a few feet of sunbaked lawn to a dusty white van parked next to her Malibu. Sarah felt a rush of relief as the van started down the driveway. Seeing Trevor had brought back too many memories—of high school, of Roy, and of Flash—but she smiled and waved before she glanced down at her watch. She'd been in Two Shot all of an hour and already the past was coming back to haunt her.

As soon as he was gone, she hauled her luggage out of the car and carried her overnight bag up a rough staircase made of halved logs. The loft was just big enough for a queen-size bed. With slanted ceilings and a curtained window under a peaked eave, it felt like a sanctuary. She shucked off her work clothes and pulled on her favorite pair of yoga pants, then slipped on a tank top and hoodie.

Trotting downstairs, she sank into the overstuffed cushions and stared at the fireplace. It was hardly the right time of year for a fire, but dancing flames would add a nice, cozy touch. Maybe coming back to Two Shot wouldn't be so bad with a place like this to stay. All that was missing was someone to enjoy it with.

She gave herself a mental slap as an image of Lane appeared in the back of her mind. That "someone" needed to be someone who wasn't a rodeo cowboy, didn't spend half his life on the road, and didn't accuse her of having an affair with his brother.

She eyed the kindling stacked under three massive logs inside the fireplace. A cylindrical box of extra-long matches beside it was a clear invitation.

Come on, baby, light my fire.

Striking a match on the rough stone hearth, she held the flame to the kindling and watched the wood catch and burn.

With the match still flaring in her hand, she eased to her feet and lit a pyramid of candles on the mantel, then moved to the coffee table and lit a few more that were interspersed with round river rocks on a tray. The room jumped to life in the gentle flicker of flames, but there were deep shadows in the corners that spooked her a little. Getting out another match, she lit a few more candles and the shadows melted away.

Rummaging in her bag, she pulled out a file on energy law she'd printed out from the Wyoming legislative website. Flicking on a lamp with a copper-colored shade, she settled down on the sofa to read. She'd just cover a little bit of the material. Just enough so she could think about strategies while she got ready for bed. That would take her mind off Two Shot. And Lane.

She adjusted a pillow under her head and started reading. Some people would fall asleep over something as dull as a regulatory bill on oil drilling and exploration, but Sarah was always interested in legislation that affected her work. The legal language was a little obscure sometimes, but it was like a puzzle, trying to figure out how the law would change the way the company made decisions and the way she'd approach the locals about the drilling…it was fascinating, really…fascinating…

Half an hour later, she blinked her eyes open to see the fire reduced to a heap of embers. Rubbing her eyes, she glanced around at the candles. Several had burned down to stubs, and one was just a guttering pool of wax melted into the river rocks. Rising, she turned out the lamp and blew out the ones on the coffee table. Even in her sleep-subdued state, she couldn't help pausing to appreciate the way the room looked with just the candles on the mantel and the few lighting the corners.

Appreciation only lasted for a second before she realized the candles on the mantel were perilously close to an Indian weaving that hung on the stone wall above the fireplace. How had she not noticed that when she lit them?

She stood up on her tiptoes to blow them out and had the crazy thought that she should make a wish, like a kid with a birthday cake. What would she wish for?

Pictures of Lane flashed into her mind. Lane in the moonlight. Lane in the light from the truck's dashboard. Lane looking into her eyes in that intense, private way that made her feel like she was the only woman in the world.

She swept away the images quick as she could. A wish shouldn't be wasted on yourself, especially when what you wanted was bad for you and impossible to boot. She painted a mental picture of Kelsey instead, holding Katie in her arms. Closing her eyes, she wished her sister happy, healthy, and headache-free.

As a kid, she'd always been disappointed when her wish didn't come true the instant the candles went out. Now she knew better, but she couldn't help imagining Kelsey waking in her bed, putting a hand to her forehead, wondering where the headache had gone.

The grating of a key in the cabin's front door chased the image right out of her head.

Trevor probably had a key, but she doubted he'd use it. Maybe she'd wasted that wish on herself after all.

And maybe her wish had come true.

CHAPTER 24

LANE HAD SEEN SARAH'S CAR OUTSIDE THE CABIN, SO HE KNEW she was there, but the lights inside were dim. The possible consequences of walking in on a woman in the middle of the night didn't hit him until he opened the cabin door and spotted her standing at the mantel clutching the fireplace lighter in one hand like a gun, her eyes wide.

"It's just me."

The cabin was a cave of soft golden light. She had the whole place lit up with candles, and he could smell the scent of sulfur, as if a few had just been blown out. It smelled like a birthday party, the sulfur mingling with the vanilla scent of the candles to bring back memories of family and childhood. It made him smile, but she didn't smile back.

Of course she didn't. The last time she'd seen him, he'd implied that she was sleeping with his brother.

But for now, he needed to lighten the mood a little. Quick, before she flicked the lighter to life and set his hair on fire.

"Were you expecting someone else?" he asked.

"No. Of course not." She set her fists on her hips, a movement that threw her shoulders back and thrust her breasts against the thin fabric of her top. He couldn't help staring at her. She was dressed in clingy gray pants that followed every curve. The wide waistband spanned her hips just below her belly button, leaving a tempting swath of skin below a tiny tank top. She didn't have a bra on under the top and the warm light of the flames seemed to highlight the full curves of her breasts, forming soft shadows between and below them.

She was evidently unconscious of the picture she created. Too busy being mad, probably.

"What are you doing here?" she asked. "You scared me to death."

"It's my house." He mirrored her pose and gazed around the room, pointedly pausing as he took in the candles in each corner. "So were you expecting someone, or were you having a romantic evening all by yourself?"

She scowled. "You probably think I'm expecting your brother."

"No." He did his best to look contrite. "I know you better than that. It just surprised me, seeing his car. I said something stupid and I'm sorry." Searching for a change of subject, he moved across the room in three long strides and picked up a sheaf of papers that were scattered on the floor by the sofa. "House Bill 70. Couldn't you find a book to read?"

She snatched the papers away, flushing.

"That's the one that lets energy companies harvest their mineral rights without first getting permission from a landowner, right? I should think you'd be discussing that with Eric."

She shrugged one shoulder. It was a gesture that defined her, elegant and careless but with an athletic, body-conscious grace that made him want to touch her.

"There's nothing to discuss," she said. "It gives us the right to drill, build roads—whatever we need to do."

He sighed. "Look, I don't want to argue about that now."

"Good." She started to stretch, but midway into lifting her arms above her head she seemed to notice her skimpy clothes and clasped her arms over her chest. "Because I'm going to bed."

"We need to talk."

"I thought you didn't want to argue."

He stepped around the coffee table and stood beside her in the warm glow of the fire. The rest of the cabin was freezing cold and he wondered why she hadn't turned on the heat. Maybe the power was out. That would explain the candles.

But it seemed as though all the heat and light in the room

COWBOY CRAZY   185

emanated directly from Sarah. She turned to face him, a reflection from the candles flickering in her eyes and making them more compelling than ever.

"I said we need to *talk*. We don't have to argue every time." He was using the same soothing drawl he used with nervous animals, but he knew this wouldn't be an easy conversation. Once she found out he'd told Eric she was from Two Shot, she'd be furious. She'd probably think he'd done it on purpose. He'd argue that point, but he wouldn't fight her when she told him what an idiot he'd been.

She seemed to have accepted his apology for his stupid accusation outside her apartment. But he knew her anger would return once he told her he'd spilled the beans about her hometown. Something in her life had made her as defensive and quick to kick as an abused filly. If only he could find a way to explain what he'd done that would help her understand he hadn't meant to do her harm.

Small talk, he told himself. *Just make small talk until you figure it out.*

He said the first thing that came into his head that didn't involve her clothes or her body. "Smells like birthday cake in here."

"I just blew out some candles."

"Did you make a wish?"

Now her normally pale skin was rosy with embarrassment from the swell of her breasts to her smooth forehead. Suddenly, he knew what she'd wished for.

He brought one hand up and brushed her cheek, smoothing her hair out of the way. When she didn't flinch, he bent and kissed her, closing his eyes and letting his own wishes flow into the kiss. He wished he didn't have to tell her what he'd done. He wished she knew how he felt about her.

Somehow, despite all his wishing, the kiss broke and they stood just inches apart, Sarah looking up into his face. She looked slim as a sprite in the firelight, her eyes bright as the flames. He stroked her cheek again, but this time he kept going, running the back of his hand down her neck, tracing the curve where it met her shoulder, drifting down to laze over the swell of her breast. He let his hand slide off into the air just before he grazed her nipple.

He could see her body wanted him, but she was poised to flee any minute. She'd pull away if he went too far.

––⁓––

Sarah knew she wasn't going to make it through this encounter unscathed. Lane had looked good in the rodeo ring—rugged and handsome and tough. He'd looked striking at the office, masculine and hot and wonderfully alive. But here, in the warm light from the fire and the candles, he looked...human.

He was giving her that intense stare again, and she could feel all her barriers falling. It happened every time. Why couldn't she resist him? She should turn away. Go up to the loft, and sleep off whatever weird effect he had on her.

But his collar was crooked. She reached up to fix it, and somehow her fingers ended up nested in the hair at the nape of his neck. Then his lips were on hers. She was pressing her breasts to his chest, looping her arms around his neck, and when he deepened the kiss she was lost all over again.

Suddenly he hefted her up into his arms with about as much effort as if he'd lifted a bag of groceries. Still kissing her, he edged around the coffee table and kicked the legal papers aside, then fell back onto the sofa with her in his lap. The impact made their mouths mesh together even harder, and he pulled away and ran his thumb over her lower lip as if checking for damage. Finding none, he kissed her again, once, twice, three times, each kiss brief and gentle enough to make her ache for more.

He lowered his arm and tilted down onto the cushions.

Suddenly she was sprawled out like a wanton Cleopatra, Lane's body pressed to hers. He rested on his elbows so he wouldn't crush her, but there was nothing to keep his hips from pressing against hers. The yoga pants didn't provide much of a barrier and she could feel him growing hard against her belly as he carefully placed one kiss on the high point of her cheekbone and another on the tender skin at the corner of her eye. Then he kissed the bow of her lips and the curve of her jawbone, and trailed a string of kisses down her neck that set off a chain reaction where every nerve sparked under her skin.

He was kissing her alive like the prince in a fairy tale—only princes were never this hot. Princes were boys, pale and slender and gentlemanly. This was a man—a highwayman storming the ramparts to steal the princess's heart.

She tilted back her head, opening herself to more kisses and closing her eyes to shut out the room around them. She felt only the warmth of the embers, the heat of his touch, and darkness, deep delicious darkness, all around them. He kissed the curve of her breast just above the scooped neck of her tank top and she had to resist the impulse to reach up and tug it down. She felt a strange urge to bare her throat like an animal in heat.

A low noise in his throat echoed the urge and she arched her back so her skin pressed against his lips. Gently, he tugged the neck of her top down and kissed his way down the curve, pulling the fabric away as he went and only stopping when his lips fastened over her nipple and his tongue flicked out to touch it.

She flexed her hips as he tightened his lips and sucked, pulling all the resistance out of her and leaving only need. She reached down and hooked her thumbs in his belt loops, snugging his hips against her and letting loose with a sinuous motion that left no doubt in either of their minds as to where this was headed.

Opening her eyes, she looked down to see his rough, stubbled jaw shadowing the smooth skin of her breast. Her squirming had hauled the yoga pants down on her hips until they barely covered her, leaving a long stretch of bare belly exposed.

Lane moved one big hand down to trace the stretched waistband, his fingers grazing the untouched skin just above the danger zone and sending ripples of pleasure from her belly to her core. She tugged at his belt loops, but that wasn't getting her anywhere. She reached for his belt buckle, surprised to find a simple metal clasp.

"No prize buckle," she said.

"The prize is inside," he murmured against her breast.

She made quick work of the buckle and the fly and slid her fingers over the thin cotton beneath, feeling the outline of his cock hard under her hand. He made a strangled noise and shimmied her yoga pants farther down, then slid his fingers under the stretched cotton and grazed her curls. She gasped. He was getting ahead of her. She hadn't done enough for him yet. Grabbing his wrist, she pinned it to the sofa and worked her hand around the length of him, opening her eyes to watch his face.

His eyes were narrowed. "Are we still keeping score?"

Caught. He was right. She was still thinking that way.

"I'm not trying to win," she said. "I'm just trying to keep things even."

He smiled. "You're always trying to win, sugar."

He kissed her again, harder this time, and his hand slid into her panties. Her thighs turned to jelly, her stomach to sweet warm syrup as her body opened and warmed to him. She closed her eyes and let the world wash away again, leaving only his touch and his kiss and the soft flicker of firelight in the depths of her subconscious.

<hr />

Lane felt the thrill of triumph rising in his chest and knew his brain was slipping into competition mode. He was calculating his moves, gauging his chances, sensing Sarah beneath him like a rider feels the bull.

That was no way to treat a woman. Sex wasn't a contest to be won. Not with Sarah. It was something to share, a give-and-take, a blending of minds and hearts.

He looked down into her face. What worked for her? What would give her pleasure? What would make her arch and sigh and finally surrender? What would make her *his*?

No. Scratch that last thought. He didn't want to tame her; he wanted to make her love him.

He stroked the slick sweet heart of her, watching her face, seeing the flickers of pleasure and ecstasy on her face, and then something almost like pain crossed her features. She bit her lip and opened her eyes, and there was helplessness in her gaze. It was what he used to want from a woman, but not this time. Not from her. He slowed his touch and simply cupped her in his hand, letting his warmth give her comfort, and the fear went away.

They lay that way for a while, his head resting on the slope of her breasts, and when he was sure she'd stilled and calmed, he kissed his way down her body again, lower this time, slipping the soft stretchy pants down her hips and away, running his hand up and down the silky smoothness of her legs.

Then the dance began as the two of them worked their way into a rhythm that harmonized and blended like a gospel choir. When her body pulled taut and she threw her head back, he felt the shimmer of her orgasm spread from her body to his, shooting through him like a flame on a fuse and bringing every nerve in his body to light.

He held her, waiting for her shudders to subside, but she struggled upright and tugged his T-shirt over his head. Suddenly they were sitting side by side, her naked, him nearly so since his jeans had somehow followed her yoga pants to the floor. She looked down at his boxers and smiled.

"Oh, look. Little bucking horses," she said. "Do you have cowboy jammies too?"

He felt himself blushing like a girl. "They were a gift," he growled. "That's my college mascot. And no. I don't wear jammies."

"Good." She considered the boxers, that little crease appearing between her eyebrows. "You went to the University of Wyoming?"

"Don't sound so surprised."

"I'm not, I just…"

"I mostly went to do college rodeo."

"What was your major?"

"Agriculture."

"Like…"

He realized her school probably hadn't even had the option. "A lot of chemistry, biology, environmental studies. Law, even." He glanced toward the papers scattered on the floor. "Water rights, stuff like that."

He wasn't about to mention mineral rights. That might bring back the real world. Just in case she thought of it, he flipped her hair back over her shoulder and kissed her again, and the thought of college and mineral rights and everything else faded to black.

He didn't know how the embrace broke, or even how they ended up engaged in the slow dance of seduction again. Somehow she shed her clothes and his were gone too, flung to the floor in a move so unconscious it felt utterly natural. It was a little more awkward to grab the jeans back and fish for the condom he kept in his wallet, but he found it and slipped it on in no time.

She set her hands on his shoulders and flexed her thighs to rise, then lowered herself onto him, letting the tip of his cock just touch her, just barely.

He steadied her with both hands, letting her guide the pace, and she tightened her grip on his shoulders and let him slide inside. He could feel her taut body softening and spreading, taking him in bit by bit until they were rocking together, her thighs tightening and releasing like a rider posting a trot.

She was amazing, with her pale skin washed in candlelight, her head tossed back, her hair hanging in a swaying curtain behind her. Up until now, he'd been conscious of every move, thinking of her pleasure as well as his own, but now instinct took over and he closed his eyes as the tension built, mounting up and up, out of control. When she arched herself backward and let out a cry, his own ecstasy started at his center and spiraled outward, running through his veins and filling his mind with a shimmering sweet smoke that only cleared when the sensation slowed and finally stopped.

They both opened their eyes and stared at each other in wonder. He'd expected fireworks, but fireworks were man-made. He and Sarah together were a force of nature.

She closed her eyes and wrapped her arms around him, pulling him close. He slowed his breathing to match hers. This moment was better than mastery. She might be his right now, but he was hers too. They belonged to each other, and somehow that made him feel like he belonged in the world.

CHAPTER 25

SARAH SAT UP AND CLUTCHED HER KNEES TO HER CHEST. The faint flush of pink lighting the cabin's windows told her the sun would be up soon. She'd been dreaming of Lane, and…

Wait a minute. That wasn't a dream. She'd gone and done it again.

She'd planned to work for a while by the toasty warmth of the fire, then climb the ladder to bed. Instead she'd—what had she done?

She didn't want to think about it. She smelled coffee wafting from the kitchen and knew Lane was probably waiting there for her. She pondered a few casual greetings that might be appropriate for a man she only really knew in the biblical sense. Would a simple "good morning" be enough? "Hello, sleepyhead" hardly seemed appropriate. Maybe "thanks for the memories" would be best. Then she could walk out the door and get on with her life—if only she had a place to live it.

In any case, she needed to be dressed before she tackled the job. Climbing the steps to the loft, she rummaged through her overnight bag. Pulling out a double-breasted navy blazer, she gave it a longing look, then tossed it over the footboard. It would reveal nothing of her body, but she'd stand out like a princess in a pigpen if she wore that into Two Shot. She unfolded a simple white shirt and a pair of "relaxed fit" jeans. The baggy cut might not be professional, but it would get her past Lane and she'd probably look like every other woman in Two Shot: relaxed, casual, and a little on the frumpy side.

Sliding her feet into her old boots, she grabbed her purse in case she needed to make a quick exit and started down the steps. Lane was probably sitting in the rustic breakfast nook, waiting to ambush her with some witty comment. She pictured the two of them sitting across the table from each other, eye to eye over steaming mugs of coffee. What would she say? Worse yet, what would *he* say?

She paused, one hand on the wrought iron railing, the other hooked into the strap of her purse. She had a lot to face this morning. Lane was the least of her problems.

Luckily, she'd thought out a plan before Lane had turned up and hijacked her brain. She was going to start her pro-drilling campaign at Suze's Diner with a hearty breakfast and, hopefully, some friendly conversation with the natives. She'd never been the type to ease her way into cold water a toe at a time. If she had to face the folks she'd been so eager to leave behind—the folks she'd spurned in high school and pretty much ignored since she left for college—she wouldn't do it one person at a time. She was a jump-in-the-deep-end kind of girl.

But facing down the people of Two Shot was a day in the kiddie pool compared to facing Lane. That situation was a product of gut thinking and bad, bad decision-making. He had a way of making her forget all her resolutions and revert to instinct. Hell, he had a way of making her rip her clothes off and have sex with him. The man was like a mind-altering drug—or maybe a mind-erasing one.

The whole situation was crazy, and one of her rock-solid rules in life was to steer clear of crazy and stay in the right-thinking, rational world. Just because she'd jumped the track last night didn't mean she couldn't get right back on the rails.

Lane was probably banking on a companionable morning cuppa Joe, the kind where you shared the milk and passed the sugar bowl. It was sort of flattering. He could have slipped out before she woke up, but apparently he wanted to share the morning-after warmth. But she'd shared too much already. Way too much.

She gave the scent of coffee one last longing sniff and dodged out the door to find the Malibu parked in the turnout all by its solitary self. Lane wasn't waiting for her. He'd left before she was even awake. He must have left the coffeepot warming for her, but that was the extent of his morning-after efforts.

Unlocking the Malibu, she climbed inside. She didn't care that he'd left. She hadn't wanted to explore their emotions, or talk about the relationship they didn't have.

The last thing she needed was a cowboy hanging around. Even if he outgrew or survived his determination to test himself on the backs of bucking horses and bulls, ranching was damn near as risky a business as rodeo. Your livelihood depended on the sun and stars, the rain and the hail, the freeze and the thaw—all elements nobody but God could control. There was no regular paycheck, only sporadic flushes and equally frequent dry spells when the crops didn't grow, the animals got sick, and cattle prices dropped to nothing despite the impossibility of keeping the damned things alive.

She'd loved that life, ridden the ups and downs with all the enthusiasm of a drama-addicted teenager, but the steady grind of corporate life fit her better now that she'd grown up.

Starting up the Malibu, she swept down the drive, almost bottoming out in a washout. Turning toward town, she breathed a sigh of relief as civilized blacktop hummed under her wheels. It was time to quit thinking about her personal life and start thinking about work.

And that was a relief, because her personal life was way too complicated.

She hadn't driven more than a few hundred feet before her cell phone rang. Pulling onto the road's narrow shoulder, she put the car in park and picked up her phone. *Gloria*, the screen said.

Great.

"Hello?"

"Sarah! I have a new boyfriend! And I owe it all to you." She started a little singsong to the tune of "Glory Hallelujah." "Thaaank you, thank you, thank you, thaaaank you! Thaaank you, thank you..."

Slumping her shoulders, Sarah suppressed a groan. She always felt like a killjoy dealing with Gloria's peppy enthusiasm. "Eric?"

"Yup! It was great," Gloria said. "I'm telling you, he's just as wild as his brother once he's out of that handsome suit. We…"

Sarah couldn't help waving her hand in the air even though Gloria couldn't see her. "Stop," she said. "I don't want to know."

She really didn't. After seeing Eric scamper off in his birthday suit, the prospect of hearing about his and Gloria's sexcapades was about as attractive as hearing about Kelsey's trysts with Mike. Eric was kind of like a brother to her, she realized. There was really no sexual attraction there at all.

"Well, it was one heck of a night. And I was wondering…"

Sarah could hear Gloria breathing heavily, like she always did when she was nervous. She pictured her friend sitting at the back of the coffee shop, twisting the tie of her apron in her hands like a little kid confessing to robbing the candy jar.

"Wondering what?"

"If he could come over tonight." Once the words started, they came out in a rush. "I thought maybe you could go out with Lane or something, because I said I'd make him dinner and he said no, we'd get takeout, and then he got all cute, like. He has this thing he does where he lifts one eyebrow and looks at my boobs and I'm telling you, it's so sexy I…"

"Gloria, stop." Sarah slumped over and thunked her head on the steering wheel.

"Oh." All Gloria's spunky enthusiasm was gone. "You're mad."

"Mad? I moved out, Gloria. Did you not notice my stuff was gone?"

Gloria sighed into the phone. "I *knew* it. I knew he was the one you wanted. But remember I said how Lane was right for you? Well, it's true. I know you probably want Eric, but he says opposites attract and he doesn't feel that way about you."

Sarah rolled down the window, but she managed to resist the

urge to throw the phone into the ditch. "I'm not mad about that. I'm..."

She paused, realizing there was no way to explain her feelings of betrayal to Gloria. As far as her roommate was concerned, it was open season on all men, all the time. Sarah's insistence that she stay away from Eric had gone in one ear and out the other.

"I'm really happy, Sarah," Gloria said in a little-girl voice. "I really like him. I think he might be The One. I'm sorry you're mad."

"I'm not mad," Sarah said. "It's just that my sister needs me to stay there."

"Oh!" Judging from Gloria's tone, the dim corner of Starbucks where the staff took their breaks had probably brightened considerably. That made Sarah feel a little better about the whopper she'd just told. Kelsey didn't need her—not one bit. She had Mike back, and the last thing they needed was Sarah's disapproving presence in the limited space of the trailer.

But she could hardly go back to the apartment and watch Eric and Gloria do whatever it was they were doing.

"Maybe we could double-date!" Gloria said.

"Um—right. Except I don't think Lane and I are going to work out. But Gloria, can I ask you a question?"

"Sure." Perky Gloria was back in full force. She lowered her voice to a conspiratorial whisper. *"It's huge."*

It took Sarah a moment to figure out what she was talking about, and then she had to thunk her head a couple more times to get the image out of her head.

"No. No, no, no. I don't want to know anything about Eric's— you know. I just wondered—did you tell him anything about me?"

"No. I just checked to make sure you and him weren't, like, doing it in the office. Because you're like a sister to me, and that would be weird."

Weird indeed. Sarah ran her fingers through her hair and rested one hand on the wheel. "You didn't tell him I was from Two Shot?"

"Nope. Didn't tell him a thing. I didn't even tell him we were roommates, but he kind of figured that out."

"Okay." Sarah sucked in a deep breath. It came a little easier now that one worry had been eased. "Thanks. I have to go now. But hey—I'm glad you're happy, okay?"

"Thanks!" Gloria giggled. "I sure am. And have fun with your sister!"

Sarah thought of Mike and sighed. "Yeah. Yeah, I'll try."

CHAPTER 26

ONCE SARAH HAD FINISHED TALKING TO GLORIA, THE DRIVE into town was too short. Before she'd even had time to think about who might be at the diner, what they might say to her, and how she should respond, she found herself guiding her car into a parking space a half block from her destination.

Stepping out of the car, she rummaged for change. When had Two Shot put in parking meters? Back when she'd lived here, nobody had wanted to come to town bad enough to pay for parking.

She shoved in a dime and cranked the lever, then fed in another. Thirty minutes should be long enough to get breakfast, make some connections, and get out. If things went wrong, she could use the expiring meter as an excuse for leaving—as long as it really was expiring. Because she had no doubt that someone passing on the street would notice a new car in town and take note of how much time was on the meter. Two Shot had its share of champion busybodies, and they didn't have much to do but gossip.

In fact, one of them was hustling toward her right now.

"Eddie." She couldn't help smiling at the white-clad figure. Eddie Johnston had been chief cook and bottle-washer at Suze's when she'd worked there in high school, and apparently he still was. He wore the cowboy uniform of a boldly striped cotton shirt and jeans, but a grease-spattered apron decorated with handprints in various shades of egg, orange juice, and maple syrup took the shine off the outfit. An old-fashioned white cap that made her think of hot dog vendors at a ballpark was perched on his thinning hair.

The progress of Eddie's hairline was a sign of how long she'd been gone. It had moved up his forehead and was obviously headed on an inexorable march up and over his crown, but his wide grin, bracketed by deep smile lines and punctuated by a dimpled chin, was still the same. So were his protuberant eyes, which bugged out even more at the sight of her.

"Hey, don't you have some hotcakes to flip?" She'd thought long and hard about her approach, and come to two resolutions: Keep it light, and act as though she'd never left. As though she'd never scorned the town and all it represented. As if she hadn't savored the long-sought experience of leaving Two Shot in a cloud of dust and moving on to bigger, better things.

"I gotta feed the meter before that danged marshal catches up to me and slaps a ticket on my truck." He stepped toward her, then away, then toward her again, clearly divided between good citizenship and good manners.

"Well, don't let me keep you." She gave him a perky smile. "I'll see you at Suze's."

There. That was easy. She walked away, leaving Eddie to hurry down the sidewalk toward his truck, which was propped half on, half off the curb a few cars down. Eddie had been notorious for his bad driving when she'd been in high school, to the point where the driver's ed teacher issued a warning to steer clear of his red-and-white pickup.

Some things never changed.

But the encounter with Eddie was just the way she wanted things to go, and that made her feel a little better about her prospects. She could do this. She'd been away from Two Shot for years, and people had probably forgotten what a snob she'd been.

Not that snobbery had been the real reason behind her retreat from the friendships and connections of her childhood. The truth was, she'd felt ashamed after Roy died and they lost the ranch. She knew she'd failed her family, and she'd figured everyone else knew it too. But she couldn't bring herself to hang her head in shame, so she'd tossed her hair and walked away whenever folks tried to throw her a pity party.

She resisted the urge to toss it now and set off down the street. She'd crossed about three sidewalk squares before Eddie caught up with her.

"I got it all taken care of now." Eddie wasn't the brightest dog in the kennel, but he was the good-natured one that never snapped back when the others chewed his ear. "I put another dime in yours too, just in case. Mel don't have much to do but watch them meters, so you gotta be careful."

"Mel's still the sheriff?"

"He likes folks to call him the Marshal. He's got the first five seasons of *Gunsmoke* on DVD, and he can make that squinty face good as James Arness. He says it gets criminals to confess just like that." He snapped his fingers.

"Two Shot has criminals?"

"Naw. Mel does all his squintin' at folks who forget to feed the meters."

Sarah paused to wait for the light at the corner of Main and Jewel Streets, but Eddie jaywalked without even looking right or left.

"How long have we had a traffic light?" Sarah asked.

"Two weeks. Nobody pays any attention to it 'cept Mel. Between that and the parking meters, he's like a dog chasin' his tail. He quit the poker group, you know. Says he got no time for games."

"You're kidding." The poker group had been running as long as Sarah had been alive. It included the town barber and a couple of retired ranchers.

"Yep. And now he says it's illegal to gamble in public places, so they can't play in the diner anymore."

He escorted her up the diner steps and held the door, causing the cowbell dangling there to clang out its usual announcement of a new arrival. Fortunately, everybody looked up and saw Eddie, then went back to whatever they were doing. It gave her a chance to step inside and take a deep breath, remembering all the resolutions she'd made. She wasn't going to talk about Carrigan. Not this first day. She was going to reestablish herself as part of the town first.

Scanning the spinning stools and vinyl booths to the left of the door, she felt an acute sense of déjà vu. There was Mr. Jenson, who'd retired from teaching English at the high school a year before Sarah had graduated. There was the poker group, looking bored without their cards to distract them. There was Joe Reynolds, slouched at the counter all by his lonesome. Joe had never had a regular job that she knew of but had a talent for fixing stuff that kept him busy all around Two Shot. He didn't talk much, which was a blessing because he'd seen under everybody's sink and into their basements over the years. He probably knew more secrets than the CIA.

There were a few people she didn't know at the counter and in the booths, probably truckers and tourists passing through. She let the door swing shut behind her and glanced to the right. There were only two tables over there, and one of them was reserved for the staff so they could drink Suze's rotgut coffee on their breaks. The other one was occupied by...

Lane.

He was sitting by the window, chatting companionably with Trevor over scrambled eggs and toast. He hoisted a thick white mug of coffee to his lips, his eyes fixed on her over the rim. Telltale crinkles at the corners told her he was smiling as he sipped.

Dammit. She'd been glad he was gone, but now he'd never know it. He probably thought she'd tracked him like a bird dog running for a downed duck.

Reflexively, she backed away and slammed into the door, setting the bell to clanging. Everybody in the place looked up to see what the racket was about this time and she froze, plastered against the glass.

—∾—

Lane watched Sarah bounce off the diner's front door to the accompaniment of the clanging cowbell. Every head in the place turned toward her. He waited for the usual greetings, the inside jokes and backslapping comments that acknowledged every Two Shot native, but the diner was remarkably silent. Evidently Two Shot didn't like her any better than she liked Two Shot.

She had her best smile on, the one she always wore to the office, but it was trembling at the edges as she glanced around the room. Finally her gaze settled on an older man who always perched at the counter. Lane knew he was a retired English teacher from the high school. Sarah had probably been teacher's pet.

"Hi, Mr. Jenson," she said.

He turned briefly and offered her a scowl that reminded Lane of some grim hero of literature—Captain Ahab, maybe. It was a look that would send most people skittering out the door, but Sarah stood firm.

"How are you?" she asked in a louder voice. "Remember me? Sarah Landon?"

A hushed murmur swept through the diners. Some of them obviously hadn't known who she was, but judging from the way they all turned away, they'd heard of her. There were no hellos, not even a few casual nods. He could swear the temperature in the room dropped ten degrees.

Mr. Jenson gave her a scowl and kept on eating. She kept on smiling, but her eyes brightened and he could tell she was holding back tears. He couldn't really blame her. She might not like the town. She might have made escaping it her lifetime goal. But he'd always figured growing up in a place like Two Shot was like being part of a big, extended family. A troublesome, pain-in-the-neck family, but still a family. And didn't families forgive each other?

People must have heard who she was working for. He'd been viewed with suspicion, even hostility, when he'd first moved to the ranch and started spending time in town. They didn't welcome outsiders and they definitely weren't embracing energy development with open arms. Maybe it was because there were so many older residents and they were resistant to change. Or maybe they'd seen the cautionary tale playing out in Midwest and didn't want to experience the same kind of boom-to-bust disaster. In any case, Sarah obviously had her work cut out for her.

She turned to the man on the next stool, who was downing a short stack like it was the last food on the planet and some alien might snatch it away.

"Joe," she said.

Joe might not be the friendliest guy in the world, but he never seemed to care about folks one way or the other. He treated everyone with the same distant, laconic attitude.

But he wasn't even speaking to Sarah.

She stood in the aisle, clasping and unclasping her hands.

"Hey, sweetheart," said a gruff voice. "You can sit with me."

It was a trucker, heavyset and unshaven, wearing a wrinkled denim shirt and oil-streaked jeans. His black leather motorcycle boots had chains across the instep. Sarah had evidently dealt with his kind before, and she wasn't desperate enough to deal with one again. "No, thank you." She shot him a killing glare. "And I'm not your sweetheart."

Great. She could have sassed him off, dismissed him with a laugh, but instead she'd confirmed everybody's bad opinion by being rude and snooty. Somebody needed to save this woman from herself.

Lane hooked his boot around a rung of the empty chair beside him and pulled it away from the table. "Join us?"

Judging from her grateful smile, she'd never been so happy to see him. She crossed the diner in three long steps and dropped into the chair.

"Hey. Heard you two got together in the Love Nest last night." Trevor's tone was just a shade too loud for normal conversation. "I didn't know you were…you know." He waggled his eyebrows. Trevor had never been famous for tact. Lane was just grateful he didn't demonstrate with a hand gesture.

A flush turned her face to a becoming pink. "Lane just needed a place to stay. I was at the cabin, so I…he slept on the sofa."

"Oh." Trevor grinned. "Well, excuse me. I saw the way he looked at you when you walked in, and I could've sworn he was picturing you naked."

"He does that with all the girls." There. The old Sarah was back, flippant and fun. He breathed a sigh of relief and was surprised to realize how much he'd tensed, suffering through her ostracism with her.

"I guess you noticed a lot of people know you're here for Carrigan," he said, nodding toward the crowd. Most of the diners had returned to their meals, but a few were still leveling hostile stares in her direction.

"You say that like you're not a Carrigan yourself," she said.

"I might be a Carrigan, but they know I'm not a part of this project." He finished his last forkful of egg and sat back. "Nobody around here is too happy about the drilling, as you might have noticed."

The diner's owner, Suze, a heavyset blonde who'd been whipping around the room removing plates and taking orders with her usual efficiency, paused by their table. "You want something?"

This should be interesting. Lane was sure Suze would be the toughest nut for Sarah to crack. The place was hung with dream catchers and cheap prints of wolf packs howling dramatically at the moon. Between the decor she'd chosen and the Birkenstocks on her feet, Lane was sure Suze wouldn't take kindly to an invasion from the Carrigan Corporation.

"Oh, hi, Suze." Sarah gave the woman a smile, but the waitress was all business.

"You want something or what?"

"No, thank you." Sarah rose and laid a dollar on the table, despite the fact she hadn't eaten anything. She was blinking fast, clearly hurt by Suze's deliberate snub. "I need to get going."

"You do that," Suze said. "You just do that."

CHAPTER 27

SARAH SAT IN THE CAR AND SEETHED, STARING AT THE PARKING meter. She had fifteen minutes left, but she'd practically been kicked out of the diner. Not physically, but emotionally. And it hadn't felt good.

Gripping the wheel with both hands, she rested her forehead on the cool plastic. The morning hadn't been a total loss. She knew more now than she had when she'd arrived.

She knew everybody hated her.

She couldn't say she was surprised. She'd dreaded her first encounter with the town. But it had been even worse than she expected. Sure, she'd been a bitch in the years before she'd left, but she'd been a kid, a kid with a lot of problems. Couldn't they give her a break?

Apparently not. Lane said they knew she was there as a Carrigan representative, but why would they assume that was a bad thing? One look around that diner would make it clear to any-body that the town was fading away. There wasn't a single person in there under forty, and few under sixty. Carrigan would bring better roads, more money for public services, and jobs for peoples' children, so they could stay in their hometown.

So why weren't they glad to see her? Heck, they should be clamoring for a chance to talk to her. Suze should have been asking if she'd need more tables for the workers. Joe should have been checking to see if he could get a job working electrical on the rig. Mr. Jenson had a son somewhere, and a daughter. Why wasn't he asking about employment opportunities for his kids?

Someone had gotten there before her. Someone had put a neg-ative spin on the Carrigan deal.

Was it just a coincidence that Lane was right there to watch her get the big freeze?

She didn't want to think about it. Shoving the key in the ignition, she cranked the engine to life and blinked a few times, telling herself it was the rising sun that had her eyes stinging. She distracted herself by poking the presets on the radio, looking for a station with soothing music. She'd finally settled for a scratchy, barely there NPR broadcast of a Brahms symphony when her phone rang.

She dug it out of her purse and squinted at the small screen, her vision blurred with the tears she refused to cry.

Eric. Just what she needed. He probably wanted a progress report. What was she going to tell him? Progress was negative. The company had been better off before she'd arrived in town. Her stomach clenched painfully and it took her a moment to recover enough to answer.

"Hello?"

"Sarah." There wasn't a hint of his usual bantering humor in his tone. "You're in Two Shot."

"Yes." *Why did he have to call so fast? She needed time to think things through.*

"I understand you've been there before."

This time, there was no mistaking his tone. He knew. Lane hadn't just set the residents of Two Shot against her; he'd blabbed to Eric too.

He cleared his throat. "I also understand there's a lot of negative feeling there toward you, and it's bleeding over to the project."

"I don't know, Eric. I just got here. I'm working on…"

"I've gotten three phone calls, Sarah, from three different people, all of them telling me they don't want Carrigan there."

"Who was it?"

"They were anonymous. But two of them mentioned you by name. They said you didn't have the town's best interests at heart."

A cloud passed over the sun and she felt suddenly cold. "When did you get those phone calls?"

"Last night."

Last night. No one had known she was there last night.

No one but Lane.

She felt like a whirling, spinning tornado of emotions. Despair. Fear. Regret. Anger. Anger. *Anger.*

Lane hadn't just betrayed her the morning after. He'd done his dirty work before they even got together. He'd apparently spread rumors and lies about her, then gone to the cabin and worked his charm on her afterwards. She smothered a sob so Eric wouldn't hear it, feeling like she'd explode from the force of the shame building inside her.

She'd known their liaisons probably didn't mean anything to Lane—but there had been a tiny glimmer of hope in her heart that believed his feelings were more than skin-deep. A foolish, girlie part that hoped for a happily ever after with a man who set her on fire like nobody ever had before.

Instead, he screwed up her life, used her, and then sat back and watched the damage he'd done. He was worse than uncaring; he was cruel, savoring a side dish of victory along with his eggs and bacon.

She'd known this was a game to him. She'd recognized a part of herself in him—the part that always wanted to win at any cost. She'd gotten caught up in playing the game with a worthy contender. But she hadn't considered the price of losing.

"Eric, I have a solid understanding of the small-town mentality. Being raised in Two Shot is an advantage."

"Not when you've burned all your bridges and moved on. Look, Sarah, you're clearly not the best person for this project. You've set us back. I want you out of there."

"Okay." She sucked in a deep breath. "So you want me back in Casper?"

She stared at the face of the parking meter and waited for his response.

And waited. And waited. Maybe she should put another dime in the meter.

Finally, she couldn't stand the silence. "Eric?"

"I'm taking you off the project."

"Is there another project?"

"Not really."

"Are you firing me?"

He sighed. "Look, Sarah, I'm sorry, but I hired you to build positive feelings in the community, and frankly, you've had the opposite effect." He cleared his throat. "I hope you know this isn't personal. It could make things awkward, because…" He cleared his throat again.

"Because you're dating Gloria?"

"Yes. I know it might surprise you, but…"

"It doesn't surprise me. Gloria's a great person." She realized what she was saying was true. Gloria was always upbeat, always positive. Sarah was going to miss her.

"Well, thanks. I'm glad you understand." His tone was kinder, but it wasn't friendship or caring; it was pity. "I'm going to hook you up with HR, okay? They'll tell you when to pick up your next check."

She couldn't pick it up. There was no way she could walk into that building and face all her coworkers after getting fired.

"They can send it to me."

She was speaking into a dead line. Eric had put her on hold.

"Human Resources," said a nasal, mechanical voice. Sarah recognized the speaker as the woman who'd scheduled her interview four months earlier. "Miss Landon?"

"Yes," Sarah said.

"Would you like your final check mailed? I'll need your current address."

Sarah lowered the phone, staring straight ahead out the windshield. She didn't have an address. She'd figured on staying at Kelsey's, but that was impossible now. And she didn't have any savings because she'd been supporting Kelsey and Katie as well as herself.

Maybe she could just keep feeding dimes into the meter and live in her car.

"I'll pick it up." Her voice cracked on the first word and she ended up whispering into the phone.

"Pardon?"

"I'll pick it up." She managed to speak up, but her tone was angry and irritated. The woman didn't deserve that; she was just doing her job. How many times had Sarah treated someone that way? How many times had she disregarded the feelings of someone who couldn't serve her ambition? She'd done it over and over in Two Shot, and she realized now she'd done it at Carrigan, too. No wonder everyone hated her. She'd always been proud of her ambition, but it was really just a socially acceptable way to be self-centered.

"Thank you," she choked out.

Pressing the "End" button, she tossed the phone on the seat and put the car in gear. It wasn't easy to see through the tears, but somehow she'd make it to the so-called Love Nest and gather her things.

Hopefully Lane wouldn't come to see the fruits of his victory, because she had a feeling her tears would only mean extra points to him.

CHAPTER 28

SARAH CRAMMED THE CLOTHES SHE'D WORN THE DAY BEFORE
into her bag and zipped it shut. Hefting it in one hand, she stag-
gered down the loft stairs and set it on the floor by the front door.
She cocked her wrist and shoved her sleeve up to check her watch,
then swore softly. Her watch was gone. Had she left it on the
nightstand?

She climbed the stairs and checked. Nope. Glancing around
the room, she tried to think where she'd left it. Maybe it was in the
bathroom downstairs. Or on the coffee table, next to the candles.
Maybe she'd taken it off when she and Lane...

Don't think about it.

Trotting back down, she grabbed her messenger bag and put it
beside the overnight bag, then made a concerted search for the watch,
scanning every horizontal surface. Maybe it was in the kitchen.

Wait, she hadn't even been in the kitchen, had she? Not since
she first arrived. Still, maybe she'd taken it off then. She stood in
the doorway, scanning the room. No watch, but there was a note
taped to the front of the coffeemaker.

She strode over and snatched it off, nearly ripping it in half
when the tape didn't give way.

Good morning, Sunshine!

The greeting was followed by a happy face, with rays coming
off it to make it look like the sun. What kind of a man drew happy
faces? It didn't seem very Lane-like. If she were still playing the
game, she'd hang onto the note and tease him about it. Yesterday it
would have made her smile.

*Have some coffee and come to Suze's when you wake up. I'll
introduce you to some people.*

He'd signed it with a flourish that was obviously the product of
years of autograph signing.

So he'd actually told her to go to Suze's—invited her right into
the lion's den. Nice. That way, when he was done trashing her, he
could point her out to all his friends and watch her get the big
freeze.

"Don't do me any favors," she muttered.

She scanned the counters, searching for the watch. She wanted
to be out of the Love Nest before he came back to torture her some
more. But it was her stepfather's watch, the one thing she had from
him. She'd started wearing it the day he died, and it was the one
thing in the world she didn't want to leave behind.

She crumpled the note in her hand and went back to the living
room. She needed a system. She'd search each piece of furniture in
turn, methodically and thoroughly, starting with the sofa. Tossing
the pillows aside, she lifted the cushions to search underneath. She
was down on her hands and knees peering under the sofa when
the front door opened.

"Hey," said a familiar voice.

She sat up too fast and got dizzy, but there was no mistaking
the tall figure that stood on the doormat. She simply stared at him,
waiting for her vision to clear. She'd been so intent on leaving that
she hadn't thought about what she'd say if Lane found her there.

So she wouldn't say anything. She needed to find that watch,
and then she'd walk away. With no job at the oil company, there
was no reason to speak to Lane Carrigan ever again.

That was about the only good news she could think of.

Lane watched Sarah sit up. She was swaying slightly, her skin pale, her eyes unfocused. Had she come home and hit the liquor cabinet or what? As he stepped toward her, holding out a steadying hand, she got back down on her hands and knees and scuttled around the side of the sofa, peering beneath it.

"You looking for something?"

"No, I'm trying to see the world from a cockroach's point of view." She sat up. "Have you seen my watch?"

"Everybody's seen your watch." He glanced at her wrist and noticed for the first time that the clunky Timex she always wore was missing. "Why do you wear that, anyway? Did it belong to an old boyfriend or something?"

"None of your business." She ducked her head under an end table, still searching. "I can't leave without it."

"So don't leave." He sat down on the edge of the sofa to admire the way her sweet ass stuck up in the air, but the minute she realized what he was doing, she tried to pop back up on her knees and hit her head on the bottom of the table.

"Ow."

He knelt down beside her but she scooted away, her hand feeling for the bump on her noggin. "Why the hell would I stay?"

"Because you need to go back to the diner and try again. You should have stuck it out, Sarah. These people won't respect you if you run away. You'll never get them to accept the Carrigan project that way."

She shrugged and stood up, still gazing around the room in search of her watch. "I'll never get them to accept it anyway."

He squinted at her, trying to figure out where the spunky Sarah he knew had disappeared to. She wore an air of defeat he'd never seen before. Looking at her slumped shoulders and downcast eyes, he felt like a hard fist had grabbed his heart and squeezed it.

"Look," he said. "You know I don't want the drilling here. But I hate to see you just give up like this."

"I didn't give up. Not willingly. Your brother fired me."

"My brother…" He swallowed. Shit. Eric must have heard something somehow. It wasn't too surprising. Once Sarah had left the diner, the conversations around the diner's scarred table-tops focused on nothing but her and the Carrigan project—and nobody had anything very nice to say about either one. Knowing Eric, there was someone else from Carrigan keeping a finger on the pulse of the town. But man, that was quick. How had news traveled so fast? "My brother fired you? Already?"

"Yes, *already*. And don't act so surprised."

She walked over to the mantel, scanning its surface. That watch must be some kind of family heirloom. She was still focused on finding it, even though she'd just lost her job.

And getting fired had to be devastating for her. He was sure she needed the money, plus she was one of those people who would answer the question "Who are you?" with her job description.

"You won, okay?" She moved over to a cabinet in the corner and pushed a couple of candles to one side, still searching. "Game over. I'm gone. Maybe you and Trevor should have a beer or something to celebrate."

"What the hell are you talking about?"

Actually, he had some idea what she was talking about—part of it, anyway. She'd caught on to the fact that relationships were about winning for him. Despite his efforts to change his thinking last night, she still thought he was tallying points with every word.

But he only recognized it because she was like that herself. So she ought to like it, or at least find it charming and roguish. But she'd turned to face him now, and she didn't look charmed. She looked angry. But that was a big improvement over that lost look she'd had a moment before.

"I'm talking about your little smear campaign. I'm talking about how you got a couple of flunkies from town to make anonymous phone calls about me."

"Smear campaign? Anonymous phone calls?" He went over her words in his mind. "Hell, Sarah, I'm not that bad."

"You might not have realized he'd fire me," she conceded. "But I know it was you, Lane. Nobody else knew I was in town until this morning."

"Nobody knew?" He flipped through the events of the previous day in his mind. "Trevor knew. And Emmy, who cleans the house." She looked startled for a moment and he knew she genuinely hadn't remembered that fact. "And if Trevor knew, Gena did too, and she and Emmy both work for Suze." He reached her in two long steps and took her wrists in his hands, turning her to face him. "Suze has been against the project from the start. Remember how she used to go on about the environment?"

She nodded, looking doubtful.

"And anyway, what makes you think I'd sneak around and make anonymous phone calls? You know me better than that. Don't you?"

She refused to meet his eyes.

"Look, Sarah. You're right. I don't want the project to succeed. But I don't want you to fail, either." She started to tug her hands away, but he held fast. "You know there's something between us. Something that matters a lot more than your job."

He shook her slightly. "We're just alike. You're the first woman I ever met who's as competitive as I am, who can give me a run for my money and everything else I've got. I want to see where we're headed. I think it might be a good place for both of us." He put his hands on her shoulders and figured he was getting to her when she didn't shrug him off. "Come on. You feel it too. You're lying to yourself if you don't admit we're great together."

She stared down at the floor, her teeth nibbling at that lower lip until he was afraid she'd chew it off. Finally, she looked up into his face, her eyes searching his. Normally that kind of gaze from a woman made him flinch and look away, but for the first time, he wanted a woman to know exactly what he was thinking.

—◆—

Sarah pulled herself out of his arms and turned to the mantel, moving a framed photo of the two brothers with their father to one side, pretending she'd suddenly remembered the watch.

Lane was right. The phone calls probably came from Suze. Once again, she'd assumed the worst of him. She needed to open up a little, trust people. But there was one thing she needed more than a mental makeover.

"I can't stay here," she said. "I don't have a job."

"Work for me. I need some help around here. You'd earn your keep."

"That's ridiculous. I told you I'm afraid of horses."

"That's what you told me. But I don't believe you." He waved toward the window. Far beyond the drive where her car was parked, she could see horses grazing in a faraway field. "And my horses aren't scary. They're a pretty mellow bunch, mostly rescues."

"Rescues? I didn't know that. I thought you raised roping horses."

"I do. But it seems like every time I go to a sale I see a good horse nobody wants. Sometimes they just need to be fattened up and treated right, sometimes they just need a place to get old and die. Trust me, I've got some horses over there that wouldn't scare a baby."

The idea of a horse rescue somehow didn't jibe with her image of Lane. He was always about being the biggest, the best, the strongest, the bravest. She'd never seen this side of him—although come to think of it, he had taken in Willie. And he was certainly patient with her.

It didn't matter. She was leaving. Turning, she scanned a book-case filled with Western history tomes and old rodeo magazines.

There was no way the watch could be there, but she searched it anyway. It gave her time to think.

The whole thing was hopeless. She needed to leave Two Shot behind—again. More thoroughly this time. Kelsey didn't seem to want her help anymore, so it would be easy to move on.

She'd leave Lane behind too. She stepped away from him and scanned the room, spinning in a slow circle. "I have to go. I'm going to have to leave without my watch." She blinked back hot tears at the thought of losing Roy's watch. It was the one part of her old life she wanted to take with her, and the one part that seemed utterly and completely lost. "Leave me a message if you find it, okay?"

"If I find it for you, will you come see the horses?"

Maybe he'd taken it. Maybe he thought she wouldn't leave without it.

"You took it, didn't you?"

"No. But I bet I know where it is. Check your purse."

"I already did."

"Check it again."

She walked over to the door where her oversized bag was slouched against her suitcase. Lifting the flap, she rummaged through its contents. Wallet, hairbrush, makeup bag…

Watch. Damn.

"You put it in there. You tricked me."

"You tricked yourself. I didn't put it there. It's just the only place it could be. It was logic."

She gave him a disbelieving stare.

"I'm not that devious, Sarah."

She had to admit that was probably true. He liked to win and get what he wanted, but his methods were pretty straightforward. Strength and sex appeal, not scheming.

"Come on." He opened the door and gestured toward the sun-baked scenery outside. "The horses are waiting."

CHAPTER 29

Sarah strode past Lane as he held open the passenger door to his pickup.

"I'll take my own car," she said. "That way I can just go."

He gave her Malibu a scornful once-over. "That car's not made for the ranch roads. You're going to get a flat."

"That'll be my problem." The old car was like her—tougher than it looked. Besides, she doubted the ranch roads were much worse than the lane to the Love Nest.

She was wrong. The Malibu bottomed out twice on the rutted road. Deep truck tracks were carved into the surface, frozen, then dried to rocklike permanence. She steered to one side so at least two wheels were on a level surface, gritting her teeth as weeds scraped her door.

There was nowhere to turn around, and stopping would bring Lane to her rescue. He'd take her to the ranch and she'd be stuck there. She didn't want to spend any more time in the company of horses than she had to. Or in the company of Lane Carrigan.

He turned onto a weed-choked two-track after about a quarter-mile, passing under a massive log ranch gate decorated with a set of elk horns flanked by two mule deer racks. It was atmospheric but not ostentatious, so it didn't prepare her for the view as she steered the Malibu around a rutted bend in the road.

The barn rose up before her, tall, ancient, and weathered. Wide, welcoming doors at the front slid open to either side, offering a glimpse of the shadowed interior. A hay door at the top framed stacks of gleaming straw.

Generations of ranchers had embellished and added to the basic edifice. On one side, old lean-to additions tilted against its solid mass like chicks round a hen, but on the other a modern new addition stretched out, with wide windows over dutch doors that indicated nearly a dozen individual stalls. A few chickens and something that looked like a pheasant pecked in the driveway, adding a homey barnyard feel.

Old corrals built of a haphazard assortment of poles and boards created a free-form patchwork that stretched from the barn, undulating over the hills like a roughly stitched quilt. Linked in a complex network by every imaginable type of gate, each square was polka-dotted with horses in colors ranging from black to palomino. The corrals gave way to a pasture surrounded by miles of crooked, weathered fence, with more horses scattered over the yellowing grass that stretched to the horizon.

The place looked like a picture-book ranch—or a scene from her adolescent fantasies of some future paradise. She felt like a goose-girl again, a barnyard princess, and this was her kind of castle.

The house, though, was less of a dream and more of a nightmare. Someone had concluded that if *big* was good, *enormous* was better. The result was a place so grandiose that it looked absurd. The high stone front was set with massive carved doors that looked large enough to admit a herd of cattle. The stone section was topped by a cathedral-style log edifice that was mostly windows. Two-story log-and-stone wings flanked the center, and a round tower rose from one side. The top story of the tower was even higher than the cathedral roof, and it had windows all around. Sarah could only imagine the view from inside.

She heard Lane's truck door slam behind her and the crunch of his boots on the gravel drive.

"Grandaddy grew up poor." He gave the house a rueful smile. "He wanted to make sure everybody knew how much money he'd made."

She shot him an irritated look. "You thought Trevor had to have this all to himself last night?"

He looked away, squinting toward the corrals as if he hadn't heard her.

"This place must sleep about fifty," she said.

"There are only twelve bedrooms. Each one has a different theme, so its fun to switch around." He shrugged. "I wanted to give him his privacy. I hadn't warned him I was coming."

"You didn't warn me either, and I had to keep a lot closer quarters with you."

"Yeah, that worked out pretty well."

"Dog." She suppressed the urge to smile as he stepped up to the corral fence and rested his elbows on the top. Joining him, she propped one foot on the bottom rail and watched three horses sidle toward them. There was a pretty sorrel with a white blaze, a slightly bony palomino, and a roan that didn't look to be much more than a yearling. The sorrel stretched her neck as she approached, testing the air.

"They're gorgeous," she said. "Well, except for the palomino."

"That's Tony," Lane said. "He had a rough time. He'll be a good-looking boy once he gets some food in him."

"Poor thing. But they're all quarter horses, aren't they?"

"I'm partial to 'em."

She couldn't really blame him. The horses all had strong hind-quarters, broad chests, and beautiful heads, wide at the forehead and tapering to an almost delicate muzzle. Their eyes were curious and soft, and she felt an urge stirring inside her—an urge she'd managed to suppress for over a decade.

Lane watched her stroke the sorrel's nose, the corners of his eyes crinkling as his smile widened. "That's Sadie," he said. "She's my project horse right now. Just turned three and learning fast."

"She's beautiful," Sarah murmured.

"Want to ride her?"

Sarah pulled her hand away and stuck it in her pocket. "Nope. I told you, I'm scared."

"You don't look scared."

"It only happens when I try to get on."

It was the closest she'd come to telling anyone about what had happened, but Lane's phone interrupted with a loud beep, startling the animals into jerking their heads back.

"I have to take this." He turned toward the house as he fished his phone from his pocket. "Be right back."

—◇◇◇—

Once they figured out she wasn't bearing food, the horses lost interest in Sarah and went about the usual equine business of standing in the sun, rolling in the dirt, and taking turns nibbling the itchy spots on each others' withers. She watched them for a while, then moved past a couple of empty corrals toward the back of the barn. The sun felt good on the back of her neck, and the scent of green grass, hay, horse manure, and that indefinable mix of sage, dirt, and pine that defined Wyoming brought back memories of her childhood. Some of the horses reminded her of the ones she'd ridden in her childhood—chestnuts and bays, palominos and blacks. Even the path she was walking was familiar, a dirt trail pounded flat by the passage of boots about a foot from the fence line. Shoving her hands in her pockets, she kicked away a few loose stones and followed it for a while.

She was so lost in her memories that she didn't notice where she was until she thought of Lane and looked back. He was nowhere to be seen, probably because she'd turned the corner of the barn and made her way past the farthest corral to a high-fenced round pen set off by itself.

Nostalgia squeezed and softened her heart. She'd spent some of the most meaningful hours of her life in her stepfather's round pen. It was where you taught horses the basics—where you taught them to trust and work in partnership. Circling the walls, she reached the gate and glanced inside. There was a horse standing in the center of the pen, staring at her. She stared back, sucking in a quick, stunned breath.

Flash.

She'd lost her mind. Or maybe she'd really gone back in time. Because this was Chromium Flash. Once you worked with horses long enough, they became as distinct from each other as humans. No other horse reflected sunlight with that gleaming shade of copper-penny red. No other horse had quite the same breadth between the eyes, the set of the ears, the tapered muzzle.

This was no flashback, no fond memory. This was the past rising up like a ghost from the grave in the form of a horse, stamping one foot and blowing as if he recognized her. She put a hand to her forehead in a vain effort to combat a dizzy spell and the horse lifted his head, startled.

"Flash," she whispered.

He was just as she remembered him, his coat bright, the color tarnishing gradually to black on the legs and muzzle. His dark skin deepened the shadows that defined his powerful muscles, and the copper glow gave added definition to a build that was already incredible. He was a big horse, probably sixteen hands, with the solid presence only quarter horses had. He swung his head toward her and she saw the long-lashed eyes considering her as they always had, making up his mind whether he'd cooperate today. Evidently he decided he would, because he turned and walked slowly toward the gate, taking his time, his black mane fluttering in the breeze.

She couldn't breathe. She needed to get her heartbeat under control. Horses sensed your mood, and hers was a mixture of wonder and fear that probably echoed the horse's feelings as he paused with one hoof raised, poised to flee.

"Flash," she whispered. "It's okay." She turned her body slightly away from him and looked away, resisting the temptation to make eye contact. Stallions sometimes saw that as a challenge, and Flash had been wild and unpredictable—even ill-tempered at times. But Roy had taught her that no animal had a truly bad nature. Every quirk of character had its roots in something—a past trauma, an ache or pain.

But they had never found the root of Flash's problems. He'd been fast to flinch and quick to kick from the day they'd bought him. Roy had been convinced he could figure out what was bothering the horse and turn those hair-trigger reactions into something positive. But though Sarah had been able to ride the horse in several rodeos and rack up a few wins on him, Flash never really changed. No matter how they pampered him, he always seemed to be under some kind of strain, his coat shining with a little too much sweat, his muscles rippling and twitching with nerves. Once in a while he'd explode, seemingly at nothing, but Sarah had always managed to avoid the flailing hooves.

Her stepfather hadn't been so lucky. But despite what had happened to Roy, Sarah had never seen Flash as a killer. When he kicked, it was out of fear or pain; they just could never figure out what was scaring him or hurting him.

Roy would have forgiven him. Roy forgave easily, totally and unreservedly. It was a quality Sarah envied and had never been able to imitate.

"Take your time. Easy." She was soothing herself more than the horse. He watched as she got a grip on her nerves, breathing in through her nose, out through her mouth. If you thought about your breath, you centered and slowed, and a calm spirit drew horses like magic. If you were genuinely at ease, even the most frightened horse would want to trust you.

She kept Flash in her peripheral vision and tried not to think about the past, but the images flickered in her mind's eye like a runaway movie on a tattered screen. She heard Roy's shouts, saw him bleeding in the dirt at the bottom of the ramp. She remembered swinging the trailer door closed on the trembling horse before racing to the house to call for help.

Panic, loss, and regret swirled through her heart as she gripped the top rail of the fence with white-knuckled fingers. She'd mourned Roy in the weeks that followed, but privately, in her sixteen-year-old heart, she'd mourned the horse too. He'd been a teenaged girl's dream, the stallion only she could ride, and she'd wept to think of some other trainer making him into the miracle she'd been praying for. She hadn't known what had happened to Flash, and she'd told herself she didn't care.

But the truth was she'd cared a lot. And all that caring had simmered for years behind the mask of indifference she'd put on the day the check came.

Surely the buyer knew he'd stolen that horse. Flash's conformation and bloodlines were unbeatable. He'd been remarkable in the arena on his good days, stopping and spinning with textbook perfection. She'd been sure she could ride him to a championship if she could just find the key to calming him. If she'd just had a little more time…

Breathe, she told herself *Breathe. Breathe slow. Breathe easy.* Gradually her grip on the fence loosened and she felt her equanimity return. Along with it came her old confidence—a confidence she'd only ever felt with horses. Working with people was an effort; working with horses had been intuitive and easy.

The horse was three feet from the gate now. Stretching his neck, he sniffed the air in front of her face and took a step closer until they stood face to face, sharing breath. She closed her eyes.

This was the point in getting to know a green horse she'd always loved—the moment when her mind and the horse's melded in a silent communion that was filled with promise and understanding. But in Flash, there had always been an underlying agitation, like a white-water stretch frothing over stones in a stream. It was a part of himself he hadn't been willing to share, a secret fear he hadn't let her see.

This horse didn't have that. His mind was as smooth as a summer lake. It was obvious his confidence in himself had never been shaken. This animal's past was nothing but cool breezes and sun on the meadow.

Somehow, somebody had saved her horse.

CHAPTER 30

SARAH STARED AT THE HORSE. IF SHE'D DIED AND GONE TO heaven, this was exactly what she would have wished for: a second chance with Flash. A chance to start him fresh, before whatever had damaged him had done its work.

But it's impossible. He'd be old. This horse isn't old.

She shrugged off her doubts and fumbled to undo the latch. There was no point in second-guessing this. Maybe she was dreaming. Maybe she really had died.

She didn't care. When the gate closed behind her with a metallic clang, she felt like she'd shut out the real world and walked into the dream. The round pen was its own universe, a place out of time.

She straightened her shoulders, an almost imperceptible movement, and took on the leader's role in her mind. The horse reacted instantly, arching his neck and backing one step away. He stood stock-still, poised between submission and flight.

He chose flight. Good horses always did.

Sarah heeded him around the ring, keeping just behind his flank, urging him into a lope with nothing but her own intent and the subtleties of body position. He moved beautifully, his mane and tail sailing behind him as his hooves ate up the ground.

Anyone watching would have said they were just a woman standing still and a horse running, but there was so much more going on beneath the surface. They were testing each other, deciding who would lead and who would follow. She could feel the horse considering his options, and finally he slowed almost imperceptibly. The circle grew smaller as he bowed his body and eased into a trot, bobbing his head down once in a while and working his mouth.

He was getting tired of running. He was asking to stop.

But it wasn't time yet. She stiffened slightly and took a step backward. Breaking into a lope again, the horse kept one eye on her, watching for permission to slow. She stepped left, and like a dance partner he caught the cue and dropped into a trot, neck arched and tail high. He was flirting with her, trying to charm her into giving way.

Not gonna happen, buddy, she thought. *Not yet.*

She took another step and he dropped his head and smoothed out his gait. She remembered riding in the round ring while Roy stood in the center offering advice.

Move your right leg back. He's not flexing.

Get back on your seat-bones, girl—you're not a jockey.

Relax. Stop thinking so hard. Let it be.

She so wished he could share this moment, see this horse. She wished she could finish this training session and sit in the barn with him afterward, dissecting every move she'd made, talking technique, figuring out what worked for the horse, what worked for her. Roy had trained her like he'd trained the horses, with deep understanding and an almost eerie sense of what she was thinking.

God, she missed him. She blinked away tears, realizing she'd lost her concentration. To work with horses you had to be present, a conscious participant in the process. She'd broken that rule and the horse had stopped. She swiped at her cheeks, chiding herself for losing focus, but when he stepped up and pushed at her with his nose the tears started again.

The horse shoved the length of his muzzle against her arm and she rested her head on his neck, feeling a rare, easy kinship with the animal. She'd never been able to bond with Flash like this. Never. He'd always held a piece of himself apart. Now he was giving his whole heart.

She buried her face in his mane, breathing in the sweet scent of him and struggling to smother her tears. He stood patiently, letting her recover, easing her turmoil with his own level calm.

Stepping back, she sniffed and wiped her nose on the back of her hand. She didn't know where Lane had gone, but she was glad he hadn't witnessed her emotional breakdown. And she was glad she'd had a chance to be alone with this horse—whoever he was.

Because she knew it couldn't be Flash—he was too young. Flash had to be his sire, so whoever had bought him had bred him.

"Where did you come from, baby?" she murmured to the horse. "And what happened to your daddy?"

She wasn't sure she wanted to know.

Lane stood a few feet from the gate, watching Sarah perform the intricate dance of teaching a horse to be tame.

Much as Lane loved rodeo, bronc bucking was a sad reminder of the old way of training horses—the fast, brutal method of riding an animal to a standstill. In the real world, a horse that had been bucked out gave up, and then he wasn't a whole horse anymore. He'd be your servant, but he'd never be your partner.

The new methods were respectful but not soft. There was no doubt who was the leader and who had to follow, but neither horse nor rider was diminished by the process if you did it right.

And Sarah did it right.

He'd been worried the sight of Cinnamon Chrome would freak her out. There was no way anyone who'd ever seen Flash wouldn't know this was his colt. It was like the sire had been reincarnated into the son—like Flash had come back to life again, whole and healthy.

Lane's grandfather had offered to buy Lane a horse the summer he'd turned twenty-one, hoping the idea of training horses would lure him away from the rodeo ring before he got hurt. He'd been willing to pay a high price to keep his grandson safe, and Lane could have bought any horse at the sale.

But the moment he'd seen the big red dun snorting and racing in manic circles around the sale barn corral, he'd thought *mine*.

Flash had been his first rescue. He couldn't figure out why nobody wanted the horse, but there was no telling where he would have ended up if Lane hadn't bought him. Maybe he'd have gone back to his owners, whoever they were—but it was also possible he'd end up on a truck en route to a Mexican slaughtering plant.

He'd never been able to ride the horse—but he'd been able to breed him and keep those bloodlines alive. Cinn was just one of the colts that looked like clones of their sire.

He watched Sarah crying and resisted the urge to help her. She wasn't the kind of woman who appreciated sympathy. He should go, give her time to recover.

But if she was going to have an emotional breakdown in the ring, somebody had to look out for her safety. You never knew how that kind of thing might affect a horse. Cinn didn't have the unpredictable blowups that had made his sire so dangerous, but he was still a stallion.

Lane watched from a respectful distance as she rested her cheek against the horse's neck. Judging from her heaving shoulders, she was having a hard time getting hold of herself. He'd never seen her like this—broken down and utterly beaten.

He was relieved when she bowed her head, blinked, and straightened her shoulders. She patted the horse a few times as if assuring the animal that she'd recovered. Then she stepped back and wiped her eyes with the back of her hand.

He moved toward the gate and Cinn whinnied in recognition. Sarah spun to see what had riled up the horse, and he was hoping she'd smile when she caught sight of him. But her face was still streaked with tears, and she looked anything but happy.

"Tell me where he came from," she said, nesting her fingers in the horse's dark mane. "Who bought Flash? I need to know. Because whoever bought him ruined my family's life."

CHAPTER 31

SARAH AND LANE SQUARED OFF A MERE HALF SECOND BEFORE a jaunty tune cut through the air. Sarah slapped at the pockets of her jeans until she found her cell phone in her back pocket. Jerking it out, she cut off Blondie's "Call Me" mid-song.

"Kelsey." She stepped away from Lane. "What? No! Where is she?"

Lane frowned. Even the newest rookie trainer knew you didn't bring a cell phone into the round pen. Maybe she wasn't such a natural after all. Anyone could make a mistake, but she was carrying on a conversation instead of flicking the phone off and taking care of the horse. And she wasn't even trying to project a calm demeanor. She was damn near as tense as the horse, snapping out her words, stamping a foot hard on the ground.

He was getting madder by the minute until he noticed that her face was growing paler each time she paused to listen to the caller. Finally, she shoved the phone back in her pocket and strode to the gate, opening it and sliding through. She tried to latch it behind her, fumbled with the mechanism, tried again, and failed. Lane reached over and fixed it.

"My sister's sick," she said. "Unconscious. She gets migraines, and Mike thinks—he thinks she's having a stroke."

"I'll drive you over."

"I've got it."

She ran to the Malibu and flung open the door. With all the clothes heaped in the backseat it looked like the cars parked on the street in city alleys, the ones homeless people crammed all their belongings into. Smushed up against the window he could see a shoe, a purse, and a pack of pink girlie razors.

It took her three tries to get the key in the ignition, and then she shoved the car in reverse and backed over a grocery bag. She shifted, lurched forward a few feet, stalled the engine, then flailed at the shift knob and backed over the bag again. She swiped away a tear while she struggled to get the car back in first and Lane tapped on the window.

"Slide over."

She shook her head, still struggling with the transmission while he opened the door.

"I mean it. Slide over. You're in no shape to drive."

"She has headaches," she said, sliding into the passenger seat. "I thought they were migraines. But what if..."

"Don't think about it."

He got behind the wheel and gunned the Malibu down the driveway. Sarah leaned forward, as if she could urge the car on like a racehorse.

"Drive faster," she said. "It's on County Road Six. You know that blue single-wide on the edge of town? That's Kelsey's." She clenched her fists and pounded her thighs. "I need to be there now. Please, Lane. Faster."

———~~~———

For once, Lane obeyed an order. He drove like he rode, careening around corners and skidding at stop signs with no regard for safety, but the ambulance still beat them to Kelsey's. It was parked in the yard when they drove in, a boxy, decrepit vehicle with old-fashioned bug-eyed headlights and red faded paint on the side spelling out "Two Shot Emergency" arched above a first aid cross.

Sarah spilled out of the passenger seat while he threw the shifter into park. A pair of good ol' boys in jeans and snap-button shirts had Kelsey strapped to a gurney. They were trying to load her in the back of the vehicle, one struggling to collapse the folding legs of the gurney while the other pumped up a blood pressure cuff. Mike was across from the technician, balancing Katie on one arm. The child's sleep-flushed cheek was pressed into his shoulder, but her eyes were open, watching as Sarah ran to them. Sarah felt a squeeze in her heart at the sight of her niece limp in Mike's arms.

Katie had been young when Mike and Kelsey had broken up, but she seemed to be wasting no time turning into a daddy's girl—which was bad news for everyone if he left again. Sarah reached for the child, but Mike spun slightly away and pretended to be involved in stroking down her hair.

His own shaggy locks were spiked up from his forehead. Sarah knew he ran his fingers through it, front to back, when he was nervous. She knew because he was always nervous when he talked to her. Which was as it should be; after what he'd done to her sister, he should be nervous.

"One thirty over eighty," said the EMT.

"Is that good?" Mike asked.

"It's okay." Sarah stepped up beside him. "Kelsey? How are you?"

"She's not conscious, ma'am," the EMT said.

"What's wrong?"

"That's what we're trying to figure out."

She turned to Mike. "What happened?"

"Nothing, really. She just passed out. She had one of her headaches. She said it really hurt, and then she passed out. I called 911, and then I called you." He kicked at the dirt with the toe of his boot.

"Where are they taking her?" Lane asked. Sarah had almost forgotten he was there.

"Casper," said the driver.

"Isn't there a doctor closer to here?"

The driver shook his head.

"Damn, Casper's an hour away."

"Forty-two minutes is the record," the driver said.

Lane started to respond, but just then the second EMT managed to get the legs on the gurney to collapse and they slid Kelsey into the ambulance.

"Ready to go," he said.

Mike turned and tipped Katie toward Sarah. The little girl stirred, blinked sleepily, and held out her arms.

"I thought you could take Katie over to the hospital, meet 'em there," Mike said.

"You're staying here?" Sarah knew he was a bastard, but she didn't know he was that much of a bastard.

"Course not. I'm riding in the ambulance."

Sarah was about to argue when the EMT crouching beside Kelsey lifted a cautionary hand. "Ma'am?" he said to Kelsey. "Ma'am? Can you hear me?"

Kelsey's eyes fluttered open. "Uh?" She tried to talk, but all that came out was gibberish.

"Speech ataxia," said the EMT. "Probably a vascular constriction."

Sarah swallowed, feeling an ache in her throat as Kelsey's eyes widened. Vascular whatever. It was a stroke. Kelsey couldn't talk. How would things be if she didn't recover? She and Mike would be all Katie had left.

They'd better start getting along.

"Wha..." Kelsey looked from side to side, panicked.

"It's okay. I'm here, Sis," Sarah said.

Kelsey moved her mouth, obviously trying to speak, but nothing came out. Finally, she closed her eyes again and clenched her fists.

"She's trying," said the EMT.

Kelsey opened her eyes again, this time looking past Sarah. "Mike?" she said. "Mike?"

The exhale of Sarah's relief that her sister could speak whooshed out, and she wished all her jealousy and misgivings could go with it. But her heart felt heavy as she took Katie from Mike and watched him slip into the ambulance and take Kelsey's hand.

"Momma?" Katie rubbed her eyes and looked up at Sarah, puzzled.

"Momma's resting." Sarah patted the child's head. "You've got the car seat, Mike. Come on. I'll ride with Kelsey."

Mike tossed a set of keys at her. They fell to the ground at her feet. "Take Kelsey's car," he said. "The seat's in it."

"But…"

"I'm not leaving her."

Now he wasn't leaving her. Sarah was tempted to say something snarky, but the EMT crouching on the other side of the gurney leaned out and pulled one of the doors closed. "We're wasting time here," he said.

"Come on." Lane picked the keys up and tossed them in the air, nodding toward Kelsey's gray-primered Camry. "Let's go."

"Let's?"

"You're in no shape to drive. Besides, my truck's at the ranch, remember?"

Sarah sighed and headed for the car. She bent and slid the sleepy Katie into the car seat, struggling to fasten the belt and shoulder straps as the child slumped like a sack of potatoes. She was used to taking care of Katie, but since they never left the yard she wasn't well versed in car seat technique. As she tried to fasten the shoulder straps into the buckle, Katie woke and widened her eyes.

"Momma?"

"Momma's going on a ride in the big truck," Sarah said. "We'll go meet her, okay?"

"Momma!" It wasn't a question now, it was a demand. "Want Momma!"

"Honey, we're going to get her, okay? Just hang on." Sarah tried to shove the buckle closed, but Katie struggled and set up a wail. "Hurting me, Aunt Sarah! Hurting meeee!"

Sarah felt the hot pressure of tears behind her eyes. Tucking her hands under her niece's armpits she hoisted her a little higher in the seat and slid the buckle home. She muttered some comforting nonsense Katie usually loved, but the child screwed up her face and let out a wail that rose in deafening concert with the ambulance siren as the vehicle pulled away from the curb.

"Mommaaaaaaaa!" She flapped her arms like a helpless baby bird. "Aunt Sarah is hurting meeeee!"

Sarah unhooked the buckles and sat back, feeling as helpless as a three-year-old herself. There was no other way the buckle could go, was there? She bent down and picked up her niece, cradling the child against her chest. Katie calmed almost immediately, lapsing into heartbroken hiccups.

Sarah bounced the child gently. This she could handle, but how the hell was she going to get to the hospital?

"Here." Lane had scooted into the backseat and was holding the straps on either side of the car seat apart. "Put her in. I'll help."

Katie held out her arms to Lane, grunting in protest when Sarah tightened her grip.

"Ride," she said. "Want ride."

"Oh, fine." Sarah set her in the seat and watched in wonder as Lane slid buckles and tightened belts like a pro. Katie smiled at him the whole time.

"Like tacking up a horse," he said, grinning up at Sarah. "Nothing to it."

CHAPTER 32

KATIE BANGED HER CHUBBY LEGS AGAINST THE SEAT, FLAILING her arms as Lane piloted the Camry through the wide, banked curve of the highway entrance. Trapped by the car seat, she looked like a baby bird trying to fly.

"There's nothing closer than Casper?" he asked.

"No." Sarah gripped the shoulder harness with one hand, the door handle with the other. "When Katie got a fever last month, Kelsey had to drive her all the way to town. It takes almost an hour."

"Forty-two minutes." Lane accelerated onto the highway and they all rocked back in their seats. Katie made a happy gurgling sound.

"Kid's got the need for speed," he said.

"So do we." Sarah clenched her hands in her lap.

"We'll get there." He reached over and patted her thigh, but she was too preoccupied with Kelsey to feel more than a faint spasm of lust from his touch. "At least we haven't caught up to the ambulance yet. I'm kind of surprised. That thing's an antique."

"It'll be a miracle if it doesn't break down before it gets to the hospital. When I was a kid they could barely keep it running. I can't believe it's still going, but when it's all you've got…" She grimaced, spreading her hands hopelessly.

"Can't they get a grant or something?"

"Lane, you've seen Two Shot. It's not exactly prosperous." She clenched her hands tighter. "You think it's quaint and old-fashioned, but this isn't a Norman Rockwell painting. It's real life. Keeping it from changing isn't doing the people who live there any favors."

He didn't respond.

"If you approved the drilling we might eventually be able to attract a doctor or something. Kelsey says there's nothing right now. There was an older lady in town who was a retired nurse, but she passed last year."

"What about tourism? I'm not the only person who likes small towns."

"There are no hotels. No events, except the Humboldt Rodeo. We're not really on the way anywhere, unless you're a trucker headed for Lincoln, and trust me, those guys can't even spare the money for a two-dollar tip."

"But you've seen Midwest. They ruined it. It's like a slum without a city."

"It might not look pretty, but they got a health clinic out of the deal. And old people dying for lack of a doctor really spoils the picture, you know?"

He was silent.

"It's not a toy town, Lane. It's real people with real lives."

She thought of Kelsey, lying in the ambulance, maybe conscious, maybe not, and suddenly the inside of the car felt close and hot. She couldn't catch her breath and tears glossed her eyes so the world looked like an Impressionist painting. Lane patted her thigh again but this time he left his hand there. It was tempting to let it lie, but then she thought of Kelsey bouncing her way south while people like Lane clung to their pretty views and quaint towns and she shook him off. When she leaned her forehead against the window the cool glass felt like a wet washcloth and she managed to blink away some of the tears.

"Open your window a little," Lane said. "You look like you're going to faint."

She hated to follow orders, but she opened the window a crack and sucked in air.

"You lost somebody, didn't you? To this…this problem." His

tone was gentle and she felt the heat of tears behind her eyes. Again. Dang, she was turning into such a girl.

"My stepfather. He was in an accident, and he…" She had to swallow down the ache in her throat to keep going. "He didn't make it to the hospital." She gestured at the road ahead, though the ambulance was still nowhere in sight. "Those guys don't have the training to help somebody with a skull fracture. And now Kelsey…"

She rocked her head back and forth against the glass, closing her eyes. "Just get us there, Lane. Just get us there."

Sarah didn't say another word until Lane pulled into the ambulance lane and stopped at the hospital's glass back doors.

"I'll bring Katie in," he said.

She started to object, but heck, she trusted him, and Katie had looked at him like he was Barney the Dinosaur or something. The kid was probably starved for male attention. She'd spent a few days with her father now, but a drop of rain couldn't make up for a year-long drought.

Sarah stepped out of the car and slammed the door. "See you in there."

She headed inside at a fast walk and almost bumped into the automatic door as it slowly slid open. Glancing around the tiny waiting room, she spotted Mike slouched sideways in a chair against the wall. He was gazing wearily up at a large-screen TV where Nancy Grace was railing about some new travesty of injustice—with the sound off, thank God. Mike had one leg over the arm of the chair and looked like a cowboy waiting to ride.

He straightened when he saw her. "Where's Katie?"

"Lane'll bring her in."

He looked like he had a few questions about that, but she shot him a glare. "How come you're out here? Where's Kelsey?"

"They wouldn't let me back there. Said they'd call me when they finished her tests."

"Was she conscious?"

"Oh, yeah. The whole way here. She was talking and everything. Her head's still hurting, but the pain was letting up." He looked sheepish. "I tried to call you, but your cell was off or something."

She jerked the phone out of her purse and stared at the screen. He was right. It was off.

"Dang," she said.

He grinned.

"What's so funny?"

"Haven't heard you talk like that in years," he said.

She was grateful for the interruption when Lane came through the door, carrying a sleepy Katie in one arm.

"Daddy!" The kid held out her arms and leaned toward her father, spilling from Lane's arms into Mike's. Sarah did her best to ignore the knifepoint of jealousy as it drove deeper and twisted.

"Where's Momma?" Katie asked, leaning back to look up at her father's face.

"She's at the doctor," he said. "We have to wait."

Katie nodded sagely. "Does she need a shot?"

At least one person in the family got regular medical care. Sarah had taken Kelsey and Katie to Casper for pediatrician appointments several times, worried that Kelsey's rattletrap car would leave them stranded on the highway.

"No shot," he said. "But she might take a while. You want to play over there? Look at the train."

He pointed toward a play area with a brightly painted wooden locomotive and an assortment of toys and books. Katie stared for a moment, her little jaw dropping, then nodded with outsized enthusiasm and struggled in his arms. He released her and she toddled over to the train, climbing onto the seat and gripping a spinning steering wheel with her chubby fists. Sarah started out of her seat, but Mike gestured for her to stay.

"She'll be okay," he said. "Kelsey likes her to play by herself sometimes. So she's not so needy."

Sarah nodded, feeling left out yet again. Normally she was privy to all Kelsey's latest childcare techniques, but now Mike was her partner in raising Katie. That was how it should be, but how long would Mike stay? And if he walked, what would it do to Katie?

"You can depend on me this time," he said, as if he'd read her thoughts. "I won't leave again."

Lane mumbled something about coffee and lurched out of his chair, leaving Sarah alone with the last person she wanted to talk to.

"I know I was an asshole," Mike said.

At least we agree on something.

"I was a kid," he said. "Just a dumb kid."

Two things.

"I never should have got married, but I love Kelsey, you know? I knew she was the one for me, and she wanted to, so..." He spread his hands helplessly. "I can tell you I never looked at another woman. That wasn't what it was about, okay?"

Sarah nodded.

"I just felt like nothing was ever going to change, you know? Like I was locked into this same thing, night after night. It's hard having a kid."

"You might have thought of that when—"

"I know." He rolled right over her as if he knew what she was going to say. He probably did. His screwups were pretty easy to figure out, even for a dumb rodeo cowboy. "But after the store closed, I couldn't find a job, and I was just—I was useless."

Three things.

"I tried the rodeo 'cause it was all there was, you know? And I thought I'd be better at it. Turned out I sucked."

Sarah was losing count of all the things they agreed on. Was that four or five?

"So we got the divorce, and I was paying best I could, and then I got the job at Carrigan and I thought she'd be pleased, you know? And then she wouldn't even talk to me. I was up there in the boonies, couldn't go see her no matter how bad I wanted, and it was like she was gone, her and Katie just gone, and I'd lost my chance. I blew it. Just blew the best thing I ever had."

Sarah nodded. Mike's eyes were suspiciously shiny. He'd never seemed like a very sensitive guy—he was always laughing, always joshing with the boys, but now he seemed different. Maybe he was growing up.

It was about time. In fact, it was damn near too late.

"But Kelsey gave me another chance," he said. "She forgave me. Can you believe that?" He set his elbows on his knees and ducked his head down, hiding his face while he got himself under control. Finally, he looked up. "She loves me no matter what. She waited, and she never gave up on me."

"I know." Sarah's heart ached for her sister. She'd blamed Mike for all Kelsey's problems, but maybe it was Sarah who'd stressed her beyond what she could take.

"When I came back, I was so scared she'd throw me out, but she wouldn't. She couldn't. 'Cause when Kelsey loves you, she loves you all the way." He ducked his head again. "I gotta go." He stood and patted his pockets, blinking fast. "I quit smoking, but I think I'll go stand outside anyway, okay?"

Sarah nodded and tried to smile, but her lips wouldn't cooperate. Thankfully, Katie chose that moment to shout out, "Aunt Sarah. Watch me!"

Sarah found she could smile for Katie, and she watched the little girl slide down from the seat of the train, run around the back of it, and climb back into the seat from the opposite side.

"Watch me again!" The child repeated the whole process, then slid from the seat and ran to Sarah, throwing herself into her arms with the abandon and trust only a three-year-old can have. "Did you see me? Did you see?"

"I did, honey. That was great." She hugged Katie and gave her a loud, exaggerated kiss. Katie giggled, squirming to the floor. She started toward the train, then paused, one finger in her mouth.

"Where did Daddy go?"

"Outside. He'll be right back."

"Oh. That's okay." Katie flailed one hand in a gesture Kelsey called her princess wave. She did look for all the world like a ruler granting sufferance to one of her many subjects, and that wasn't too far from the truth. She sure ruled Sarah's heart. "I love him anyway."

"That's good." Sarah almost meant it. A kid needed a father. Nobody knew that better than her. Roy had been everything to her, filling a hole in her life she hadn't even known existed until he came home with her mother one night and stayed. She'd never known her own father, but she'd felt the lack of one. Roy had taken that emptiness away, and then he'd gone again. She'd never wish that kind of loss on Katie.

"I love you, Aunt Sarah," Katie said.

"I love you too, hon." She remembered what Mike had said about Kelsey. "I love you all the way."

She looked up to see Lane striding into the room, juggling two Styrofoam coffee cups and a handful of sugar packets and one-shot creamers.

"All the way?" He lifted his eyebrows in a teasing question. "I didn't think you were that kind of girl."

"I'm not." She gave him a wry half smile. "I need to work on it."

CHAPTER 33

THEY DIDN'T LEAVE THE HOSPITAL UNTIL WELL AFTER midnight. Kelsey and Mike fell asleep in the backseat, snuggled together beside Katie's car seat. They'd been holding hands, Kelsey's head resting on Mike's shoulder. It had actually made Sarah smile. Maybe her heart was thawing a little where Mike was concerned.

She and Lane made small talk on the way back to the ranch, mostly about Kelsey. Sarah filled him in on what the doctor had said. It wasn't a stroke, just an especially severe migraine that had tightened up some capillaries. The doctor gave her migraine medication, much to Sarah's satisfaction, and ordered her to take it. Lane actually seemed to care, which would have warmed her heart if she'd been able to forget about the horse. How had he ended up with Flash's colt? Had he been the buyer, the person who put the last nail in the coffin of her family's ruined life? She counted surreptitiously on her fingers. He was six years older than her, so that would have made him twenty-one when it all happened.

It could easily have been him.

He pulled the Malibu to a stop outside the Love Nest. She opened her door, then closed it again. She'd never been so emotionally exhausted, but there was no way she could sleep until she found out if Lane had bought Flash.

She didn't know what she'd do with the information. She knew the buyer shouldn't bear the blame for the loss of the ranch. But all her life, she'd nursed a burning resentment toward the person who had profited from her family's misfortune.

She turned toward him, bending one leg and tucking it beneath her. There was no moon tonight, so she could barely see his face.

"It was you, wasn't it?" she asked. "That bought Flash."

"Yes."

"You stole him. You know that, right?"

"I put up my hand. It's not my fault nobody else did. I would have paid more if anyone else had bid." He reached over and stroked her arm. "What happened to your family wasn't my fault."

She knew he was right. But blaming the shadowy buyer had always been easier than blaming herself. It had been up to her to help the family recover from the perfect storm of disaster that had struck them when they least expected it. And she had failed.

"If nobody had bid, I could have gotten him back," she said, as much to herself as to him. "I could have worked with him more, settled him down, taken him to the rodeo a few times. We could have gotten triple that price for him. I just needed a little time to get over things."

"Do you really think anyone would have let you do that?" he asked. "You were a kid, Sarah. From what I heard, they wouldn't even let anyone open the trailer."

"They," she said bitterly. "There was no *they*. It was my mother that locked him in there."

"Look, Sarah, I'm sorry. I didn't know anything about all this when I bought the horse."

"Just like you didn't know Two Shot didn't have a doctor," she mumbled.

"What does that have to do with anything?"

"Everything," she said. "It's how you operate. You say you like the dust and dirt, but you don't know what it's really like. So you just ignore the reality and tell yourself you're one of us just because you can ride a horse and get some dirt under your nails once in a while."

"No," he said. "That's not how it is."

"Then how is it? You didn't think about the fact that someone was depending on the sale, just like it never occurred to you that people in Two Shot have to drive an hour for medical care."

"Forty-two minutes," he said. "I'm sorry, Sarah."

"Sorry won't bring back Roy," she said. "He died in the ambulance on the way to the hospital. They didn't know what to do for him. Sorry won't bring back the ranch, either. The bank took it when we couldn't pay the mortgage. And it won't bring back my mother, who drank herself to death and left me and my sister alone in that damn gossip-ridden town, with everyone pointing their fingers and judging us." She sniffed. "And it won't get me back my horse. Dammit, I loved him, Lane. I was the only one who could ride him, you know that? And he raced for me. He went all out just for me."

To her horror, she realized she was crying, tears streaming down her face.

"What happened to Flash?" she asked.

"I had him about five years," he said. "He got colic. He's gone."

She knew it. She'd known the horse she'd worked with yesterday couldn't be Flash. He'd been too pure, too clean. When she'd worked Flash, she'd felt his secrets like a tangle of wires in his head, complex and impenetrable. The horse she'd worked yesterday was a blank slate. It was as if someone had taken Flash and wiped his mind clear of whatever was wrong with him.

She glanced out the window, the long span of sage and rock blurring as the tears tried to come back. She'd known it couldn't be Flash. But some little light had burned on in the depths of her heart, hoping it was her horse.

Lane watched Sarah struggle to control her emotions. Why couldn't she just cry? Why did she have to be so strong all the time? She'd had a hard life. But why did she have to hold herself so firmly in check when she was with a man who...

Who loved her. He didn't want to finish that thought, but the truth wasn't something he could deny anymore. He loved her, and she thought he'd destroyed her life.

Great. This might be the one fight he couldn't win.

"I'm sorry, Sarah. I wish—I didn't know. Nobody bid on the horse. For all I knew, he had nowhere to go. You know where those horses end up when nobody wants them."

She looked away and he knew he'd struck a nerve. But he didn't want to hurt her. He wasn't here to make her face facts; he was here to help her any way he could.

"The horse you worked yesterday is named Cinnamon Chrome."

"Cinnamon Chrome," she muttered. "Son of Chromium Flash."

He nodded. "We call him Cinn, and believe me, it fits. He's got the devil in him, but you were great with him." He paused. "He's yours if you stay."

"Stay?" She looked at him like he'd suggested she go get a knife and stab herself. "*Stay?*"

"Sure." He pretended he didn't notice the pallor that had washed over her face, followed by a flood of color that made him wonder if she was going to explode like a human volcano. "Trevor can do ground work, but he can't ride."

She turned to him suddenly as if she'd just woken from a deep sleep.

"Why does he work for you?"

"He doesn't just work for me. He owns half the operation. That's why it's called the LT. Lane, Trevor."

"You gave him half your land?"

"Not the land. The operation. The cattle, and the horse revenues."

"Why?"

"Because I owe him." Now it was his turn to stare moodily out the window. "The night Trevor had that accident, he and I were partying together. I knew he was too drunk to drive, but I was too busy talking some buckle bunny into my bed to stop him."

"That doesn't make you responsible."

"Friends look out for each other. And I didn't. He'd be his old self today if I hadn't let him walk out that door." He turned to look at her. "How come you take care of your sister like you do?"

"Same thing." She fooled with a button on her shirt, avoiding his eyes. "After Roy died, I went off to college. Left her with Mama and nobody to take care of her." She heaved a heavy sigh and he wondered how those slim shoulders supported so much weight. "She turned to Mike, and when he left—I thought maybe I could make up for the way I'd left her."

"She seems to be doing okay now," he said.

"No thanks to me. I've made a lot of mistakes."

"Who hasn't? Maybe you ought to stop trying to fix the past and take care of yourself."

A faint smile gave her face a little of its old glow. "Maybe you should too."

"We could do it together. I'm serious. Come work at the ranch. If you could ride that hellion of a stallion, you can ride anything. Cinn would be your signing bonus."

It was a ridiculously generous offer, and judging by her expression, she knew it. But just when he thought she might say yes, she looked away. He caught the glimmer of a tear on her lower lashes.

"Lane, you don't understand. I can't."

She was right. He didn't understand. Something was still holding her back—some hidden fear he hadn't found yet.

"So where are you going to go?"

She looked over at the darkened Love Nest.

"I don't know," she said. "I'll think of something." She faced him, and a small spark of the old Sarah leapt in her eyes. "It's not really your concern, okay?"

"No, it's not. But I want it to be."

She started to speak, but he held up one hand in a "stop" gesture.

"Look, I know that's the last thing you want right now. But I want to help."

"Then leave me alone."

He took a deep breath. "Actually, I can do that. I need to get on the road and build up some points if I'm going to make the finals this year, anyway. Frankly, I should have gone to Amarillo. And then—then you made me want to stay."

He remembered the softness of her skin in the dark, the glow of her eyes when he made love to her, and wondered if she was thinking the same thing. She looked up at him and there was no trace of that passion in her eyes now. She was still processing the fact that he'd been the man who bought Flash. He'd lost her for good, all because of something he'd done ten years earlier.

All he'd done was buy a horse. Anyone would have done it. But she was right—it had never occurred to him to wonder about Roy's family, or the fact that his good fortune was someone else's disaster.

And she was right about another thing. He liked playing cowboy, but he didn't know a damn thing about what that life was really like. He hung out with the young guys and shared their carefree hours at the rodeo, but when they got in their trucks and went home to their wives, with or without prize money, he really had no idea what happened. He might as well be his brother, perched on his leather throne looking down on the streets of Casper. He didn't know a damn thing about real life, any more than his brother did.

"I'll be on the road for a week, maybe two," he finally said. "Hell, I could stay out for three. Trevor can handle things here. So you're welcome to stay in the cabin for a while."

"I'm leaving."

"Sarah, you've had a shock. I hate to think of you hitting the road like this."

"Like what?" She shoved out her chin, trying to look tough.

"Like a basket case." She shot him a dirty look, but she couldn't deny it was true. "Stay as long as you need to. Take a little time to think. A couple of days, a couple of weeks... Whatever you need."

She looked from him to the window, then back at the man. She really didn't have any place to go, but she wasn't about to tell him that.

"I can take care of myself," she said. "Don't do me any favors."

"Hitting the road isn't doing a favor for most women." He did his best to resurrect his usual cocky grin. "Most of 'em want me to stick around."

She didn't answer and he opened the car door. "Stay, Sarah. At least for today, tomorrow, as long as it takes to work things out. And if you're still here when I get back, the job offer's open."

"I'll be gone," she said as he opened the door. "I might stay the night. I need to make some plans. But you can come back after that. And you won't hear from me again."

———∿∿∿———

Sarah woke in the morning with an emotional hangover. She felt drained, as if someone had wrung out her heart and left just a shriveled husk behind.

The day before had been like the world's wildest bronc ride. She'd had that magical moment of reunion with the horse she'd thought was Flash. Then the near-disaster with Kelsey, and the realization of her own shortcomings. And to top it off, she'd discovered that the man she—loved, maybe—was the villain in the life story she'd constructed to cope with her own shortcomings.

She felt like she'd been dropped in the dirt by the ultimate bucking horse. She could feel the fall in her bones; it was like she was bruised right down to her soul.

Rifling through the unfamiliar cupboards, she finally found a coffee cup. Like the rest of the cabin's meager supply of dishes, it was made of heavy white china decorated with ranch brands and rodeo scenes. She poured herself a cup of the coffee she'd set brewing the night before and took a long sip while she pondered her future.

At least her lack of material goods made her mobile. As she headed for the front porch, she started to formulate a plan. She'd stay at Kelsey's for a while. Mike would just have to put up with her, because she needed to regroup, redesign, and restore her life. Getting fired from Carrigan wouldn't help her professional reputation any, but she'd only been there a few months. Maybe if she just left the job off her resume entirely...

Kind of like she'd left any reference to Two Shot out of her conversations about her past. Yeah, that had worked out just great.

She leaned against the log wall and scanned the prairie, drinking in the long, featureless vista as she sipped her coffee. Maybe it was time to stop the sins of omission and face the truth. It wasn't like the truth was so terrible. She'd gone from relative poverty to success in the business world. That was something to be proud of, right? Anyone could be born to success. It took a special kind of determination to claw your way up from poverty. She was a small-town girl who'd made good—or at least that's what she'd been yesterday.

Today, she was a small-town girl who'd failed. She was right back where she'd started—in Two Shot country. And she could moan and cuss about that all she wanted, but the truth was it was time to start clawing her way to success again.

CHAPTER 34

THE VIEW FROM THE PORCH WAS BLEAK, JUST A FLAT PLAIN scattered with rocks and sage, but the longer Sarah looked the more she felt like she belonged here. This was the landscape she'd grown up with. The subtle greens and golds broken by gold and gray rocks and pale, parched earth were the colors of home.

It was a good day for horses, the kind of day she'd loved as a girl. The heat of the sun was tempered by a gentle, lilting breeze, just enough to cool the skin without raising dust. The Wyoming sky was a hard gemstone blue, and the grass glistened like gold tinsel. It would be a perfect day to spend with Flash Junior. What had Lane called him? Cinnamon Chrome. Cinn.

She squinted at the dusty, disreputable car parked in the drive, with all her earthly possessions jammed inside. She was in transit, moving from her old life to something new and unknown. This wasn't the destination she had in mind, but that didn't mean she couldn't pause and rest, let herself out to play like a dog taking a roadside break on a long car trip.

She checked her watch, thinking of Roy as she always did when she looked at the no-frills Timex with its bold, simple numbers. It was early, not even six yet. She was hungry, and she didn't have the energy to cook. In any other town, she'd have found a diner and gone for breakfast.

She took a long sip of coffee and set the empty cup on the porch rail, glancing down at the watch again. Her stepfather would have told her to stick it out in town, force them to respect her. He would have been ashamed of the way she'd turned tail and run. Gentle as he was, he'd had a core of iron, and he'd wanted Sarah to have that inner steel too.

"All right, Roy," she muttered, stepping off the porch and heading for the car. She didn't know for sure what her future held, but she knew she was going to be in Two Shot for a while if she stayed with Kelsey. Sooner or later, she'd have to tackle Suze and her customers. She might as well do it now.

The trip to town went far too fast. Parking spaces were in surprisingly short supply, and she was forced to pull in almost two blocks from the diner and walk. Her experience the other day had grown in her mind to the point where she fully expected to hear hissing from the few cars that passed by, but everyone was just going about their business.

She swung into the diner and slid into a booth near the door, glancing around the room. Joe was at the counter again, but it was early and only two members of the poker gang sat in the corner booth. Nobody seemed to be paying any attention to her, so she slid the menu out from behind the napkin holder and perused the familiar offerings.

"Can I get you something? Coffee to start?" Sarah looked up and was relieved to see that Suze wasn't her waitress this time. Instead, a white-aproned teenager stood over her. The girl had lovely clear skin and flushed cheeks, but she was tall and raw-boned, a farm-girl type clearly going through an awkward stage, and her thick wire-framed glasses didn't help. Judging from the way she held the order pad just inches from her nose, they didn't do her much good.

"Cheese omelet," Sarah said. "And does Eddie still make those home fries with onions and peppers?"

"Yup. Home-style potatoes." The girl scribbled down the order with her tongue poking out of the corner of her mouth. "Something to drink?"

"Coffee and a small orange juice, please."

"Okay." The girl lowered the order pad but didn't leave the table. She stood over Sarah, shifting awkwardly from one foot to another.

"You're her, aren't you?" she finally said. "The girl who got that scholarship and left."

Sarah swallowed, her throat suddenly dry, and nodded. For a little while there she'd thought she might get through breakfast without any complications, but clearly her reputation had preceded her.

She met the girl's eyes, which wasn't easy since they were flicking nervously around the room, lighting on everything but Sarah. They looked foggy and misshapen behind the thick glasses. "Yes, I did."

To her surprise, the girl slid into the booth across from her and leaned forward eagerly. "I want to go too," she said, clasping her hands together. "I want to leave so bad."

Sarah looked again and saw past the tawdry uniform, the unkempt hair tumbling out of a tightly rubber-banded bun, and the thick glasses. She caught a glimpse of her old self in the girl's breathless anticipation of a world full of wonders beyond Two Shot.

"How are your grades?"

"They're good. I'd have straight As if it wasn't for Phys Ed." She made a wry face and Sarah was reminded of Carol Burnett, only this girl wasn't playing her awkwardness for laughs. "I got a C in it last semester. We did volleyball, and I'm scared of the ball. Same thing with basketball. I try to catch it, but I flinch and then it's gone. Or it hits me." She put a hand to her chest as if remembering the ball's last assault.

Sarah hadn't been much for team sports either, but there had been other options that worked for her.

"Have you tried track?"

The girl sighed and gazed out the window, her cheeks flushing again. "My legs get tangled up and I fall down."

Sarah suppressed a smile. The girl was long-limbed as a colt, and apparently just as clumsy. "It'll change. You're going to be pretty when you grow up."

"Oh, no." The girl's blush looked almost painful now as it suffused her neck and chest. "I'm homely, and my eyes…" She made a helpless gesture toward the glasses. "But I'm smart." She said the last line with a hint of defiance. There might be hope for her despite her lack of confidence.

"You're not homely. You're just young. What grade are you in?"

"Tenth."

"Have you looked at scholarships? Thought about where you want to go to college?"

"I want to go to Vassar," the girl said, looking away and twirling a wayward strand of hair around one finger. "Like you did."

"That C in gym might keep you from being able to do that." The girl's face fell, and Sarah hurried to turn the conversation to something positive. "But there are lots of good colleges out there. What do you want to study?"

"Science." The girl's voice had dropped almost to a whisper and she glanced around the room as if afraid someone might hear. "Maybe engineering."

"They have a good program in petroleum engineering at UW."

"No. I want to go someplace better. Someplace farther away."

Sarah looked into the girl's glowing face and saw her old, hopeful self, setting off into a world that had proven to be as much of a struggle as life in Two Shot.

The girl straightened self-consciously, clearly forcing herself to be brave. "Don't tell me I can't. That's what everybody says." She tugged at her hair so hard Sarah winced. "I can do it."

"I know you can," Sarah said. "Just don't forget what matters, okay?"

"Grades?"

Sarah shook her head, smiling. "Home. The people who love you. Don't leave them too far behind. And don't ever forget where you came from."

"I'm from *Two Shot*," the girl said scornfully. "What good is that?"

"You might be surprised." Sarah stifled a smile. "It could come in handy sometime."

The swinging doors thwapped across the room, revealing Suze with her hands on her big hips, glaring at the waitress. The girl flinched guiltily.

"Emmy?" Suze's tone was harsh. "What are you doing?"

"Sorry, Suze, it's my fault," Sarah said.

"Don't you be filling her head with your Carrigan crap," Suze growled.

"I don't work for Carrigan anymore."

"Oh? How come?" Suze swung one hip sideways to rest against the table and casually considered her fingernails as if checking her polish. The move was so absurdly feminine and out-of-character that Sarah knew immediately that Lane was right about those phone calls.

Sarah narrowed her eyes as Suze's glance flickered up to her face, then back down to her nails. She'd been bold enough to leave anonymous phone calls, but she couldn't look Sarah in the face.

Sarah thought back to those long conversations she'd had with Suze when she was still living in Two Shot. Suze had always argued passionately for animals, for conservation, for the environment. Sarah should have realized she'd be against the drilling. Why had she assumed it was Lane?

"Apparently, some people in Two Shot don't want Carrigan here." She struggled to keep her tone conversational instead of combative.

"Those rigs are ugly," Suze said. "I like my plains unspoiled. I like to look out and see for miles, the way you can now, without a house or a factory or even a phone pole in the way. There's hardly anyplace left in the world like this anymore." She waved toward the window with such an expansive gesture that Sarah looked out and half expected to see Venetian canals or craggy Alps instead of a line of empty storefronts and crumbling garages.

"But people need jobs," Sarah said. "Do you really think your pretty view trumps making a living?"

Suze glowered at her for a moment, then focused on the waitress and twitched her head toward the double doors. "Back to work."

The girl scurried off, and Suze started to follow. Impulsively, Sarah reached out to stop her. She didn't really mean to grab the tie of the woman's apron, but the knot unraveled as the woman whirled to face her.

"Sorry," Sarah said. "I just wondered if you could sit a minute."

"Nope."

"Please. You lost me my job, Suze. I need to know why."

"Wasn't just me."

"Are you saying you didn't orchestrate the whole thing? I know who holds the power in this town. Just talk to me a minute."

Suze was the least vain person Sarah had ever met, but the mention of power made her sigh like a beleaguered starlet as she plumped down into the booth across from Sarah. "Okay. What?"

Sarah gazed pointedly around the diner. "Not many people here this morning."

Suze shrugged. "Some days are busier than others."

"I noticed that Best's Store is boarded up."

Suze shrugged again, her heavy shoulders rising and falling with exaggerated carelessness.

"If something doesn't change, Two Shot's going to die," Sarah said.

"We get by. There's ranching, in case you forgot."

"It's harder and harder to make a living that way. Who do you know that ranches without a day job to pay the bills? You know what they say. Behind every great cowboy is a wife who works in town."

Suze snorted. "Maybe. But there are jobs. They can always work for me."

Sarah nodded toward the kitchen. "You think that girl should wait tables all her life?"

"She could."

"Not much of a future for a bright kid."

"Good enough for most people." Suze shot a disdainful glare across the table. "Not good enough for you, I guess."

"But Carrigan would bring something better. They'd—"

"Don't tell me what they'd do." Suze snorted and everyone in the diner turned as if a volcano had erupted in the corner. "You think they'd give the jobs to Two Shot folks? They bring in out-of-towners for those rigs. I know. I met some of 'em. A bunch came through here on their way to Casper. Caught Emmy out back after her shift and teased her 'til she cried. Don't know what they woulda done to her if Eddie hadn't happened to go out there." She pressed her lips together. "They gave Eddie a hard time too, but they finally left."

"They're not all like that."

"Don't care. Two Shot's not ready for change." She nodded toward the door again. "Emmy's not ready." She jabbed a finger toward Sarah. "You tell her to go to UW, 'cause if she goes out of state folks'll eat that girl alive."

"She'll learn."

"That's what I'm afraid of." Suze's expression softened and for a moment she looked almost motherly. "It's not just the view I want to save. I want the people to stay the same too." She settled deeper into the booth, her hostility fading. "I been all over before I got here. Two Shot people's good folks. There's not many like 'em left in the world."

Sarah looked around at the other customers—the poker group in the back in their striped cowboy shirts and Carhartt jackets, Joe sitting at the counter in a T-shirt and worn denim overalls, his battered cowboy boots propped on the rail. Eddie was at the counter, his simple face creased in concern as he watched Suze and Sarah argue.

The place was pretty much the same as it had been when she'd left all those years ago. She felt a sudden wave of warmth curl around her heart. She'd longed to leave Two Shot, but it wasn't such a bad place to come back to, even when it didn't want you.

At least she knew what to expect. All the time she'd been gone, Two Shot had hung in the distance like a safety net poised to catch her if she fell. It really was like a family. That's why it had hurt so much when they'd been so cold the day before.

But looking at Suze, she knew that like a family, they'd all forgive her eventually.

CHAPTER 35

LANE PULLED INTO THE PARKING GARAGE ACROSS FROM THE Carrigan building, cruising down an empty row to take a space at the end. The garage had been built by the city in some unrealistic fit of optimism during the last boom. The police department used it, so there were half a dozen cop cars parked on one side, but other than that he had his pick.

He strode down the short stretch of sidewalk and through the swinging doors to the Carrigan building. Standing in the elevator, he glanced at his reflection and quickly looked away. He'd made the mistake of gussying up for the visit to Carrigan headquarters, and now he knew where the expression "dressed to kill" came from. His brand-new Wranglers were so stiff he could barely bend his knees, and the bolo tie at his throat was slowly strangling him to death.

He wasn't sure why he'd felt compelled to citify himself that morning. It wasn't like he needed to impress Eric. Eric knew who he was no matter what he wore.

But it was about time he took things more seriously as far as the company was concerned. Sarah had convinced him of that much. He'd always felt a responsibility to the communities surrounding their operations, but he'd believed it was a responsibility to preserve and protect the status quo. Sarah had made him realize that wasn't all they needed to do. He'd been right in his conviction that drilling rigs and trailer towns ruined the landscape. But he hadn't thought about the fact that people might be more than willing to trade their pristine landscape and quaint towns for things that were more essential to survival, like medical care and law enforcement.

The West was going to change. It was his job, and Eric's, to make sure it changed for the better. It had been Sarah's job too, up until the day before. Maybe he could do something about that too.

"Hey, bro." Eric lowered his feet from the desk, where his polished loafers had been crossed casually on the shining wood. "What's with the new duds?" His face changed from mockery to dread in an instant. "Oh, shit. You're looking for Sarah."

"Nope. I heard."

"It wasn't anything personal. I just—she couldn't..." He waved a hand helplessly. "Two Shot's the only game we've got going right now, and she couldn't do us any good there. She—wait. How did you hear?"

"I was there."

"With Sarah?" A smile spread over Eric's face. "I guess she can do one of us some good in Two Shot."

"It wasn't like that."

"Okay. Whatever. But I'll give her a good recommendation wherever she ends up. She's good at what she does—she just can't do it in Two Shot."

"That's between you and her."

"Exactly. So why are you here? Must be serious. You shaved and everything."

"I shave."

"Yeah, once a week, whether you need it or not."

Lane settled into the chair in front of the desk and stretched his legs out. Sitting there with Eric lording it over the big mahogany desk always made him feel like some kind of supplicant. But today, he was just that.

"I want to talk to you about Two Shot."

"Not again," Eric groaned. "Lane, the project's going forward. You can't stop it."

"I'm thinking about a conservation easement." Lane leaned back in his chair and folded his hands over his stomach, smug as if he'd just laid out a winning poker hand. "It won't entirely prevent you from drilling on the ranch, but it'll make it a pain in the ass."

Eric paled. "Great. Do the people of Two Shot know what you're doing to them? Hijacking the jobs and money we bring in?"

"The jobs and money come too late. You bring all those people into those small towns, there's nowhere for them to go. You see it over and over. People slap up substandard buildings to house them. The men come on their own, because their wives won't bring their families to these godforsaken little towns. You need to put some things in place before things get going. And if you do, I'll cancel the easement."

"What kind of things?"

Lane shrugged. "Ask the townspeople. You could get together with all those pillars of the community, just like you were going to have Sarah do. But instead of trying to talk them into giving us free rein, figure out how to help them get grants, loans, that kind of thing. And maybe Carrigan could get things started with a grant of their own."

"You want me to shell out money before we even *start*?"

"Dad would have done it. If he'd have seen Midwest, he'd have wanted to prevent it from happening again."

"So this grant..."

"They need a medical clinic and an ambulance. Right now if something happens at the drilling site you have to drive all the way to Casper. And law enforcement—the place doesn't even have a real police station."

"That's millions of dollars."

"And how much will you take out of the ground?"

Eric was silent.

"Plus when people see what you've done, it'll be that much easier to get going in other places. Responsibility brings rewards. That's what Dad always said."

"Don't bring Dad into this."

"Why not? He's the reason you do all this." Lane gestured around the room. "You're still trying to please him."

Eric scowled. "It's easy for you to make fun of that. You were always getting pats on the back with all your sports stuff."

"He didn't have any respect for that. Not once he figured out that winning at bronc busting didn't translate to winning in business. He'd be proud of you, Eric. Especially if you do this."

Eric moved a couple of pens from one side of his blotter to the other, then back again.

"Look, I'm not here to harangue you. I just wanted to make that suggestion."

Eric huffed out a laugh. "Your suggestions sound a lot like demands."

"Yeah, well, kind of." Lane rose. "You want to drill on the ranch, you need to do something for the town. Otherwise, there's going to be trouble."

"We own those rights." The bravado in Eric's voice clashed with the tempo of his pencil-tapping, which was taking on the frantic urgency of a heavy metal drum solo. "You can't stop us."

"No, but I can make it hell for you to make so much as a tire track on the property. And if you try to get around it, I can make it news."

Eric sighed. "How am I supposed to get all that done? We're an oil company, not a community development company."

"Dunno," Lane said. "You're the business guy. I'm just a dumb cowboy, remember?" He looked up at the ceiling as if searching for answers. "Maybe you need to hire somebody who knows what the town needs. Somebody who lived there."

——◆——

Sarah pulled the Malibu to a stop at the fork in the road and quickly recited the Robert Frost "The Road Not Taken" poem in her head.

No, this wasn't a case of taking the road less traveled; both roads were equally scarred and pitted, so she couldn't even figure out which one that was. This was a matter of taking the right road.

She should go back to the cabin, grab the few belongings she'd left there, and leave. But what she wanted to do was go to the ranch and see Cinn just one more time, maybe even spend the day with him.

It would be a rash, impulsive move, the kind of thing Sarah Landon never did. She'd spent the last ten years building her career by avoiding that kind of self-indulgence. She'd taken the hard road, over and over, denying herself the freedom of turning off her predetermined path. She'd been disciplined and hardworking, responsible and dependable.

And where had it gotten her? To the crossroads of Nowhere Street and Disaster Road. What the hell did it matter which way she turned? Either way, she was screwed.

So she might as well go play with that horse.

She'd have to talk to Trevor first. Yesterday's getting-to-know-you session hadn't required anything but herself and the horse, but to go any further she'd need a halter, a lead, maybe a lunge whip for ground training.

That would mean facing Trevor's teasing, and probably a bunch of questions about Lane. Maybe she should just hunt down the equipment and find the horse. It was wrong, she knew, to just go on and do what you wanted with an animal. But what had Lane said?

He's your horse if you stay.

Well, she was staying, wasn't she? Maybe just for today, but still—that made him hers.

CHAPTER 36

DEEP DOWN, SARAH KNEW SHE WAS BEING FOOLISH. SHE WAS liable to get attached to the horse, and then it would be even harder to leave. The best insurance would be to make plans. That's what she'd done for the past decade: map out a plan of attack and stick with it.

Taking out her cell phone, she dialed Kelsey's number.

"Hi, Kelse?"

"Sarah." Her sister sounded relieved and angry all at once. "Where have you been?"

It was the way she sounded when she couldn't spot Katie on the playground and then the girl popped out of the bushes laughing. When had Kelsey become such a mom? It was like their roles had switched.

"I stayed at the ranch."

"With Lane?"

"No."

"That's too bad. He was nice."

"Yeah, he seems that way, but he's not. Kelsey, he was the one who bought Flash."

"Flash?" Kelsey sounded stunned. "Wow, what a coincidence. That's amazing. Does he still have him?"

"No." Sarah could barely get the words out through clenched teeth. "He bred him, though. He has a colt that—well, it could be the same horse."

"Cool."

"Cool? Is that all you have to say?"

"Yeah. You loved that horse. Isn't it cool to see his baby?"

"Kelsey, he stole Flash, remember? Two thousand dollars. The horse was worth twenty."

"I know, but we had to sell him fast and—well, that's how it worked out. It's not like we could have kept him."

"I could have kept him."

"How? Without Roy…"

"It would have been hard, but I could have done it. I could have taken him to rodeos again, won some prize money."

"How? How would you have gotten him there? Who'd drive the truck? You had to be in the trailer with him or he'd kick it to bits."

Sarah gripped the phone so hard her hand hurt. "Never mind, Kelse."

She didn't need to be reminded that she should have been in that trailer. Instead she'd been putting on mascara. Primping while Roy got killed.

Kelsey knew her so well she could even read her silences. "Sarah, it wasn't your fault."

"It doesn't matter."

"It does to you. I know it does."

"If I'd been there, Roy would be alive."

"No, he…"

"That's not what I called about anyway. I need to tell you something." Damn, this was the hardest phone conversation she'd ever had. "I lost my job."

"Oh, Sarah."

"It'll be okay," Sarah said. "You've got Mike now. He's still working, right? So you and Katie'll be okay?"

"We'll be fine. But it's not all about me, you know." She muttered something Sarah could barely hear. It sounded like "it never was."

"What did you say?"

"I said it never was." Kelsey sounded defiant, as though she was letting loose something she'd kept bottled up a long time. "It was never about me. It was about you needing to be—I don't know. Needing to be needed."

Sarah didn't know how to respond.

"Sorry," Kelsey added. "But that's what Mike said. Look, I'm grateful," Kelsey sounded sullen, "but if you hadn't always been there taking over, I might have listened to his message. I know you were trying to help, but…"

"Kelsey, he left you and you collapsed. What the hell were all those headaches about?"

"They were about being stressed," Kelsey admitted. "You helped, and I appreciate it. But I'm okay now, all right? I don't need help. I can make it on my own." She paused for a moment. "With Mike. I know you think it's wrong to take him back, but the whole thing was mostly a misunderstanding."

"Okay," Sarah said. The phone suddenly seemed heavy in her hand.

"What we need to talk about is you," Kelsey said. "I can't believe you're still harping on the whole deal with Flash. Come on, what's done is done. I'd forgotten all about whoever bought him. I remember you made him into some kind of bogeyman, some evil outside force that ruined our lives. Well, he didn't."

"We lost the ranch, Kelsey."

"We lost it because Roy made bad decisions. He gambled on that horse, and he lost. There was something wrong with Flash, you know? I was scared to death of him."

"I loved him."

"I know you did, but he was screwed up. Nobody could deal with him. So stop blaming everything on somebody who took a load off our hands."

Sarah felt like the air had been sucked out of the car. Her sister blamed Roy for what had happened to them. Roy, who had saved their family and died. Died for her, in a way.

"Look, I have to go." She had no idea where. She wasn't about to ask Kelsey for a place to stay anymore.

She pulled the phone away from her ear and heard her sister

protesting in a tinny, faraway voice. "No, wait. Sarah, we need to talk about this."

"I'm fine."

"No, you're not. Jeez, Sarah, let it go. What are you hanging onto all this stuff for? You have to forgive him." Her tone softened. "You have to forgive yourself. What happened with Flash didn't ruin our lives. It was just the way things went, okay? It wasn't your fault."

"Sure." Sarah tried to sound casual. "I know that."

Kelsey sighed. "So what did you call about?"

"Nothing," Sarah said. "Just letting you know where I am."

"Which is where?"

Sarah looked out the window at the acres of sagebrush stretching from the car, the faint blue mountains in the distance. "The Carrigan ranch," she said. "Or the LT or whatever. I think I might stay here for a while."

She clicked the phone off and eased down the road to the ranch, nursing the Malibu over the ruts and ridges. Going slow wasn't such a bad thing anyway; it gave her time to think.

By the time she reached the ranch, she'd thought, all right. She'd managed to wipe everything Kelsey said out of her mind and focus on the horse ahead of her. Horses had always been like that for her. When you worked with a horse, it was you and the animal. The rest of the world faded away.

Today, that would be a good thing. She shut off the engine and stepped out of the car, breathing in the scent of old wood, hay, and sunshine as she stared out at the complex network of corrals.

Which were empty.

Not only was there no red dun stallion, there were no horses at all.

She strode into the barn and was greeted with a chorus of impatient whinnies. The graceful heads of a dozen quarter horses hung over stall doors at regular intervals down the long wood alleyway, their soft eyes gazing expectantly at her. There was a dull thud as one of the more impatient critters kicked at his stall door.

"Hey, babies, what's wrong? Didn't anybody let you out?" She stopped at the first stall, where a pretty sorrel mare was nosing at the sad remnants of yesterday's grain. "Didn't they feed you?"

"I'm working on it," said a voice from the end of the alley. She squinted into the sunshine streaming in the doorway at the far end of the barn. She could barely make out Trevor's silhouette in the shadowed depths of the barn as he wheeled around with a bucket of grain in his lap. He was dragging a hose as well.

Sarah bent and took the hose, then remembered her manners. "Can I help?" she asked. It looked like he was handling everything okay, but it couldn't be easy.

"Sure. Since my usual helper didn't show up this morning, I was just going to top off the buckets, but they really should be dumped and rinsed. That one especially." He wheeled to the nearest stall and scooped out some grain for the eager occupant. "She's not going out with the others today. She got a good kick from somebody yesterday and her leg swole up."

Sarah looked in at the mare. She did indeed have a swelling on her right front cannon bone. Grabbing the bucket that hung next to the stall door, she turned to Trevor. "What about hay?"

"Sure. A couple flakes each."

He spun to a stop in front of the next stall, which held a gray gelding who was a little on the thin side. "Only two scoops for you, buddy." He turned to Sarah. "This one's a poor keeper, has trouble keeping weight on, so he gets a cup of sweet feed, too."

Sarah reached up to stroke a red dun nose that had poked out of the third stall on the right.

"Cinn," she said. "Good boy."

"That's not Cinn. That's Sonic," Trevor said. "Another son of Flash."

"How many are there?"

"Just the two." He angled her a hopeful glance. "You taking the job?"

"No, I just like horses, and it seems as though you could use the help." She cussed herself mentally even as the words flew out of her mouth. The guy was doing fine. It just seemed like he shouldn't have to handle all this on his own.

"We usually have somebody, but she called in at the last minute. Could you do it just for today? Takes me a while and these guys don't like waiting."

"Who would call in and leave you with everything?"

"Somebody who likes their job at the diner better than working with horses."

Sarah remembered him mentioning a high school girl who'd come to clean the cabin. "Emmy?" she asked.

"That's her. She's a good kid, really. She's just young. Doesn't think."

"She waited on me this morning."

He flashed her a smile. "You went back to Suze's?"

"Sure did."

"Always knew you had spunk. How'd it go?"

"Better."

"Good. It'll keep on getting better, too." He sobered. "You ought to stay, Sarah. Quit that job with Eric and work for us. We've got to find somebody, and frankly, not everybody can handle Lane."

Apparently he didn't know she'd been fired. "Yeah, well, I can't handle Lane either."

"I heard different." The grin was back. "But seriously, we need some help. Emmy won't do it because she doesn't want to do ranch work. Only reason she took the part-time position was to make money. I think she's kind of scared of the horses, and let me tell you, that girl is clumsy with a capital C. She manages to feed the horses a little grain, but mostly she spills it."

Sarah smiled.

"It is kind of funny sometimes, but not today. I guess she thought Lane was still going to be here today." He sighed. "I thought he was going to be around too. He said he was getting off the road for a week or two, and then he left first thing this morning."

So Lane hadn't planned on leaving. He'd done it for her, and now Trevor had to deal with the fallout.

"Well, I'll help for today," she said, gathering another bucket. "Where's the sweet feed?"

<center>~~~</center>

Sarah stabbed the manure fork into the ground and watched the horses milling in the corrals. The smile on her lips felt strained, as if she hadn't used those muscles for a while, but she felt genuinely happy for the first time in weeks—maybe months. There were a few new foals in the pens, spring babies who'd just passed the gangly, wobbly stage and were gallivanting about while their mommas watched indulgently. An older mare stood in the shade next to the barn, one leg cocked, eyes closed as she simply enjoyed the sunshiny day. Sarah felt herself relax too, picking up on the mare's calm. That feeling of peace hadn't been there for a long time. Once in a while her conversation with Kelsey crept into the back of her mind, but she shook it off and kept working.

She'd spent the morning feeding horses and turning them out, following Trevor's directions as to what horse went where. Then she'd spent an hour mucking stalls, forking the leavings into a rusty old trailer that she'd hauled out to the manure pile with an ancient, wheezing tractor. She'd forked it all back out again until beads of sweat rolled down her back, prickling the skin between her shoulder blades, and she was pretty sure she'd streaked her face with grime from wiping off the sweat. Her hair hung lank and damp over her forehead. She hadn't felt this good in years.

She'd forgotten how therapeutic hard work could be. You didn't have to think or strategize when you cleaned stalls; you could just shut down your mind and shovel.

What if this was her job? What if she went to a place like this every day instead of an office? She felt like herself here, not like an imposter. Maybe Lane was right and she needed to find her old self again.

But she couldn't do it here, with the man who bought Flash. Could she?

Maybe Kelsey had a point. Maybe she should stop blaming "the buyer" for all that had happened to her family. Now that she'd put a face on the shadowy figure who'd haunted her all these years, he seemed a whole lot less demonic.

But if she stopped blaming him, she'd have to blame herself. Because it wasn't Roy's mistake that had cost her family everything. It was her vanity that had cost Roy his life, and her failure that had lost Flash.

She grabbed a halter from a nail on the wall and threaded her way through the corrals, following the path pounded in the dirt. Horses lifted their heads as she passed, watching her briefly, then returning to their grazing. When she reached the corner of the barn, she looked at the round pen and smiled.

Cinnamon Chrome. He was three years old, barely started. And he was waiting for her.

As she approached, the horse jerked his head up and snorted, seeming to react to something inside the pen. Maybe a leaf had flipped up in the breeze, or a shadow shifted and spooked him. He'd seemed like a calm boy yesterday, but something was definitely setting him off. As she watched, he broke into a trot and moved past the gate out of sight. She watched him circle past it two more times before she got close enough to see what was happening.

The horse was loping in a circle around the pen, and at the center of the circle was Trevor. He spun his chair nimbly with one hand so he could keep the horse running. As Sarah stepped up to the gate, he gave her a grin.

"Lane said you worked this guy a little yesterday. He seemed to have some doubts you'd keep it going, so I figured I'd come out and make sure he didn't forget what he learned." He edged the chair to the right and Flash broke into a lope. "Seems like he's doing good. Must be somethin' to see after what happened with Flash, huh?"

"I don't want to talk about it." Hearing Trevor mention Flash again felt like being punched in the gut. She started to back out of the gate, but he turned the chair to face her.

"You can pretend it didn't happen if you want." His tone was casual and conversational. Did he not know what he was doing to her? Even the horse had paused, one front foot in the air, stunned by the tension in the air.

"I probably wouldn't talk much about my issues either if I didn't have to," Trevor continued. Obviously, he knew—but he wasn't going to stop. "Sometimes I think it's lucky for me my scars are on the outside. People ask, I tell, and in the long run I feel a lot better for letting it out." He smacked his chest twice with his fist. "You keep it in here, it'll either eat you up or turn you hard."

She swung through the gate and closed it.

"Hey, wait. Can you hold that for me?"

She couldn't say no. Cinn was still poised and ready to run at the slightest movement, but when Trevor wheeled through the gate the horse bent to crop a few strands of grass at the edge of the ring.

"I've got some stuff to do in the house." He nodded toward the halter. "See if you can get that on him and lunge him a little. But don't work him too long. You know two twenty-minute sessions'll get you a lot farther than one long one, right?"

"Right."

"And when you're done, go ride that chestnut if you want." He nodded toward a muscular gelding in a nearby corral. "He's got a big motor, needs to be loped out every day. When you're done with that, stop up to the house for a bite of lunch and I'll give you more. Work's never-ending around here."

She eyed him a moment, thinking she'd say no. She'd planned to just visit Cinn and go. But there was a day's honest work to be done, and in her heart she wanted to do it.

She wasn't sure she could. But she wanted to.

She nodded, and he grinned. "Enjoy your second chance," he said.

CHAPTER 37

SARAH TIGHTENED THE CINCH ON THE WESTERN SADDLE she'd put on the chestnut gelding, then grabbed the horn and pulled it to one side, then the other. Solid. She'd been amazed at how swift and sure the process had felt, as if she'd been doing it for years.

She had done it for years, but those years were a long time ago.

Pulling out a stirrup, she measured it against the length of her arm. Yup, she had it right. There was no excuse to put off the next step.

The horse turned and watched her as she fussed with the cinch again. He seemed to be wondering why she kept tugging and adjusting everything, why she didn't just get on and ride already.

She was wondering too. Sure, it had been a long time. She hadn't really been lying when she'd told Lane she was afraid of horses. But after the session with Cinn, she'd hoped she might be over it.

Lifting the reins from the horse's neck, she looped them in one hand while she set her foot in the stirrup. Grabbing the saddle, she bounced on her right foot like she had so many times before. Before...

Don't think about it. Just ride.

The horse turned his head slightly and rolled back an eye to watch her as she bounced again. Flash used to do that. He'd done that the last time she'd seen him, looked back at her with his eye rolling, and then...

She took her toe out of the stirrup and held onto the saddle, resting her forehead on the sun-warmed leather. She could do this. She could. She remembered her sister's words.

Jeez, Sarah, let it go. What are you hanging onto all this stuff for?

"Sorry, boy," she said to the horse. He nodded once as if he understood, or maybe he was just trying to ease the pressure of the reins. She fed out a little more and prepared to mount again. As she shifted her weight to the stirrup, the horse stamped one hind hoof. Like Flash. He'd been impatient sometimes, antsy. She felt her heart rate amp up and knew she had to calm herself before she could ride.

She pulled on the stirrup leather, opening the buckle so she'd have something to do if Trevor came out. She'd tell him she'd gotten the length wrong. She'd have to tell him something, because she couldn't tell him she was unable to ride.

Maybe if she walked the horse a while she could visualize the ride. Roy had taught her to do that over and over whenever she'd come up against a problem—a tendency to run at the barrels too hard, or a subconscious ill-timed tug on the reins. He'd make her walk the course, picturing herself on horseback, doing it right. It helped. When she'd mounted again, the problem would be gone.

She lifted the reins over the horse's head and led him along the fence. The horse moved at a level, easy pace. He was clearly a cooperative animal, a gentle soul. She pictured herself on his back, moving easily, her body in sync with his. The picture came easily and she wanted to mount up right there, but she forced herself to finish a full circuit of the arena.

She stopped by the gate and set her foot in the stirrup.

You can do it.

The horse tossed his head, picking up on her tension, and lifted one front foot, then the other, rearing up slightly on his back legs. He settled but the image was stuck in her head, Flash dancing, rearing, almost pulling her arm off.

She shook her head, bringing herself back to the present, and rested her head against the horse to take a few long breaths. Then she set about the work of unsaddling the horse just as she'd unsaddled Flash all those years ago. It was bright daylight now, not moonlight, but the feeling was the same.

Defeat.

She still couldn't ride. In all the years that had passed since that dark night with Flash, she'd been right not to try. The fear was too strong, the memories too vivid. It was time to put the horse away and then go talk to Trevor. She'd had her second chance, and she couldn't take it.

She was heading for the house when a pickup pulled into the turnout in front of the barn. "Hemsworth Farriery," it read. "Custom Shoeing, 20 years experience."

The guy who stepped out of the truck looked like he must have started shoeing horses at age ten in order to get that much experience under his worn leather belt. He was short but broad in the shoulders with impossibly muscular arms. The belt encircled a slim waist and almost bony hips, but his leg muscles swelled under his worn jeans. If she hadn't known the kind of workout the art of farriery imposed on its practitioners, she would have thought he was some kind of obsessive gym rat.

As he approached, she realized his dark hair was shot with gray and his face was lined from sun exposure, like Lane's and so many other ranchers'. Men were lucky. Up to middle age, wrinkles only made them rugged, while the shoe-leather look just didn't work for women.

"Trevor finally hire a new hand?" The man stuck out his hand. "Dan Hemsworth," he said. "Here to check a few feet."

"My name's Sarah. Who do you need to work on?" Sarah decided she'd avoid the question about hiring. She'd just help the guy, and then she'd go talk to Trevor. Find out when Lane was coming back. She'd have to stay until he returned. She couldn't leave Trevor dependent on Emmy. So in a way, she was a new hand—a temporary one. One who couldn't ride, but hopefully nobody needed to know that. Nobody but Trevor. She knew he wouldn't let it go.

The farrier grabbed a clipboard from a toolbox in the back of the pickup. "I need Tally, Ollie, and Trip," he said.

She realized she had no idea of the names of most of the horses. She'd called all the geldings "boy" and "buddy" in her head while she'd worked, the mares "girl" and "baby."

He must have seen her confusion. "First day?"

She nodded. For some reason, she was reluctant to explain that she was just a temp. Less than a temp, really. What did you call a stable hand who couldn't ride?

"Let's go in and I'll show you the ones I need," he said.

He pointed out the horses and she led them out one by one. He worked in the alley, cross-tying the horses back near the sliding doors. The late-afternoon sunlight slanted in and bathed man and horses in golden light as he bent over and held their feet upraised between his muscular thighs, shaping their hooves, adjusting their shoes, and hammering out new ones where needed.

"I'd better take a look at Cinn too," he said when he'd finished the third horse. "Gotta keep tabs on him. Guess they never did figure out what caused his sire's problems, but I'm damn sure not going to let it happen to him."

Despite the sunshine, Sarah felt a sudden chill. "What problems?"

The man shrugged his broad shoulders. "Carrigan didn't know. Somewhere along the way the horse had probably fallen or something. There were no outward signs 'cept for the way he kicked and bucked. Took a lot of tests to find the problem, but Lane doesn't give up, you know? He wants something, he sticks, like he sticks to a bull."

Sarah nodded. Lane was persistent. He'd stuck with her, and she hadn't made it easy.

"So what was wrong with him?"

"Pinched nerve in his neck." He led the gelding back to his stall and steered him inside, then unbuckled the halter and lifted it off his head. "You wouldn't have ever guessed it. Most horses would be short-strided, show it in their gait. But it's instinct for animals to hide their pain, and that horse was strong enough to keep it covered up. Lane had a hell of a time figuring out what was wrong with him, but he just kept trying." He stroked the horse's nose with the effortless camaraderie of a true horseman as he exited the stall, latching the gate behind him. "It's just lucky that animal had a buyer who could afford to fix him," he said. "By the time they got it figured out, I think Carrigan had spent three times what the animal was worth."

"What all did he do?"

The farrier shook his head. "A lot more than most people would have. He hauled that horse all the way down to the vet school at Colorado State, and let me tell you, that was no small feat. Never saw a horse that hated trailers the way that one did."

They were both silent for a moment. Sarah didn't know what the farrier was thinking about, but she was thinking of Flash and the reason for his fear of trailers.

"So the vet figured out the problem?" she finally asked.

"After a few thousand dollars in tests. That horse spent almost six months there. Once they figured out what it was, there was surgery, recovery, therapy—for a while they had him swimming every day."

Sarah sat down on a bale of hay, her legs weak. "It must have cost a fortune," she muttered.

She was talking more to herself than to the farrier, but he was a friendly guy and kept on talking. "Sure did. Just figuring it out, let alone fixing it." He shoved his hands in his pockets and leaned against the stall door. "Guess the folks that sold him didn't know. Thought the horse was just difficult, and he ran for 'em anyway. Daughter was a barrel racer. Let me tell you, that animal had heart. To get through the pain he was suffering and make those turns—it must have hurt like hell. That horse was a goddamn hero."

Sarah jerked to her feet, swallowing hard as she steadied herself against the wall. "I need to go get Trevor for you. He'll write you a check or whatever."

The farrier waved her away. "No need. Got a contract, so Lane just pays me monthly. Where's Cinn hanging out today?"

She wanted to get out of there more than she'd ever wanted out of anywhere. She needed to sit somewhere quiet and process the information about Flash. Lane was no villain. Really, she was the bad guy in this story.

Because she'd tortured the horse she loved, tortured him every day. She'd thought she was being patient, working through what she and Roy had believed were psychological issues. They'd had him checked, X-rayed, analyzed—nobody had been able to find anything wrong.

To get through the pain he was suffering and run anyway…that horse was a goddamn hero.

Lane had been the best thing that ever happened to Flash. He'd saved him. Given him the gift of a few pain-free years at the end of his life.

She led the farrier out of the cool barn and over to the sun-baked corral where she'd left Cinn. She could see Flash in the glowing red of his coat, the graceful curve of his back, the breadth of his chest and the elegant beauty of his head.

"How long did Flash live after the surgery?"

"Couple years. Long enough to enjoy being nothing but a stud for a while." The farrier laughed. "He got the life he deserved after all, even if it was only for a while. Once he recovered from the surgery, he was a sweetheart. Everybody's favorite. Cinn's got the same personality."

Sarah watched him slip a halter over the horse's head and clip on a lead rope. As he led the stallion back to the barn, the world blurred in front of her, the sharp stems of grass blending into patches of yellow light and blue shadow, the sun blurring to a watercolor glow, the corral fences becoming sharp dark strokes against the light. She tripped over a tussock of grass and realized she'd veered off the path.

"You okay?" the farrier asked.

"Fine," she said. "I just need to go, um, up to the hayloft. I left something up there. You got everything you need?"

He nodded as the horse's hooves hit the wood of the barn floor. "Sure," he said. "Take your time."

She climbed the rickety ladder to the loft like demons were nipping at her heels. She hadn't left anything up there. She hadn't even been up there yet—but she needed to be alone and the loft at her stepfather's ranch had always been her thinking place. Hoisting herself up from the ladder, she made her way through a narrow space between stacks of hay and straw and finally sat down on a bale positioned near the hay door. Looking out, she could see the drive curving away, the crooked fence line strung beside it. The gigantic house was behind the barn, so from here it looked like any other ranch—a remote outpost on the plains, just one more of the many efforts to fence and tame the West. The grass was scrubby and scattered with sage and rocks, the trees sparse and tortured by the wind. Far beyond the fence posts, a rock outcropping reared up, bronzed by the sun against the darkening sky.

The familiar scent of hay, straw, and dust carried her back to the past. The day they'd packed up and left, relinquishing the house and empty barn to the bank, she'd gone up and sat in the hayloft. She hadn't mourned that day. She hadn't cried. She'd just been angry, cursing in her head over and over the man who'd bought Flash. She'd spent her whole life blaming everything that went wrong on that one man, as if he'd been a seed of trouble that grew roots and shoots that strangled every aspect of her life.

Her mother's retreat from life and the way she'd crawled into a bottle and stayed there. Kelsey's pregnancy and rushed marriage, her outsized determination to build a happy home. Sarah's own push for safety and security, the years she'd spent at school struggling to master her new world—she'd blamed it all on the buyer. He was like a bogeyman, hiding in every corner, darkening every incident with his ominous shadow.

And he didn't exist. Lane was no monster. He hadn't stolen her horse; he'd saved him.

She plucked a piece of straw from the bale and stared down at it. Why hadn't he told her about Flash's problems?

She remembered the way he'd cut off the conversation about the horse, turned away, and left. She'd had the sense he was about to say something and then thought better of it—and now she knew he'd let the chance to defend himself pass. The man who always wanted to win had thrown the game rather than tell her that her troubles weren't the fault of some outside force. There was no one left to hate but herself.

Lane seemed so rough on the outside, with his jokes and insults, his endless teasing—but somehow, in a very short time, he'd come to understand her like no one else. He'd seen all her flaws, her pride and stubbornness, her determination to hold onto the grudges that defined her past, present, and future, and he'd chosen to walk away and give her time, rather than ripping away the shield she'd carried all these years. He was willing to be the bad guy and bear the blame if it helped her heal from the pain of her past.

Resting her elbows on her knees, she lowered her head into her hands and let the tears fall.

Twenty minutes later, the farrier shouted out a goodbye. She answered in a cracked, quavering voice, then waved from the hay door as he climbed into his truck and drove away. She watched until the plume of dust kicked up from the truck faded away, and then she let herself cry some more.

CHAPTER 38

LANE DUG HIS HEELS INTO THE SIDE OF A BLACK-SPECKLED BULL named Dalmatian and tensed to give the nod. Shifting his weight, he tightened the rope wrapped around his riding glove, then reached up and shoved his hat down hard. The arena was clear, the crowd hushed, the clowns and pickup men standing off to the side. If only he could clear his mind and quiet the thoughts whirling through his brain.

He stared down at the bull's blunt horns, but all he could see was Sarah. That would be all right if he could see her naked, but the pictures that kept flashing through his mind were surprisingly tame. Her flushed embarrassment after he'd kissed her. Her serious, sedate dance with the horse when she didn't know he was watching. Her face, bright with fury when she'd confronted him about Flash.

He worked his fingers deeper into the glove and tugged himself closer to the bull's broad shoulders. He just didn't feel right. Maybe if he rewrapped his hand. He unwound the rosined rope and carefully laced it around his hand, tight but not too tight, staring down at the process but still thinking about Flash.

What had happened to the stallion wasn't Roy Price's fault, but it had been a mistake to work the horse like he did. And though Lane managed to keep the animal comfortable, he couldn't be ridden. His potential never would have paid off. Roy had gone out on a limb buying the horse, and sooner or later, that limb would have come crashing down.

But it seemed like the one good thing Sarah had held onto all her life was her unshakable belief in her stepfather. She probably had great memories of Flash too, since she'd ridden him successfully on the barrel racing circuit. If he told her what had been wrong with the horse, she'd be horrified to learn she'd put the animal through excruciating pain.

If hating Lane helped her, he'd let her do it. That way she'd keep believing in her father and in herself. He was doing the right thing.

It took him a half second to realize he'd nodded his head at the thought and the cowboy by the gate had taken it as a signal. The iron bars swung aside and Dalmatian leapt for the opening, rearing up so high he almost dumped Lane off the back.

Damn. He wasn't ready on the rope. He hadn't settled into his seat. Worst of all, he wasn't ready mentally. He felt his legs sliding backward. The rope burned his palm as it slid through his grip, twisting away. For a long, suspended second he looked down from the top of his arc and saw the bull kicking up dust, the wide-eyed wonder of the cowboy at the gate watching him fly up and away, and the faces of the crowd, a blur of color and light, tracing his descent.

The arena fence rose to meet him, the metal bars speeding closer, closer—and then a shuddering clang reverberated through every bone in his body. Stars exploded inside his head and faded to a deep, black darkness and the last thing he knew was pain.

By the time she trudged up the wheelchair ramp to the house, Sarah was a mess. Her boots were dusty, her hair flecked with hay. She'd splashed her face over and over with cold water from the spigot in the barn, and though it had washed away the swelling from her tears, it had left her face ruddy and pink.

She needed to talk to Trevor and find out where Lane was so she could tell him she knew she'd misjudged him. Hell, she'd misjudged her whole life, and she was ready to start over. She'd start by apologizing to Lane.

Not that it would make much difference. She'd shown her worst side to him. He knew she was angry and stubborn and hopelessly deluded. He knew the image she'd presented to the world was a false front, like a grand facade on the street side of a rickety, tumbledown shack. She'd just as soon never face him again.

But she needed to bite the bullet and tell him he was right. She hadn't been giving her true self a chance. If she could, she'd take the job he'd offered, but she could hardly work as a stable hand when she couldn't bring herself to get on a horse. Her riding days were over. She'd proven that this morning.

It was a shame, because she'd come to another conclusion during her long, hay-scented crying jag. Lane had been right when he'd said Two Shot made her what she was today. The specter of her past had always urged her on like a trainer with a lunge whip, pushing her to try harder. If she could stay, she could somehow pay the town back, make amends. But with no job, there was no future for her in Two Shot.

Halfway up the wheelchair ramp to the house, she almost turned around. What if she went back to the barn and tried again? Maybe a different horse would help. But those painful memories and the heart-pounding panic that accompanied them weren't something she could face again.

Trevor was just hanging up the phone when she stepped into the kitchen. She'd kicked her boots off on the porch, so he didn't hear her stocking feet on the hardwood floor.

"Is he conscious?" he was asking.

Sarah stopped. His tone was hushed, as different from his usual bantering tone as it could be. Dread coiled in her stomach and she reached out and touched a hand to the counter to keep her balance.

"Okay," he said. "Thanks." He turned and caught sight of Sarah. "I'll send somebody right over."

He clicked the phone off and set it on the counter, then lowered his head and closed his eyes as if marshaling all his strength.

"Lane's hurt," he said. "Bucked into the fence."

Sarah felt heat behind her eyes. "Is he okay?"

"Dunno." Trevor's face flushed and his lips whitened, as if he was holding back emotion. "It's a head injury. They're working on him, but he's unconscious."

She pictured him in an ambulance and felt her lungs squeeze shut. The thought brought back the pictures she'd been trying to avoid—a man killed by an animal. Roy in the driveway, Roy in the ambulance, his ruddy skin gray and lifeless.

No. Lane Carrigan was upright and vital and most of all strong. He couldn't end up that way. She couldn't let the fate that had taken away Roy steal the only other man she'd ever—loved?

That couldn't be right. Hell, she wasn't even capable of love. Lane had given her every reason to love and trust him, and she'd still blamed him for her reception in Two Shot. Blamed him for what had happened to her family.

"Oh, God," she said to Trevor. "When he left—I said terrible things to him. I need to get to him. I need to tell him I didn't mean it."

She hated herself even as she said the words. Trevor was losing his best friend, and all she could think of was herself. But she couldn't stop replaying their parting in her head. She'd told Lane to hit the road and he'd walked away without defending himself, sparing her the pain of knowing the truth.

She needed to tell him she knew about Flash, and that she was sorry. Picturing him lying in the dirt of the arena, hurt and helpless, she knew there was one more truth she needed to face. One more puzzle piece in her future she needed to slide into place.

She loved Lane Carrigan. He couldn't possibly love her back—not after how she'd behaved. Even a good man had his limits. But she needed to tell him.

"Where is he?" she asked.

"Casper," he said.

"Casper? Where was the rodeo?"

"Humboldt."

"But…" She paused, stunned. "He said he was going away. Staying somewhere else."

"Yeah, he said he was going to stay in the trailer, then leave for Amarillo tomorrow or the next day."

So he'd had nowhere to go. He could have stayed at the ranch.

"Why?"

The minute she asked the question, she prayed Trevor didn't know the answer. Hopefully Lane hadn't told Trev she was a basket case, that she was delusional, that she blamed him for all her problems and he was afraid to be alone in the house with a crazy woman. Because that was the only reason he would have stayed in the cramped trailer instead of his own cozy Love Nest.

"Dunno." Trevor shrugged and spun the chair away from the counter.

Sarah breathed a sigh of relief. One thing about rodeo cowboys—they were not given to introspection. It was a quality she'd often criticized, but right now she was grateful for it.

"Can you drive the van?" Trevor held up his hand. It was shaking like an aspen leaf in a high breeze.

"Sure." She was shaking a little herself, but Trevor didn't need to know that.

Lane did, though. Lane needed to know everything.

She was through with keeping secrets.

CHAPTER 39

LANE BLINKED, SQUINTING HIS EYES AGAINST A GLARING WHITE light. He'd expected to wake up in the arena, possibly to an enormous hoof descending on his head or a high-speed view of the crowd flashing by as he hurtled through the air. But all he saw was light shimmering around him, plus occasional shadows, blurred at the edges, that came and went.

The light. He'd heard about that. It meant he was dying. How the hell had that happened? He pondered that question for a while, remembering the bull, the flight through the air, and the metal fence post. Oh, yeah.

He was supposed to go toward the light, right? But he couldn't even move. Come to think of it, most people couldn't move when they were dying, so how the hell were you supposed to go toward anything? He tensed his muscles, but all that did was make his ribs hurt. It got the shadows moving, though. They flashed in and out of sight, making a constant and incomprehensible noise, like quacking ducks.

If heaven was full of ducks, he was in trouble. About his only contact with a duck had been shooting one on a hunting trip in 1998. He'd fed some once too, when he was a kid, but he doubted a few chunks of bread tossed into a scummy pond would offset cold-blooded duck murder. If ducks controlled the pearly gates, he was out of luck and headed for hell.

Oh, well. He'd never really expected to make the cut for heaven anyway. Too much carousing. Too many women.

Still, he'd done a few good things in his life. He'd done his best to make it up to Trevor for the mistake he'd made that night. He'd insulted the guy the entire time, but that was just to make everybody feel more comfortable.

And he'd helped a few horses. Flash, especially. If he did nothing else in his life, he'd always be proud he'd given that horse a chance to escape the pain he'd suffered so long.

And that brought him to Sarah. Had he helped her? Probably not. He'd done his best, but she was still deluding herself, believing in her stepfather and blaming Lane for all her family's troubles. She didn't realize families had troubles no matter what the circumstances.

Look at his own family. His father, who had died stern and disapproving even though a stroke had robbed him of the ability to express his disappointment in his sons. His brother, driving the company onward as it ate up land and sucked out communities' souls along with the precious oil beneath them.

But not this time. He'd prevented that from happening to Two Shot. He was pretty sure he'd convinced his brother that taking responsibility for the community would have earned their father's approval. And if that didn't work, he'd had paperwork done up on the conservation easement, and Trevor didn't know it yet but he had power of attorney if anything happened to Lane.

Anything like this.

He closed his eyes and listened to the quacking of the ducks for a while. They sounded pretty riled up. And they were pretty big ducks. One in particular loomed over him. He felt it brush against his hand, and then something stroked his face. A feather? A wingtip? Man, he was in trouble.

The duck moved away and the light hit his eyes like a laser, sending a sharp, shooting pain straight to the back of his head. He closed his eyes and tensed. It was like he'd been shot. Damn, he shouldn't have done that to a poor innocent duck. It hadn't even been good eating. The thing was tough as an old saddle and tasted like a bad chicken gone worse.

The wingtip brushed his face again and he opened his eyes. Things were starting to come into focus now. The illumination he'd taken for the light at the end of the tunnel to heaven was actually just a big lighted square in one of those cheap drop ceilings. The shadows weren't ducks; they were people. Thank God. He wasn't dead. He might have come close—but he was alive and clearly in the hospital.

He hadn't died; he'd just been delusional. And that meant he had a second chance at life.

What was he going to do with it?

Well, first of all, he'd be nicer to ducks. Maybe he could dig a pond at the ranch, make a little duck country club for them. He pictured a duck lounging by a swimming pool on a duck-sized chaise lounge with an umbrella drink in his hand and almost laughed.

"Did he just laugh?" someone asked. It was a woman's voice, probably a nurse. It reminded him of Sarah, but no way would Sarah be here. Sarah hated him now.

The sharp pain came again, but this time it hit his heart.

"I think he did laugh," said a low, masculine voice. "But did you see him flinch?"

He knew that voice. It was Trevor. If Trevor had set foot in a hospital, Lane had to be in pretty bad shape.

He squinted, struggling to make out the shapes that had blurred into shadows again. He wanted to see that nurse. She really sounded a lot like Sarah. Maybe it was. Maybe...

No, it couldn't be. If he was lucky, Sarah was still at the ranch finding the woman she was meant to be. He was hoping to have one more shot at redemption before she gave up on him completely.

But there was no way she'd come running if he got hurt. She still thought she could blame everything that ever happened to her on one single bad guy, and the bad guy was him.

That was the other thing he'd do with his second chance. It had been wrong to let her go on believing something from outside yourself could destroy your whole life. He didn't mind playing the bad guy if she needed one, but realizing she was in control of her own life would set her free. Nobody could take success away from her if she was true to herself.

That's what he'd tell her, but he'd find a way to tell it that sounded a little less corny.

The edges of the shadows sharpened and for a second he thought he could see, but then he realized he was still hallucinating. He had to be, because the woman sitting beside him really was Sarah—but she was dressed in gloriously dirty cowgirl clothes. She was the Sarah he'd been hoping to find, her hair windblown and tangled with little bits of straw dangling here and there. And she wasn't wearing a shred of makeup. Her face was pink and unadorned except for a smudge of mud across her forehead.

She looked like a girl from Two Shot, Wyoming, like a woman who'd shed those prim little suits and forbidding frowns forever. She looked like a woman who held a horse and pressed her cheek against its neck, the woman who kicked rocks and danced in worn-out boots, a woman who made love in the bed of a pickup in the moonlight, a woman who danced the simple, timeless dance of trust with a horse when she thought nobody was looking.

The curtain's metal rings zinged across the rod as a nurse whipped it back.

"Looks like he'll be okay," she said. "He'll have one heck of a headache, and he might not be much use for a few days, but tests show no real damage."

Her voice didn't sound one bit like Sarah's. In fact, if he couldn't see her, he'd think he'd been right about the ducks. But Sarah was there, standing beside the cot, and Trevor was sitting in his wheelchair in a corner of the cubicle, his eyes suspiciously bright.

"He was never any use anyway. Can we take him home?"

"Soon as he's okay to get up."

Sarah—it really was Sarah—smiled at him and he almost thought he was dying again, she glowed so bright. The last time he'd had a wreck he'd seen her holding that horse and he'd thought she was some sweet equestrian angel come to take him away. Now he knew she was no angel.

But if she'd just drop her guard she'd be the kind of woman he needed. He reached out a hand and brushed a strand of hair away from her face. She reached up at the same time and he trapped her hand in his. He knew what they meant now when they said you'd been struck by Cupid's arrow. He felt like that duck, downed by a single shot.

"It's you," he said.

"Yeah." She even talked like a small-town girl now. Maybe he really had died and gone to heaven.

"No, I mean, it's really you."

She laughed and spread her arms. "That's for sure. Complete and unadulterated. Unbathed, too. Sorry. I was playing with your horses all day."

Playing. That's just what he'd hoped she'd do.

"Don't be sorry." He squeezed her hand and felt his own heart expand in response. "This is the way I love you."

The smile faded. "You don't mean that."

"Sure I do." He'd vowed to tell her the truth, and there it was. Something in her heart called to his, and no matter who she decided to be from here on out, he'd always love her. "I know you don't want to hear it. I know you think I took your life away from you. But Sarah, I didn't. I…"

"I know." Her eyes brightened with unshed tears and she looked even more like an angel as she wrapped her other hand around his. "I know what happened with Flash. I know you helped him, and you didn't steal him. You saved him." Her voice dropped to a whisper. "I think you might have saved me too."

He didn't know what to say to that, so he figured he'd talk about the horse. He suspected the two of them would do that a lot if they ended up together, and that was fine with him. "I was lucky. I could afford the best vets, the best tests to find out what was wrong. You would have done the same thing."

"I know. You're right." She smiled and she seemed okay now, the hoarseness gone from her voice. "We ran up one heck of a vet bill trying to figure it out. But then we had to give up and work around it."

A single tear escaped her eye, flowing in a slow, crooked line down her cheek. "He suffered. I feel so bad."

"You couldn't know."

"It's just—if a horse is hurting, he's supposed to limp. It should show in his gait. Flash never showed it."

"He just powered through it. He never stopped trying, and he wouldn't admit to weakness." He reached up and wiped the tear away with the pad of his thumb. "He was a lot like you. You were hurt, and you just powered through it."

"I did it all wrong."

"You did your best, and it was damn good. You took care of your sister, and you built yourself a future."

"Which came crumbling down when your brother fired me."

"It didn't fall down. It just changed." He reached up and stroked her jawline and she turned her head, rubbing her cheek on his hand like a cat. He cupped it, loving the feel of her warm skin against his palm, and watched her close her eyes. She might be tough, she might be hard as nails when she needed to be, but there was a sweetness at the core of her that he wanted to cherish. Sarah would always take care of herself, but he'd be there for her when things went wrong. Always.

"You know you have a future on the ranch if you want it," he said.

She pulled away and shook her head. "I can't, Lane. I just— can't." A shadow crossed her face and he knew there was still some-thing holding her back. "But whatever I do from here, wherever I go, you're part of it." A tear welled up in the corner of one eye and she swiped it away. "I guess I always knew it. Dangit, remember that first day you came to the office? I knew you could see right through me. At first I thought it was a sex thing, but it was more." She bit her lip. "A lot more."

She bent down and brushed his lips with hers. It felt so good he tried to rise, but that pain shot through his head again and he couldn't. But she bent again, and this time it was more than a brush. She kissed him with all the passion and power he'd sensed was hiding behind the mask. When she finally drew away, her face was flushed.

"I love you, princess," he said.

"Don't call me that." She said it reflexively, but this time she said it with a smile. "I'm not like that. I'm not precious and prim and spoiled like a princess. I'm real, and I could kick your butt if I wanted to."

"I know that. I always did," he said. "I'm just glad you figured it out too."

CHAPTER 40

Sarah watched Lane muscle a wheelbarrow full of hay bales into the shed that housed some of his older mares. As far as she could tell he never got rid of a horse once he'd bought it, no matter how difficult, elderly, or infirm the animal was.

She adjusted her new straw hat, which was already smushed and dirty from hard work. It was time to stop focusing on horse crap and start straightening out a few things. She and Lane had spent about a quarter of their time in the barn, a quarter in town, and a generous, heavenly half in the loft of the Love Nest.

But neither one had wanted to bring up the future.

"We need to talk," she said.

"I hate it when you threaten me," he said, turning away from the mare. "That's just mean."

"Lane, I'm serious."

He turned back to the mare. "That's even worse."

She tugged on his shirtsleeve and he turned to face her. After all the time they'd spent together over the past week, she should have been used to him—but the light of his smile still made her take a step back.

And then a step forward.

This was where they both belonged. Standing in the sun-streaked grass, breathing in the clean summer air, and kissing like their lives depended on it. She moved her hands up his chest, then down, savoring the strong, square strength of him. When she swept her hands down his sides to his back, he shuddered and she felt a thrill of triumph.

But this wasn't talking. And talking was what they needed to do.

He must have felt her stiffen because he stopped and looked in her eyes. "Here? Now? Do we have to?"

"Yes." She took his hand and led him over to the shady side of the shed, where a few oblong hay bales rested against the wall.

"You're not going to tell me you're leaving, are you?" He shot her a mock stern glare. "Don't tell me I have to hog-tie you in the barn to keep you."

"No." She put a hand on his knee. "I'm not leaving."

"But something's changing. You're looking at me like you feel sorry for me."

"I know we work well together, Lane, and I think the last day or two you've just assumed I'm going to work for you."

"Honey, the last day or two I've just assumed you're going to marry me."

She widened her eyes, stunned.

"Oops." He slid off the hay bale and suddenly he was kneeling at her feet like a prince in a fairy tale. He reached for her hands, but she tugged them away. What the hell was he doing? Proposing? Had he said "marry me"?

She wasn't ready for this.

"Lane…"

"Shh. I need to think. I was going to write a little speech, but now I spilled the beans and I'm going to have to think of it on the fly."

"Lane, it's okay. You can work on the speech later."

"Is that a yes?" His smile was boyish and eager. Hell, she could just say yes, tumble off the hay bale into his arms, and get back to that kiss. She could marry him and stop worrying about everything. She even had a job—a job she could actually do.

Which was what she needed to talk to him about.

"Can we put off the personal decisions for now? I need to talk to you about work."

"Okay. Let me tell you about the benefits we offer here at the LT Ranch." He lowered his voice. "The first one is sex on demand."

He looked so serious she had to laugh. "Lane, I get that anyway."

"True. But if you work for me, it'll be permanent. Of course, if you marry me..."

"Lane. I'm serious."

"I know. We're going to have to work on that."

"I got a job."

The playful light left his face and he rose. Sometimes she forgot how beat up he'd been by that last bull. He was still moving slowly, clearly feeling the aches and pains.

"A job."

She took a deep breath. "With your brother."

He smiled, but it was clearly an effort. "He hired you back?"

She took a step back and held out her arms. "Meet the new Executive Director of Community Development for the Carrigan Corporation."

He groaned. "I didn't see this coming."

"Oh, come on." She smacked his arm. "You're the reason the job even exists."

"And you're taking it."

"I already did." She grinned. "It's exactly what I need."

—⁓—

Lane felt Sarah's words like a blow to his chest. Sure, he'd planted the idea of a community liaison in Eric's head. But it had never occurred to him that it could be the first step toward losing Sarah.

Not that he wanted to trap her at home. It was good for her to have options, to step into her new life willingly. But over the past few days, he'd become more and more certain she was happy at the ranch. She belonged here. He could no longer even picture her putting on that straitlaced suit every day, going back to the corporate world. She might come back at the end of the day, but it wouldn't be the same. In the future he'd pictured, they were both immersed in this world—the world of the ranch, of horses, of building a life on the LT Ranch.

"This isn't what I had planned," he said.

"I know. But you can't always have what you want." She bit her lower lip. "I'm sorry. It's what I have to do."

He nodded, staring into the distance, his mind whirring like a revving engine as he thought of ways to change her mind.

What could Eric give her that he couldn't? When he'd first met her, he'd thought they would never make a couple. He'd thought she liked the clothes, the boardrooms, the fancy wine and gourmet food. He'd called her princess, and he'd thought the name fit—but now he knew better.

She was a part of this world—not the one she'd left behind.

"Do you really want to go back to the corporate stuff?"

He saw the answer in her eyes and his heart leapt with a shot of hope. But he could see her struggling to overcome the reluctance that was at her core.

"Yes," she said. "Yes, I do. I have to."

"Why?"

She fidgeted, clasping and unclasping her hands. He hadn't seen her do that since she'd left Carrigan. Was he going to have to watch the old, brittle, struggling Sarah come back? Was he going to have to live with a woman who was lying to herself every day?

"It's a chance to give back to Two Shot."

That wasn't the defense he'd expected.

"You were right when you said the town made me what I am," she continued. "I owe a lot to Two Shot, and Eric's going to give me a chance to pay it back." She set her hand on his arm. "What you did was a good thing, Lane. We're going to get the things we need before the drilling even starts. But I was wondering. Does this mean you're going to let them on the land?"

"I'll deal with that when it happens," he said. "And if it does, it'll be all right. I can get a conservation easement. They can only drill if they do it clean. They can't disrupt the landscape or screw up the water."

She nodded. "Then everybody wins. Including me. I get a chance to really make a difference."

He nodded. Much as he wanted her on the ranch, he could see that her motives were good. She knew what the town needed. She knew the people and the problems. And for a while, anyway, she'd be based in Two Shot.

But what would happen when the project was over? Eric would want her to move on to another community. And he'd lose her.

"When do you start?" he asked.

"Day after tomorrow."

"Okay." He stood. "I need to make a couple of calls."

He sure as hell did. He needed to sign on for a couple of rodeos, see if they'd accept a late entry. He'd been saving the news of his retirement from rodeo for a time when he and Sarah were alone, but when he pictured her going off to work in the morning, heading into town, he knew his days would be long and empty. He might as well climb back on the bulls.

He was making his calls from the ranch house kitchen when Trevor wheeled into the room.

"July fourteenth," Lane was saying. "I can make that."

Trevor waited until he'd hung up, then shot him a questioning glance. "Thought you were hangin' up your spurs."

"I changed my mind."

"That got anything to do with the redhead out there in the barn?"

Lane had left Sarah sitting on the bench by the barn door, working leather conditioner into a saddle that had dried out in the summer heat. She'd nodded when he'd said he had work to do. Just nodded and let him go.

He was going to have to learn that move.

"Heard she's going back to work for your brother."

"Yup." Lane tried not to sound resentful. "She's pretty excited about it."

"Really?" Trevor shook his head. "I don't think so. I think she'd rather work here."

"I thought so too, but she had a choice and she made it."

"Not much of a choice when you can't get yourself on the back of a horse."

Lane turned, narrowing his eyes at Trevor. "What do you mean? You were the one who told me what a great rider she was."

"*Was* is the operative word, though. Girl can't talk herself into the saddle. I saw her the other day trying to get on Ollie. She must have tried half a dozen times. Then she came in with some lame excuse why she couldn't lope him out. Haven't seen her try again."

Lane stared at him, then glanced out the window where Sarah was bent over the saddle. He'd tried twice to get her to go riding. Both times she'd made an excuse.

"I don't know what happened, but she can't bring herself to do it. Looks scared to me," Trevor said.

"Sarah's not scared of anything," Lane said. "She's sure as hell not scared of horses."

"No, I don't think it's horses." Trevor spun his chair and motored out of the room. "It's something in her own head." He turned back to Lane. "Remember when you took me home from the hospital?"

Lane nodded. It hadn't been easy.

"Getting in that truck was the hardest thing I ever did, but it wasn't my legs that were the problem," Trevor said. "It was my head. I thought I was going to die every minute."

Lane remembered that ride. Trevor had gone so pale he'd almost turned around and taken him back to the hospital. He'd been sure the guy wasn't ready to cope with real life, but his friend had been fine once they'd pulled into the driveway.

"When I was getting in the truck, I kept seeing the accident. I hadn't remembered it up to then. But the minute I heard that engine run, it was all I could see." Trevor paused. "That's how

Sarah looked when she tried to get on that horse. I could feel it, just watching her."

"Why didn't you tell me?"

"Girl didn't know I was looking." Trevor spun away again. "And I figured she'd find her own way to tell you. Some things just ought to be private, but she needs help. Don't tell her I told on her, okay?"

Lane stood at the window a minute, watching Sarah. Then he took off through the front door at a run.

CHAPTER 41

SARAH LOOKED UP AS LANE JOGGED PAST HER. HE WAS HEADED into the barn, probably to do something with the horses. She bent closer to the seat of the saddle she was working on, pretending to be absorbed in the task. A lot of Lane's tack needed work. He probably couldn't sit still long enough to take care of it.

The ranch really did need help. Over the past few days, she'd realized that while Trevor knew everything there was to know about quarter horses and cattle, one man couldn't do everything.

But she couldn't seem to overcome her fear, and it was better for Lane to just think she'd chosen to work for his brother. Someday, he'd figure out she couldn't ride. It was inevitable. But it was also inevitable that on that day, they'd start to grow apart. Horses and ranch work were Lane's life. He needed a woman who could work by his side, on horseback and off.

She returned her focus to the saddle, living in the moment, forgetting the past and future as she rubbed oil into the intricate flower designs of a World Champion Bull Rider prize saddle. Maybe she'd make the tack room her pet project until she started her new job, just lose herself in the quiet work and the warmth of the sun on her skin.

She was definitely absorbed in her work when hoofbeats hit the floor behind her. She turned to see Lane standing at the barn door between two horses. On one side he held the gelding she'd tried to mount the other day. In the other hand he held a big red stallion groomed like he was entering a halter class. His coat gleamed like polished copper.

Both horses were fully tacked up and ready to ride.

"What—"

"We're going for a ride," Lane said. "Ready?"

"No." She shook the saddle in her lap. "I'm kind of busy. You let this stuff dry out much more, it'll start to crack."

"I don't care about the saddle," he said. "Come on."

"Lane, this is your championship saddle. It shouldn't even be out here."

"We can argue about that later. I'll look forward to it." He held out the stallion's reins. "Come on."

"Lane, I'm…no."

"Just walk him, then."

She expected him to mount the gray but he walked a little ahead of her, leading her down a dirt two-track that led away from the barn and angled up a slight hill. The grass was dappled with wildflowers on the south-facing slope, and she wished for a moment that she was riding. But even the thought brought back a mental glimpse of hooves pawing the air, a rolling eye, a horse's mouth drawn back in a terrified grimace. She stopped a moment to recover, but Lane missed the sound of hoofbeats behind him and turned.

"What's wrong?"

"Nothing." She drew in a long breath, blew it out again. "I need to sit down."

"Can you make it to that rock up there?" He pointed toward a long, low boulder.

"Sure. Okay."

Her mind roiled while she trudged up the hill behind him, reluctant as a convict en route to the gallows. It was stupid to think she'd be able to hide her fear from Lane. He was bound to figure it out eventually, unless she left him—and that just wasn't something she could do. Not now, not ever. She'd told him the truth in the hospital—this wasn't just about sex. He was the one for her, the only one. And that meant she had to share everything, including her fears.

She'd been thinking about giving up on Lane, letting him go. But she never gave up anything without a fight. If she couldn't ride, she was going to have to tell him why.

"You know, this would be a lot easier if you'd ride instead of walking," he said.

"I can't," she said.

"Sure you can. You rode Flash, for God's sake."

"Not when it mattered." She sat back down so abruptly she almost bruised her tailbone.

"Tell me about it."

He sat beside her and the whole story spilled out. The quiet night, the locked trailer, the surreptitious saddling of the horse. His sudden change from docile mount to kicking, screaming chaos. The feeling of total defeat as she led him back to the trailer, back to his unknown fate, back to the road that would take him away from her.

"I couldn't do it." Somehow, in the telling of the story, she'd ended up with her head on Lane's shoulder. His shirt was wet with tears and getting wetter, but he didn't seem to mind. His arm circled her protectively and she felt her secrets spilling with her tears. "I couldn't do it, and I knew they'd take him and it would be over. And then when he sold so cheap, I knew I should have tried again and it was too late. I failed, Lane. My family lost everything, and all because I was scared."

He pulled her face to his shoulder and rocked her back and forth, to and fro, the motion soothing as a cradle. "You weren't scared, honey. You were traumatized. You saw your dad die. You can't just shake that off."

"But I had to. And I should have. Soldiers do it." She was spilling words faster and faster. "They see people die and they still do what they have to do."

"You weren't a soldier. You were a kid."

"But I gave up. I gave up and I let it happen."

"And now you're giving up again."

She jerked away from him. "What?"

"Do you really think you'll be happy as long as you can't ride? Do you really think you can hang out here and see the one thing in the world you can't do and not grow to hate it? What happened wasn't your fault, but you're not a kid anymore. You can't give up now."

She sniffled and hunched her shoulders, feeling almost as miserable as she'd felt the day they'd taken Flash. "I did try. I can't do it."

"Yes, you can." His eyes met hers, challenging and unwavering. "You can get on that horse and ride away from your past, leave it behind you forever. Or you can stay on the ground and keep wallowing around in it. Your choice."

She hunched lower, reminding herself that she loved this man. And he loved her. He was doing what he thought was best. He didn't realize he was killing her.

"You weren't scared of anything when you rode Flash."

"I'm not that girl anymore."

"No, maybe not. Maybe you don't want to be." He knelt beside her. "Fear is a choice, Sarah. I'm scared every time I get on a bull. But I get on anyway."

"Yeah, but you're an idiot."

"I'm a rodeo cowboy."

"Same difference." She sniffed, then took a deep breath. "Okay. I'll try." She stood and reached for the reins in his hand. "Give me Ollie."

"You're riding this one."

"Lane, I can't do that. He looks just like…"

"There's an old saying in rodeo: 'When you get thrown off the bucking bronco, you got to get back on the bronc that throwed you.'"

"And in business we have a definition of what crazy is: Doing the same thing over and over expecting a different result."

They stood inches apart, their eyes meeting in a challenge just as they had on that first day. He lifted his chin and gave her just the faintest hint of a smug smile and she snatched the reins from his hand.

She led Cinn a few feet away and gathered the reins in her hand. She waited for the inevitable flashback to begin but the horse just stared back at her, his eyes soft. She felt his spirit in her mind, the calm, untangled sense she'd had at their first encounter.

"Go on," Lane said. "He'll take you wherever you want to go."

She bunched the reins in her hand and walked around to the side of the horse. Tipping the stirrup toward her, she pushed her toe in and felt a surge of panic. She closed her eyes.

"Open your eyes," Lane said. "Open them and look at me."

She opened her eyes and he was there, at the horse's shoulder, his eyes meeting hers. Now she could feel him too, the strength of him, and love hit her like a wave. It lifted her heart, sweeping it up, swinging it sideways, and settling it into the saddle like a leaf washing up on the shore. She was still watching his face when she realized she'd done it.

She was on horseback.

She looked straight ahead and saw the horse's muscled neck, his dark, coarse mane, the tufted ears pointed forward, and suddenly she was awash in memories—but they were good memories. She could hear the rodeo announcer, the murmur of the crowd. For a moment she and the horse hung suspended out of time, hovering in the hot summer air like a hummingbird in the second before it darts for a flower.

She gazed down the trail and thought *go*.

Cinn went, his muscles bunching and loosening in a rocking, casual walk. The rhythm was so comforting and familiar she couldn't resist rocking forward in the saddle and giving him a nudge, just the barest nudge. And then he was jogging, arching his neck and flashing his feet out like a parade horse, and she had to laugh and give him another touch of her heels.

Lane had been right. It was like riding a bicycle. She was a little unsteady at first, but she was finding her balance as muscle memory kicked in.

And sitting high in the saddle, she felt in control for the first time in years. She hadn't realized how much of her life she'd handed over to the Carrigan Corporation and the other companies she'd worked for. There was something to be said for the Western life after all.

Turning, she loped back to Lane and sat back on her seat-bones the way Roy had taught her. Cinn slid to a halt on the dry dirt trail, his hind legs gathered beneath him, his front feet kicking up dirt. Lane grinned while Ollie blinked in the puff of dust they'd raised.

"Well, I suppose you're ready to ride off into the sunset now," he said teasingly.

"Nope." She tightened one rein and the stallion danced in a tight circle, impatient to be off. She turned and grinned at Lane, feeling happier than she'd felt since she was a kid. "I was thinking we ought to ride to the Love Nest. Come on, Lane. Race me."

EPILOGUE

THE RED RIBBON FLUTTERED FROM SARAH'S HANDS AS SHE made her fourteenth effort at tying it to a tilting fence post. There was a pretty stiff breeze blowing, promising a late-afternoon rainstorm, but it really wouldn't be that hard to get the job done if Lane would quit trying to help her.

"I've got it." She shoved him sideways and grabbed the runaway end of the ribbon.

"Do you need some help?" Sarah turned to see Emmy standing beside her, hands clasped shyly behind her back. But her shoulders weren't slumped, and as Sarah stepped away, she took the ribbon and tied it into a quick, assured bow around the post.

"They teach you that at UW?" Lane teased.

"No. They're teaching me what kind of formations you look for to find oil, and how to access it, and—oh." She paused, mortified, and proved her newfound confidence hadn't affected her ability to blush. "You don't want to hear about that, do you? You're against it."

"Not if it's done right," he said. "Just learn how to do it right, and then make sure it happens when you get your first job." He grinned. "Maybe you could work for Carrigan. What do you think, Bro?"

Eric had taken off his jacket and was carefully rolling his shirt-sleeves to the elbow. "Probably. But she'll be done with graduate school by the time you and I agree on anything."

"I hope so," Lane said. "But at least I'll have one engineer on my side."

Emmy nodded enthusiastically, then frowned. "I'm on Sarah's side, though."

Lane rolled his eyes. "Everybody loves my wife." Sarah punched his arm and he winced. "Me most of all."

Gloria, who was honoring the occasion with a magnificently inappropriate sequined red dress, gave Sarah a friendly nudge with her shoulder. "I told you the cowboy brother was the one for you." She glanced over at Eric, who had flung his jacket over his shoulder with a *GQ* flourish. "Opposites attract."

Lane grinned and settled an arm around Sarah's shoulders. "Sometimes opposites aren't as different as they seem," he said. "Sometimes, deep down, they belong together."

A crowd gathered gradually. First the poker gang arrived, decked out in their Sunday best. Sarah had never seen most of them in suit jackets before, let alone ties and shiny shoes. Joe was probably wearing his best clothes too, but that just meant there weren't any holes in his jeans or swear words on his T-shirt.

Kelsey and Mike picked their way across the uneven ground, Mike lugging Katie in his arms. She was almost too big to carry, and she started squirming the moment she saw Lane and Sarah. Mike set her down and she ran across the open field, dodging sagebrush with her arms outstretched. She slammed into Lane's legs and looked up at Sarah, then at Lane, her smile as wide and sunny as the summer sky.

"Hey, short stuff." Lane rumpled her hair and the smile widened. Catching sight of Willie, she toddled off to watch as he dug furiously at an old prairie dog hole.

Suze arrived late, but the crowd parted for her like the Red Sea as she made her way to the front where Lane and Sarah were standing by the fence post.

"You all are determined to do this, aren't you." It wasn't a question, it was a statement.

Sarah nodded. "It's green construction, though. All local materials so it blends with the landscape, and most of the power will be wind and solar."

She scanned the crowd. Just about everybody in town had showed up, even Eddie, who stood at the back in his ever-present white cap and apron.

"Suze, who's manning the grill?" Lane asked.

"Nobody." Suze folded her arms over her ample chest and scowled. "Place is closed for the ceremony."

"Wow," Lane said with a glint in his eye. "I don't think the diner's ever been closed before. If we'd known the ribbon-cutting was that important to you, we'd have done it after hours."

"It's not important to me," she grunted. "Eddie wanted to come, and when he gets a bug up his butt about something there's no stopping him."

"Well, hopefully we'll have a doctor who can deal with the bug issue," Lane said.

Suze snorted. "You gonna cut that ribbon or talk all day?"

"Talk all day," Sarah said. "You can't have a ribbon-cutting without a speech."

"Crap," Suze mumbled, backing into the crowd.

Sarah scanned the crowd and caught sight of Trevor in the front row. He grinned, giving her a wave. He was the only one who knew how hard her road had been, and they'd formed a fast friendship.

"Speech!" somebody at the back of the crowd yelled.

"Get on with it!" hollered another voice.

Sarah cleared her throat. "I'll make this quick," she said.

Cheers rose from the crowd. Small-town folks weren't much for standing in one place, and she was eager to get to the end of her speech too.

"A lot of you know there was a time in my life when Two Shot wasn't my favorite place in the world."

There was a smattering of laughter.

"There was a time in my life I couldn't get out of this town fast enough," she continued. "And now there's no place I'd rather be." She smiled at Lane, who stood in his typical pose, legs apart, arms folded over his chest, totally unaware that he stood head-and-shoulders above every man in the crowd.

In her eyes, he stood above every man in the world.

"I wanted to leave Two Shot because I felt like I was stuck. Like the town would never change. It would always be Two Shot, Wyoming, Population 245. It would never grow, and neither would I.

"I was right about being stuck, but the town wasn't the problem. I was the one who needed to change. And thanks to Lane and to all of you, I did.

"But Two Shot is changing too," she said. "We're getting the Carrigan Clinic built, and soon there'll be a police station too." She glanced at Lane. "The Roy Price Memorial Building, named after my stepdad. And there's one other thing that's changing." She scanned the crowd, then focused on Lane as she delivered the last line of her speech.

"In about six months, the population will be two hundred forty-six." She put a hand on her belly and waited for the news to sink in.

The crowd caught on right away, whooping and cheering, but Lane stood as if he was frozen to the ground despite the summer heat.

"Two hundred forty-six?" he said as the cheers died down.

"Two hundred forty-six," she said. "And number two hundred forty-six is going to be a little Carrigan cowboy. Or maybe a cowgirl."

He took a step forward, still looking stunned, and then a smile spread across his face and he swept her into his arms. She clasped her hands around his neck and he lifted her into the air. She watched the landscape whirl past as he spun her in a circle, the landscape and then the crowd, a sea of smiling faces. Her family.

He set her down and Emmy handed her an enormous pair of silver scissors that glinted in the sunlight. With Lane's arms draped over her shoulders, she snipped the red ribbon and stepped away.

As the bow unfurled and the ribbon fell, she and Lane stepped through the opening and they each grabbed a waiting shovel. As the blades dug into the hard Wyoming earth, she felt like she was breaking ground on much more than a medical clinic or even a new era for Two Shot.

She was breaking ground on a whole new life.

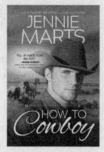

CADE CALLAHAN STOOD IN THE HOSPITAL GIFT SHOP STARING at the colorful display of get-well tokens. A fluffy white unicorn with a purple horn and a glittery pink-and-purple mane caught his eye. Allie had loved unicorns as a little kid—she'd called them "princess ponies." But he was wrestling with the notion that now she might be too old for a stuffed animal.

If she was, she could always toss it. At least he was trying, he thought as he snagged the unicorn from the shelf. He considered a card but figured that might be a little too much. Besides, he doubted he'd find a card that read, *Sorry I was a shitty dad. Get well soon.* For now, the unicorn would have to do.

He grabbed two bottles of water and threw a couple of Reese's Peanut Butter Cups onto the counter, thinking they might want them on the drive up the mountain. He was already dreading the trip. His back hurt from sleeping in the chair next to her hospital bed, and between the two of them, they were grumpier than a grizzly who'd stepped in a hornet's nest.

I'm the grown-up, he reminded himself. Which meant he needed to be the better person, no matter how many of his buttons his thirteen-year-old daughter pushed. And if there were an Olympic event for pushing one's parent's buttons, Allison Raye would take home the gold *and* the silver.

As the teenage cashier rang up the items, his eye caught on the shelf of paperbacks behind her. He gestured to the books. "Do you have any YA?" he asked, recalling the conversation he'd had earlier with his daughter about the Kindle app on her phone. It was probably the longest one they'd had yet. Even though she'd rolled her eyes at his lack of knowledge of the young adult genre, he'd still gleaned three important pieces of information from the conversation: one, her phone was at home on the charger; two, her Kindle took the place of any real friendships she might have; and three, she was still a bookworm who loved to read.

The cashier turned to peruse the shelf and pointed to three books along the bottom. "It looks like we only have these three."

"Okay, I'll take them."

"Which ones?"

"All three."

"Sure." She added the books to his total, then slid them into a bag.

Allie was asleep when he got back to her room. He paused in the doorway to look at her and had to swallow back the emotion burning his throat. He and her mother had had their share of struggles, but he couldn't believe Amber was gone. And the thought that Allie could have died in that car accident too hit him like a punch to the gut.

He blinked back the sudden burn of tears as he peered at the dark purple bruises around her eyes and along one of her cheeks. A thin line of stitches ran next to her hairline—they weren't sure if she'd hit her head or something in the cab had flown by and cut her when the car rolled. Her right arm was bandaged and secured in a cream-colored splint, and her left leg was constrained in a blue boot, only sprained and thankfully not broken.

She looked so small, so young, like the little girl he remembered. He hadn't seen his daughter in almost a year. He'd contacted Amber a few years back, told her he wanted to try to see

Allie more often, but she'd stalled and always seemed to have some excuse for why it wouldn't work. When Allie got a cell phone, he'd tried to call her, but the few times they'd talked had been stilted and awkward with neither of them knowing exactly what to say.

That's bullshit, he thought as he forced himself to step into the room. *I should have tried harder.*

Her eyes fluttered open, and a hard knot tightened in his chest as he saw the array of emotions flash in her eyes with each blink. They changed from almost glad to see him to confused to angry, then to agonizingly sad as the realization of her mother's death must have hit her again.

She winced as she tried to push herself up in the bed with her good hand but waved Cade off as he took another step toward her. "I got it."

He stayed where he was, not sure how to help her and knowing she wasn't ready to accept his help yet anyway. It used to feel like walking on eggshells around each other—now it felt more like land mines.

The nurse had said she'd be able to leave before lunch, and she'd changed into the shorts and one of the T-shirts his cousin Bryn and neighbor Elle had bought for her when they'd come down to Denver after they'd heard about the accident. The T-shirt was red and yellow and referenced being a Gryffindor on the front.

"Nice shirt," he said.

"Thanks. Cousin Bryn and your other friend Elle bought it for me. Apparently they stalked me on Insta and figured out my size and that I love Harry Potter."

"I don't know what Insta is, but I'm glad you like the things they brought." He held out the unicorn. "Here, I got you something too."

"What's this?" she said, peering down at it.

"A peace offering. And an apology, I guess. And just something I thought you'd like."

"Wow. That's a lot of mileage to get out of one stuffed animal."

He shrugged. "I like to consolidate. I also mix my peas into my mashed potatoes and gravy."

She wrinkled her nose. "Gross."

"What? It keeps them from rolling off the plate." He'd been trying to make her smile—just one instant of her lips curving up—and he thought he might have had it. But then her face shut down again as she pushed the unicorn into the tote bag with the rest of her things. "They gave me a bag with my stuff in it, but I don't know if I want it anymore."

The hospital had given him a bag with his ex-wife's things as well. He'd taken a quick look inside—enough to see some clothes, a pair of sneakers, and a streak of blood across the front of Amber's purse. Being on the rodeo circuit, he was no stranger to blood, but it was different when it belonged to the mother of his child who had been alive and breathing less than twenty-four hours ago. He'd twisted the bag closed and stowed it behind the seat in his truck.

He picked up the plastic bag with his daughter's name written on the front. "I'll take care of it." He passed her the bag of books, as if in trade. "Here. I got you these too. The cashier said they were all YA."

A hint of a smile pulled at her lips as she peered into the bag. "They are. I've read one of them already."

He held out his free hand. "That's okay. I can take it back."

She shook her head and pulled the bag of books to her chest. "No, I'll read it again." She narrowed her eyes, then barely lifted one eyebrow. "The unicorn is cute, but you should have led with the books."

He turned away to hide his smile. At least he'd gotten something right.

A nurse pushed a wheelchair into the room. "You ready to break out of this joint?" she asked Allie.

"So ready." The girl pointed to the chair. "Do I have to ride in that thing?"

The nurse crossed her arms over her chest. She'd been with them since the night before and most of the morning and seemed immune to his daughter's snark. "First of all, yes. It's a requirement. And second of all, you're not going to be walking anywhere today. We're sending you home with crutches, and you'll be using those and that boot you're wearing for the next few weeks at least."

"Fine." Allie plopped down in the seat.

They had already completed the paperwork for her release, and Cade had taken a load of stuff down to the truck earlier that morning. He picked up the rest of her things and followed them down the hall.

The drive up the pass took just over an hour but felt like five. The cab of the truck was thick with awkward silences and uncomfortable attempts at conversation. Mostly his.

To say Allie wasn't thrilled about heading to Bryn's ranch was an understatement. She'd assumed they were going back to her house, but Cade wasn't ready for that. And he wasn't sure Allie was either. He promised her they'd go by her house on their next trip down, but for now, he was trying to keep her mind on her recovery.

Cade's efforts to ask about her school or how she was feeling were met with wisecracks or exaggerated shrugs, so he'd finally just turned on the radio and let his daughter sulk.

She wrinkled her nose at the country music station. "Is this the only kind of music you listen to?"

"No. I'll listen to whatever. You can choose."

She shook her head. "I guess I don't really care either. You can leave it, SD."

He furrowed his brow as he turned the volume down. "So, what's with this SD business?" She'd used the initials several times.

Allie lifted one shoulder. "It's just a nickname I have for you."

"What does it mean?"

She shrugged again and kept her gaze trained out the window.

"I don't think I like it," he told her.

"Oh well."

"Can't you just call me Dad?"

She turned back to him, her eyes narrowed as she leveled him with a cool stare. "No. I can't. You haven't earned that title in a long while. I haven't even *seen* you in close to a year."

He swallowed at the guilt churning its way up his throat like a bad bout of heartburn.

"That wasn't my—" He stopped. He was going to say it wasn't his fault—that Amber had moved them again and hadn't given him her new number for months. And that even when he'd called, she'd always had a reason why he couldn't talk to his daughter. But telling Allie that wouldn't do any good. He didn't want to speak poorly of Amber, especially right now, and it probably was his fault too. He should've tried harder, pushed Amber to put Allie on the phone or insist she return his call. "How about you just call me Cade? I didn't earn it either, but that's my name."

Slumping further into the seat and turning back to the window, she offered him that slight lift of her shoulders coupled with a mumbled "Whatever." Which he now took as her way of agreeing with him.

Glad that's settled. He glanced at the dashboard clock before returning his focus to the road. Only forty-five more minutes of awkward silence to go.

Close to an hour later—traffic up the mountain had been a bear—he turned the truck into the driveway of the Heaven Can Wait Horse Rescue.

Allie lifted her head and sat up straighter in the seat. "Is this it?"

"Yep." He and his brother had been coming here to visit his grandparents since he was a kid, but he tried to see the small farm from her eyes. An old yellow two-story farmhouse with a wide front porch sat on one side of the drive, and a large barn with faded red paint sat on the other. Two nice-sized corrals flanked either side of the barn, and chickens roamed inside the fence surrounding a small chicken coop. The bunkhouse sat beyond the barn, and Cade could see a couple of barn cats lying in the sun on the front porch.

The farm was a little worse for wear, but Bryn had added homey touches in the cheery blue pillows on the porch swing and the array of colorful pots spilling over with flowers on the steps. She had a fenced-in garden next to her house with neat rows of vegetables and tall green cornstalks reaching for the sun. Several of the rescued horses stood in one corral, and a couple dozen head of cattle filled the other and the pasture beyond.

"It's pretty old," Allie said, leaning forward to peer through the front window.

"This used to be your great-grandparents' farm. I came here quite a bit with your uncle Holt when we were kids. Us and Bryn and her brother, Bucky, used to run all over this place."

"What kind of name is Bucky?"

He shrugged. "He just goes by Buck now. I used to see him a lot on the rodeo circuit." Allie's shoulders tensed, and he figured he'd better change the subject quick. She'd always blamed the rodeo for keeping him away and not visiting her more often. "My grandpa left this farm to Bryn when he died. She always loved it, and now she's turning it into a horse rescue. It's pretty cool."

She offered him one of her noncommittal shrugs as they pulled up in front of the bunkhouse. "Is that your dog?" she asked, derision in her tone as she pointed to a mangy canine standing in the pasture behind the bunkhouse. His body was thin, and he stood perfectly still, watching them approach through one good eye. His other was a wreck of scar tissue and damage.

He huffed. "No. Not even close. That's a coyote. He's been hanging around here a lot this summer. I think he's looking to get into the chicken coop and steal a hen. Zane, that's Bryn's fiancé, he's been calling him Jack, for the one-eyed jack in a deck of playing cards. He's pretty small and scrawny for a coyote, probably the runt of his litter. Which is why I think Bryn feels sorry for him and has been tossing him scraps. You'll soon learn your cousin Bryn has a heart the size of Montana, and she can't resist a wounded soul."

"Is he dangerous? The coyote?"

"He could be. Most coyotes are assholes." He held up one hand. "Sorry. I mean jerks. But if you don't mess with him, he shouldn't mess with you. And he's an odd one. You don't usually see 'em this close to the house. I'd be more worried about stepping on a rattler or running into a bear than tangling with that coyote."

"A *bear*?" Her voice raised almost an octave.

Ugh. He was just making this worse. "Don't worry. I won't let anything happen to you." Did he really just say that? The whole reason he'd all but disappeared out of her life was because he *had* let something happen to her.

He didn't know if she was thinking the same thing as she turned away and pushed open the door. This was their new start. He needed to show her he wanted her here. He got out and quickly rounded the back of the truck as she wrestled with the crutch. Her left arm was in a sling, making the use of two crutches impossible. "Welcome home, Allie Cat," he said, as he reached to help her.

"I got it," she said, her mouth set in a tight line as she wedged the crutch into the pit of her good arm. She took a clumsy step forward and had to grab the side of the door to steady herself. "What are you looking at?" she sneered at the row of horses watching her from the edge of the corral.

"I'd say they're staring because you're the first three-legged animal they've seen, but you haven't met Lucky, Bryn's dog. He's missing a leg and runs and hops all over this place." He glanced toward the farmhouse. "I'm surprised he and Zane's dog, Hope, haven't come out to greet us yet. They must not be home. Do you have a dog?" He had a sudden anxious concern that they'd left an animal alone in their house, forgotten in the trauma of the accident.

Allie shook her head. "No. I've always wanted one, but Mom wouldn't let me get one. She said I wasn't old enough for the responsibility. I think *she* just didn't want the responsibility." Her breath caught, as if she'd just remembered that her mom was dead.

Cade caught the well of tears in her eyes before she lowered her gaze to the hand gripping the crutch. He reached an arm out trying to think of something to distract her thoughts. "You want to come over and meet the gang? They seem pretty curious about you."

She looked skeptical but allowed Cade to help her hobble over to the fence, where four horses waited to greet her.

"This is Beauty and her colt, Mack," Cade said, resting a hand on the neck of the quarter horse. "She was Bryn's first rescue. She was waiting on a couple of scumbags at the diner where she works and found out they were taking her to slaughter. Zane left her a hundred-dollar tip for his breakfast so she could buy the horse off 'em."

"A *hundred-dollar tip*? He must have *really* wanted that horse."

"I think he really wanted the girl."

"Ahh," Allie said with a nod that was probably more knowing than her thirteen years should have allowed. "And she got the colt too?"

"She did. Although she didn't know it at the time. The horse was pregnant when she got her." He nuzzled the chin of the gray standing next to Beauty. "This is Prince. They rescued him from an abandoned farmhouse. And this little old man…" he said, scratching the head of the mini-horse who was stretching his nose through the rungs of the fence to sniff at Allie. "Is Shamus. He was dumped here anonymously. But he's real friendly. You can pet him."

"What do you mean by dumped?" She tentatively reached a hand out to touch the side of the mini-horse's neck.

"I mean Bryn came home one day, and this guy was tied to her porch."

"That's awful."

Cade shrugged. "Yeah, but it worked out pretty well for him. He was a mess when he got here, but now he's happy and playful.

You gotta watch out for him and Otis, the ornery goat that runs around here. Shamus has a way of escaping the corral, and he and that dang goat are always getting into trouble. Elle found them in the house one afternoon eating a piece of cake."

Allie giggled. He wasn't sure if it was from his comment about the cake or from the way Shamus was nibbling at her hand, but he loved the sound of it. "His nose is so soft. It's like velvet."

The rev of an engine had them turning to watch a small white compact SUV as it headed down Bryn's driveway and stopped a short distance away. A woman stepped out and held her hand up to shade her eyes as she peered around, then offered them a wave. "Is this the Heaven Can Wait Horse Rescue?"

Cade nodded. "Yep. You lookin' to drop one off or pick one up?"

"Neither," she said with a charming laugh as she headed toward them.

She smiled as she approached, and he was struck by the openness of her grin. She was wearing a black pencil skirt, a pink silk blouse, and high-heeled black boots. She looked completely out of place on the farm as the dust of the driveway clung to her fancy boots, but he found his lips curving into a dopey smile as she drew nearer.

His smile didn't matter apparently, because her attention was completely focused on his daughter. "You must be Allie," she said, reaching out a hand to shake, then pulling it back as she realized the move would be difficult for the girl. "I'm Nora. I'm going to be your physical therapist."

Cade turned to Allie and said, "She's a good friend of Elle's and agreed to help us out. She's gonna be staying out here on the farm, so we don't have to drive to Denver every day."

"Whatever." She shrugged in that loose-shouldered way that teenagers had, as if her bones were made of cooked spaghetti noodles. "Welcome to Podunkville, Colorado, otherwise known as the edge of isolation. Hope you don't need cell-phone service."

"It's not that bad," Cade told the woman.

Allie tilted her head toward him. "This is my SD," she said by way of introduction.

Nora's brow furrowed. "SD?"

"It's her nickname for me," he explained, offering his own shrug that he hoped wasn't as annoying as the teenager's. "Except she won't tell me what it means." He cocked an eyebrow at his daughter. "I'm thinking it stands for 'Super Dad.'"

"I can assure you it does *not* stand for Super Dad," Allie said with a snort.

As he'd done with the majority of her salty comments lately, he ignored it and held out his hand to the physical therapist. "Cade Callahan. Thanks for coming."

The woman nodded. "Nice to meet you. Nora Fisher. And I'm happy to help." Her gaze traveled over him in a way that had a shot of heat creeping up his spine. "You're not exactly what I was expecting."

"No?" He had a moment of wondering what she *had* been expecting and if he was better or worse than she imagined. *What the hell?* He couldn't remember the last time a woman's opinion of him mattered. Especially one he'd just met.

She shook her head. "Sorry, that was rude. I just meant from Elle's description, I thought you'd be much older."

He grinned. "Yeah, that sounds about right. She probably said I was crotchety—she likes to tell me I remind her of a grumpy old man."

Allie huffed, then muttered, "She got the grumpy part right."

He ignored her as he shrugged. What could he say? He *was* kind of grumpy most days. And his daughter hadn't exactly seen him at his best. But now they were on the ranch and with the horses, the place where he felt the most at ease. He gestured to the small herd of horses still watching them from the corral. "We just got here ourselves, and I was introducing Allie to the crew. You want to meet them?"

"Sure." Nora nodded and smiled, but the nervous look that crossed her face told him her thoughts were probably more along the lines of *un*sure.

City girls.

He went through the horses' names again, stroking their necks as he repeated their stories to Nora.

"The little one is the funniest," Allie said, scratching the mini-horse's ears. Shamus stretched his neck through the fence again and nudged her hip, sniffing at her front pocket.

"He's checking to see if you brought him any treats."

"What kind of treats does he like?"

"That horse will eat anything. The guy who left him here said his favorites were macaroni and cheese and jelly beans."

"Jelly beans?" Allie chuckled. "I can understand macaroni and cheese—that's my favorite too—but what kind of horse eats jelly beans?"

"Not this one. Not anymore. Now he just gets carrots and apple slices and horse treats. We'll bring him out something tomorrow." Although he just might bring the mini-horse a jelly bean. Shamus was making more headway with his daughter in the last ten minutes than Cade had in the last two days. But he did just find out that macaroni and cheese was still her favorite.

Nora smiled with them but hung back a little, not as bold as Allie had been in petting the animals. "I don't have much experience with horses. In fact, I don't think I've ever been this close to one before."

"Me either," Allie admitted.

"Really?" Cade asked. "I've been around horses my entire life. I get along with them better than I do most people. Present company excluded." He hoped. Although so far in the compatibility battle, the horses were still winning. "You couldn't have asked for better horses to hang out with for your first time. This is a real sweet bunch."

"Which one is yours?" Nora asked, glancing around at the other horses in the corral.

"Mine's in the barn. She's the palomino in the first stall. I'll give you a tour later, but I think for now, I'd better get Allie inside." He reached for her elbow, but she pulled it away.

"I told you, I can do it myself."

He raised his hands in surrender. What else could he do? Her personality was as prickly as a pissed-off porcupine. One minute she was laughing and petting the horses, the next she's firing off a shot at him. "Fine. Do it yourself."

The teenager tried to take a step forward but the crutch slid on some loose gravel, and she started to pitch forward. Cade reached out to grab her before she fell, but after he'd steadied her, she pushed him away again. "I can do it."

"Hold on. I brought you something that might help," Nora said, heading back toward her car. She popped the hatchback and pulled out a wheeled contraption. "It's a knee scooter. It'll make your mobility much easier," she said as she wheeled it back toward Allie. She bent her leg and rested it on the center platform. "You put your knee here, then you can wheel yourself around and not have to use the crutches."

Allie passed the crutch to her dad and positioned herself on the scooter. He watched as she awkwardly inched forward.

"This is much easier," Allie said, getting the hang of the scooter. It was still a little wonky since she could only use one hand, but it offered her much more stability than the single crutch had. "Thanks." She offered Nora the smallest of smiles.

Better than what he'd been getting lately.

"Are you okay to give me a few minutes to get her settled, then I'll come back and help you get unloaded?" he asked Nora.

"Oh, yeah," she said, waving away his concerns. "Take your time. I'll just hang out here with the horses. We'll get to know each other."

He grinned as she inched just a smidge closer and tentatively reached out to pat Shamus's head.

The bunkhouse was small, and it only took a few minutes to give Allie the tour and get her settled in her new room. It was obvious his cousin and Elle had been in there, and they had transformed the second bedroom into a welcoming space. A new floral comforter covered the bed and a mess of matching pillows lined the headboard. Fresh-cut flowers tucked into a mason jar sat on the dresser next to a basket of miniature bottles of soaps and lotions. A fresh bottle of water was on the nightstand along with an assortment of magazines and paperback novels.

"Did you do all this?" Allie eyed him skeptically.

He shook his head. "Nah. I mean I've been working on setting up this room for you in case you wanted to visit, so I got the new bed and the desk and the dresser and nightstand. But the flowers and the bedding and that basket of good-smelling stuff was all your cousin Bryn and her friend Elle. And they definitely get credit for that jumble of useless pillows."

"Why would they do all this? For me?"

"They're good people, and they wanted you to feel welcome. Bryn did all this kind of stuff for me when I first got here too. Maybe not the flowers and frou-frou pillows, but she has the gift of hospitality, just like our grandmother did, and it makes her happy to do things for other people."

"Huh. Just seems like a lot to do for someone she doesn't even know."

"Yeah. It takes a little getting used to, but once she's brought you over a pan of warm cinnamon rolls, you find a way to accept it." He reached out to touch her shoulder, then drew his hand back. "And she does know you. I told you, she met you several times when you were little."

"Oh, you mean before you left us."

ABOUT THE AUTHOR

After dabbling in horse training, chicken farming, and organic gardening, Joanne Kennedy ran away from home and ended up in Wyoming, where the unique blend of past and present inspires her to write contemporary Western romances with traditional ranch settings. She is the author of ten novels, including the RITA-nominated *One Fine Cowboy* and *How to Handle a Cowboy*, which was named one of *Booklist*'s "Best Romances of the Decade."

She lives in a secret mountain hideout on the Colorado border with three dogs, two cats, and her husband, who is an airline pilot and volunteer fireman. When not reading, writing, or loving a man in uniform, she obsesses over birds, horses, wildflowers, and squirrels.

Joanne loves to hear from readers and can be contacted through her website, joannekennedybooks.com.

Also by Joanne Kennedy

Cowboy Trouble
One Fine Cowboy
Cowboy Fever
Tall, Dark and Cowboy
Cowboy Crazy
Cowboy Tough

COWBOYS OF DECKER RANCH
How to Handle a Cowboy
How to Kiss a Cowboy
How to Wrangle a Cowboy

BLUE SKY COWBOYS
Cowboy Summer
Blue Sky Cowboy Christmas